Pocket Book of
British Ceramic Marks

Also by J. P. Cushion
(in collaboration with W. B. Honey)

HANDBOOK OF POTTERY AND
PORCELAIN MARKS
(fourth, revised edition)

Pocket Book of
British
Ceramic Marks

including

Index to Registered Designs

1842–83

compiled by

J. P. CUSHION

lately Senior Research Assistant of the
Department of Ceramics
Victoria and Albert Museum, London

faber and faber
LONDON · BOSTON

First published in 1959
by Faber and Faber Limited
as Pocket Book of English Ceramic Marks
Second edition 1965
Second impression 1967
Third impression 1969
Fourth impression 1970
Fifth impression 1972
Third enlarged edition, revised and reset 1976
First published in Faber Paperbacks in 1983
Reprinted in 1986
Printed in Great Britain by
The Thetford Press Ltd., Thetford, Norfolk
All rights reserved

British Library Cataloguing in Publication Data

Cushion, John P.
Pocket book of British ceramic marks,
including index to registered designs, 1842.83.
—Enlarged ed.
1. Pottery—Great Britain—Marks—Identification
2. Porcelain—Great Britain—Marks—
Identification
I. Title
738'.0278   NK4230

ISBN 0-571-13108-5

Acknowledgements

The author wishes to express his gratitude to the many officers and colleagues at the Victoria and Albert Museum, numerous collectors, English Ceramic Circle members and ceramic dealers, all of whom have assisted him in the recording of elusive marks for the guidance of future seekers.

Thanks are also recorded to Mr. Murray Fieldhouse, editor of *Pottery Quarterly*, and to the members of The Craftsmen Potters Association, who have assisted him in the collection of the marks and particulars of the present-day studio potters. The author is indebted to Mr. Geoffrey Godden for information concerning the dates of nineteenth-century factories and potters.

Thanks for information concerning recently established factories, closures, take-overs etc. are due to the proprietors of *Tableware International* (formerly *Pottery Gazette and Glass Trade Review*, established 1877), and to Mr. Terence Woolliscroft of Milton, Stoke-on-Trent, who so generously carried out the research concerning the recent, and often very complicated, changes of proprietorship of many Staffordshire factories. Mr. Woolliscroft noted that by January 1972 only one hundred and forty-four factories (individual producing units) remained in the Stoke area, employing thirty-four thousand workers.

Contents

MARKS

Preface: Scope and Arrangement
of the Book

This pocket-book of ceramic marks has been produced especially to answer the requirements of the collector and dealer who has long needed such a guide when on 'pot-hunting' expeditions. In order to restrict the bulk of this volume the marks shown here have been confined to those of Great Britain and Ireland; Continental and Far Eastern marks are dealt with in the *Handbook of Pottery and Porcelain Marks*.

The marks recorded here are restricted to true factory marks and those others which by their frequent occurrence, or in other ways are of actual use in helping to identify the place and period of manufacture of a piece.

The arrangement is in alphabetical order of towns, subdivided into names of factories or owners, again alphabetically. The pottery centre of Staffordshire is treated in a separate section from the rest of England.

As far as practicable the marks are shown in facsimile (space has not permitted full-scale reproduction in all cases), the chief exception being those numerous modern marks consisting of the names or initials of the maker, or of the place of manufacture, which are reproduced by using printers' type, as has so often been done in the marks themselves on the actual wares.

The scope of this book has been extended to include many nineteenth- and twentieth-century marks not hitherto recorded, and brought right up-to-date by showing the marks of modern studio-potters.

To help the enquirer, an approximate date or period

is given for every mark together with the name of the principal proprietor where of interest, and a word or so of description of the type of ware on which the mark is generally found.

*   *   *

This enlarged and revised new edition of the *Pocket Book of English Ceramic Marks*, includes that part of the Class IV Design Index which relates to pottery and porcelain (Appendix B, page 288). It is included by the kind permission of the Public Record Office and will enable readers not only to date their wares by using the tables on pages 284–287, but also to determine the name of the manufacturer or person or firm, who initially registered the design to protect it from 'piracy' for a period of three years, by consulting the Index (i.e. Appendix B).

Historical Note and Methods
of Marking

The practice of marking ceramic wares as a guide to the manufacturer is a very old one and was carried out by the Romans on their red-wares, but it is not until the sixteenth century in Europe that the soft-paste Italian 'Medici' porcelain appears with a fully developed factory-mark, i.e. the sketch of the dome of Florence Cathedral in underglaze blue.

It was not until 1723 that the Meissen (Dresden) factory in Saxony adopted as a regular factory-mark the crossed swords of the arms of Saxony; this mark was invariably painted in underglaze blue on the base of the article in the Chinese manner. Other European porcelain and faience factories quickly followed the lead of Meissen and in 1766 the porcelain makers of France were required by law to use a mark which had been previously registered with the police authorities.

The practice of marking was never regularized throughout the eighteenth century with the result that factories which were proud of their reputation used a recognized mark, whilst the less important factories either left their wares unmarked in the hope that they would be mistaken for those factories whose style they were copying, or alternatively, used a mark similar enough to a famous one to be mistaken for genuine. The crossed swords of Meissen were used on numerous imitations and quite openly copied on Bow, Derby, Worcester and Lowestoft.

Many of the marks encountered on ceramics are

merely those of painters or workmen and are not a sure guide to the place of manufacture even when identified, for these people were of a very nomadic nature and often worked in many different factories in the course of their career. The throwers and 'repairers' (a term used for the workers who assembled the various parts of figures, etc.) invariably used a mark scratched in the body prior to the biscuit firing. These marks when under the glaze can safely be treated as genuine, but otherwise they should be closely examined for the burr or raised edge which is unavoidable when scratching soft clay, to ensure the mark has not been ground in after firing in order to deceive.

Painters and gilders generally used one of the colours in their palette or gilt, to mark the wares upon which they worked, this information was probably solely for the benefit of the management and for purposes of payment, which was often on a piecework basis.

Not to be confused with the names of potters are those of London dealers, who during the eighteenth and nineteenth centuries had goods made and decorated to their specific orders.

The marks used on English wares were applied in several different ways, including the incising (or scratching) on the unfired clay we have mentioned above. The other marks impressed in the body at this stage are also a reliable guide and usually were names of the factory, place or proprietor, made up of printers' type and stamped in one operation.

Painting or transfer-printing under the glaze in blue (also in green after 1850) was a most common method of marking wares and may be accepted as genuine, at least as far as knowing the piece was marked at the time of manufacture.

14

The practice of marking by painting, transfer-printing, or stencilling over the glaze in enamel-colours, are methods which are always liable to be fraudulent, as it is possible to add these type of marks at any time after the piece has been made.

The beginner should approach all marks with caution and it is important to learn to detect the difference between the various materials, (i.e. earthenware, hard-paste porcelain, soft-paste porcelain and bone-china, etc.); this would enable him to immediately realize that a neat gold anchor on a Chelsea-type figure cannot possibly be of that factory if the body is a hard continental paste and not the soft-paste as used at Chelsea. Finally do remember that many nineteenth-century factories include the date of their establishment in their mark and those early dates do not signify that the piece in question was made at that date, and also, that grandmother, who died at the ripe old age of one hundred and one, did not necessarily acquire the piece of china she has passed down to you at her birth.

Notes on Wares Made in
Great Britain and Ireland

The English late-medieval wares are not only of great artistic interest, but historically important as the direct ancestors of the Staffordshire wares. Little is known of the places of their production, the finer specimens perhaps being made in monasteries, and though of coarse materials the jugs and pitchers are often of great beauty of form and bear simple but effective decoration.

In the fifteenth and sixteenth centuries smaller neater jugs appear with a rich copper-green glaze together with a hard red pottery with dark brown or black glaze sometimes decorated with trailed white slip or with applied pads of white clay.

A rare and distinct class of sixteenth-century English pottery comprises cisterns, stove-tiles and candle-brackets finely moulded in relief and covered with a green or yellow glaze.

English pottery tradition before the industrial period was rooted in the medieval use of lead-glazed earthenware. The sixteenth-century Cistercian pottery was the immediate forerunner of the Tickenhall and Staffordshire slip-wares, and the tradition of the last in turn gave vitality to the 'Astbury' and 'Whieldon' wares made in the same district in the eighteenth century.

The impulse towards refinement, which had been inspired by the Elers brothers (who made fine red wares in the Chinese style) and by the vogue of porcelain, also led to the making of a fine white salt-glazed stoneware in Staffordshire, where the industrializing process was finally carried through by Josiah Wedgwood. His cream-coloured ware was immediately imitated at numerous neighbouring potteries as well as at Leeds, Liverpool, Bristol, Swansea, Sunderland, Newcastle, Portobello and elsewhere, quickly securing a world-wide market.

Aside from the main English tradition are the decorative stonewares of Wedgwood, products of the neo-Classical enthusiasm.

Tin-glazed ware, largely inspired by Italian, Dutch and Chinese models, was made at London, Bristol, Liverpool, Dublin and Glasgow, but had little effect on the main current of the English tradition as represented by the wares of Staffordshire, where delftware (as this is called) was never made. English delftware was painted in high-temperature colours; overglaze enamels were used only on very rare examples and were probably the work of Dutch independent enamellers.

The seventeenth-century stoneware of Fulham, inspired at first by the Rhenish and Chinese wares, produced the isolated phenomenon of Dwight's admirable figures; that of Nottingham, though typically English, was of minor importance, reflecting latterly something of the Staffordshire style.

English porcelain of the eighteenth century is remarkable for its variety of composition. Soft-pastes of French type ware made at Chelsea, Derby and Longton Hall; soapstone pastes at Worcester, Caughley and Liverpool; and hard-paste at Plymouth and Bristol. From about 1750 onwards for several decades Derby was a most productive factory and a large proportion of the surviving English porcelain figures were made there. At Bow the use of bone-ash from 1747 heralded the type of porcelain which towards the end of the eighteenth century became and still remains the English standard body; this last was a hybrid porcelain in which some part of the kaolin was replaced by bone-ash. At Nantgarw and Swansea a belated soft-paste was made in the period 1813–22.

None of the factories enjoyed royal or princely protection or subsidy and most were short-lived. Chelsea, and possibly Worcester, alone reached the standard set by the chief manufacturers of France or the many establishments supported by the rulers of small states in Germany; the porcelain of the first-named, however, ranks with the best ever made in Europe. The unsophisticated charm of Bow and Lowestoft is of a different order and typically English.

From the absence of marks, the English porcelains are difficult to identify. The chief factories were those named above, but other early manufacturers may have existed in Limehouse, Lambeth, Kentish Town, Vauxhall and Greenwich.

The ceramic art of the nineteenth century suffered no less than others from misdirected effort and mistaken enthusiasms. While the early part of the century lived largely on the artistic capital of the preceding period, the later part was chiefly occupied with the deliberate revival of former styles.

Yet in spite of unfavourable conditions the native genius of the English potters did succeed in producing wares which are both beautiful and of permanent value; the simple 'cottage china' and lustre wares of the New Hall type and its kindred earthenware; Worcester, Derby, Spode, Coalport and other porcelains which were its opulent contemporaries and successors, the charming blue-printed ware, and the entirely English brown stonewares of the Midlands and Lambeth. A singular use of glazed Parian is to be noted in the wares of Belleek in Co. Fermanagh, Ireland, where a pottery was started in 1863. Vases in naturalistic shell-forms were especially characteristic.

At the end of the century the revival of handicraft makes its appearance with De Morgan and the Martin Brothers, heralding the studio pottery of the present day.

AMESBURY (Wiltshire)
Zillwood, W., late 18th-
early 19th centuries
pottery

W.Z.
incised

ASHBY-DE-LA-ZOUCH
(Leicestershire)
Thompson, J., *c.* 1815–56
general pottery

JOSEPH THOMPSON
WOODEN BOX
POTTERY
DERBYSHIRE
impressed
and other printed marks

Wilson & Proudman
Coleorton Pottery
1835–42, general pottery

WILSON &
PROUDMAN
impressed

ASHTEAD (Surrey)
Ashtead Potters Ltd.
1926–36, earthenware

AYLBURTON (Gloucestershire)
Leach, Margaret, 1946–56
Taena Community, 1951–56
and Upton St. Leonards, Glos.
where L. A. Groves also
used mark. Studio-pottery

impressed

BARNSTAPLE (Devon)
Baron, W. L., 1899–1939
Rolle Quay Pottery
earthenware

BARON. BARNSTAPLE
incised

20

Brannam, Ltd., C. H.,
Litchdon Pottery, 1879–
earthenwares

C. H. BRANNAM
BARUM
incised

    as from 1913–

C. H. BRANNAM LTD.
impressed

printed or impressed, 1929–

impressed, 1930–

C. H. BRANNAM
BARUM DEVON

BELPER (Derbyshire)
Belper Pottery 1809–34
stonewares
(transferred to Denby 1834)

BELPER
impressed

BENTHALL (Salop)
Pierce & Co., W., *c.* 1800–18
earthenwares

W. PIERCE & CO.

Salopian Art Pottery Co.
1882–*c.* 1912 earthenwares,

SALOPIAN
impressed

BILLINGHAM (Cleveland) and
elsewhere
Dunn, Constance, 1924–
studio-pottery

incised

BIRKENHEAD (Merseyside)
  Della Robbia Co. Ltd.
  earthenwares, *c.* 1894–1901

DELLA ROBBIA
impressed or incised

  top initial that of decorator

BISHOPS WALTHAM
(Hampshire)
  Bishops Waltham Pottery
  decorative earthenwares
  only from 1866–7 in
  Greek revival form

BISHOPS
WALTHAM
printed

BOVEY TRACEY (Devon)
  Bovey Tracey Pottery Co.
  earthenwares, 1842–94
  Bovey Pottery Co. Ltd.
  1894–1957
  also
  'Blue Waters Pottery'
  c. 1954–57

B.T.P. CO.
printed or impressed

c. 1937–49   1949–56

  Devonshire Potteries Ltd.
  earthenwares. 1947–
  also
  'Trentham Art Wares'
  1959–

TRENTHAM
ART WARE

Ehlers, A. W. G.
  Lowerdown Cross, 1946–55
  studio-potter

incised or painted

22

Leach, David, 1956–
(also at St. Ives *c.* 1932–56)
  'LD' for Lowerdown
  Pottery

impressed

BOW (London)
(Stratford High St., Essex)
c. 1747– *c.* 1776
soft-paste porcelain
  early marks, *c.* 1750

incised

  presumably 'repairers'
  marks 1750–60

incised

impressed

probably mark of
'repairer'
Mr. Tebo (Thibaud?)

impressed

marks on blue-painted
wares 1750–70

underglaze blue

on figures and other late pieces
and
'anchor and dagger'
period, *c.* 1762–76

in red

in underglaze
blue and red

23

in red   in underglaze blue

         in underglaze   in underglaze
         blue and red   blue

 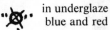

on blue-and-white
cups, in underglaze
blue   in underglaze blue

BRADFORD (W. Yorkshire)
  Booth, Frederick, *c.* 1881
  earthenware
	F.B.

BRAMPTON (Derbyshire)
  Knowles & Son, Matthew
  stonewares, *c.* 1835–1911
	KNOWLES

Oldfield & Co., *c.* 1838–88 earthenware	J. OLDFIELD OLDFIELD & CO. impressed

Pearson Ltd., James
  Oldfield and London
  Potteries. stonewares
  19th century—1939
  1920–
	J.P. LTD.
	impressed or printed
	from 1907
	
	Bramfield Ware

24

BRAUNTON (N. Devon)
Braunton Pottery Co. Ltd.
earthenwares, 1910–
　　mark of *c.* 1947–
(moved or finished by 1972)　printed or impressed

BRAUNTON
POTTERY
DEVON

BRISTOL (Avon)
(Lund & Miller's factory)
soft-paste (soapstone)
porcelain 1748–52, then
transferred to Worcester

BRISTOL
BRISTOLL
in relief

(Cookworthy & Champion's factory)
hard-past porcelain
1770–81, transferred
from Plymouth

underglaze blue,
blue enamel, red or
gold

　early mark during
　Cookworthy's
　ownership (also used
　at Plymouth)

in blue enamel

　underglaze blue
　and blue enamel

blue
enamel

tin-glazed earthenware
(delftware) *c.* 1650–

mark of John Bowen,
painter, apprenticed
1734

yf. 1ˢᵗ : Septʳ
1761
Bowen - fecit,
in blue

25

initials of Michael Edkins,
delft-painter and his wife
on plate dated 1760

M̈ B
j7 60
in blue

Bristol Pottery
c. 1785–1825
earthenwares

BRISTOL POTTERY
impressed or painted

Coombes, a china-mender
c. 1775–1805
  in pale brown lustre

Coombes
Queen St
Bristol

Fifield, William (b. 1777,
d. 1857) painter on
Bristol pottery
c. 1810–55

W.F.
W.F.B.
W. FIFIELD

Pardoe, Thomas (d. 1823)
painter at Derby,
Worcester, Cambrian
Pottery, Swansea,
factories, independent
decorator of pottery and
porcelain in Bristol
c. 1809–20

Pardoe
28 Bath St.,
Bristol
Warranted

Pardoe, Bristol
painted

Pardoe, William Henry
(son), decorator at
Cardiff and elsewhere
c. 1820–35

PARDOE, CARDIFF

Patience, Thomas
18th century stoneware

PATIENCE
impressed

26

Pountney & Allies Bristol Pottery *c.* 1816– 35, earthenware	P. P. & A. P.A. B.P.
printed, impressed or painted	P.A. BRISTOL POTTERY
impressed	
Pountney & Goldney Bristol Pottery, 1836–49	POUNTNEY & GOLDNEY (or as above)
impressed Pountney & Co., 1849– Bristol Victoria Pottery	BRISTOL POTTERY P. & CO.
1849–89	POUNTNEY & CO.
1889–	POUNTNEY & CO. LTD.
c. 1954– now Cauldon Bristol Potteries Ltd.	*Bristol* founded ✕ in 1652 *England*
Powell, William (& Sons) Temple Gate Pottery *c.* 1830–1906, stoneware	POWELL BRISTOL
impressed *c.* 1830–	BRISTOL TEMPLE GATE POTTERY

Ring, Joseph 1785–
(*d.* 1788), cream
coloured earthenware
continued by partners
until 1812

RING & CO.
impressed

BROSELEY (Salop)
Maw & Co. Ltd., 1850–
tiles and art pottery
from *c.* 1875
c. 1880–

MAW & CO.

FLOREAT MAW
SALOPIA

BURTON-ON-TRENT (Derbyshire)
Bretby Art Pottery, Woodville
Tooth & Ault 1883–87
Tooth & Co. 1887–
earthenwares
Henry Tooth *c.* 1883–1900

c. 1914–

CLANTA
WARE

Woodward, James
Swadlincote Pottery
'Majolica' earthenware
1859–88

printed or impressed

CASTLE HEDINGHAM (Essex)
Hedingham Art Pottery
Bingham, Edward
1864–1901
reproduction of medieval
and Tudor type wares

applied in relief

28

incised signature
1864–1901

E. BINGHAM
CASTLE HEDINGAM
ESSEX

early 20th century

ROYAL ESSEX ART
POTTERY WORKS

CASTLEFORD (W. Yorkshire)
Clokie & Masterson
earthenware, 1872–81

C. & M.
CLOKIE &
MASTERMAN
printed or impressed

Clokie & Co., 1888–1961
earthenware
(Ltd. after 1940)
printed

Dunderdale & Co., David
Castleford Pottery,
c. 1790–1820
earthenware and
stoneware

D.D. & CO.

D.D. & CO.
CASTLEFORD

Gill, William (& Sons)
Providence Pottery
1880–1932

printed

Hartley's (Castleford)
Ltd., Phillips Pottery
c. 1898–1960
stoneware and earthenware;
decorative art wares
from 1953

HARTROX

29

Nicholson & Co., Thomas
earthenware, *c.* 1854–71

T.N. & CO.
printed with name
of pattern

Robinson Bros.
Castleford & Allerton
Potteries
stoneware, 1897–1904

R.B.
printed or
impressed

Robinson & Son, John
stoneware, 1905–33

J.R. & S.
impressed

CAUGHLEY (Salop)
Turner, Thomas
c. 1772–1799 (then taken over by John Rose
of Coalport factory)
soft-paste porcelain and
black basaltes
(*see also* 'Benthall')

SALOPIAN
Salopian
impressed

printed or painted in
underglaze blue *c.* 1772–95

$\mathcal{S}$ $\mathcal{S}_X$

$\mathcal{S}_o$

printed or painted
c. 1772–95

$\mathbb{C}$ $\mathbb{C}$

printed mark usually
Worcester
open printed crescent
also on Coalport

$\mathbb{C}$ $\mathbb{C}$

printed

Chinese type mark

CHEAM (Surrey)   HENRY CLARK
Clark, Henry, 1869–80   CHEAM POTTERY
earthenware   impressed or incised

CHELSEA (London)
c. 1745–1784 soft-paste porcelain
(1770–84 known as 'Chelsea-Derby'
period under William Duesbury)

rare incised mark on
'triangle' period
1745–*c.* 1749

usual triangle mark

rare mark of 'crown   incised
and trident', 1745–*c.*
1750 in underglaze blue

'raised-anchor' mark
c. 1749–52, latterly
picked out in red

in applied relief

'red-anchor' mark
1752–*c.* 1758
occasionally painted in   painted in red
blue or purple

31

c. 1750–56
painted in underglaze blue

'gold anchor' mark
c. 1756–69
(also seen on Chelsea-
Derby wares as late
as 1775)

in gold

rare 'repairers' mark
(not Roubiliac)

impressed

Chelsea Pottery, 1952–　　　CHELSEA POTTERY
(Rawnsley Academy Ltd.)　　　incised
impressed or
incised, 1952–

Vyse, Charles, 1919–*c.* 63　　　C.V.　　C.V.
studio-potter　　　　　　　　　CHELSEA

painted mark with
year-date added

19 34

CHELSEA

P. & CO.

CHESTERFIELD
(Derbyshire)
　　Pearson & Co., 1805–　　　　PEARSON & CO.
　　Whittington Moor　　　　　　WHITTINGTON
　　Potteries　　　　　　　　　　MOOR
　　　　1805–*c.* 1880　　　　　　impressed

1880–

from *c.* 1925 renamed as
Pearson & Co. (Chesterfield) Ltd.

Barker Pottery Co.
1887–1957
stoneware
    printed or impressed
    mark 1928–1957

CHURCH GRESLEY (Derbyshire)
    Green & Co. Ltd., T.G.
c. 1864– earthenware
and stoneware
    printed mark *c.* 1888–

    mark of *c.* 1930, numerous
    other late marks all
    include 'T. G. Green
    & Co., Ltd.'

CLEVEDON (Avon)   1879–1920
    Elton, Sir Edmund
    Sunflower Pottery
    1879–1930   1920–30

Elton

Holland, William Fishley
studio-potter, 1921–
earthenware

FH

                        incised

33

Holland, Isabel Fishley
pottery figures, 1929–42

I. HOLLAND

Holland, George Fishley
earthenware, 1955–

CLIFTON JUNCTION
(nr. Manchester)
  Pilkington Tile & Pottery
  Co. Ltd., earthenwares
  and tiles, (decorative
  pottery, 1897–1938,
  1948–57)

P
early incised mark

  factory mark, VIII for
  1908

VIII

  c. 1914–38

'ROYAL LANCASTRIAN'

marks of notable designers:

Lewis F. Day

Walter Crane

C. E. Cundall

R. Joyce

Jessie Jones

G. M. Forsyth

Gladys Rodgers

W. Mycock

34

COALPORT (Salop)
John Rose, *c.* 1796–
(transferred to Stoke-on-Trent
c. 1926)

rare early mark in red   COALBROOKDALE

1815–25 on many wares
decorated in Swansea
style

impressed

c. 1810–25, in underglaze
blue

underglaze blue mark
c. 1810–20

C. B. DALE

marks used from *c.* 1820

1830–50

JOHN ROSE & CO.
COALBROOKDALE
SHROPSHIRE
35

c. 1851–61, painted or gilt

c. 1861–75, 'c'
Coalport, 's',
Swansea, 'N', Nantgarw

painted or gilt

printed mark c. 1870–80
incorporating Patent
Office Registration
mark

c. 1875–81, printed or
painted
late marks c. 1881–
'England' added 1891
'Made in England'
c. 1920

COALPORT A.D. 1750

wares made for London
dealer A. B. & R. P.
Daniell c. 1860–1917

large size anchor mark
on Coalport copies of
Chelsea, also on
Continental wares
without 'c'

CODNOR PARK
(Derbyshire)
  Burton, William,
  c. 1821–32, stoneware

W. BURTON
CODNOR PARK
impressed

CROWBOROUGH (Sussex) & REDHILL (Surrey)
  Walford, J. F., 1948–
  studio-potter

DARTINGTON (S. Devon)
  Trey, Marianne de
  studio-potter, 1947–
  Shinners Bridge Pottery

incised or painted

  Haile, T. S., *c.* 1936–43,
  1945–8, studio-potter

impressed

DENBY (Derbyshire)
  Bourne & Son Ltd.,
  Joseph, *c.* 1809–
  stoneware

BOURNES
WARRANTED

  Joseph Bourne, 1833–60
  'Son' added 1850

J. BOURNE & SON
PATENTEES
DENBY POTTERY
NEAR DERBY
impressed

DENHOLME (W. Yorkshire)
  Taylor, Nicholas
  1893–1909
  earthenware

N. Taylor
Denholme
incised

DERBY (Derbyshire)
  c. 1750–1848
  soft-paste porcelain
    early marks of Planché
    period c. 1750–56

Derby

incised *1750*

Derby Porcelain Works
1756–1848
  'William Duesbury &
  Co.' c. 1760

WD·Co

incised

  'N' seen on dishes, etc.
  c. 1770–80

N

incised

  'Chelsea-Derby' marks
  c. 1770–84

in gold

  c. 1770–82, in blue or
  purple

incised model numbers
on figures, c. 1775–
early 19th century

No 314

No 195

common Derby mark
1782–, incised, purple,
blue or black
c. 1800–25 in red
enamel

mark of Isaac
Farnsworth 'repairer'

mark of Joseph Hill
'repairer'

'size' mark

'Duesbury & Kean',
c. 1795
in blue, crimson or purple

blue-painted mark in
imitation of Meissen
c. 1785–1825

Robert Bloor Period

printed in red
c. 1820–40

printed in red
c. 1830–48

mark in imitation of
Sèvres, *c.* 1825–48
in blue enamel

39

Locker & Co., King Street factory
c. 1849–59

similar marks used also
by:
Stevenson Sharp & Co.
1859–61
'Courtney late Bloor'
1849–63

Stevenson & Hancock
1861–1935, this mark
also used after 1935
when King St. factory
was taken over by Royal Crown Derby
Porcelain Co. Ltd.

Derby Crown Porcelain Co. Ltd. Est. 1876
c. 1878–90, together   Derby
  with year mark as
  shown in table on next
  page   impressed

printed

Royal Crown Derby Porcelain Co. Ltd.
1890–
  printed mark of *c.* 1890
  'England' from 1891
  'Made in England'
  added from *c.* 1920
  together with year
  mark
(Part of Royal Doulton Tableware Ltd. from 1973)

TABLE OF DERBY YEAR-MARKS,
1882–

1882	1883	1884	1885	1886	1887	1888

1889	1890	1891	1892	1893	1894	1895

1896	1897	1898	1899	1900	1901	1902

1903	1904	1905	1906	1907	1908	1909

1910	1911	1912	1913	1914	1915	1916

1917	1918	1919	1920	1921	1922	1923

1924	1925	1926	1927	1928	1929	1930

1931	1932	1933	1934	1935	1936	1937

1938	1939	1940	1941	1942	1943	1944
I	II	III	IV	V	VI	VII

1945	1946	1947	1948	1949	1950	1951
VIII	IX	X	XI	XII	XIII	etc.

Derby Pot Works
creamwares, *c.* 1750–80

T. RADFORD SC.
DERBY

Thomas Radford,
engraver of prints
found on some
Cockpit Hill wares

RADFORD fecit
DERBY POT WORKS

Potts, W. W.
St. George's Works, *c.*
1831–, earthenware
(also at Burslem)

marks indicating
patent printing
processes, 1831 & 1835

DONYATT (Somerset)
Rogers, James, 19th century
(with descendants)
sgraffiato slipwares

Jas Rogers
Maker Octr 10th
1848

    impressed on jug
    dated 1864

ROGERS & SONS
CROCK STRETT
POTTERY

EAST HENDRED (Oxfordshire)
Thompson, Pauline
studio-potter, 1950–

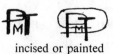

incised or painted

EAST HORSLEY (Surrey)
Moore, Denis & Michael
Buckland
Green Dene Pottery
1953–
    (initials also used)

impressed or painted

FARNHAM (Surrey)
Hammond, Henry
studio-potter, 1934–40,
1946–

incised   impressed

Barron, Paul
studio-potter, 1948–

B

impressed

FELIXSTOWE (Suffolk)
Kemp, Dorothy, 1939–
studio-potter

incised or impressed

FERRYBRIDGE (Yorkshire)
Ferrybridge Pottery, 1792–
known as Knottingley Pottery, 1792–1804

1792–6, *c.* 1801–34   TOMLINSON & CO.
                            impressed or printed

Wedgwood, Ralph, *c.*   WEDGWOOD & CO.
1796–1801

c. 1804–   FERRYBRIDGE
                             impressed

Reed & Taylor, *c.* 1843–56	R. & T.	R.T. & CO.
Woolf & Sons, L., *c.* 1856–83	L.W.	L.W. & S.
Poulson, Bros., Ltd. 1884–97	P.B.	P.BROS
Sefton & Brown, *c.* 1897–1919	S.B.	
Brown & Sons, T., *c.* 1919–	T.B & S.	

43

FREMINGTON (Devon)
  Fishley, Edwin Beer
  1861–1906, earthenware

E. B. FISHLEY
FREMINGTON
N. DEVON
  incised

FULHAM (London)
  Dwight, John, 1671–
  salt-glazed stoneware

no certain
marks

De Morgan, William
  c. 1872–1907
  decorator of earthenwares made to order
  from other factories, and own wares
    impressed mark, 1882–
    '& Co.' added after 1888

marks used at Merton Abbey, 1882–88
made own tiles from *c.*
1879, and wares from 1882

  impressed or painted
  1882–

Sands End Pottery, 1888–97
(period of partnership with
Halsey Ricardo)

1898–1907, partnership with
Frank Iles, Charles & Fred
Passenger at Fulham

decoration continued
until 1911, four years
after De Morgan retired

all impressed

earthenwares were decorated
in De Morgan style at
Mrs. Ida Perrin's studio,
Bushey Heath, 1921–33
by Fred Passenger

Fulham Pottery & Cheavin Filter Co. Ltd.
vases & commercial pottery
1889–present

FULHAM POTTERY
LONDON

1948–　　　　　　　impressed

GATESHEAD (Tyne and Wear)
　　Durham China Co. Ltd.
　　general ceramics, 1947–57

printed or impressed

HENLEY-ON-THAMES
(Berkshire)
　　Hawkins, John & Son
　　china and glass dealers
　　closed about 1935

'FAMOUS HENLEY CHINA'
EST. 1867
HAWKINS
HENLEY-ON-THAMES

HEREFORD
   Godwin & Hewitt, tiles
   1889–1910, mark printed
   or impressed

HONITON (Devon)
   Honiton Art Potteries
   Ltd., earthenware, *c.*
   1881–, printed or
   impressed *c.* 1915

THE HONITON
LACE ART POTTERY
CO.

   Collard, C., 1918–1947
   printed or impressed

COLLARD HONITON
ENGLAND

   Hull, N. T. S., 1947–1955

N.T.S. HULL

   1947–

HONITON POTTERY
DEVON

   Hull, Norman
   Norman Hull Pottery
   1947–55

NORMAN HULL
POTTERY

HORNSEA (Humberside)
   Hornsea Pottery Co. Ltd.
   earthenware, *c.* 1951
     printed or impressed, 1962–

HULL (Humberside)
   Longbottom, Samuel
   earthenware, late 19th
   century, closed 1899

S.L.
impressed

IPSWICH (Suffolk)
  Balaam, W., 1870–81
  Rope Lane Pottery
  slipwares

W. BALAAM
ROPE LANE POTTERY
IPSWICH
impressed

ISLEWORTH (London)
  earthenware, *c.* 1760–
  1825, Shore, J.
  Shore & Co.
  Shore & Goulding
    (*Note:* S. & G. seen on Wedgwood type wares
    are Schiller & Gerbing, Bodenbach, Bohemia.
    See Pocket-Book of German Ceramic Marks)

SHORE & CO.
S. & CO.
S. & G.
ISLEWORTH

JACKFIELD (Salop)
  Craven Dunnill & Co.
  Ltd., tiles, 1872–1951

CRAVEN & CO.

JACKFIELD

KEW (Surrey)
  Duckworth, Ruth
  studio-potter, 1956–

painted or incised

KILMINGTON MANOR (Wiltshire)
  Pleydell-Bouverie, Katharine
  stoneware, 1925–
  studio-potter
  (also at other addresses)

incised or stamped

47

LAMBETH (London)
  Coade & Sealy, 1769–
1811, artificial stoneware

'Coade Lambeth'

Doulton & Watts
stoneware and earthenware
c. 1815–1858
  c. 1826–1838
  on early brown salt-
  glazed wares

  c. 1826–1858

  all marks impressed
  moulded or incised

Doulton & Co.
Lambeth, *c.* 1858–1956
Burslem, *c.* 1882–
  c. 1869–77, decorated
  coloured wares, year often
  appears in centre after 1872

DOULTON
LAMBETH

  '4D' mark on decorated
  salt-glaze

  Note: 'England' added
  after 1891

c. 1877–80   *c.* 1880–1902

  mark on mural tiles
  c. 1879–1900

on wares decorated with
coloured clays
c. 1887–1900

underglaze decorated
earthenware

c. 1872–73

c. 1873–1908

underglaze decorated
earthenware, c. 1881–1910

'Carrara' ware, stoneware
covered with translucent
crystalline enamel
c. 1888–1898

'Silicon' ware, unglazed
stoneware, c. 1882–1912

fine earthenware and china,
made at Burslem
c. 1882–1902

standard impressed mark
c. 1902–22
c. 1927–36

Lambeth stoneware
c. 1922–

Burslem factory marks   DOULTON
c. 1882–1902

                    DOULTON
                                        & SLATERS
                                         PATENT
c. 1900–   ROYAL   ROYAL
                                  DOULTON   DOULTON
                                   FLAMBE   KALON
c. 1960–   ENGLISH
                                  TRANSLUCENT
                                      CHINA

selection of initials used
by Doulton decorators:
Atkins, Elizabeth, *c.* 1876–82   *EA*
Banks, Eliza, *c.* 1876–84   *E/B*
Barlow, Arthur B., 1871–8   *AB 3*
Barlow, Florence E., *c.* 1873–1909

Barlow, Hannah B., *c.* 1872–1906

Barnard, Harry, *c.* 1880–90

Butler, Frank A., *c.* 1872–1911

50

Butterton, Mary, *c.* 1874–94	
Capes, Mary, *c.* 1876–83	
Dewsberry, David, 1889–1919	D.Dewsberry
Dunn, William, E., *c.* 1883–95	
Lee, Frances E., *c.* 1875–90	FEL
Marshall, Mark V., 1879–1912	M·V·M
Pope, Frank C., 1880–1923	F·C·P
Raby, Edward J., 1892–1911	E.Raby
Rowe, William, 1883–1939	WR
Simeon, Henry, 1894–1936	
Simmance, Eliza, *c.* 1873–1928	S
Tinworth, George, 1886–1913	

A full-list of painters, modellers and designers are shown in *Royal Doulton* 1815–1965 by Desmond Eyles, London, 1965, together with full guides, etc. to precise dating

Green, Stephen
Imperial Pottery
stoneware, *c.* 1820–58

impressed marks

STEPHEN GREEN
IMPERIAL
POTTERIES
LAMBETH

Stiff, James
London Pottery, *c.* 1840–
1913 stonewares
    c. 1863

J. STIFF

J. STIFF & SONS
impressed

LANGLEY MILL (Nottingham)
Lovatt & Lovatt, 1895–
stoneware and earthenware
printed or impressed marks
          c. 1900–

now Langley
Pottery Ltd. (1967)   *c.* 1900–   *c.* 1931–62

LEEDS (W. Yorkshire)
  c. 1770–1881
creamware, earthenware and stoneware

Green Bros., 1770–

LEEDS *POTTERY
impressed

Humble, Green & Co., 1774–76

Humble, Hartley, Greens & Co., 1776–1780

LEEDS POTTERY

LEEDS *POTTERY

Hartley, Greens & Co. 1781–1830

LEEDS *POTTERY

1800–1830

LEEDS.POTTERY

HARTLEY GREENS & Co
LEEDS * POTTERY

LEEDS*POTTERY.

all marks impressed

LEEDS*POTTERY

HARTLEY*GREENS*&*Co
LEEDS*POTTERY

HARTLEY
LEEDS

HARTLEY*GREENS & Co
LEEDS * POTTERY

1780–1810
impressed or enamelled

LP

Britton & Son, Richard
1872–8, earthenware
  initials found on variety
  of transfer-printed wares

R.B. & S.
printed

Rainforth & Co. 1800–17
Petty's Pottery, 1817–46
earthenware & creamware

RAINFORTH & CO.
PETTYS & CO. LEEDS

printed or impressed

Burmantofts
art-pottery, 1882–1904
  marks impressed

BURMANTOFTS
FAIENCE

Leeds Fireclay Co. Ltd.
earthenware, *c.* 1904–14

L.
F.C.

decorative wares, made
up until 1914, after
which only commercial
& utility wares were
produced

LEFICO

GRANITOFTS

Yates, William, *c.* 1840–76
(retailer only)

YATES
LEEDS
printed or painted

LETCHWORTH
(Hertfordshire)
  Cowlishaw, W. H.
  1908–14, earthenwares

ICENI WARE
impressed

LIVERPOOL (Merseyside)
  Chaffers, Richard, 1743–65
  tin-glazed earthenware
  and soft-paste porcelain
    dated example referring
    to son:

Richard ✕ Chaffers ~ 1769 ~

Christian, Philip
c. 1765–1776

'CHRISTIAN'
impressed

Billinge, Thomas
engraver, *c.* 1760–80

Billinge Sculp
Liverpool

Sadler, John & Green,
Guy, printers only, their
work seen on tiles,
Wedgwood's creamware,
Longton Hall, etc.,
1756–1799

J. Sadler, Liverpool

Green, Liverpool

Abbey, Richard
engraver and printer
1773–80, potter from
1790

ABBEY
LIVERPOOL

R. Abbey, sculp.

Johnson, Joseph
engraver, second half
18th century

'I. JOHNSON,
LIVERPOOL'

Herculaneum Pottery
earthenware and procelain
c. 1793–1841
Worthington, Humble
& Holland, 1794–1806

HERCULANEUM

impressed or printed marks, *c.* 1796–1833

1822–41

HERCULANEUM POTTERY
impressed or printed
in blue

Case, Thomas & Mort, John, 1833–1836

   printed, usually in red

Mort & Simpson

   'Liver' bird printed or impressed, *c.* 1836–41

Gibson, John & Solomon, earthenware, early 19th century

JOHN GIBSON
LIVERPOOL
1813

LONDON
VARIOUS RETAILERS OF POTTERY & PORCELAIN

Allsup, John, 1832–58
   printed

JOHN ALLSUP
ST. PAUL'S CHURCH-
YARD, LONDON

Blades, John
c. 1800–30

BLADES LONDON

Bradley & Co., J.
decorators and retailers
c. 1813–20

J. BRADLEY & CO.

Brameld, J. W.
c. 1830–50
partner of
Rockingham Works

I. W. BRAMELD

at various
London addresses

Daniell, A. B. & R. P.
c. 1825–1917
    printed mark on wares
    of Coalport, etc. made
    to order for Daniell's

Dreydel & Co., Henry
late 19th century
    mark of wares made
    to order both in England
    and on Continent

Goode & Co. (Ltd.), Thomas
c. 1860–present
'Ltd' from 1918
now in South Audley St.

Green & Co., J.
1834–42 at St. Paul's
Churchyard, elsewhere
until *c.* 1874

Haines, Batchelor & Co.
1880–90

    H.B.
    printed

Hales, Hancock &
Goodwin, Ltd., 1922–60
(Hales, Hancock & Co.
Ltd., and Hales Bros.)

    H.H. & G. LTD.
    printed

Hart & Son 1826–69	H. & S. printed
Howell & James *c.* 1820–1922 (also retailers of materials for amateur decorators)	HOWELL & JAMES

Mortlock, J.
1746–*c.* 1930
    many marks used
    including name of such
    manufacturers as
    Mintons
	MORTLOCK
	
	MORTLOCKS
	OXFORD STREET

Pearce, Alfred B. 1866–1940	ALFRED B. PEARCE 39 LUDGATE HILL LONDON
Pellatt & Co., Apsley *c.* 1789– (also glass retailers)	APSLEY PELLATT & CO.
Pellatt & Green *c.* 1805–30	PELLATT & GREEN LONDON
Pellatt & Wood *c.* 1870–90	PELLATT & WOOD

Phillips, *c.* 1799–1929
    c. 1858–97
    c. 1897–1906
    c. 1908–29
	
	W. P. & G. PHILLIPS
	PHILLIPS & CO.
	PHILLIPS LTD.

Walker, William   WALKER MINORIES
c. 1795–1800

MINOR FACTORIES AND STUDIO-POTTERS
IN LONDON

Benham, Tony, 1958
  mark written or incised
  with year, studio-potter
(now at Wateringbury, Kent),

Billington, Dora
studio-potter, 1912–

incised or painted

Briglin Pottery Ltd.   BRIGLIN
earthenware, 1948–   impressed

Dalton, William B.
stoneware and porcelain

studio-potter, 1900–   incised or painted
c. 1955
(In U.S.A. from 1941)

Eeles, David   D.E.
studio-potter, 1955
Shepherd's Well Pottery
London, then in 1962
to Mosterton, Dorset

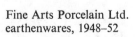

Fine Arts Porcelain Ltd.
earthenwares, 1948–52

printed

Fry, Roger, Omega
Workshops *c.* 1913–19,
studio-potter

Groves, Lavender
studio-potter, 1952–

Leach, Jeremy   J.L.   J.L.
studio-potter, *c.* 1959   D.S.

Martin Bros. (Robert Wallace, Walter, Edwin
and Charles), studio-potters, stoneware,
1873–1914
   1873–5   R. W. Martin fecit

     1873–4

     1874–8

     1878–9

    SOUTHALL   MARTIN
    MARTIN   SOUTHALL
    POTTERY   POTTERY

     1879–82

     1882–

all marks either incised or impressed together
with month and year

Mills, Donald
studio-potter, 1946–55

Murray, William Staite
studio-potter, 1919–62
in S. Rhodesia from 1940

W. S. MURRAY
(date)
LONDON

Northen & Co., W.
Union Potteries,
Lambeth, stoneware,
1847–92, '& Co.'
added 1887

W. NORTHEN
POTTER
VAUXHALL
LAMBETH

O'Malley, Peter
studio-potter, 1953–

Parnell, Gwendolen
studio-potter, 1916–36

CHELSEA CHEYNE
(date)
G.P.

Parr, Harry
studio-potter, *c.* 1919–
c. 1948

HY PARR
CHELSEA (date)

Powell, Alfred & Louise
decorators of Wedgwood
earthenwares, *c.* 1904–39

61

Powell, John
painter and retailer
c. 1810–30

Powell
91, Wimpole St.

Richards, Frances E.
studio-potter, 1922–31
   mark incised

Rie, Lucie
studio-potter, *c.* 1938–
   mark impressed

Samuel, Audrey
studio-potter, 1949–

A S

Smith & Co., Thomas
stonewares, 1879–93

T. SMITH & CO.
OLD KENT ROAD
LONDON

Stabler, Harold &
Phoebe, earthenware
designers and potters
b. 1872–*d.* 1945 (wife
d. 1955)

Phoebe Stabler
(date)

Stabler (date)

Vergette, Nicholas
studio-potter, 1946–58

Walters, Helen
studio-potter, 1945–
(now Helen Swain,
mark 'HWS')

1945–53   1953–

White, William J. W.W.
Fulham Pottery (date)
stoneware, *c.* 1750–1850

W. J. WHITE
incised dated marks (date)

LOWER DICKER (Sussex) U.C. & N.
U. Clark & Nephews, THE DICKER
1843–1946, earthenware SUSSEX
1933– DICKER WARE
Dicker Potteries Ltd. 1946–59

LOWESBY (Leicestershire) LOWESBY
Lowesby Pottery
Fowke, Sir Frederick
c. 1835–40
earthenwares

LOWESTOFT (Suffolk)
soft-paste porcelain
c. 1757– *c.* 1800
decorators numbers,
to approx. 17, painted
on inner wall of foot-
rim, *c.* 1760–75
copies of Worcester

1 3 5

7 9 13

and Meissen marks
c. 1775–1790

Allen, Robert, *b.* 1744, *d.* 1835
decorator at Lowestoft factory
and independent enameller
from *c.* 1800

Allen
Lowestoft

painted

MADELEY (Salop)
Randall, Thomas M.
c. 1825–40, decorator of
English and Sèvres porcelain;
with factory at Madeley
for production of soft-paste
imitations of Sèvres

T MR
Madeley
S

painted

MALVERN (Worcestershire)
Woods, Richard, *c.* 1850–
retailer only

R. WOODS
printed

MANCHESTER
Sutcliffe & Co., *c.* 1885–1901
decorative tiles

printed or impressed

MANSFIELD
(Nottinghamshire)
Billingsley, William
1799–1802
painter and gilder

BILLINGSLEY
MANFIELD
painted

MEXBOROUGH
(S. Yorkshire)
Emery, James
earthenware, 1837–61

J. EMERY
MEXBRO

incised

Rock Pottery
Reed, James, *c.* 1839–49

REED
impressed

Mexbro Pottery
Reed, John, *c.* 1849–73

Sowter & Co., *c.* 1795–
1804, Mexborough Old
Pottery
  marks impressed

SOWTER & CO.
MEXBRO

S. & CO.

Wilkinson & Wardle
Denaby Pottery, 1864–6
earthenware

Wardle & Co., John,
Denaby Pottery
earthenwares (including creamware)
1866–70
  printed mark

JOHN WARDLE & CO.

MIDDLESBROUGH
(Cleveland)
  Linthorpe Pottery, 1879–90
  earthenware (art pottery type)

LINTHORPE
impressed

    incised, impressed or
    painted signature of Dresser

Chr. Dresser

    Tooth, Henry, manager
    1879–1882

H   H T

Middlesbrough Pottery Co.
1834–44
earthenware and
creamware

M.P. CO.

MIDDLESBRO'
POTTERY CO.

65

Middlesbrough   M.E. & CO.
Earthenware Co.
1844–52, earthenware
   initials used with various
   printed or impressed marks

                  MIDDLESBRO POTTERY
                  (with anchor)
Wilson & Co., Isaac   I.W. & CO.
Middlesbrough Pottery   MIDDLESBRO'
1852–87   impressed

MORTLAKE (London)   KISHERE
   Mortlake Pottery, *c.*
   1800–43, Kishere,   I.K.
   Joseph   impressed
   salt-glazed stoneware

NEW BARNET (Hertfordshire)   D.A.
   Arbeid, Dan, 1956–
   Abbey Art Centre   ARBEID
   studio-potter   painted or impressed
   (now at Saffron Walden, Essex)

NEWCASTLE UPON TYNE   DAVIES & CO.
(Tyne and Wear)   impressed
   Davies & Co., 1833–51
   Tyne Main Pottery
   earthenware

   Fell, Thomas, 1817–90   FELL
   St. Peter's Pottery   impressed
   earthenware and creamware
   1817–30

                  impressed

Fell & Co., *c.* 1830–90	F. & CO.
initials used with	T.F. & CO.
various marks:	T. FELL & CO.

Ford & Patterson	FORD & PATTERSON
Sheriff Hill Pottery	Sheriff Hill
c. 1820–*c.* 1830	Pottery
earthenware	impressed
Jackson & Patterson	J. & P.
1830–45	
Maling, Robert	MALING
Ouseburn Pottery	M
1817–59, earthenware	impressed

Maling, C. T.	MALING
Ford Pottery, 1859–90	C. T. MALING
earthenware, often	C.T.M.
with lustre decoration	

Maling & Sons, Ltd.
1890–1963
earthenwares, mark of
c. 1875–1908

1890–	*c.* 1908	*c.* 1949–63

Patterson & Co.   PATTERSON & CO.
Sheriff Hill Pottery,   printed or
1830–1904, earthenware   impressed

Sewell, 1804– *c.* 28   SEWELL
St. Anthony's Pottery, *c.* 1780–1878
earthenware (including creamwares)
1780–1820   ST. ANTHONY'S
Sewell & Donkin   SEWELL & DONKIN
1828–52
Sewell & Co., 1852–78   SEWELL & CO.
                       all impressed or printed

Taylor & Co., *c.* 1820–5   TAYLOR & CO.
Tyne Pottery   printed
earthenware

Wallace & Co., J.   WALLACE & CO.
Newcastle or Forth Bank   impressed
Pottery, 1838–93, earthenware

Warburton, John, &   J. WARBURTON
family, Carr's Hill   N. ON TYNE
Pottery, earthenware, *c.* 1750–1817

NEWTON ABBOT (Devon)   **ꟻIΛƎᴎ IIꓘIꓘOИ**
  Phillips & Co., John
  Aller Pottery, 1868–87   printed or impressed

Aller Vale Art Potteries   ALLER VALE
earthenware, 1887–1901   impressed

Royal Aller Vale &
Watcombe Pottery Co.
(Torquay) *c.* 1901–62
  impressed or printed
    1901–

ROYAL ALLER VALE

ROYAL   DEVON
TORQUAY MOTTO
POTTERY WARE

Candy & Co. Ltd.
Great Western Potteries
earthenwares, 1882–

CANDY WARE
C
N A

NORTH SHIELDS
(Tyne and Wear)
  Carr, John
  earthenware, *c.* 1845–1900

J. CARR & CO.

NOTTINGHAM
(Nottinghamshire)
  Lockett, William
  stoneware, *c.* 1740–80

'Wm. and Ann Lockett,
1755'

OXFORD (Oxfordshire)
  Blackman, Audrey
  studio-potter, 1949–
  'Astbury-type' figures

A. BLACKMAN

OXSHOTT (Surrey)
  Oxshott Pottery, 1919
  Wren, Henry, *c.* 1919–47

HW   hw

Wren, Denise, *c.* 1919–

DKW

Wren, Rosemary, *c.* 1945–
69

PINXTON (Derbyshire)
  Pinxton Works, *c.* 1796–1813
  John Coke, William Billingsley
  soft-paste porcelain
  (Billingsley, *c.* 1796–93)
  (Cutts, *c.* 1803–1813)

in red   in purple
from arms of Coke

  marks found on late
  pieces

PLYMOUTH (Devon)
  Plymouth Porcelain Works
  Cookworthy, William
  hard-paste porcelain, 1768–70
  (transferred to Bristol in 1770)
    workman's mark also seen
    on Bow, Worcester, Bristol
    and Wedgwood

underglaze-blue,
blue enamel,
red or gold

$2\!\!\downarrow$

T°

  Plymouth Pottery Co. Ltd.
  earthenware, 1856–63

P.P. COY.L
STONE CHINA

POOLE (Dorset)
  Carter & Co.
  earthenware, 1873–1921

CARTER & CO.
CARTER POOLE

  Carter, Stabler & Adams
  1921–
    'Ltd.' added 1925
    1956–
  1963– Poole Pottery Ltd.

POOLE
ENGLAND

printed

70

PRAZE (Cornwall)
　Crowan Pottery, 1946–62
　Davis, Harry & May
　studio-potters

impressed

PRESTBURY (Cheshire)
　Nowell, C. D., *c.* 1946–59
　studio-potter
　(at Disley *c.* 1946–51)

C D Nowell

PRESTBURY

PRESTWOOD (Buckinghamshire)
　Newland, William
　studio-potter, 1948–

WN

(date)

　Casson, Michael & Sheila
　studio-potters, 1953–
　　Sheila Casson, 1951–59

CM　M

W
S

RAINHAM (Kent)
　Upchurch Pottery, 1913–61
　Baker, W. & J.
　　'Seeby', name of agent
　　1945–61

UPCHURCH

UPCHURCH
SEEBY

　Rainham Pottery Ltd.
　earthenware, 1948–
　Wilson, Alfred, now
　E. J. Baker

Rainham
impressed or painted

RAMSBURY (Wiltshire)
　Holdsworth Potteries
　Holdsworth, Peter, 1945–

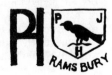

READING (Berkshire)
Collier Ltd., S. & E.
terra-cotta, *c.* 1848–1957

RICHMOND (Surrey)   Steven Sykes
Sykes, Steven, 1948–55   (signature)
studio-potter

ROCKINGHAM (Yorkshire)
Rockingham Works
(nr. Swinton) earthenware
c. 1750–1842 (porcelain
also made from about 1826)   BINGLEY
c. 1778–87   impressed

Brameld & Co., 1806–42   BRAMELD
     impressed

     c. 1826–30   ROCKINGHAM   ROCKINHGAM
               WORKS,   BRAMELD
               BRAMELD

     c. 1830–42   ROYAL
              ROCKINGHAM
                WORKS
              BRAMELD

     'griffin-mark', *c.* 1826–30
from crest of Earl Fitzwilliam,
Marquis of Rockingham

from *c.* 1830–42
     'Royal' added to title
of factory
mark in red *c.* 1826–30, puce 1830–42
'Manufacturer to the King' added to mark
in 1830–37 (William IV)

Baguley, Alfred & Isaac   'Griffin mark'
Rockingham Works   with
decorator only of   'Baguley'
porcelain in Rockingham
style, *c.* 1842–65 (Mexborough)
  c. 1865–91   printed

ROLVENDEN (Kent)
  Watson, Dorothy
  Bridge Pottery 1921–

                impressed or printed

ROTHERHAM (S. Yorkshire)   J.J. & CO.
  Holmes Pottery, 1870–87
  Jackson & Co., J.   J. & CO.
  earthenware
  Shaw & Sons, Ltd., G.   G.S. & S.
  1887–1948   printed

  Northfield Pottery   W. & G. HAWLEY
  earthenware
  Hawley, W. & G., 1863–8,
  Hawley Bros Ltd.,   H.B.
  1868–1903, 'Ltd'. added 1897   HAWLEY BROS.

  Northfield Hawley Pottery Co. Ltd.
  earthenware, 1903–19

    impressed or printed
    mark introduced about
    1898 by Hawley Bros.

Walker & Son   WALKER
earthenware, *c.* 1772–

RUSTINGTON (Sussex)
  Champion, G. H. & E. E.
  studio-potters, 1947–

RYE (Sussex)   SUSSEX WARE
  1869– mark of *c.* 1900
  pottery (including tin-glaze)
  c. 1869–1920
  (Sussex Rustic Ware)
  'S.A.W.' Sussex Art Ware
  c. 1920–39
  J. C. Cole & W. V.   RYE
  Cole, 1947–
    various marks including
    name 'RYE'
  Walter V. Cole, 1957–

Cadborough Pottery,   OLD SUSSEX WARE
  1807–71, earthenware   RYE

Mitchell, William, *c.*   MITCHELL
1840–, W. Mitchell &   M
Sons, 1859–69,
Mitchell, F. & H., 1869–71

Iden Pottery, 1961–
Townsend, D. & Wood, J. H.
studio-potters
(moved from Iden to Rye
in 1963)

74

Everett, Raymond, 1963–
studio-potter

ST. IVES (Cornwall)
Leach, Bernard, 1921–
  Leach Pottery marks
studio-pottery
  personal marks of B. Leach

Hamada, Shoji
1920–23, 1929–*c.* 30

Leach, Janet, 1956–

Leach, John, *c.* 1950–8
(at Langport, Somerset since 1964)
Marshall, William, 1954–   impressed

incised

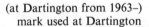

Mc. Kenzie, Warren, 1950–2

(at Dartington from 1963–)
  mark used at Dartington

Quick, Kenneth, 1945–63
(at St. Ives 1945–*c.* 55 and
1960–63)
  mark used at Tregenna Hill Pottery
  c. 1955–60

ST. MARY CHURCH (Devon) WATCOMBE
  Watcombe Pottery Co.   TORQUAY
  1867–1901   WATCOMBE
                                             POTTERY

    printed mark, 1875–1901

  Royal Aller Vale &   ROYAL
  Watcombe Pottery Co.   TORQUAY
  c. 1901–62   POTTERY

SALISBURY (Wiltshire)   PAYNE SARUM
  Payne, retailer only   printed
  c. 1834–41

SMETHWICK   TAYLOR
(nr. Birmingham)   impressed
  Ruskin Pottery, 1898–1935
  earthenware
  Taylor, W. Howson, c. 1898–

    painted or incised

    impressed mark, c. 1904–15
    with added date

STANMORE (London)   E.C./(date)
  Collyer, Ernest & Pamela
  studio-potters, 1950–

  Collyer-Nash   P.N. (Pamela Nash)

STEDHAM (Sussex)   Ray Marshall
  Marshall, Ray   (date)
  studio-potter, 1945–
  impressed mark   signature

STOCKTON-ON-TEES (Cleveland)
Ainsworth, W. H. & J. H.
1865–1901, earthenware

impressed

Harwood, J.   HARWOOD
Clarence Pottery, 19th   STOCKTON
century earthenware
  impressed mark, *c.* 1849–77

Skinner & Co., George   G.S. & CO.
Stafford Pottery   printed
earthenware, *c.* 1855–70

Skinner & Walker   S. & W.
1870–80   QUEEN'S WARE
                               STOCKTON

Smith & Co.,   W.S. & CO.   W.S. & CO.
William, *c.* 1825–55   STAFFORD
Stafford Pottery   W.S. & CO'S   POTTERY
                    WEDGWOOD

Smith, George F.   G.F.S.
North Shore Pottery
c. 1855–60, earthenware

Smith (Junr), William   W. S. JUNR. & CO.
c. 1845–84   all printed or impressed

STOURBRIDGE (West Midlands)
Sunfield Pottery, 1937–
earthenware and stoneware

77

SUNDERLAND
(Tyne and Wear)
  Southwick Pottery,
1788–99, Atkinson & Co., earthenware

ATKINSON & CO.
impressed or
printed

Deptford Pottery,
1857–1918
Ball, William,
earthenware, Ball Bros., 1884–

COPYRIGHT BALL
BROS.
SUNDERLAND

Wear Pottery
Brunton, John,
1796–1803, earthenware

J. BRUNTON
printed

South Hylton &
Ford Potteries
Dawson, John, *c.* 1799–1864
c. 1799–1848, earthenware
Thomas Dawson & Co.,
c. 1837–48, earthenware
  printed marks

DAWSON   I. DAWSON

DAWSON & CO.

FORD POTTERY J. DAWSON
SOUTH HYLTON

Garrison or
Sunderland Pottery
earthenware, *c.* 1807–65
  c. 1807–12

J. PHILLIPS
SUNDERLAND
POTTERY

  c. 1813–19

PHILLIPS & CO. DIXON & CO.

  c. 1820–26

DIXON, AUSTIN
& CO.

  c. 1827–40

DIXON, AUSTIN
PHILLIPS & CO.

  c. 1840–65

DIXON, PHILLIPS
& CO.

Wear Pottery, 1803–74 MOORE & CO.
Moore & Co., Samuel SUNDERLAND
earthenware

North Hylton MALING
Pottery, 1762–67, impressed
earthenware, Maling, William, 1762–, continued
by family until 1815

Phillips & Co., JOHN PHILLIPS
John, 1815–67 HYLTON POT
(Phillips & WORKS
Maling, 1780–1815)

Southwick Pottery, *c.* 1800–97
   c. 1800–29 A. SCOTT & CO.
                           SCOTT, SOUTHWICK
   c. 1829–44 A. SCOTT & SONS
                                 S. & SONS
   c. 1844–54 S.B. & CO.
                           SCOTT BROTHERS
   c. 1854–97 A. SCOTT & SON
                                  S. & S.

Union Pottery, UNION POTTERY
c. 1802 printed

SWADLINCOTE (S. Derbyshire)
Ault, William, 1887–1923
earthenware
   The wares of this
   pottery sometimes
   bear the signature
   of the designer
   Christopher Dresser
   and date from printed or printed
   1891–6 impressed

79

Ault & Tunnicliffe Ltd.
1923–37
(*see* Ashby Potter's Guild)

Ault Potteries Ltd., 1937–
(now Pearson & Co., Group)
   marks impressed or printed

SWINTON (Yorkshire)   DON POTTERY
Don Pottery, earthenware
1790–1893
    1800–34   GREEN
                        DON POTTERY

    1820–34, impressed or
    printed

Barker, Samuel, 1834–93

    '& Son' or '& Sons'
    added 1851–93   BARKER
                        DON POTTERY

Bingley & Co., Thomas   BINGLEY
earthenware, 1778–87   impressed

Twigg, Joseph & brothers
Kilnhurst Pottery & Newhill Pottery, *c.* 1822–81
earthenware
    impressed or   J.T.
    printed, *c.* 1822–
    impressed, *c.*   TWIGG
    1822–66   NEWHILL
    impressed, *c.*   TWIGG
    1839–81   K.P.

TONBRIDGE (Kent)
Slack & Brownlow
earthenware, *c.* 1928–34

TONBRIDGE WARE
printed or impressed

TORQUAY (Devon)
Torquay Terra-Cotta Co. Ltd.
Dr. Gillow, 1875–1909
earthenware figures, busts, etc.

impressed or printed

TRING (Hertfordshire)
Pendley Pottery, 1949–
Fieldhouse, Murray
studio-potter (now at
Northfields Studio)

incised or printed

TRURO (Cornwall)
Chapel Hill Pottery,
1872–, Lake & Son Ltd.,
W. H., earthenware

LAKE'S CORNISH
POTTERY TRURO
printed or impressed

WAREHAM (Dorset)
Sibley Pottery Ltd., 1922–
62, earthenware and
stoneware

SIBLEY POTTERY LTD
DORSET
ENGLAND
impressed or printed

WATTISFIELD (Suffolk)
Watson Potteries Ltd., Henry
earthenware and stoneware
c. 1800–; mark of about
1948, early wares unmarked

WELWYN GARDEN CITY (Hertfordshire)
Coper, Hans, 1947–
studio-potter

81

WENFORD BRIDGE (nr. Bodmin, Cornwall)
   Wenford Bridge Pottery
   c. 1939–42; 1949–
      impressed mark
   (*see also* WINCHCOMBE)

WESTON-SUPER-MARE (Avon)
   Matthews, John
   terra-cotta, 1870–88
      impressed mark with
      Royal Arms

JOHN MATTHEWS
LATE PHILLIPS
ROYAL POTTERY
WESTON-SUPER-MARE

WHITTINGTON (Derbyshire)
   Walton Pottery Co. Ltd.
   1946–56
   Gordon, William
   salt-glazed stoneware

WINCANTON Somerset)
   Ireson, Nathaniel
   c. 1730–50
   tin-glazed earthenware

IRESON
WINCANTON

WINCHCOMBE (Gloucestershire)
   c. 1926–39
   Cardew, Michael A.
   also at Wenford Bridge
   c. 1939–42
   studio-potter

mark impressed

Finch, Raymond, 1939–
studio-potter, impressed
mark used from *c.* 1926

WITHERNSEA (Humberside)
Eastgate Potteries, Ltd.
earthenware, 1955–

EASTGATE
ENGLAND
(on a gate)

WOODVILLE (Derbyshire)
Ashby Potters' Guild
earthenware, 1909–22

impressed

Mansfield Bros., Ltd.
Art Pottery Works, *c.* 1890–
1957

M.B.
impressed

WORCESTER (Worcestershire)
Worcester Porcelain Factory
1751 (Lund & Miller's Bristol factory
est. 1748, taken over in 1752)
soft-paste porcelain (soapstone)

workmen's marks
in underglaze blue

'open' crescent on painted
wares, 1755–83

83

crescent-mark with
crossed-hatched lines
on printed wares

in underglaze blue

any crescents in gilt or enamel colour
probably indicate outside decorator or
reproduction
on painted and printed
wares

painted in blue

marks on wares decorated
with 'Japan patterns'
c. 1760–75

in blue

'fretted square' mark
usually on heavily decorated
wares with scale-blue ground
c. 1755–75 (frequently seen
on reproductions)

in blue

Worcester imitation of Meissen
crossed-swords mark
c. 1760–70

in blue

printed numerals disguised as Chinese
characters, numbers 1–9, until recent
excavations at Worcester factory site these were
thought to be marks of Caughley (Salop)

'Flight' period, 1783–92
   'small crescent', 1783–92

   mark in blue, 1783–92

   mark in blue, 1788–92

'Flight & Barr' period
1792–1807   F. & B.

'Barr', *c.* 1792–1807

        B   incised   **Bₓ**

'Barr Flight & Barr' period
1807–13

                BFB
                impressed

Barr, Flight & Barr   BARR, FLIGHT
Worcester   & BARR
Flight & Barr   ROYAL PORCELAIN
Coventry Street,   WORKS
London   WORCESTER
Manufacturers to their   LONDON HOUSE
Majesties and   NO. 1
Royal Family   COVENTRY STREET

'Flight, Barr & Barr' period
1813–40

impressed

(factory taken over by Chamberlains, 1840–52)

Kerr & Binns, 1852–62

Kerr & Binns, '54' = 1854
   mark on outstanding
   examples, including decorator's
   initials (bottom left)

   standard mark, printed or
   impressed, *c.* 1852–62
   Note: crown added
   in 1862

'Worcester Royal Porcelain Company Ltd.'
(Royal Worcester) 1862–present

   standard mark, 1862–present
   early version, with 'C'
   in centre replacing crescent
   in Kerr & Binn's version
   numbers below = last 2 years
   of date

From 1867 a letter indicating the year of
manufacture was printed under the factory mark
according to the following table:

Worcester		**England**		Worcester
A 1867	G 1872	M 1877	T 1882	Y 1887
B '1868	H 1873	N 1878	U 1883	Z 1888
C 1869	I 1874	P 1879	V 1884	O 1889
D 1870	K 1875	R 1880	W 1885	
E 1871	L 1876	S 1881	X 1886	

'a' in Old English script in 1890; date letter
omitted in 1891.
'Royal Worcester England' written around mark
from 1891, after which, dots, stars and other
letters and forms were added to the mark each
year as listed below until 1963 when the year in
full is added.

1892, dot to left of crown, 1893 dot either side of
crown; dots were then added to either side of
crown until 1915, thus:

1894 3 dots	1900 9 dots	1906 15 dots	1912 21 dots
1895 4 dots	1901 10 dots	1907 16 dots	1913 22 dots
1896 5 dots	1902 11 dots	1908 17 dots	1914 23 dots
1897 6 dots	1903 12 dots	1909 18 dots	1915 24 dots
1898 7 dots	1904 13 dots	1910 19 dots	
1899 8 dots	1905 14 dots	1911 20 dots	

In 1916 the dots alongside the crown were
replaced by a star under the mark, dots were then
added to either side of this star until 1927:

1916 1 star	1922 star & 6 dots
1917 star & 1 dot	1923 star & 7 dots
1918 star & 2 dots	1924 star & 8 dots
1919 star & 3 dots	1925 star & 9 dots
1920 star & 4 dots	1926 star & 10 dots
1921 star & 5 dots	1927 star & 11 dots

then as follows:

1928 ▭ 1929 ◇ 1930 ÷

1931 ∞ 1932 ∞∞ 1933 ∞∞ ·

further dots were then added to three interlaced circles as follows:

1934 circles & 2 dots	1938 circles & 6 dots
1935 circles & 3 dots	1939 circles & 7 dots
1936 circles & 4 dots	1940 circles & 8 dots
1937 circles & 5 dots	1941 circles & 9 dots

from 1941 to 1948 inclusive there were no changes in the year-mark

1949 V	1953 W and 3 dots
1950 W	1954 W and 4 dots
1951 W and 1 dot	1955 W and 5 dots
1952 W and 2 dots	

1956 R in place of W with 6 dots	1960 R and 10 dots
	1961 R and 11 dots
1957 R and 7 dots	1962 R and 12 dots
1958 R and 8 dots	1963 R and 13 dots
1959 R and 9 dots	

From 1963 all new patterns have the year in full.

(*By courtesy of the Worcester Royal Porcelain Co. Ltd.*)

Hancock, Robert, *b.* 1730, *d.* 1817
engraver of transfer-prints
c. 1756–65

RH . Worcester

(Hancock associated with
Turner of Caughley in
1776)

initials of Hancock
and rebus of Richard
Holdship on prints

Chamberlain, *c.* 1786–1852
decorators from *c.* 1786–*c.* 1790, then
manufacturers of soft-paste porcelain
  c. 1790–1810

*Chamberlains
Worcs No276*
in red

written or printed
c. 1811–40
(under crown)

*Chamberlain's
Worcester,
& 155
New Bond Street
London,
Royal Porcelain
Manufactory*

c. 1814–16

*Chamberlain's
Worcester,
& 63 Piccadilly,
London*

written or printed

incised, *c.* 1815–25	CHAMBERLAINS ROYAL PORCELAIN WORCESTER
printed mark under crown, *c.* 1840–5 ('& Co.' from this date)	CHAMBERLAIN & CO. WORCESTER 155 New Bond St. & No. 1 COVENTRY ST. LONDON
written or printed *c.* 1846–50	CHAMBERLAIN & CO. WORCESTER
impressed or printed *c.* 1847–50	CHAMBERLAINS
printed *c.* 1850–52	

(then Kerr & Binns, p. 86)

Doe and Rogers, *c.* 1820–40 porcelain decorators	Doe & Rogers Worcester
Grainger, Wood & Co. *c.* 1801–12, porcelain rare mark	Grainger Wood & Co. Worcester, Warranted
Grainger, Lee & Co. *c.* 1812–*c.* 39 porcelain	Grainger, Lee & Co. Worcester painted

c. 1820–30 painted	New China Works
	Worcester
c. 1812–30 painted	Royal China Works
	Worcester

Grainger, George   GEO. GRAINGER
c. 1839–1902   CHINA WORKS
porcelain   WORCESTER
   painted or printed mark
   c. 1839–60
   '& Co.' added *c.* 1850   G. GRAINGER & CO.
                        WORCESTER

's.p.' for 'Semi-   G.G. & CO.   S.P.
Porcelain', *c.*   S.P.   G.G.W.
1850–   impressed or printed
initials included in   G.W.
printed marks, 1850–60
1850–89   G. & CO. W.

printed mark on copies   GRAINGER & CO.
of 'Dr. Wall' period wares   WORCESTER
c. 1860–80
printed or impressed
c. 1870–89

c. 1889–1902 ('England'
added in 1891)

letters added under mark to indicate year of
manufacture from 1891–1902:

A	1891	D	1894	G	1897	J	1900
B	1892	E	1895	H	1898	K	1901
C	1893	F	1896	I	1899	L	1902

George Grainger & Co. was taken over by
Worcester Royal Porcelain Co. Ltd. in 1889 and
closed down in 1902.

Hadley & Sons, James
porcelain and earthenware
1896–1905

Hadley

    signature on work   incised or impressed
    modelled by Hadley for
    Worcester Royal Porcelain Co.
    c. 1875–94
    printed or impressed
    1896–97

    1897–1902,   FINE ART
    impressed   HADLEY'S
                    TERRA-COTTA

    printed mark 1897–1902
    (centre ribbon omitted
    from 1900)

    printed mark, 1902–5

Locke & Co., porcelain   LOCKE & CO.
1895–1904   WORCESTER

'globe-mark', *c.* 1895–1904
'Ltd,' added in *c.* 1900

Sparks, George, *c.* Sparks Worcester
1836–54, decorator of written mark
Worcester and Coalport porcelain

WROTHAM (Kent) I.G.
Greene, John
slipware potter, *c.* 1670

Hubble, Nicholas N.H.
slipware potter, second
half of 17th century

Ifield, Thomas, Henry T.I.
& John H.I. I.I.
slipware potters whose
   initials are found on wares
   dating from *c.* 1620–75

Livermore, John I.L.
(*d.* 1658) slipware potter,
wares dated from 1612–49

Richardson, George G.R.
slipware potter, wares
dated from 1642–77 all above slip-trailed

Wells, Reginald, WELLS
(1877–1951) incised
studio-potter

93

c. 1909	COLDRUM
	WROTHAM
c. 1910–24 (at	COLDRUM
Chelsea)	CHELSEA

c. 1910   R. F. WELLS

c. 1918–51   SOON
(at Storrington,   impressed or incised
Sussex, c. 1925–51)

YARMOUTH (Norfolk)
   Absolon, William, 1784–1815
   independent enameller of
   the wares of various
   earthenwares and glass   painted in brown

STAFFORDSHIRE

Since the early seventeenth century the area in,
and around, Stoke in Staffordshire has been the
centre of the English ceramic industry.
Manufacture was first confined to earthenwares,
but later included salt-glazed stonewares,
jasperwares, bone-china and the mass of various
hybrid pottery and porcelain bodies introduced
about 1800 and later. The smaller pottery towns
are today grouped together to form
Stoke-on-Trent.
   In this section of the book, the various

94

Staffordshire potters are listed alphabetically under the names of the towns in which they potted.

Many of the more recent factories have often changed their mark many times and the following general aids to dating are often sufficient enough as a guide.

Few serious collectors seek pieces which include 'ENGLAND' in the mark, for this implies the piece was made in, or after, 1891 in order to comply with the American McKinley Tariff, which called for the country of origin to be marked on imported wares. The term 'MADE IN ENGLAND' suggests a date of about 1920.

The mass of blue-printed earthenwares are difficult to attribute if unmarked. Many have just a Royal Arms as a mark; this is a sure indication of a 19th-century date, whereas often similar marks, or 'back-stamps', include the name of the design and the initials of the potter. These initials may well be included in the index at end of the book. Versions of the Royal Arms used after 1837 lack the small inescutcheon on the quartered shield which is present on arms previous to this date.

In addition to factory marks, many wares will be found to bear the well-known 'diamond' or 'lozenge'-mark (see Appendix A, page 284). This mark was applied by either printing, impressing, or applying as a relief medallion and indicates that the design of the form or decoration had been registered with the London Patent Office and was protected against 'piracy' for a period of three years. If the numbers and letters in the four corners of this 'diamond-mark' can be accurately read, the reader should consult the key diagrams and tables on pages 284–7 to check the day, month and year the design was initially registered between 1842 and 1883. After this year wares bear only a registered number (e.g. Rd. 12345), which can be dated to the year, up until 1909.

Appendix B in this book is an abbreviated copy of the Class IV (pottery, porcelain, etc.) Index, giving the name and whereabouts of the firms registering ceramic designs between 1842 and 1883. This list is reproduced with the kind permission of the Public Record Office.

BILSTON (Staffs., now West Midlands)
Myatt Pottery Co., *c.* 1850–94
earthenware, mark of 1880   MYATT

BURSLEM (Staffs, now West Midlands.)
Albert Potteries Ltd.
earthenware, 1946–54   printed or impressed

Allman, Broughton & Co.,   A.B. & CO.
earthenware, 1861–8   printed or impressed

Baggaley, Jacob   J.B.
earthenware, 1880–6   impressed

Bagshaw & Meir   B. & M.
earthenware, 1802–8   printed or impressed

Ball, Izaac   I.B.
slipware, *c.* 1700

Bancroft & Bennett
earthenware, 1846–50

Barker & Son   B. & S.
earthenware, *c.* 1850–60   printed
          BARKER & SON
          printed or impressed

Barker, Sutton & Till   B.S. & T.
earthenware, 1834–43

Bates, Elliott & Co.   B.E. & CO.
general ceramics, 1870–5
97

Bates, Gildea & Walker,   B.G. & W.
general ceramics, 1878–81   printed

Bates, Walker & Co.   B.W. & CO.
general ceramics, 1875–78   printed

Bathwell & Goodfellow   BATHWELL &
earthenware, 1818–23   GOODFELLOW
(also Tunstall 1820–2)   impressed

Beech, James
earthenware, 1877–89
Swan Bank Works (also   J.B.
at Tunstall)   printed

Blackhurst & Bourne   B. & B.
earthenware, 1880–92   printed

Blackhurst & Tunnicliffe   B. & T.
earthenware, *c.* 1879   printed

Bodley & Co.
earthenware, 1865

Bodley & Co., E. F.   E.F.B. & CO.
earthenware, *c.* 1862–81

    SCOTIA POTTERY

    BODLEY
Bodley & Son   B. & SON
bone-china, 1874–5   printed

Bodley, E. J. D. general ceramics, 1875–92	E.J.D.B. printed, impressed or as monogram
Bodley & Harrold Scotia Pottery 1863–5, earthenware	B. & H. Bodley & Harrold printed
Boote, Ltd., T. & R. Waterloo Pottery general ceramics and tiles, 1842–*c.* 1966	T. & R.B. T.B. & S. T. & R. BOOTE printed or impressed

printed mark
1890–1906
'England' added
from 1891

Booth & Co., Thomas (also at Tunstall) earthenware, 1868–72	T.B. & CO. printed
Bridgwood & Clarke (also at Tunstall) earthenware, 1857–64	BRIDGWOOD & CLARKE impressed B. & C. B. & C. BURSLEM printed

Brown & Steventon, Ltd.
earthenware, 1900–23

B. & S.
printed
'sun-face' mark
from 1920–

Buckley, Heath & Co.
earthenware, 1885–90

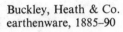

printed or impressed

Buckley, Wood & Co.
earthenware, 1875–85

B.W. & CO.
printed or impressed

Burgess, Henry
earthenware, 1864–92

H.B.
impressed or printed
under Royal Arms

Burgess & Leigh
earthenware, *c.* 1862–

B. & L.
impressed or printed

'Ltd.' added to marks
from *c.* 1919, large
variety of printed
marks from 1880,
'England' added from
1891

B & L.
printed

monogram mark
1862–

impressed or printed

Burslem Pottery Co. Ltd.
earthenware, 1894–1933

    printed

ENGLAND

Burslem School of Art
earthenware, figures, etc.
in 'Astbury' style
1935–41

impressed

Clarke & Co., Edward   EDWARD CLARKE
earthenware, *c.* 1880–87
(also at Tunstall, *c.* 1865–   EDWARD CLARKE &
77, and Longport, *c.*   CO.
1878–80)   printed

Clowes, William   W. CLOWES
general ceramics   impressed
c. 1783–96

Collinson & Co.,   C. COLLINSON & CO.
Charles, earthenware,   printed
1851–73

Cooper & Co., J.   J. COOPER & CO.
earthenware, 1922–5   ENGLAND
printed or impressed   DUCAL WORKS
      in circle
Cooper Pottery, Susie   *Susie Cooper*
('Ltd.' from *c.* 1961)   CROWN WORKS
general ceramics   BURSLEM
     c. 1930–   ENGLAND

printed mark, 1932–

Cooper China Ltd., Susie
(also at Longton, *c.* 1950–9)
china, *c.* 1959–
Member of the
Wedgwood Group

Cork & Edge
earthenware,
1846–60

C. & E.
printed with a
variety of designs

Cork, Edge & Malkin
earthenware, 1860–71

C.E. & M.
printed with varying
'backstamps' often
including pattern-name

Dale, John   J. DALE   I. DALE
'Staffordshire   BURSLEM   BURSLEM
figures', early 19th century

Daniel & Cork   DANIEL & CORK
earthenware, 1867–9   printed

Davison & Son, Ltd.
earthenware,
c. 1898–1952

mark of 1948–   printed

102

Dean, S. W.
earthenware, 1904–10

  printed mark

Deans (1910) Ltd.
earthenware, 1910–19
  printed mark

DEANS (1910) LTD.
BURSLEM
ENGLAND

Doulton & Co.
earthenware and
porcelain, *c.* 1882
(Doulton Fine China Ltd.
from 1955 and Royal
Doulton Tableware Ltd., 1973–)
  impressed name of
  new material from
  1960

see under
LAMBETH
for major
marks

ENGLISH
TRANSLUCENT
CHINA

Duke & Nephews, Sir James
various hybrid porcelains
c. 1860–3

  impressed hand

Dunn, Bennett & Co.
earthenware, 1875–
('Ltd.' added from 1907–)
(now Royal Doulton Group)
  marks 1875–1907

D.B. & CO.
printed

printed mark, 1937–   DUNN BENNETT & CO. LTD.
                        BURSLEM
                        ENGLAND

added to mark on
'Ironstone' from 1955–   'Vitreous Ironstone'

Edge, Malkin & Co.   E.M. & CO.
earthenware, 1871–1903

                       E.M. & CO.
'LTD.' added from 1899   B
                       printed

Edwards & Son, James   J.E. & S.
various pottery, 1851–82

                       EDWARDS
'Dale Hall', Burslem   D.H.
                       printed or impressed

Edwards, James & Thomas   J. & T.E.
earthenware, 1839–41

printed or impressed   J. & T. EDWARDS
                        B

Ellgreave Pottery Co. Ltd.   'Lottie Rhead Ware'
earthenware, 1921–
(Wood & Sons Ltd.)
    and other fully   'Heatmaster'
    named marks

Elton & Co. Ltd., J. F.   J.F.E. CO. LTD.
earthenware, 1901–1910   BURSLEM
    (also in monogram)   printed or impressed

104

Emery, Francis J.
earthenware, *c.* 1878–93

F. J. EMERY
printed

Evans & Booth
earthenware, 1856–69

E. & B.
printed

Ford & Co., Samuel
earthenware, 1898–1939
(*see* Smith & Ford)

S & F.

'F. & CO.' alternative to
'S. & F.'

printed

c. 1936–9

'Samford Ware'

Ford & Riley
earthenware, 1882–93

F. & R.
B

Ford & Sons ('Ltd.'
added 1908),
earthenware, *c.* 1893–1938

F. & S.
B

also 'CROWN
FORD', 'NEWCRAFT'

F. & SONS, LTD.
printed

Ford & Sons (Crownford)
earthenware, 1938–

printed, 1961–

Gibson & Sons, Ltd.
earthenware, 1885–

G. & S. LTD.
B

Gibson & Sons, Ltd.
'Harvey Pottery'
printed, *c.* 1904–9

'Royal Harvey', *c.* 1950–5
large variety of fully named marks, 1909–

Gildea & Walker, 1881–5 G. & W.
earthenware

   c. 1881–5:
$$\frac{4}{82} = \text{APRIL, 1882}$$

Gildea, James
earthenware, 1885–8

   printed mark includes
   a pattern-name

Godwin, B. C. B.C.G.
earthenware, *c.* 1851– printed

Godwin, Thomas & T. & B.G.
Benjamin, general T.B.G.
ceramics, *c.* 1809–34 printed

Godwin, Thomas THOS GODWIN
earthenware, 1834–54 BURSLEM
   STONE CHINA

Godwin, Rowley & Co. earthenware, 1828–31	G.R. & CO. printed
Hall & Sons, John earthenware, 1814–32	I. HALL HALL
c. 1822–32	I. HALL & SONS impressed or printed
Hammersley & Son, Ralph, earthenware, 1860–1905	R.H.
'& Son' added 1884–	R.H. & S. printed
Hancock, Whittingham & Co., earthenware, 1863–72	H.W. & CO. printed
Harding, Joseph earthenware, 1850–1	J. HARDING printed
Harrison & Phillips earthenware, 1914–15	H. & P. BURSLEM
	printed
Heath & Son earthenware, c. 1800	HEATH & SON impressed
Heath, John general ceramics, 1809–23	HEATH impressed
Heath, Thomas earthenware, 1812–35	T. HEATH impressed or printed

Heath & Blackhurst & Co., earthenware, 1859–77	H. & B. H.B. & CO.
Heath & Greatbatch earthenware, 1891–3	H. & G. B printed or impressed
Hill Pottery Co. Ltd. general ceramics, *c.* 1861–7	J.S.H. printed (also as monogram)
Hobson, Charles earthenware, 1865–80 's' added 1873–5	C.H. C.H. & S. impressed or printed
Hobson, G. & J. earthenware, 1883–1901	HOBSON'S printed
Hobson, George earthenware, 1901–23 printed or impressed	TRADE MARK HOBSON B
Holdcroft & Co., Peter earthenware, 1846–52	P.H. & CO. printed
Holdcroft, Hill & Mellor, earthenware, 1860–70	H.H. & M. printed
Hollinshead & Griffiths earthenware, 1890–1909	CHELSEA ART POTTERY H. & G. BURSLEM

mark includes lion and crown

Holmes, Plant & Maydew earthenware, 1876–85	H.P. & M. printed
Hope & Carter earthenware, 1862–80	H. & C. printed
Hughes, Thomas earthenware, 1860–94	THOMAS HUGHES IRONSTONE CHINA impressed
Hughes & Son Ltd., Thomas, general ceramics, 1895–1957	THOS. HUGHES & SON ENGLAND
Hulme & Sons, Henry earthenware, 1906–32 (mark previously used by Wood & Hulme)	W. & H. B
Hulme, William earthenware, 1891–1941	printed 1891–1936
printed or impressed, 1936–41	ALPHA WARE H ENGLAND
Jackson, Job & John earthenware, 1831–5	J. & J. JACKSON JACKSON'S WARRANTED impressed or printed

Johnson, Ltd., Samuel   S.J.
earthenware, 1887–1931   S.J.B.
'Ltd.' 1912–
'BRITANNIA POTTERY',   S.J. LTD.
1916–31   printed

Jones, George   GEORGE JONES
earthenware, *c.* 1854

Keeling & Co. Ltd.   K. & CO.
earthenware, 1886–1936

    K. & CO. B.

'England' usually added
from 1891
'Losol Ware', *c.* 1912–   all
    printed

Kennedy, William Sadler   W. S. KENNEDY
earthenware, 1843–54   impressed or printed

Kennedy & Macintyre   W. S. KENNEDY
earthenware, 1854–60   & J. MACINTYRE
    impressed or printed

Kensington Pottery Ltd.
c. 1937–
(also at Hanley 1922–37)
now Price & Kensington Potteries Ltd.

Kent (Porcelains) Ltd., William
earthenware 1944–62

King & Barrett, Ltd. general pottery, 1898–40	K. & B. impressed or printed
Lakin & Poole pottery and figures, *c.* 1791–5	LAKIN & POOLE L. & P. BURSLEM impressed
Leighton Pottery Ltd. earthenware, 1940–54	'ROYAL LEIGHTON WARE'
Machin & Potts general ceramics 1833–7 colour-print patent 1835	MACHIN & POTTS MACHIN & POTTS PATENT
Machin & Thomas earthenware, *c.* 1831–2	M. & T. printed
Macintyre & Co. Ltd., James, earthenware, *c.* 1860–1928, '& Co.' from 1867– (continued with industrial wares only)	MACINTYRE J. MACINTYRE J.M. & CO. printed or impressed
Maddock & Seddon earthenware, *c.* 1839–42	M. & S.
Maddock, John earthenware, 1842–55 (not to be confused with 'M' for Minton)	M printed

Maddock & Sons (Ltd.)
general pottery, 1855–
specialist hotel-ware
'Ltd.' added 1896–

various fully named
marks, and
'ROYAL VITREOUS'
'ROYAL IVORY'
'IVORY WARE'
'EMBASSY'

Malkin, Frederick
earthenware, 1891–1905

printed, *c.* 1900–5

Malkin, Samuel
slip-wares, early 18th century

S.M.
moulded in
relief

Mayer, Thomas, John
& Joseph, general
ceramics, 1843–55

T. J. & J. MAYER
printed

Mellor, Taylor & Co.
earthenware, *c.* 1880–1904

'ROYAL IRONSTONE CHINA'

printed or impressed
with name of firm

'SEMI PORCELAIN'

Mellor, Venables & Co.
general ceramics, 1834–51

MELLOR, VENABLES
& CO.

M.V. & CO.
printed or impressed

112

Midwinter Ltd., W. R.
earthenwares, 1910–
    added numbers indicate
    month and year
(*now Wedgwood Group*)

various fully-named
marks with:
'PORCELON'
'STYLECRAFT'

Moorcroft Ltd., W.
earthenware, 1913–

MOORCROFT
BURSLEM

    signature of William
    Moorcroft (*d.* 1945)

W.M.Moorcroft

    mark of Walter Moorcroft
    (son)

W.M.

Morgan, Wood & Co.
earthenware, 1860–70

M.W. & CO.
printed
(at times with bee)

Mountford, A. J.
earthenware, 1897–1901

BURSLEM
printed

New Wharf Pottery Co.
earthenware, 1878–94

N.W.P.C.O.
B
printed

Newport Pottery Co. Ltd.
earthenware, 1920–
(now Wedgwood group)

various fully named
marks

    c. 1938–66

'Clarice Cliff'

Parrott & Co. Ltd.
earthenware, 1921
(manufacture ceased *c.* 1962)

Phillips & Son, Thomas
earthenware, *c.* 1845–6

T. PHILLIPS & SON
BURSLEM
printed or impressed

Pinder, Thomas
earthenware, 1849–51

PINDER BURSLEM
printed or impressed

Pinder, Bourne & Hope
earthenware, 1851–62

P.B. & H.
printed

Pinder, Bourne & Co.
earthenware, 1862–82
(taken over by Doultons
in 1878, but name unchanged
until 1882)

P.B. & CO.

Plant Bros. Crown Pottery
porcelain, 1889–1906
(at Longton from 1898)

Plant, Enoch
earthenware, 1898–1905
(such crowns are a
common form of mark)

printed or impressed

Poole, J. E.
earthenware, *c.* 1796–
early 19th century

POOLE
impressed

Price Bros.
earthenware, 1896–1903

Price Bros. (Burslem) Ltd.   printed
earthenware, 1903–61   'star-mark', as above
until 1910

  trade-names:
  'PALM ATHLO'
  'ATHLO WARE'
  'MATTONA WARE'

Price & Kensington   PRICE
Potteries Ltd.   KENSINGTON
earthenware, 1962–   printed within wreath

Radford Handcraft   G. RADFORD
Pottery, earthenware,   BURSLEM
1933–48   printed signature

Riley, John & Richard   J. & R. RILEY
general ceramics, 1802–28

  marks painted,   RILEY'S
  printed or impressed   SEMI-CHINA

Robinson, Joseph   J.R.
earthenware, 1876–98   B
printed or impressed

Roddy & Co., E.   STAFFORDSHIRE
earthenware, 1925–8   RODDY
WARE

115

Sadler & Sons, Ltd.,
James, earthenware,
1899–
   impressed or printed
    from 1937–

ENGLAND
J.S.S.B.
impressed

SADLER
BURSLEM
ENGLAND

Simpson, Ralph
slip-wares, 1651–*c.* 1724
   name slip-trailed on front
   of large chargers

RALPH SIMPSON
slip-trailed

Simpson, John
slip wares, first half of
18th century

JOHN SIMPSON
I.S.
slip-trailed

Smith & Co., Ambrose
earthenware, *c.* 1784–6

A.S. & CO.
impressed or printed

Smith & Ford
earthenware, 1895–8
   printed (*see also*
   Samuel Ford)

S & F

Stanyer, A.
earthenware, *c.* 1916–41

A.S.
B
ENG.

A.S.
ENG.
B

impressed

Steel, Daniel,
  1790–1824
earthenwares and
'Wedgwood-type' stonewares

STEEL
impressed

Stubbs, Joseph
earthenwares, *c.* 1822–35

JOSEPH STUBBS
LONGPORT
impressed or printed

Stubbs & Kent
earthenware, *c.* 1828–30
   mark impressed or
   printed

Sudlow & Sons, Ltd., R.
earthenware, 1893–
(Part of Howard Pottery
Co. Shelton from 1965)

full-name marks
impressed or printed
from *c.* 1920–

Till & Sons, Thomas
earthenware, *c.* 1850–1928

   1861–

   'Globe-mark' from 1880
   'Tillson' ware, *c.* 1922–8

Tundley, Rhodes &
Proctor, earthenware,
1873–83, then:
Rhodes & Proctor,
1883–5, earthenware

T.R. & P.
printed

R. & P.
printed

Venables & Baines
earthenware, *c.* 1851–3

VENABLES &
BAINES

Venables & Co.
earthenware, *c.* 1853–5

J. VENABLES
& CO.
printed or impressed

117

Vernon & Son, James
earthenware, 1860–80   J.V.

1875–   J.V. & Son

J.V. & S.   J.V. junr.

Wade & Son, Ltd.,   WADE
George, earthenware   Figures
    1922–,
    1936–

    1947–

Wade & Co.   WADES
earthenware, 1887–1927   W. & CO.
    B

Wade, Heath & Co., Ltd.,   WADES
earthenware,   (with lion)
1927–

    c. 1934–   WADEHEATH
    ORCADIA
    WARE

    c. 1934–   WADEHEATH
    (with lion)

    Trade-names: 'Flaxman Ware', 'ROYAL
    VICTORIA'

Walley, John   J. WALLEY
earthenware, 1850–67   J. WALLEY'S
    WARE
    printed or impressed

Walton, John
earthenware groups and
figures, *c.* 1818–35

impressed on raised
scroll

Wedgwood & Sons, Ltd.
Josiah, general ceramics, 1759–
  very rare incised initials or   'J.W.'
  signature, *c.* 1760
  rare, *c.* 1759–69   wedgwood WEDGWOOD
  c. 1759   WEDGWOOD

Wedgwood & Bentley   WEDGWOOD
partnership, 1769–80   & BENTLEY
concerned only with
the manufacture of   WEDGWOOD
ornamental neo-classical   & BENTLEY
wares   ETRURIA

  impressed on cameos, etc.   W. & B.
  impressed or raised mark

  c. 1780–98   Wedgwood

  rare impressed mark   WEDGWOOD & SONS
  c. 1790
  printed on bone-china   WEDGWOOD
  c. 1812–22   red, blue or gold

rare printed mark on stone china, *c.* 1827–61	WEDGWOOD'S STONE CHINA
impressed mark *c.* 1840–5	WEDGWOOD ETRURIA
impressed on 'pearlware' *c.* 1840–68	PEARL
as above, post–1868	P

From 1860 the Wedgwood factory in addition to their usual name-mark, adopted a system of date-marking consisting of three letters side by side: the first indicates the month, the second a potter's mark and the third the year of manufacture. As from 1907 the first letter, which had hitherto denoted the month of manufacture, was replaced by a number indicating the cycle of year marks in use; previously there was no indication whether the piece was made in the first second, or third cycle.

This system was further changed in 1930 when the cycle number was replaced by the chronological number of the month, e.g.: January = 1, February = 2, etc., and the initial which had previously indicated the year was now replaced by the last two years of the actual date of manufacture.

Examples:	Month	Potter	Year	
	Y	O	R	May, 1863
	L	O	E	July, 1902
	Cycle	Potter	Year	
	3	O	N	1911
	4	O	A	1924

Month	Potter	Year	
3	O	32	March, 1932
11	O	48	November, 1948

Monthly marks indicated by the first letter from

1860–1864:

January	J	April	A	July	V	October	O
February	F	May	Y	August	W	November	N
March	M	June	T	September	S	December	D

1865–1907:

January	J	April	A	July	L	October	O
February	F	May	M	August	W	November	N
March	R	June	T	September	S	December	D

First cycle of year marks:

O	1860	R	1863	U	1866	X	1869
P	1861	S	1864	V	1867	Y	1870
Q	1862	T	1865	W	1868	Z	1871

Second cycle of year marks:

A	1872	H	1879	O	1886	V	1893
B	1873	I	1880	P	1887	W	1894
C	1874	J	1881	Q	1888	X	1895
D	1875	K	1882	R	1889	Y	1896
E	1876	L	1883	S	1890	Z	1897
F	1877	M	1884	T	1891		
G	1878	N	1885	U	1892		

Note: 'ENGLAND' added to mark from 1891

Third cycle of year marks:

A 1898	H 1905	O 1912	V 1919
B 1899	I 1906	P 1913	W 1920
C 1900	J 1907	Q 1914	X 1921
D 1901	K 1908	R 1915	Y 1922
E 1902	L 1909	S 1916	Z 1923
F 1903	M 1910	T 1917	
G 1904	N 1911	U 1918	

Fourth cycle of year marks:

A 1924	C 1926	E 1928
B 1925	D 1927	F 1929

the last two years of the date then appear in full.

'Portland Vase' mark printed
on bone-china from *c.* 1878
occasionally seen impressed
on earthenware, *c.* 1891–1900
Note: 'ENGLAND' added
    after 1891 'MADE IN
ENGLAND' from about 1910
'*Bone China*' added *c.* 1920

printed on creamwares
from *c.* 1940

Lessore, Emile, decorator
c. 1858–76

Thomson, E. G., decorator, *c.* 1870	E. G. Thomson
Barnard, Harry, decorator *c.* 1900	

marks on red stonewares, probably Wedgwood second-half of 18th century

impressed

Whittingham, Ford & Co., 1868–73, earthenware

w.f. & co.
printed

Whittingham, Ford & Riley, earthenware, 1876–82

w.f. & r.
printed

Wilkinson, Arthur J., 1885–*c.* 1970, earthenwares
'ROYAL SEMI-PORCELAIN', *c.* 1891–
'ROYAL IRONSTONE CHINA', *c.* 1896–
'IRONSTONE CHINA', *c.* 1910
'Clarice Cliff', *c.* 1930
'Honeyglaze', *c.* 1947
(merged with W. R. Midwinter Ltd., 1964)

many fully-named marks including:

Withinshaw, W. E., 1873–8, general ceramics

w.e.w.
w. e. WITHINSHAW
printed or impressed

Wood, Enoch
c. 1784–*c.* 1790 general
ceramics

WOOD   E. WOOD
w (***)
E.W.   w.

Enoch Wood's marks can be seen impressed, moulded or incised	ENOCH WOOD SCULPSIT
	E. WOOD SCULPSIT
	ENOCH WOOD
Wood & Caldwell 1790–1818, earthenware especially figures, etc.	WOOD & CALDWELL impressed
Wood & Sons, Enoch 1818–1846, earthenware blue-printed wares made for U.S.A. include the American eagle in mark	ENOCH WOOD & SONS BURSLEM STAFFORDSHIRE
	E.W. & S. E. & E. WOOD E. & E.W. all printed

E. WOOD & SONS
E. & E. WOOD
BURSLEM

Wood, H. J.
1884–, earthenware

many various fully-named marks including:
'Bursley-Ware' *c.* 1930–
'E. Radford' *c.* 1935–
'CHINESE ROSE' *c.* 1960–, etc.

Wood, Isaiah 1710–15, earthenware	ISA WOOD 1712 incised

Wood, John Wedge   w.w.
1841–4 (also at Tunstall   impressed
1845–60)   J. WEDGWOOD
         printed

Wood, Ralph (Snr.)   R. WOOD   Ra. WOOD
(1715–72), son of same   Ra. WOOD
name (1748–95)   BURSLEM
grandson (1781–1801)   Ralph Wood
    impressed or incised marks
    c. 1770–1801

    rebus of trees (rare)
    c. 1770–90

Wood & Son   various fully-named
1865–, earthenware, etc.   marks from *c.* 1890–
    '& Sons', from 1907
    'Ltd.' added *c.* 1910

Wood & Co., Thomas   T.W. & CO.
1885–96, earthenwares   printed or impressed

Wood & Sons, Thomas   T.W. & S.
c. 1896–7, earthenware   printed

Wood & Co., W.   W.W. & CO.
1873–1932, earthenware   printed or impressed
    mark of initials printed in 'Staffordshire
    knot', 1880–1915, with crown, 1915–32

Wood & Baggaley 1870–80, earthenware	w. & b. printed
Wood & Barker, Ltd. 1897–1903, earthenware	w. & b. Ltd. printed
Wood & Bowers 1839, earthenware	w. & b. (can be confused with Wood & Baggaley)
Wood & Clarke *c.* 1871–2, earthenware	w. & c. printed with 'lion rampant'
Wood & Hulme 1882–1905, earthenware	w. & h. b printed or impressed
Wooldridge & Walley 1898–1901, earthenware	w. & w. b printed

COBRIDGE (Staffordshire)

　　　　　　　　　　J. & G.A.

Alcock, John & George 　1839–46, earthenware and 　'INDIAN IRONSTONE'	J. & G. ALCOCK COBRIDGE impressed or printed
Alcock, Junior, John & Samuel, *c.* 1848–50 earthenware	J. & S. ALCOCK JR. printed or impressed

Alcock, John 1853–61, earthenware	JOHN ALCOCK COBRIDGE printed

Alcock & Co., Henry
1861–1910, earthenware
   fully-named mark from
   1880, 'Ltd.' from 1900
	H.A. & CO.
	printed

Alcock Pottery, The Henry 1910–35, earthenware	fully named 'coat of arms' mark printed

Alcock & Co., Samuel
c. 1828–53, general ceramics
   (Also at Burslem
   c. 1830–59)
   printed, painted or
   impressed, sometimes
   with Royal Arms or
   bee-hive
	SAMUEL ALCOCK & CO.
	COBRIDGE
	printed or impressed
	S.A. & CO.
	S. ALCOCK & CO.

Bates & Bennett 1868–95, earthenware	B. & B. printed or impressed
Birks Brothers & Seddon 1877–86, earthenware	IMPERIAL IRONSTONE CHINA BIRKS BROS. & SEDDON printed below Royal Arms
Blackhurst & Co. Ltd., John 1951–9, earthenware	J. BLACKHURST ENGLAND

Brownfield, William
1850–91, earthenware (also
porcelain after 1871) much
'parian ware'

printed, impressed
or moulded

impressed, often with
crown, from 1860–　　　　BROWNFIELD
'S' or '& Son', added 1871
'& Sons', added 1876
printed 'double-globe' mark, 1871–91

Brownfields Guild Pottery　　B.G.P. CO.
Society Ltd., 1891–1900,　　impressed
general ceramics
(Brownfield's Pottery Ltd.,
c. 1898–1900)

printed monogram

printed within circular
strap device　　　　　　　BROWNFIELDS

Cartledge, John　　　　JOHN CARTLEDGE
c. 1800, earthenware　　rare incised mark
figures

Clews, James & Ralph　　CLEWS WARRANTED
1818–34, pottery and porcelain　STAFFORDSHIRE
　　　　　　　　　　　　impressed under
　　　　　　　　　　　　crown

impressed mark on
blue-printed wares

Cockson & Chetwynd   C.C. & CO.
1867–75, earthenware

COCKSON &
CHETWYND
printed

Cockson & Seddon   IMPERIAL IRONSTONE
1875–7, earthenware   CHINA
COCKSON & SEDDON
printed under Royal
Arms

Crystal Porcelain Pottery   C.P.P. CO.
Co. Ltd., 1882–6,   printed or impressed
pottery and porcelain
  (dove sometimes
  included in mark)

Daniel, John   JOHN DANIEL
c. 1770–c. 86, earthenware   incised

Dillon, Francis   DILLON
1834–43, earthenware   impressed

F.D.
printed with various
back-stamps

Furnival & Co., Jacob
c. 1845–70, earthenware

J.F. & CO.
printed

Furnival & Sons, Thomas
1871–90, earthenware
  various 'T. F. & Sons'
  monograms

Furnivals (Ltd.)
1890–1968, earthenware
'Ltd.' added *c*. 1895

FURNIVALS
ENGLAND

c. 1905–13
(Taken over by Barratt's
of Staffordshire in 1967,
closed 1968)

1913 date included in
marks from that year

FURNIVALS
(1913)
ENGLAND

Globe Pottery Co. Ltd.
1914–, earthenware (now
Royal Doulton Group)

fully-named
printed 'globe' marks

Godwin, Benjamin E.
1834–41, earthenware

B.G.
printed with back-
stamp

Godwin, John & Robert
1834–66, earthenware

J. & R.G.
printed

Harding & Cockson
1834–60, earthenware

COBRIDGE
H. & C.
printed

Hughes & Co., Elijah
1853–67, earthenware

E. HUGHES & CO.
impressed

Hulme, William
1948–54, earthenware

printed mark

Jones, Elijah
1831–9, earthenware

fully named
impressed mark
or
E.J. printed

Jones & Walley
1841–3, earthenware

fully named
impressed or
moulded mark
or
printed J. & W.

Meakin, Henry
1873–6, earthenware

IRONSTONE CHINA
H. MEAKIN
printed with Royal
Arms

North Staffordshire Pottery Co. Ltd.
1940–52, earthenware

trade-mark registered
in 1944

Portland Pottery Ltd.
1946–53, earthenware
('P.P.C.' monogram,
Portland Pottery, Cobridge)

Regal Pottery Co. Ltd.
1925–31, earthenware

Richardson, Albert G.   REGAL WARE
c. 1920–21   A.G.R.
                                          printed

Richardsons (Cobridge) Ltd.,   REGAL WARE
1921–25   R(C) LTD.
                                          printed

Robinson, Wood &   R.W. & B.
Brownfield, 1838–41,
earthenware, printed

Sant & Vodrey   S. & V.
1887–93, earthenware   COBRIDGE
                              printed or impressed

Shaw, Ralph   Made by Ralph Shaw
c. 1740–, earthenware   October 31, Cobridge
                                        gate

Simpsons (Potters) Ltd.   fully-named marks
1944–, earthenware
    including various trade-names:
    'Ambassador Ware', 'Solian Ware', 'Loh
    Yueh Mei Kuei', 'Vogue', 'Chinastyle',
    'Marlborough Old English Ironstone',
    'Chanticleer'

132

Stevenson, Andrew
c. 1816–30, earthenware

STEVENSON
A. STEVENSON

impressed 'ship'
mark could also refer to
following potter

Stevenson, Ralph
c. 1810–32, earthenware

R. STEVENSON

marks impressed

R.S.

Stevenson & Son, Ralph
c. 1832–35, earthenware
marks printed

R.S. & S.

R. STEVENSON
& SON

Stevenson, Alcock &
Williams, earthenware *c.* 1825,
marks printed

STEVENSON
ALCOCK &
WILLIAMS

Stevenson & Williams
c. 1825, earthenware

R.S.W.

marks printed

STEVENSON & WILLIAMS

Viking Pottery Co.
1950–63, general ceramics

Walley, Edward
1845–56, general ceramics
marks impressed or printed

E. WALLEY

W.

Warburton, John *c.* 1802–25, earthenwares and stonewares	WARBURTON impressed
Warburton, Peter *c.* 1802–12, general ceramics *c.* 1810–12	WARBURTON'S PATENT printed or written under crown
Warburton, Peter & Francis 1795–1802, earthenware marks impressed	P. & F.W. P. & F. WARBURTON
Wood, Son & Co. 1869–79, earthenware	WOOD, SON & CO. printed under Royal Arms
Wood & Brownfield *c.* 1838–50, earthenware	W. & B. impressed or printed
Wood & Hawthorne 1882–7, earthenware	WOOD & HAWTHORNE printed under Royal Arms

FENTON (Staffordshire)

Bailey Potteries, Ltd. 1935–40, earthenware	BEWLEY POTTERY MADE IN ENGLAND printed
Baker & Co., W. 1839–1932, earthenware	W. BAKER & CO. printed or impressed

printed or impressed
'Ltd.' added 1893

BAKER & CO.

Barkers & Kent
1889–1941, earthenware
'Ltd.' added 1898

B. & K.
B. & K.L.
printed or impressed

Beardmore & Co., Frank
1903–14, earthenware
  impressed on printed mark

F.B. & CO.
F

printed mark

Bourne, Charles
1817–30, porcelain

C.B.
(pattern no.)

Bowker, Arthur
1948–58, porcelain

STAFFORDSHIRE
FINE BONE CHINA
OF
mark printed under crown ARTHUR BOWKER

Brain & Co. Ltd.
1903–67
porcelain

HARJIAN
ENGLAND

1905–
(now Coalport
a division of
the Wedgwood
Group at
Foley Works)

E.B. & CO.
F.
impressed or
printed within
Staffordshire
knot

135

(Coalport China Ltd., taken over by
E. Brain & Co. Ltd. in 1958)

British Art Pottery Co. (Fenton) Ltd.
1920–6, porcelain

   mark printed or impressed

Broadhurst & Sons, James
c. 1862–, earthenware
printed in mark, 1862–70   J.B.

   printed in mark, 1870–1922   J.B. & S.
   'Ltd.' added 1922

Challinor & Co., E.   E. CHALLINOR & CO.
1853–62, earthenware   printed

Challinor, E. & C.   E. & C.C.
1862–91, earthenware

             E. & C. CHALLINOR
                FENTON
                printed

Challinor, C. & Co.   C. CHALLINOR & CO.
1892–6, earthenware   ENGLAND

Clulow & Co.   CLULOW & CO.
c. 1802, earthenware   FENTON

Crown Staffordshire Porcelain Co. Ltd.
1889–, porcelain
(renamed Crown Staffordshire China Co. Ltd. in
1948)

printed 1889–1912
(Wedgwood China Div.
from 1973)
  printed marks of from
  1906, this firm makes
  bone-china reproductions
  of Chelsea 'raised-
  anchor' birds

'STAFFORDSHIRE'
with a crown within
wreath

Edge, Barker & Co.
1835–6, earthenware

E.B. & CO.
printed

Edge, Barker & Barker
1836–40, earthenware

E.B. & B.
printed

Edwards, John
1847–1900, general ceramics
  '& Co.' added *c.* 1873–9
  named marks including
'PORCELAINE DE TERRE' or
'WARRANTED IRONSTONE CHINA'
from *c.* 1880–1900

J.E.

J.E. & CO.
PORCELAINE
IRONSTONE

Elkin, Knight & Co.
1822–6, earthenware
  marks impressed or
  printed

E.K. & CO.

ELKIN KNIGHT
& CO.

Elkin, Knight & Bridgwood
c. 1827–40, earthenware
and porcelain

E.K.B.
printed

Forester & Sons, Thomas   T.F. & S.
1883–1959, earthenware

'Ltd.' added, 1891–
'Phoenix China', 1912–

Forester & Hulme   F. & H.
1887–93, earthenware   printed under bee

Hulme & Christie   H. & C.
1893–1902, earthenware   F
    mark printed with a dove

Garner, Robert   R.G.
late 18th century, earthenware   moulded

Gimson & Co., Wallis   WALLIS GIMSON &
1884–90, earthenware   CO.
    printed under beehive

Ginder & Co., Samuel   S. Ginder & Co.
1811–43, earthenware   printed

Greatbatch, William   GREATBATCH
c. 1760– *c*, 1780, modeller   printed
potter and engraver of
transfer-prints

Green, Thomas   T. GREEN
1847–59, general   FENTON POTTERIES
ceramics   printed

Green, Thomas

Green & Co., M.   M. GREEN & CO.
1859–76, general ceramics   printed

Green, T. A. & S.   T.A. & S.G.
1876–89, china   initials printed in
                                   'Staffordshire knot'

From 1889 this firm became known as
'Crown Staffordshire Porcelain Co.'

Greenwood, S.   S. GREENWOOD
late 18th century   rare impressed mark
black basaltes

Hines Bros.   H.B.
1886–1907, earthenware   impressed

                                   HINES BROS.
                                   printed

Hoods, Ltd.   H. LTD.
c. 1919–, earthenware   printed
(firm now closed)

Hughes & Co., E.   H
1889–1953, porcelain
   impressed mark, 1889–98

   impressed or printed   H.F.
   1898–1905

printed mark
c. 1908–12

various 'globe' marks
from 1912–41
1940 firm retitled Hughes (Fenton) Ltd.

Hulme & Christie	H. & C.
1893–1902, earthenware	F
(Christie & Beardmore	printed with dove
1902–3)	

Jones, A. G., Harley-	H.J.
1907–34, earthenware	
and porcelain	
initials printed with	A.G.H.J.
various trade-names:	

'FENTONIA WARE', 'PARAMOUNT',
'WILTON WARE'

Kirkby & Co., William	W.K. & CO.
1879–85, general ceramics	
'K. & Co.', also used in	K. & CO.
monogram form	printed or impressed

Knight, Elkin & Co.	K.E. & CO.
1826–46, earthenware	
	KNIGHT ELKIN
printed initials with	& CO.
variously designed	
backstamps	K. & E.

Knight, John King	J. K. KNIGHT
1846–53, earthenware	printed

140

Knight, Elkin & Bridgwood *c.* 1829–40, earthenware marks printed	K.E. & B. K.E.B.
Knight, Elkin & Knight 1841–4, earthenware	K.E. & K. printed
Malkin, Ralph 1863–81, earthenware	R.M. printed
Malkin & Sons, Ralph 1882–92, earthenware	R.M. & S. printed
Moore & Co. 1872–92, earthenware	M. & CO. impressed or printed
Moore, Leason & Co. 1892–6, earthenware	M.L. & CO. printed in shield under crown or initials alone impressed or printed
Morley, Fox & Co. Ltd. 1906–44, earthenware	M.F. & CO. printed

c. 1906–

'HOMELEIGHWARE', 1929–

Morley & Co. Ltd., William
1944–57, earthenware

Pratt & Co. (Ltd.), F. & R.　　F. & R.P.
c. 1818–, earthenware

PRATT

'Co.' added 1840　　F. & R.P. CO.

c. 1847–60　　F. & R. PRATT & CO.
FENTON
this firm is known　　MANUFACTURER'S
to have made a great　　TO H.R.H. PRINCE ALBERT
number of the popular
printed pot-lids and
similarly printed jugs,
etc. *c.* 1850
the firm was taken over in *c.* 1925
by Cauldon Potteries Ltd., who continue
original name together with their own

Pratt & Co., John　　J.P. & CO. (L.)
1872–8, earthenware　　printed

Pratt, Hassall & Gerrard　　P.H.G
1822–34, general ceramics　　P.H. & G.
printed

Pratt & Simpson　　P. & S.
1878–83, earthenware　　printed

Radford (Ltd.), Samuel
1879–1957, porcelain
　　'R.S.' monogram from
　　about 1880, 'England'
　　added 1891

various 'S.R.' monograms
used during this century

Rainbow Pottery Co.　　　RAINBOW POTTERY
1931–41, earthenware　　　　FENTON
　　　　　　　　　　　　MADE IN ENGLAND
　　　　　　　　　　　printed or impressed

Reeves, James　　　J.R.　　　　　　　　J.R.
　1870–1948, earthenware　　　　　　　　F
　printed or impressed　　　J. REEVES

Rubian Art Pottery Ltd.　　　L.S. & G.
1906–33, earthenware
　impressed or printed　　　RUBAY ART WARE
　c. 1926–33

Sterling Pottery Ltd.
1947–53, earthenware

　other marks include:
　'RIDGWAY'　　　　　　　printed

Stubbs Bros.
1899–1904, bone-china
　printed

Victoria Porcelain (Fenton) Ltd.
1949–57, earthenware
　printed

Victoria & Trentham Potteries Ltd.
1957–60, general ceramics
  lion mark as above but includes new name

Wathen & Lichfield   W. & L.
1864–4, earthenware   FENTON

Wathen, James, B.   J.B.W.
1864–9, earthenware   J.B.W.
                       F
                 printed

Wileman, James & Charles   J. & C.W.
1864–9, general ceramics   J.F. & C.W.
                     C.J.W.
  'J. Wileman & Co.'   J.W. & CO.

Wileman, James F.   J.F.W.
1869–92   J. F. WILEMAN

Wileman & Co.
1892–1925
  'SHELLEY' mark used
  from *c.* 1911

Wilson & Sons, J.
1898–1926, bone-china

               printed

FOLEY (Staffordshire)

   Hawley & Co.   HAWLEY
   1842–87, earthenware   HAWLEY & CO.
                          impressed

   Mayer, John   J.M.
   1833–41, earthenware   F
                          printed

HANLEY (Staffordshire)

   Adams & Co., John   J. ADAMS & CO.
   1864–73, earthenwares and   ADAMS & CO.
   stonewares, etc.   impressed

   Adams & Bromley   A. & B.   A. & B.
   1873–86, earthenware   SHELTON
   stonewares, etc.   ADAMS & BROMLEY
                printed or impressed

   Alcock, Lindley & Bloore (Ltd.)
   1919, earthenware
   (now Allied English Potteries)
     printed or impressed

   Art Pottery Co.   ART POTTERY CO.
   1900–11, earthenware   ENGLAND
    printed mark   (with crown)

   Ashworth & Bros. (Ltd.)
   1862–1970, earthenware   ASHWORTH
    1862–80   impressed
   (now Mason's Ironstone
   China Co. Ltd.)   A. BROS.
   Wedgwood Group from 1973

Ashworth & Bros. G.L.A. & BROS.
  printed *c.* 1862–90
  with designs including
  pattern names
  From 1862 Ashworths used mark similar
  to that of Mason's 'Patent Ironstone'
(Mason's Ironstone China
Ltd. from 1968)
  'England' added 1891

  printed mark from
  about 1880

  'LUSTROSA' trade-name
  1932–

  printed on ironstone
  c. 1957–

Baddeley, Thomas T. BADDELEY
1800–34, engraver of HANLEY
plates for transfer-prints printed

Baddeley, William EASTWOOD
1802–22, 'Wedgwood- impressed
type' ware

Bakewell Bros. Ltd. BAKEWELL BROS.
1927-43, earthenware LTD.
  printed

Bates, Brown-Westhead B.B.W. & M.
& Moore printed or impressed
1859–61, general ceramics

Baxter, John Denton I.D.B.
1823–7, earthenware J.D.B.
printed
Bednall & Heath B. & H.
1879–99, earthenware printed

Bennett & Co., J. J.B. & CO.
1896–1900, earthenware printed or impressed

Bennett (Hanley) Ltd., William W.B.
1882–1937 H
earthenwares printed or impressed

Bevington, James & Thomas J. & T.B.
1865–78, porcelains impressed

Bevington & Co., John J.B. & CO.
1869–71, earthenware H
printed in backstamp

Bevington, John
1872–92, porcelains

This mark was underglaze-blue
obviously adopted to
imitate that of Meissen on pieces made in
'Dresden' style

Bevington, Thomas
1877–91, general ceramics

T.B.

printed

Birch & Whitehead
c. 1796, 'Wedgwood type'
wares

B. & W.
impressed

Bishop & Stonier
1891–1939, general
ceramics

B. & S.
printed or impressed

printed marks
1891–
'England' added
on fully named
marks from *c.* 1899–

1936–9

BISHOP
ENGLAND

Blue John Pottery Ltd.
1939, earthenware

various 'Blue John'
printed marks

Booth, G. R.
1829–44, earthenware
  '& Co.' added *c.* 1839
  impressed mark

PUBLISHED BY
G. R. BOOTH & CO.
HANLEY
STAFFORDSHIRE

Booth & Colcloughs Ltd.
1948–54, general ceramics
(see Ridgway Potteries Ltd.)
  also trade-names:
  'Blue Mist', 'Malvern Chinaware'
  and 'Royal Swan'

various marks
including
name

Bourne, Samuel
early 18th century
pottery figures

S. BOURNE
impressed

Bournemouth Pottery Co.
(Bournemouth, 1945–52)
Hanley 1952–, earthenware

BOURNEMOUTH
POTTERY
ENGLAND

Boyle, Zachariah
1823–50, general
ceramics
  '& S.' added from
  1828

BOYLE

Z.B.   Z.B. & S.

Brown-Westhead, Moore & Co.
1862–1904
general ceramics

B.W.M.

B.W.M. & CO.

printed or impressed

149

impressed	T. C. BROWN WESTHEAD-MOORE & CO.
printed or impressed 1891–	
later marks include initials & 'CAULDON'	
Bullers Ltd. *c*. 1937–55, earthenware	BULLERS MADE IN ENGLAND painted
Bullock & Co., A. 1895–1915, earthenware	A.B. & CO. H. A.B. & CO. printed or impressed
Burgess, Thomas 1903–17, earthenware (mark of Harrop & Burgess was continued)	printed or impressed
Burton, Samuel & John 1832–45, earthenware	S. & J.B. impressed on applied tablet
Cauldon Ltd. 1905–20, general ceramics	CAULDON ENGLAND printed under crown

marks previously used by Ridgway
and Brown—Westhead, Moore & Co., used
with addition of 'CAULDON'

Cauldon Potteries, Ltd.　　ROYAL CAULDON
1920–62, general ceramics　　ENGLAND
　　　　　　　　　　　　　EST. 1774
　similar printed marks used from 1930–62,
　when factory was taken over by
Pountney & Co. Ltd. of Bristol (now
Cauldon Bristol Potteries Ltd., Redruth, Cornwall)

Ceramic Art Co. Ltd.　　THE CERAMIC ART
1892–1903, decorators　　CO. LTD. HANLEY
　　　　　　　　　　　　STAFFORDSHIRE
　　　　　　　　　　　　ENGLAND
　　　　　　　　　　　　printed

Clementson, Joseph　　　　J.C.
c. 1839–64, earthenware　　J. CLEMENTSON
　　　　　　　　　　　　printed

Clementson Bros.　　　　CLEMENTSON BROS.
1865–1916, earthenware　　with Royal Arms
and stoneware
　printed 1867–80
　various fully named printed marks with
　phoenix from 1870–
　'Ltd.' added 1910

　　　　　　　　　　CLEMENTSON BROS.
　printed, 1913–16　　　ENGLAND
　　　　　　　　　　under crown

Clementson, Young & Jameson　C.Y. & J.
1844, earthenware

Clementson & Young　　　CLEMENTSON &
1845–7, earthenware　　　YOUNG
　　　　　　　　　　impressed or printed

Coalbrook Potteries
1937–, decorative wares
  printed–

COALBROOK
MADE IN
ENGLAND

Coopers Art Pottery Co.
c. 1912–58, earthenware

ART POTTERY CO.
ENGLAND
with crown

Cotton, Ltd., Elijah
1880–, earthenware
  Trade-names: 'NELSON WARE', *c.* 1913–;
  'LORD NELSON WARE', 1956–

various fully-
named marks

Creyke & Sons, G. M.
1920–48, earthenware
  initials also used in
  monogram form
  Trade-name 'BROADWAY'
  c. 1935–

G.M.C.
printed or impressed

Davenport, Banks & Co.
1860–73, earthenware

  impressed or printed
  marks

D.B. & CO.

DAVENPORT
BANKS & CO.
ETRURIA

Davenport, Beck & Co.
1873–80, earthenware

D.B. & CO.

Davis, J. Heath
1881–91, earthenware

J. H. DAVIS
HANLEY

Diamond Pottery Co. Ltd.   D.P. CO.
1908–35, earthenware   D.P. CO. LTD.
    printed

Dimmock (Junr.) & Co., Thomas   D.
1828–59, earthenware

  impressed or printed
  'double D' monogram

Dimmock & Co., J.   J.D. & CO.
1862–1904, earthenware

firm taken over by
W. D. Cliff in *c.* 1878–
  'Cliff' used in varying   CLIFF
  forms *c.* 1878–1904   ENGLAND

  written on ribbon   ALBION WORKS
  under 'lion rampant'   printed

Dudson, James   DUDSON
1838–88, earthenware   impressed
(this firm made many
'Spaniels' and 'Rockingham-type' dogs)

Dudson, J. T.   J. DUDSON
1888–98, earthenwares
and stonewares   J. DUDSON
  'England' added 1891   ENGLAND
    impressed

Dudson Bros., Ltd.
1898–, earthenwares and
stonewares

    printed mark, 1936–45

DUDSON ENGLAND

Dudson, Wilcox & Till, Ltd.
1902–26, earthenware
    printed or impressed,
    figure of Britannia also
    used within double-ring
    with full name of firm

Dura Porcelain Co. Ltd.
1919–21, porcelain

    printed mark

Ellis, Unwin & Mountford
1860–61, earthenware

E.U. & M.
printed

Fancies Fayre Pottery
c. 1946, earthenware
    Trade-name 'KNICK
    KNACKS'
(now Bairstow & Co.)

STAFFORDSHIRE
F.F.
ENGLAND
printed or impressed

Fenton & Sons, Alfred
1887–1901, general
ceramics

A.F. & S.
impressed or printed
(also written within
circular crowned strap)

Fletcher, Thomas
c. 1786–1810, printer and
decorator

T. FLETCHER
SHELTON

Ford, Charles
1874–1904, porcelain

impressed
or printed

'Swan' mark, impressed
or printed, c. 1900–4

Ford, T. & C.
1854–71, earthenware
impressed or printed
marks

T. & C.F.

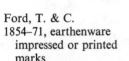

Ford, Thomas
1871–4, porcelain

numerals indicate
month and year, e.g.
JULY, 1872

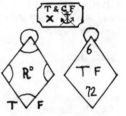

impressed or printed

Ford & Pointon Ltd.
1917–36, porcelain
(absorbed by Cauldon
c. 1921)

Furnival, Jacob & Thomas
c. 1843, earthenware

J. & T.F.
printed under
Royal Arms

Furnival & Co., Thomas
c. 1844–6, earthenware

T.F. & CO.
printed

Futura Art Pottery Ltd.
1947–56, earthenware

FUTURA
ART POTTERY LTD.
printed

Gelson Bros.
1867–76, earthenware

GELSON BROS.
HANLEY
printed

Glass, John
c. 1784–1838, earthenware
and stoneware

GLASS HANLEY
J. GLASS HANLEY
impressed

Glass, Joseph
c. 1700, slipwares

JOSEPH GLASS

Goldscheider (Staffordshire) Pottery Ltd.
1946–59, figures in
pottery and porcelain

Goldscheider
printed

Gray & Co. Ltd., A. E.
1912–61, earthenware
(known as 'Portmeirion
Potteries Ltd.' from 1962)
moved to Stoke in 1934

various printed marks
depicting ships with
factory name

    printed mark
    1934–61

Grimwade Bros. G. Bros.
1886–1900, earthenware on star within
circle

Grimwades Ltd.
1900–, earthenware
printed mark, *c.* 1900–

STOKE POTTERY

many various fully named marks including
name or trade-name:
'winton' *c.* 1906, 'rubian art' *c.* 1906–,
'vitro hotel ware' *c.* 1930, 'royal
winton ivory' *c.* 1930, 'atlas' *c.* 1934–9

Hackwood & Co. h. & co.
1807–27, earthenware and hackwood & co.
stoneware impressed

Hackwood, William w.h.
1827–43, earthenware hackwood
impressed or printed printed or impressed

Hackwood & Keeling h. & k.
1835–6, earthenware printed

Hall, Samuel hall
c. 1840–56, earthenware impressed

Hall & Read hall & read
1883–8, earthenware hanley
'H. & R.' also probably printed
used

157

Hammersley, J. & R.   J.R.H.
1877–1917, general ceramics   printed

Hanley Porcelain Co.
1892–99, porcelain

printed

Hanley China Co.   H
1899–1901, porcelain   C C°.
  printed   in knot

Harrop & Burgess
1894–1903, earthenware

printed

Heath, J.   I.H.
c. 1770–1800, earthenware

                              HEATH
                              impressed

Heath, Joshua   JOSHUA HEATH
c. 1740, earthenware   incised

Hollins, T. J. & R.   T.J. & R. HOLLINS
c. 1818–22, earthenware   impressed

Johnson Bros. (Hanley) Ltd.   JOHNSON BROS.
1883–, earthenware   ENGLAND
  impressed or printed
  name with various
  coat-of-arms, crowns,
  etc.
(now part of Wedgwood Group) Johnson Bros
                              England.

Jones & Son
c. 1826–8, earthenware

JONES & SON
printed

Keeling, Joseph
c. 1802–8, earthenware and
stoneware

JOSEPH KEELING
impressed

Keeling & Co., Samuel
1840–50, earthenware

S.K. & CO.

S. KEELING & CO.
printed

Keeling, Toft & Co.
1805–26, stonewares
in Wedgwood style

KEELING & TOFT

KEELING, TOFT & CO.
impressed

Kensington Fine Art Pottery Co.
1892–9, earthenware

printed or impressed

Lancaster & Sons
1900–44, earthenware
 '& Sons' & 'Ltd.' added
 c. 1906
 c. 1920–

L. & SONS LTD.
HANLEY. ENG.

'ROYALL & LANSAN' 1930–
'BRITISH CROWN WARE', *c.* 1935–
'CROWN DRESDEN WARE', *c.* 1935–

c. 1934–44

LANCASTERS LTD.
HANLEY. ENGLAND

Lancaster & Sandland Ltd.
1944–1968, earthenware

BRITISH
CROWN WARE

many various printed
marks including name
'SANDLAND'

CROWN DRESDEN WARE

SANDLAND
STAFFORDSHIRE
ENGLAND

Langdale Pottery Co. Ltd.
1947–58, earthenware
printed

Langdale
MADE IN ENGLAND

Lear, Samuel
1877–86, general ceramics

LEAR
impressed

Livesley, Powell & Co.
1851–66, earthenware
and stoneware

LIVESLEY POWELL
& CO.
L.P. & CO.
impressed or printed

Powell & Bishop
1867–1878, general
ceramics

P. & B.
POWELL & BISHOP
printed or impressed

Powell, Bishop & Stonier
1878–91, general
ceramics

P.B. & S.
printed or impressed

'Chinaman' mark first
registered 1880, but
continued by Bishop
& Stonier

Bishop & Stonier   B. & S.
1891–1939, general ceramics
   full name printed in   BISHOP & STONIER
   various designs, 1899–1936
   'Bishop' only used 1936–9

Lloyd, J. & R.   LLOYD SHELTON
c. 1834–52, 'Staffordshire   impressed
figures'

Lockett, Baguley &   LOCKETT BAGULEY
Cooper, 1855–60, porcelain   & COOPER

Lockitt, William H.   W.H.L.
1901–19, earthenware   H
   'DURA-WARE' 1913–19   printed in crescent

Mann & Co.   MANN & CO.
1858–60, general ceramics   HANLEY
   printed

Manzoni, Carlo
c. 1895–8, studio pottery

   incised mark including
   date

Mayer, Elijah   E. MAYER
c. 1790–1804, various   impressed
Wedgwood-type wares

Mayer & Son, Elijah 1805–34 Wedgwood-type wares	E. MAYER & SON impressed or printed
Mayer & Co., Joseph *c.* 1822–33, earthenware	JOSEPH MAYER & CO. HANLEY MAYER & CO.
Meakin, Charles 1883–9, earthenware	CHARLES MEAKIN HANLEY under Royal Arms
Meakin (Ltd.), J. & G. 1851–, earthenwares (now part of Wedgwood Group) 1890–	J. & G. MEAKIN impressed or printed
'ENGLAND' added from 1891 'Sun-face' marks from 1912– 'PASTEL VITRESOL' 'STUDIO WARE' and 'SOUTH SEAS' recent trade-names	printed
Meigh, Job *c.* 1805–34, earthenware 'Son' added *c.* 1812	MEIGH impressed OLD HALL impressed or printed J.M. & S.

Meigh, Charles — CHARLES MEIGH
1835–49, earthenware and — impressed
stonewares — G.M.
printed with device
and pattern name

printed or impressed marks of various
bodies and styles of decoration include:
'Indian Stone China', 'French China',
'Improved Stone China', 'Enamel Porcelain'

Meigh, Son & Pankhurst, — C.M.S. & P.
Charles, 1850–51, earthenware — printed

Meigh & Son, Charles — C.M. & S.
1851–61, earthenware

many of the marks — M. & S.
used by this firm
include the Royal — C. MEIGH & SON
Arms

MEIGH'S
CHINA

printed or impressed — OPAQUE
PORCELAIN

Old Hall Earthenware Co Ltd.
1861–86

O.H.E.C.
printed — O.H.E.C.(L.)

printed or impressed

mark registered in 1884 and
continued by Old Hall
Porcelain Works Ltd.
printed

Old Hall Porcelain Works   (as above)
Ltd., 1886–1902, general
ceramics

Mills, Henry   H. MILLS
c. 1892, earthenware   printed

Moore & Co.   M. & CO.
1898–1903, earthenware   printed with name
                                      of pattern

Morley & Co., Francis   F.M.
1845–58, earthenware

late form of Masons'   F.M. & CO.
Ironstone mark used
from 1845   F. MORLEY & CO.
                              printed with many
                             various backstamps

Morley & Ashworth   M. & A.
1859–62, earthenware   MORLEY &
   impressed or printed   ASHWORTH
   with pattern name   HANLEY

Neale & Co., James
c. 1776–*c.* 86, all manner
of wares in Wedgwood
style
   '& Co.' added *c.* 1778

N   NEALE
I. NEALE
I. NEALE. HANLEY

NEALE & CO.
impressed

Neale & Bailey
c. 1790–1814, earthenware

NEALE & BAILEY
printed or impressed

Neale, Harrison & Co.
1875–85, general ceramics

N.H. & CO.
printed

Neale & Palmer
c. 1769–76, earthenwares
in Wedgwood style

NEALE & PALMER
impressed

Neale & Wilson
c. 1784–95, earthenware
and Wedgwood-type wares

NEALE & WILSON

NEALE & CO.
impressed

New Hall Porcelain Works
1781–1835, hard-paste
porcelain 1781–*c.* 1812
bone-china, *c.* 1812–35

printed on bone-china

New Hall Pottery Co. Ltd.
1899–1956, earthenware

  printed, *c.* 1930–51

New Pearl Pottery Co. Ltd.   PEARL POTTERY CO.
1936–41, earthenware,   printed
'Royal Bourbon Ware'

Palmer, Humphrey   PALMER
c. 1760–78, earthenware
and Wedgwood-type
stonewares

impressed

Pankhurst & Co., J. W.   J.W.P.
1850–82, earthenware
    '& Co.' added *c.* 1852   J. W. PANKHURST

Pearl Pottery Co. Ltd.
1894–1936, earthenware
    1894–1912

printed or impressed

    printed in various
    forms, 1912–36   P.P. CO. LTD.

Physick & Cooper   P. & C.
1899–1900, earthenware   over crown

Art Pottery Co.   ART POTTERY CO.
1900–11, earthenware   over crown

Coopers Art Pottery Co.   printed as above
c. 1912–58, earthenware

166

Podmore China Co. 1921–41, porcelain	'P.C. CO.' monogram under crown
Pointon & Co. Ltd. 1883–1916, porcelain	POINTONS STOKE-ON-TRENT printed with coat-of-arms
Poole, Richard 1790–5, earthenware	R. POOLE impressed
Ratcliffe, William *c.* 1831–40, earthenware	R HACKWOOD printed or impressed

printed in underglaze blue

Ridgway, Job *c.* 1802–8, earthenware	R J.R. printed (J.R. also used by John Ridgway)
Ridgway & Sons, Job *c.* 1808–14, earthenware	RIDGWAY & SONS impressed or printed
Ridgway, John & William 1814–*c.* 1830	J.W.R. J. & W.R. J. & W. RIDGWAY printed or impressed

Ridgway & Co., John *c.* 1830–55, general ceramics	JOHN RIDGWAY J.R. JHN RIDGWAY
printed or impressed marks usually including name of pattern	I. RIDGWAY '& CO.' added *c.* 1841
Ridgway, Bates & Co., J. 1856–58, general ceramics	J.R.B. & CO. printed
Bates, Brown-Westhead & Moore, 1859–61, general ceramics	B.B.W. & M. printed or impressed
Brown-Westhead, Moore & Co. 1862–1904, general ceramics	*see p.* 149
Cauldon Ltd. 1905–20, general ceramics	*see p.* 150
Cauldon Potteries Ltd. 1920–62, general ceramics	*see p.* 151
Ridgway & Robey *c.* 1837–9, figures marks very rare	RIDGWAY & ROBEY HANLEY STAFFORDSHIRE POTTERIES
Ridgway, Morley, Wear & Co., 1836–42 earthenware	R.M.W. & CO. RIDGWAY, MORLEY WEAR & CO. printed

Ridgway & Morley   R. & M.
1842–44, earthenware   RIDGWAY & MORLEY
                               printed

Ridgway & Abington   E. RIDGWAY & ABINGTON
c. 1835–60, earthenware   HANLEY
                              impressed

Ridgway, Son & Co.,   W.R.S. & CO.
William, c. 1838–48   W. RIDGWAY, SON
                          & CO. HANLEY
                               printed

Ridgway, Sparks & Ridgway   R.S.R.
1873–79, earthenware   also printed in
                            'Staffordshire knot'

Ridgways
1879–20
   mark of 1880–

   'RIDGWAYS' and 'ENGLAND' in various
   marks from c. 1905–20
   RIDGWAYS (BEDFORD WORKS) LTD.
   1920–52, earthenware
   'RIDGWAYS' and/or 'BEDFORD' in variety
   of marks used from 1920–52
This firm became 'Ridgway & Adderley Ltd.'
in 1952, Ridgway, Adderley, Booths &
Colcloughs Ltd.' from 1955 and in same year
'Ridgway Potteries Ltd.'
(part of Allied English Potteries, Ltd.
from 1952, now Royal Doulton Group)

name of American firm, JONROTH
John R. Roth & Co. J.H.R. & CO. monogram
seen on some Ridgway printed
exports, *c.* 1930–56

Rigby & Stevenson R. & S.
1894–1954, earthenware printed

Rivers, William RIVERS
c. 1818–22, earthenware impressed

Robinson & Wood R. & W.
1832–6, earthenware printed

Salt, Ralph 'SALT'
c. 1820–46, earthenware impressed on scroll

Sandlands & Colley, Ltd. full name &
1907–1910, general 's.c.' monogram
ceramics printed under crown

Scrivener & Co., R. G. R.G.S.
1870–83, general ceramics

  printed or impressed R.G.S.
  & CO.

Sherwin & Cotton
1877–30, tiles
  impressed

Shorthose & Co. SHORTHOSE & CO.
c. 1817–1822 written
  impressed or printed

Shorthose & Heath   SHORTHOSE &
c. 1795–1815, earthenware   HEATH
      impressed or printed

Shorthose, John   S
1807–23, earthenware

  impressed marks   SHORTHOSE

Sneyd & Hill   SNEYD & HILL
c. 1845, earthenware   HANLEY
  printed   STAFFORDSHIRE
      POTTERIES

Sneyd, Thomas   T. SNEYD
1846–7, earthenware   HANLEY
      impressed

Stevenson, William   W. STEVENSON
c. 1802, earthenware   HANLEY
  rare impressed mark

Swinnertons Ltd.
1906–71, earthenware
(Allied English Potteries   SWINNERTONS
Ltd.), mark printed   HANLEY
  c. 1906–17, later marks all include
  full-name of firm

Sylvan Pottery Ltd.
1946–, earthenware

  'B' included in mark
  prior to 1948

Studio Szeiler, Ltd.
c. 1951–, earthenware printed or impressed

Taylor, George   G. TAYLOR
c. 1784–1811, earthenware   GEO. TAYLOR
                                   impressed or incised

Taylor, Tunnicliffe & Co.   T.T.
1868–, general ceramics   T.T. & CO.
(now electrical &   printed
industrial wares only)

Thomas & Co., Uriah
1888–1905, earthenware

printed or impressed

Toft, James (*b.* 1673)   James Toft
Ralph (*b.* 1638),   Ralph Toft
Thomas (*d.* 1689), slipware   Thomas Toft

Unwin, Mountford &   U.M. & T.
Taylor, *c.* 1864, earthenware   printed

Unwin, Holmes &   U.H. & W.
Worthington, *c.* 1865–8   printed
earthenware

Upper Hanley Pottery Co.   U.H.P. CO.
c. 1895–1902, then at   ENGLAND
Cobridge until 1910
earthenware   impressed or printed
  'Ltd.' from 1900

Wardle & Co.
1871–1910, earthenware
Wardle Art Pottery Co. Ltd.
1910–1935, earthenware

WARDLE
impressed

printed, *c.* 1885–90

printed, *c.* 1890–1935

Wardle & Ash
1859–62, earthenware

W. & A.
impressed

Weatherby & Sons, Ltd.
1891–, earthenware
   c. 1925–

J.H.W. & SONS

FALCON WARE

   c. 1936–, (trade-name)

WEATHERBY WARE
printed

Wellington Pottery Co.
1899–1901, earthenware

printed or impressed

Westminster Pottery Ltd.
1948–56, earthenware

   1952–, (trade-name)

CASTLECLIFFE WARE

Whittaker & Co.
1886–92, earthenware

W. & CO.
printed

Whittaker, Heath & Co.
1892–8, earthenware

W.H. & CO.
printed

Wilson, Robert
1795–1801, earthenware

impressed marks

WILSON

C

Wilson, David
c. 1802–18, general ceramics

WILSON
impressed

Winkle & Wood
1885–90, earthenware

printed

Worthington & Harrop
1856–73, earthenware

W. & H.
printed

Wulstan Pottery Co. Ltd.
c. 1940–58, earthenware

printed

Yates, John
c. 1784–1835, earthenware

J.Y.

printed or impressed

LANE DELPH (Staffordshire)
  Edge, William & Samuel
  1841–8, earthenware

W. & S.E.
printed

Harrison, George
c. 1790–5, earthenware

G. Harrison
impressed

Mason, William
c. 1811–24, earthenware

W. MASON
printed

Mason, Miles
c. 1792–1816, porcelain
  marks impressed *c.* 1800–16

M. MASON
MILES MASON

  printed mark on
  chinoiserie patterns

Mason, G. M. & C. J.
1813–29, earthenware
(ironstone)

G.M. & C.J. MASON

G. & C.J.M.

  impressed marks
  c. 1813–25

MASON'S PATENT
IRONSTONE CHINA

  patented in 1813

PATENT IRONSTONE
CHINA

  standard mark of
  c. 1820, continued by
  Ashworth (*c.* 1862)
'Mason's Ironstone China
Ltd.' from 1968–
(a Division of Josiah
Wedgwood & Sons Ltd., 1974)

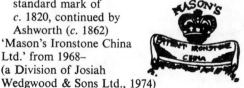

printed mark with
pattern number *c.* 1825–

Mason & Co., Charles
James, 1829–45,
earthenware, (ironstone)
  printed

FENTON
STONE WORKS
C.J.M. & CO.
GRANITE CHINA

  printed

C.J. MASON & CO.
LANE DELPH

  c. 1840–

'MASON'S CAMBRIAN ARGIL',
'MASON'S BANDANA WARE'
impressed or printed
c. 1825–40

Mason, Charles James
c. 1845–8, earthenware
(ironstone), also at
Longton, 1851–4

Morley & Co., Francis
1845–58, earthenware
(Hanley)

printed
F.M.
F.M. & CO.
F. MORLEY & CO.

Morley & Ashworth
1859–62, earthenware
(Hanley)

M. & A.
impressed or printed

Myatt, late 18th- early
19th centuries,
earthenware

MYATT
impressed

Pratt, William
c. 1780–99, earthenware

PRATT

LANE END (Staffordshire)
Abbott, Andrew
c. 1781–3, earthenware

ABBOTT POTTER
impressed

Abbott & Mist
1787–1810, earthenware

ABBOTT & MIST
impressed or painted

Aynsley, John
1780–1809, engraver of
prints for earthenwares

'*J. Aynsley Lane End*'
printed

Barker, John, Richard &
William, *c.* 1800
earthenware

BARKER
impressed

Batkin, Walker & Broadhurst,
1840–5, earthenware

B.W. & B.
printed

Booth & Sons
1830–5, earthenware

BOOTH & SONS
impressed

Bott & Co.
c. 1810–11, earthenware

BOTT & CO.
impressed

Carey, Thomas & John CAREYS
c. 1823–42, earthenware impressed or
printed with anchor

Chesworth & Robinson C. & R.
1825–40, earthenware printed

Chetham & Woolley CHETHAM &
1796–1810, earthenware WOOLLEY
LANE END
incised

Cyples, Joseph CYPLES
c. 1784–1840
(initials of various I. CYPLES
potters in this family impressed
rarely used)

Deakin & Son
1833–41, earthenware
printed mark

Everard, Glover & E.G. & C.
Colclough, *c.* 1847– printed
general ceramics

Floyd, Benjamin B.F.
c. 1843, earthenware printed

Goodwin, Bridgwood & G.B.O.
Orton, 1827–9 G.B. & O.
earthenware

Goodwin, Bridgwood & Harris   G.B.H.
1829–31, earthenware

Goodwins & Harris   GOODWINS &
c. 1831–8, earthenware   HARRIS
          printed

Griffiths, Beardmore &   G.B. & B.
Birks, 1830, earthenware   printed

Harley, Thomas   HARLEY
1802–8, earthenware   T. HARLEY
          impressed

   printed or written

          T. HARLEY
          LANE END

Harvey, Bailey & Co.   H.B. & CO.
1833–5, earthenware   printed

Heathcote & Co., Charles   C. HEATHCOTE & CO.
1818–24, earthenware   printed

Hilditch & Son
1822–30, general ceramics

   printed in various
   surrounds

Hulme & Sons, John   HULME & SONS
c. 1828–30, earthenware   printed

179

Lockett, J. & G. *c.* 1802–5, earthenware	J. & G. LOCKETT impressed
Lockett, John 1821–58, earthenware	J. LOCKETT impressed
Lockett & Co., J. *c.* 1812–89, earthenware (also at Longton 1882– 1960, and 1960– Burslem)	J. LOCKETT & CO. impressed or printed
Lockett & Hulme 1822–6, earthenware	L. & H. L.E. printed
Mayer & Newbold *c.* 1817–33, general ceramics	M. & N.
marks painted or printed	MAY^R & NEWB^D

MAY^R & NEWB^D

Opaque China
M&N

Plant, Benjamin
c. 1780–1820, earthenware
marks incised

B Plant
Lane End

Plant, Thomas
1825–50, earthenware

T P

painted

Ray, George, modeller
early 19th century

G. RAY
Lane End

Turner, John (also entered under Longton) *c.* 1762–1806, earthenware and porcelain	TURNER I. TURNER
early impressed marks	

TURNER

printed or impressed from 1784 after Turner was potter to the Prince of Wales	
impressed, *c.* 1780–6 1803–6	TURNER & CO.
painted on earthenwares 1800–5	*Turner's Patent*
Turner & Abbott *c.* 1783–7 (Abbott probably only agent) earthenwares and stoneware in Wedgwood style	TURNER & ABBOTT impressed

LONGPORT (Staffordshire)

Bodley & Son, E. F. 1881–98, earthenware	E.F.B. & SON
trade-mark, 1883–98	

Bourne, Edward　　　　E. BOURNE
1790–1811, earthenware　impressed

Corn, W. & E.　　　　　W. & E.C.
1864–1904, earthenware
(also at Burslem *c.* 1864–　　W.E.C.
1904, nearly all marks
　are late and include 'ENGLAND' (post-1891)

Davenport & Co., W.
c. 1793–1887, general
ceramics; 1798–1815　　　　Davenport

c. 1815–60　　　　　　DAVENPORT
　'Davenport' or 'DAVENPORT'
　is impressed with or　　
　without anchor

　marks on 'Stone-China'　　
　c. 1815–30

19th century mark to　　
about 1860, including
last two numerals of
year
　anchor mark alone *c.* 1820–40　　

many printed wares of 1820–60 bear
name of pattern and 'DAVENPORT'

182

printed on porcelain
c. 1815–
three numerals denote month and last
two numerals of year made
'Manufacturers of China to His Majesty
and the Royal Family' on porcelain
c. 1830–37

DAVENPORT
LONGPORT

impressed *c.* 1850–70

DAVENPORT
PATENT

printed in underglaze-blue
c. 1850–70
(sometimes in enamel
colours prior to 1830)

This mark was used
from *c.* 1830–45 in puce
and from *c.* 1870–87
in red

DAVENPORT
LONGPORT
STAFFORDSHIRE
printed under crown

printed on earthenware
c. 1881–7

DAVENPORTS LTD.

Liddle, Elliott & Son
1862–71, general
ceramics

L.E. & S.
impressed or printed

Mayer & Elliott
1858–61, earthenware
    number of month and
    last two numerals of year

$\mathcal{M}^{\&}_{\mathcal{E}}$
printed

impressed, e.g. $\dfrac{6}{59}$ = June, 1859

Phillips, Edward & George 1822–34, earthenware	PHILLIPS LONGPORT
printed marks	E. & G.P.

Phillips, George
1834–48, earthenware
   name with or without knot,
   sometimes 'Longport' also
	PHILLIPS

Rogers, John & George *c.* 1784–1814, earthenware	ROGERS
impressed marks	J.R. L.
Rogers & Son, John *c.* 1814–36, earthenware	as above and
	J.R.S. ROGERS & SON
Smith, Ltd., W. T. H. 1898–1905, earthenware	W.T.H. SMITH & CO. LONGPORT printed with 'globe'

Wood & Son (Longport)
Ltd., 1928–, earthenware
   'ROYAL BRADWELL
   ART WARE' trade-name
	ARTHUR WOOD
	full name printed in
	variety of marks

Wood, Arthur
1904–28, earthenware
   mark impressed or
   printed
	A.W.
	L
	ENGLAND

LONGTON HALL (Staffordshire)
  c. 1749–60, porcelain
    rare marks painted in
    underglaze blue

LONGTON (Staffordshire)

Adams & Co. Harvey
1870–85, general ceramics

H.A. & CO.
over crown
printed

Adams & Cooper
1850–77, porcelain

A. & C.
printed

Adderleys Ltd.
1906–, general ceramics

  printed mark 1906–26
  many other marks all
  including full name of firm

Adderley, J. Fellows
1901–5, porcelain

  printed marks

J.F.A.

Adderley, William Alsager
1876–1905

W.A.A.

W.A.A. & CO.

  and 'sailing-ship' trade-
  mark as above

185

Adderley Floral China Works
1945– bone-china
decorative wares
   printed mark
(Royal Doulton Group
from 1973)

Aldridge & Co.
1919–49, earthenware

ALDRIDGE & CO.
LONGTON
impressed

Allerton & Sons, Charles
1859–1942, general
ceramics
   printed or impressed
   marks, *c.* 1890–1942
   Many other fully named
   marks also used

C.A. & SONS

CHAS. ALLERTON &
SONS
ENGLAND

Alton China Co. Ltd.
1950–7, bone-china

ALTON
BONE CHINA
printed

Amison, Charles
1889–1962, porcelain
   impressed initials, 1889–

   printed mark of 1906–30
   '& Co.' added 1916
   '& Co. Ltd.', 1930

   further late marks include
   'Stanley' and 'Staffordshire
   Floral Bone China'

C.A.
L.

186

Anchor Porcelain Co. Ltd.   A.P. CO.
1901–18, porcelain
    impressed marks   A.P. CO. L.

    impressed or printed
    'anchor-mark', 1901–15
    'ROYAL WESTMINSTER CHINA' printed
    with 'A.P. CO. L.', 1915–18

Aristocrat Florals & Fancies   ENGLISH
1958–, bone-china decorative   Aristocrat
wares (Wedgwood Group   Florals
from 1973)   BONE
                                      CHINA

Asbury & Co.   ASBURY
1875–1925, general ceramics   LONGTON
    printed marks

                                      A. & CO.

                                      TRADE MARK

Avon Art Pottery
1930–69, earthenware
    recent mark, printed   MADE IN
(seemingly merged with   Avon Ware
Elektra Porcelain Co., 1962)   ENGLAND

Aynsley & Co., H.   H.A. & CO.
1873–, earthenware   L.
    'Ltd.' added 1932
    late marks include
    name in full

Aynsley & Sons, John AYNSLEY
1864–, porcelain impressed
  various later marks include full name and
  'ENGLAND' added from 1891
(now Aynsley China Ltd.–Waterford Glass Co.
Ltd.)

Baddeley, William EASTWOOD
1802–22, earthenware impressed
(Wedgwood-type)

Baggerley & Ball B. & B.
1822–36, earthenware L.
  printed in blue
  within oval frame

Bailey & Sons, William
1912–14, earthenware
  printed mark

Bailey & Batkin BAILEY & BATKIN
1814–*c*. 27, earthenware
including lustreware
  marks impressed or moulded B. & B.

Bailey & Harvey BAILEY & HARVEY
1834–5, earthenware impressed
including lustre

Balfour China Co. Ltd. BALFOUR
1947–52, bone-china ROYAL CROWN
(then known as: POTTERY
Trentham Bone China printed with crown
Ltd.)

Barker Bros. Ltd.   B.B.
1876–, general ceramics   impressed
   large variety of other printed marks
   including such trade names as:
   MEIR CHINA, MEIR WARE, TUDOR WARE
   and ROYAL TUDOR WARE
(Alfred Clough Ltd.)

Barlow & Son Ltd., T. W.   B. B. & S.
1882–1940, earthenware   rare impressed
                              marks
   marks used from about 1928 include
   'CORONATION WARE'

Barlow, Thomas   B.
1849–1882, general ceramics   impressed

Barlows (Longton) Ltd.   B. Ltd.
1920–52, earthenware   impressed
   later marks include 'MELBAR WARE'

Baxter, Rowley & Tams   B.R. & T.
1882–5, porcelain   impressed

Beardmore & Edwards   B. & E.
1856–8, earthenware   printed

Bentley & Co. Ltd., G. L.   G.L.B. & CO.
1898–1912, porcelain   LONGTON
   'Ltd.' added from 1904

Beswick & Son   B. & S.
1916–30, porcelain   printed or impressed
  'ALDWYCH CHINA', trade-name also used by
  Bridgett & Bates, former prop's.

Beswick Ltd., John   BESWICK
1936–, earthenware   ENGLAND
(Royal Doulton Group 1973)   printed

Blackhurst & Hulme   B. & H.
1890–1932, porcelain
  early mark of printed
  initials, later full   THE BELGRAVE
  mark used from *c.* 1914   CHINA
                     B. & H.
                     L
                  ENGLAND

Blair & Co.
1880–1930, porcelain
  'Ltd.' added *c.* 1912
  (LONGTON) added *c.* 1923
  early impressed 'B'
  up until about 1900
  'BLAIRS CHINA, ENGLAND'
  impressed or printed
  c. 1900–
  printed mark of *c.* 1900–

Blyth Porcelain Co. Ltd.   B.P. CO. LTD.
c. 1905–35, porcelain   printed in
  'DIAMOND CHINA'   varying forms
  also used from *c.* 1913

Boulton & Co.
1892–1902, porcelain

B. & CO.   B. & CO.
L
printed or impressed

Bradbury, Anderson & Bettanny
1844–52, general ceramics

B.A. & B.
printed

Bradley, F. D.
1876–96, porcelain

BRADLEY
impressed

Bradleys (Longton) Ltd.
1922–41, porcelain
  mark printed with crown

BRADLEYS
LONGTON
MADE IN
ENGLAND

Bridgett & Bates
1882–1915, porcelain
  'ALDWYCH CHINA' trade-name from *c.* 1912

B. & B.
impressed or printed

Bridgett, Bates & Beech
1875–82
  printed or impressed mark

Bridgwood & Son Ltd.,
Sampson, 1805–, earthenware
(porcelain until *c.* 1887)

BRIDGWOOD & SON

  impressed or printed marks
from *c.* 1850–

S. BRIDGWOOD &
SON

S.B. & S.

other various printed marks include
full name of firm or initials

'Parisian Granite' mark
c. 1870–, printed

Britannia China Company   B.C. CO.
1895–1906, porcelain   impressed

    other fully-named marks
    also used
    1904–6

printed or impressed

British Anchor Pottery Co. Ltd.
1884–, earthenware
(from 1971, Hostess Tableware Ltd.)
    printed or impressed
    1884–*c.* 1913

other various marks include full
names and such trade names as:
REGENCY, MONTMARTRE, RICHMOND,
HOSTESS and TRIANON

British Pottery Ltd.   B.P. LTD.
c. 1930–, agents only   printed

Brough & Blackhurst   BROUGH &
1872–95, earthenware   BLACKHURST
               printed or impressed

Burgess Bros.	"BURCRAFT"
1922–39, earthenware	BURGESS BROS.
'Burgess Ware' also	MADE IN ENGLAND
used	printed
Capper & Wood	C. & W.
1895–1904, earthenware	printed or impressed
Cara China Co.	CARA CHINA
1945–, porcelain	printed
Cartlidge & Co., F.	F.C.
1889–1904, porcelain	F.C. & CO.
'& Co.' added *c.* 1892	printed or impressed
Cartwright & Edwards, Ltd.	C. & E.
c. 1857–	printed or impressed

Cartwright & Edwards, Ltd.
c. 1857–
(Alfred Clough Ltd.)
   printed mark of 1912–
   'Ltd.' added *c.* 1926–
   trade names of 'Norville'
   & 'Baronian' ware used
   with 'C. & E.' from *c.* 1930–

Chapman & Sons, David
1889–1906, porcelain
   'Atlas' mark of 1889–1906

Chapmans Longton Ltd.   STANDARD CHINA
1916–*c.* '67 porcelain   crown
   printed 1916–30   ENGLAND
(now Paragon China Ltd.)

193

various other marks including trade-names of:
'ROYAL STANDARD' and 'ROYAL
MAYFAIR', (from 1973 part of Royal Doulton
Group)

Chetham	CHETHAM
1810–34, earthenware	impressed
'& Son' added 1818	

Chetham, Jonathan Lowe	J.L.C.
1841–62, earthenware	printed

Chetham, J. R. & F.	J.R. & F.C.
1846–69, earthenware	printed

Chetham & Robinson	C. & R.
1822–37, earthenware	printed

Chew, John	J.C.
1903–4, porcelain	L
	impressed

Clare China Co. Ltd.	BONE CHINA
1951–, decorators	CLARE
printed mark, possibly	MADE IN ENGLAND
taken over by Taylor &	with crown
Kent	

Clough's Royal Art	'ROYAL ART POTTERY'
Pottery, 1961–69,	ENGLAND
earthenware	with crown
mark also used by	printed
Alfred Clough Ltd.	
(Royal Art Pottery), 1951–61	

Transferred to Alfred Clough, Ltd., Longton
under name of Barker Bros. Ltd. in 1968

Coggins & Hill   C. & H.
1892–8, porcelain   printed or impressed

Colclough & Co.   R.S. monogram
1887–1928, general ceramics
  printed marks   'ROYAL STANLEY WARE'

Colclough, H. J.   H.J.C.
1897–1937, general ceramics   L
  various marks including 'H.J.C.' and/or
  'VALE CHINA'

Colclough China Ltd.   Colclough
1937–48, porcelain   GENUINE
                 BONE CHINA
  late printed marks   MADE IN ENGLAND

Collingwood Bros. Ltd.   COLLINGWOOD
1887–1957, porcelain   early impressed mark

  initials used with crown   C.B.
  c. 1887–1912   L
  later marks fully named

Collingwood & Greatbatch
1870–1887, porcelain

  printed or impressed
  (crown also used
  alone)   C. & G.

Cone Ltd., Thomas	T.C.	T.C.
1892–*c.* 1967	L	LONGTON

earthenware — printed or impressed
  mark of 1892–1912
(moved to Meir in 1964)
  printed 1912–35 T.C. monogram
  'Alma Ware' 1935–
  'ROYAL ALMA' 1946–68

Conway Pottery Co. Ltd. CONWAY
1930–, earthenware POTTERY
  mark printed from 1945– ENGLAND

Cooke & Hulse COOKE & HULSE
1835–55, porcelain printed

Cooper & Dethick C. & D.
1876–88, earthenware printed

Co-operative Wholesale Society Ltd.
1922, porcelain and
from 1946 also earthenware
  printed mark on porcelain
  from *c.* 1946, also
  'Clarence Bone-China'

  'Crown Clarence'
  earthenware from 1946–
  also 'Balmoral'
(from 1971–, Jon Anton Ltd.)

J. H. Cope & Co. Ltd. C. & CO.
1887–1947, porcelain impressed or printed

printed with 'back-stamps' J.H.C. & CO.
from *c.* 1900
'WELLINGTON CHINA' with crown *c.* 1906–
'WELLINGTON CHINA' and profile of Duke
c. 1924–1947

Cotton & Barlow C. & B.
1850–5, earthenware printed

Cyples & Barker CYPLES & BARKER
1846–7, earthenware impressed

Day, George STAFFORDSHIRE
1882–9, earthenware
  printed mark

Day & Pratt DAY & PRATT
1887–8, porcelain printed or impressed

Decoro Pottery Co. TUSCAN
1933–49, earthenware DECORO
  various fully-named POTTERY
  printed marks

Denton China (Longton) Ltd. DENTON
1945–, porcelain CHINA
(Aynsley China Ltd.)

Dewes & Copestake D. & C.
1894–1915, earthenware L
  various printed marks
  including initials

197

Diane Pottery Co.
1960–, now closed,
porcelain
  various printed marks
  with full name

DIANE
POTTERY
LONGTON
STAFFORDSHIRE

Dinky Art Pottery Co. Ltd.
1931–47, earthenware
  printed mark

MADE IN
DINKY WARE
ENGLAND

Dixon & Co., R. F.
1916–29, ceramic retailers
and importers

various marks
include 'D.C.'
for Dixon & Co.

Dresden Floral Porcelain Co. Ltd.
1945–56, porcelain
  printed mark

Dresden Porcelain Co.   D.P. CO.   D.P. CO.
1896–1904, porcelain   L

printed or impressed

  printed mark 1896–1903

Edwards & Brown   E. & B.
1882–1933, porcelain   L
  impressed or printed mark 1882–1933
  'E. & B.L.' with 'DUCHESS CHINA', 1910–33

Elektra Porcelain Co Ltd.
1924–71, earthenware
  printed mark of 1924–
(now Allied English Potteries)
  similar mark 'VULCAN WARE' *c.* 1940–

Elkin, Samuel   S.E.
1856–64, earthenware   printed

Elkin & Newbon   E. & N.
c. 1844–5, earthenware

Fell & Co., J. T.   EMBOSA WARE
1923–57, earthenware

            MADE BY CYPLES
printed or impressed   OLD POTTERY
               1793

Finney & Sons Ltd., A. T.   DUCHESS
1947, porcelain   BONE CHINA
  trade-name in a variety   printed
  of styles

Flacket, Toft & Robinson   F.T. & R.
1857–8, earthenware   printed

Floral China Co. Ltd.
1940–51, porcelain
  printed mark

Forester & Co., Thomas
1888–, earthenware
  printed mark

Forester & Sons, Thomas
1883–1959, general ceramics
   'Ltd.' added 1891
   printed, 1891–1912
   later marks include
   'PHOENIX CHINA'

T.F. & S.

Gallimore, Robert
1831–40, earthenware

R.G.
impressed

Gallimore & Co. Ltd.,
1906–34, earthenware
   mark impressed or printed

Gladstone China (Longton)
Ltd., 1939–1952,
porcelain
   printed mark until
   1961 after firm became:
Gladstone China
1952–, porcelain

GLADSTONE
BONE   CHINA

MADE IN ENGLAND
various marks with
'Gladstone Bone China'

Green & Clay
1888–91, earthenware
   printed or impressed

Grove & Stark
1871–85, earthenware
   printed or impressed
   'G.S.' impressed
   monogram also used

G. & S.
printed

GROVE & STARK
LONGTON

Hallam & Day 1880–85, earthenware	H. & D. printed, often with Royal Arms

Hammersley & Co.　　　　H. & C.　　H. & CO.
1887–1932, porcelain
(Hammersley & Co., Longton) Ltd.

from 1932–present
　　crown mark used without
　　initials, 1887–1912
　　many various fully-named marks from 1912–
(now Carborundum Group)

Hammersley & Asbury　　　　H. & A.
1872–5, earthenware　　　printed, sometimes
　　　　　　　　　　　　　with 'Prince of Wales'
　　　　　　　　　　　　　feathers

Hampson & Broadhurst　　　H. & B.
1847–53, earthenware　　　printed

Harvey, C. & W. K.　　　　C. & W.K.H.
1835–53, general ceramics
　　name also printed with　　　HARVEY
　　Royal Arms and 'REAL　　printed
　　IRONSTONE CHINA'

Hawley, Webberley & Co.
1895–1902, earthenware
　　printed mark

Hewitt & Leadbeater
1907–19, porcelain
then Hewitt Bros. until
c. 1926　　　　　　　　printed

Hibbert & Boughey   H. & B.
1889, general ceramics   printed with crown

Hill & Co.   H. & CO.
1898–1920, porcelain   impressed or printed

Holdcroft, Joseph   printed or
1865–1940, general ceramics   𝗛𝗝   impressed
(Holdcrofts Ltd., *c.* 1906–,   1865–1906
later Cartwright & Edwards Ltd.)
   mark of 'H.J.' monogram on globe from
   1890–1939

Holland & Green   H. & G.
1853–82, earthenware   LATE HARVEY
                                    printed or impressed

Holmes & Son   H. & S.
1898–1903, earthenware   LONGTON
   other marks include   impressed or printed
   full name

Hudden, John Thomas   J.T.H.
1859–1885, earthenware   J.T. HUDDEN
                                        printed

Hudson, William   W.H.
1889–1941, porcelain   printed
   printed mark 1892–1912
   other later marks
   include 'SUTHERLAND
   CHINA'

202

Hudson & Middleton, Ltd.
1941–, porcelain
　various late marks
　include 'SUTHERLAND'
　and 'H.M.' with lion

Hulse & Adderley
1869–75, general
ceramics
　printed mark as
　used later by
　W. A. Adderley & Co.

H. & A.

Hulse, Nixon & Adderley　　H.N. & A.
1853–68, earthenware　　printed

Jackson & Gosling　　J. & G.　　　　J. & G.
1866–1968, porcelain　　　　　　　　L
　'Ltd.' added *c.* 1930　　impressed or printed
　variety of marks including trade-name of
　'Grosvenor China'

Jones (Longton) Ltd., A. E.
1905–46, earthenware
　printed or impressed
　c. 1908–36
　other 'Palissy' mark continued by
　Palissy Pottery, Ltd., now a subsidiary of
　Royal Worcester, Ltd.

PALISSY

ENGLAND

Jones & Co., Frederick   F. JONES LONGTON
1865–86, earthenware   impressed or printed

Jones & Sons, A. B.   A.B.J. & S.
1900–, porcelain   A.B.J. & SONS
(A. B. Jones from 1876)   A.B. JONES & SONS
  large variety of marks including
  initials, full name and/or trade-name of
  'GRAFTON' or 'ROYAL GRAFTON'
(acquired in 1966 by Crown House Glass Ltd.)

Jones, Shepherd & Co.   J.S. & CO.
1867–8, earthenware   printed

Jones, Josiah Ellis   J.E.J.
1868–72, earthenware   or full name
                               printed

Kent, James   JAMES KENT
1897–, general ceramics   ENGLAND
  'Ltd.' added 1913   with Royal Arms &
  printed mark of   'ROYAL SEMI CHINA'
  1897–1915
  various shield or 'globe' marks with full name
  or J.K.L. or J.K., from 1897–present, when
  'Old Foley' is used

Lawrence (Longton) Ltd., Thomas
1892–1964, earthenware
  printed or impressed
  marks include name
  'Falcon Ware'

204

Leadbeater, Edwin
1920–24, porcelain
   printed or impressed mark

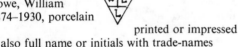

Ledgar, Thomas P.   T.P.L.
1900–5, general ceramics
   impressed or printed mark

Lockett & Sons, John   J. LOCKETT & SONS
1828–35, earthenware   impressed

Longton New Art Pottery Co.   KELSBORO'
Ltd., 1932–66, earthenware   WARE
   various printed marks

Longton Porcelain Co. Ltd.   L.P. CO.
1892–1908, porcelains   monogram

Longton Pottery Co. Ltd.   L.P. CO. LTD.
1946–55, earthenware   printed

Lowe, William
1874–1930, porcelain

                         printed or impressed
  also full name or initials with trade-names
  'ROYAL SYDNEY WARE', 'COURT CHINA'

Lowe, Ratcliffe & Co.
1882–92, earthenware
   printed or impressed

Mackee, Andrew   A.M.
1892–1906, general ceramics   L.
         impressed or printed

Malkin, Walker & Hulse   M.W. & H.
1858–64, earthenware   printed

Martin, Shaw & Cope   MARTIN SHAW
c. 1815–24, general ceramics   & COPE
         IMPROVED CHINA
         printed

Mason, Holt & Co.   M.H. & CO.
1857–84, porcelain   printed or impressed

Massey, Wildblood & Co.   M.W. & CO.
1887–9, porcelain   printed

Matthews & Clark   M. & C.
c. 1902–6, general ceramics   L.
   printed mark in frame

Mayer & Sherratt   M. & S.
1906–41, porcelain   L.
         under crown
   also other printed marks including trade-name
   of 'MELBA CHINA'

McNeal & Co. Ltd.
1894–1906, earthenware
   printed

Middleton & Co., J. H.
1889–1941, porcelain
  various printed marks
  with trade-name of
  'DELPHINE'

Moore Bros. MOORE
1872–1905, porcelain printed or impressed

  'Bros.' added 1872–1905 MOORE BROS.

  printed from *c.* 1880 MOORE (with globe)

  printed mark, 1902–5
Bernard Moore
continued at Stoke
until 1915

Morris, Thomas
1892–1941, porcelain

  early printed mark, from
  c. 1912 trade-name of
  'CROWN CHELSEA CHINA' used

New Chelsea Porcelain Co. Ltd.
  from 1913 many marks used
  including anchor and
  'Chelsea', 'New Chelsea'
  or 'Royal Chelsea'

New Chelsea China Co. Ltd.
1951–61, porcelain

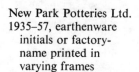

New Park Potteries Ltd.
1935–57, earthenware
    initials or factory-
    name printed in
    varying frames

N.P.P. LTD.
NEW PARK
POTTERIES
LONGTON
NEW PARK

Osborne China Co. Ltd.
1909–40, porcelain

'Osborne China'
with torch

Palissy Pottery Ltd.
1946–, earthenware
(subsidiary of Royal
Worcester Ltd.)

    variety of printed marks include,
    'Palissy Pottery' or 'Palissy Ware', etc.

Paragon China Ltd.
1920–, porcelain
    large variety of marks
    include 'Royal Arms'
    and 'Paragon'
(now an Allied English
Potteries Ltd. company)

Pattison, J.
c. 1818–30, earthenware

JOHN PATTISON
incised

Plant, Benjamin
c. 1780–1820, earthenware
B Plant Lane End.
incised

Plant & Co., R. H.
1881–98, porcelain
'R.H.P. & CO.'
in knot under a
winged crown

Plant, Ltd., R. H. & S. L.
c. 1898–1970, porcelain
    numerals under
    mark indicate last
    two numerals of year
    made. From 1973:
'TUSCAN CHINA'
trade-name in
many various
forms
'WEDGWOOD–ROYAL
TUSCAN DIVISION'

Plant & Sons, R.
1895–1901, earthenware
P. & S.
L
printed

Poole, Thomas
1880–1952, general ceramics

    impressed or printed
    crown, 1880–1912
    (common mark)
    early form of 'ROYAL
    STAFFORD CHINA' used
    from 1912–

Poole & Unwin
1871–6, earthenware
P. & U.
printed or impressed

Proctor & Co., J. H.
1857–84, earthenware

WARRANTED
P
printed or impressed
under crown

Procter, John
1843–6, earthenware

J.P.
L
printed or impressed

Procter & Co. Ltd., G.
1891–1940, porcelain
  with or without 'L'
  for Longton
  'GLADSTONE CHINA'
  from 1924–40

G.P. & CO.
L
printed

trade-name

Ratcliffe & Co.
1891–1914, earthenware

printed

Redfern & Drakeford Ltd.
1892–1933, porcelain
  printed or impressed
  mark, 'BALMORAL
  CHINA' added in
  1909–33

Regency China Ltd.
1953–, porcelain

Reid & Co.
1913–46, porcelain

   'PARK PLACE CHINA'
   c. 1913–24

   'ROSLYN CHINA'
   c. 1924–46
   (see ROSLYN CHINA)   all printed

Riddle & Bryan   RIDDLE & BRYAN
c. 1835–40, earthenware   Longton
                  printed

Robinson, W. H.   W.H. ROBINSON
1901–4, porcelain   LONGTON
   printed mark in   BALTIMORE CHINA
   circle under crown

Robinson & Son   R. & S.
1881–1903, porcelain   L.

   'Foley' is a name   FOLEY CHINA
   used by several potters

Roper & Meredith   R. & M.
1913–24, earthenware   LONGTON

Roslyn China   FINE
1946–63, porcelain   BONE
   printed mark also   Roslyn
   used by Reid & Co.   China
                 MADE IN
                 ENGLAND

Rowley & Newton Ltd.   R. & N.
1896–1901, general ceramics   printed or impressed
   'R. & N.' often with lion 'rampant'

Royal Albion China Co.   ROYAL ALBION CHINA
1921–48, porcelain   L
   printed marks   ENGLAND
                                    with crown

Royal Stafford China   variety of marks
1952–, porcelain   with
   printed marks   'ROYAL STAFFORD'

Salisbury Crown China Co.
(Salisbury China Co. from
1949)
c. 1927–61, porcelain

   printed mark of *c.* 1952

Salt & Nixon, Ltd.   S. & N.
1901–34, porcelain   L
   various marks with initials
   & 'SALON CHINA'   printed

Shaw & Sons (Longton) Ltd., John
1931–63, general ceramics

   printed mark of *c.* 1949
   various other marks,
   include 'Burlington'

212

Shaw & Copestake
1901–, earthenware
  various printed or impressed
  marks with trade-name of 'SYLVAC'

Shelley Potteries, Ltd.
1925–67, porcelain
(now Royal Albert Ltd.)
  various printed marks
  with 'SHELLEY' (Royal Doulton Group)

CHINA
SHELLEY.
ENGLAND

Shepherd & Co., Alfred   A. SHEPHERD & CO.
1864–70, earthenware   printed

Shore & Co., J.   J.S. & CO.
1887–1905, porcelain   printed

Shore, Coggins & Holt   S.C.H.
1905–10, general ceramics   L
  initials printed under   *ENGLAND*
  crown

Shore & Coggins
1911–*c.* 67, porcelain
  mark of *c.* 1930, other
  marks include trade-name
  'Bell China' (now Royal Doulton Group)

Smith, Sampson   S.S.
c. 1846–1963, general   impressed
ceramics

'S.S.' monogram used in a variety of
marks during this century and 'WETLEY
CHINA' or 'OLD ROYAL CHINA'

Stanley & Lambert   S. & L.
c. 1850–4, earthenware   printed

Stanley Pottery Ltd.
1928–31, general ceramics

  same printed marks as
  used by Colclough & Co.

Star China Co.   S.C. CO.
1900–19, porcelain   printed with crown
                or star with
       'THE PARAGON CHINA'

Stevenson, Spencer & Co. Ltd.
1948–60, porcelain
  fully named marks
  with 'WILLOW' or
  'ROYAL STUART'

Sutherland & Sons, Danial   S. & S.
1865–75, general   impressed or
ceramics   printed

Swift & Elkin   S. & E.
1840–3, earthenware   printed

Tams, John J.T.
c. 1875–, earthenware (or as monogram)
  printed marks

J. Tams
'& Son' added 1903–12 J.T. & S.
'LTD.' from 1912, with trade-marks:
'NANKIN WARE', 'ELEPHANT BRAND',
'TAMS REGENT' and 'CHININE'

Tams & Lowe T. & L.
1865–74, earthenware printed

Taylor & Kent T. & K.
1867–, porcelain L
  printed or impressed
  variety of named or initialled marks
  with 'KENT' or 'ELIZABETHAN'

Thorley China Ltd. THORLEY CHINA
1940–70, decorative LTD.
porcelain printed under crown
(last six years in Fenton)

Tomkinson & Billington T. & B.
1868–70, earthenware printed

Townsend, George G. TOWNSEND
c. 1850–64, earthenware printed

Trentham Bone China Ltd.
1952–7, porcelain
  printed

215

Turner, John
c. 1762–1806, Wedgwood-
type earthenwares and
stonewares

TURNER
impressed

> printed or impressed
> from 1784

> impressed *c.* 1780–6,
> 1803–6
> painted mark on
> 'ironstone' type ware
> 1800–5

TURNER & CO.

Turner & Abbott
c. 1783–7, Wedgwood-
type wares

TURNER & ABBOTT
impressed

Universal Pottery (Longton) Ltd.
1949–62, general ceramics
various printed marks
with 'Universal Ware'

Unwin, Joseph
1877–1926, earthenware
figures, etc.

UNWIN
moulded in
relief

Wagstaff & Brunt
1880–1927, general
ceramics

W. & B.
LONGTON
printed

Wain & Sons, Ltd., H. A.
1946–, earthenware

Waine & Co., Charles
1891–1920, porcelain
   printed, 1891–1913
   'Ltd.' from 1913

C.W.
or as monogram

Walker & Carter
1866–72, earthenware
(at Stoke 1872–89)

W. & C.
printed

Walton, J. H.
1912–21, porcelain

   printed or impressed

Warrilow, George
1887–1940, porcelain
   '& S.' or '& Sons'
   and 'Ltd.' added
   from 1928

G.W.

G.W. & S.

G.W. & S. LTD.

Rosina China Co. Ltd.
1941–
   various marks with
   trade-names 'Rosina'
   or 'Queen's' China

Wayte & Ridge
c. 1864, general
ceramics & figures

W. & R.
L
printed

217

Wedgwood & Co. Ltd., H.F.　　H.F.W. & CO. LTD.
c. 1954–9, general　　ISLINGTON
ceramics　　printed

Wild Bros.　　J.S.W.
1904–27, porcelain　　or in monogram
　　W. Bros.

Wild & Co., Thomas C.　　T.W. & CO.
1896–1904
　printed or impressed　　T.C.W. with crown

Wild, Thomas C.
1905–17, porcelain
　printed mark, 1905–7

Wild & Sons (Ltd.), Thomas C.
1917–*c.* 72, porcelain
　various printed marks
　with trade-name
　'Royal Albert', now Royal Doulton Group

Wild & Adams　　W. & A.
1909–27, earthenware　　printed or impressed
　'Ltd.' from 1923
　various marks with 'ROYAL CROWN'

Wildblood, Richard Vernon
1887–8, porcelain

　printed

Wildblood & Heath
1889–99, porcelain
  printed

Wildblood, Heath & Sons
1899–1927, porcelain

  'Ltd.' added from 1915

Williamson & Sons, H. M.
c. 1879–1941, porcelain

  various marks of 'W. & Sons',
  'H.M.W.' or 'Heathcote
  China'
  printed mark of *c.* 1908–

Winterton Pottery (Longton) 'WINTERTON'
Ltd., 1927–54, earthenware printed over crown

  'Bluestone Ware'

Wood & Co., J. B.
1897–1926, earthenware

  late printed or impressed
  mark

Woolley, Richard   WOOLLEY
1809–14, earthenware impressed

Yale & Barker	Y. & B.
1841–53, earthenware	printed

MIDDLEPORT (Staffordshire)	FIVE TOWNS CHINA
Five Towns China Co. Ltd.	CO. LTD.
1957–67, porcelain	ENGLAND
name with various	
printed marks	

SHELTON (Staffordshire)	ASTBURY
Astbury, mid-18th	incised or impressed
century, earthenware	

Astbury, Richard Meir	R.M.A.
1790–, earthenware	impressed

Baddeley, John & Edward	B
1784–1806, earthenware	I.E.B.
impressed initials	I.E.B.
then:	W
Hicks & Meigh	HICKS & MEIGH
1806–22, earthenware	impressed or
and 'Ironstone'	printed
then:	
Hicks, Meigh & Johnson	H.M.J.
1822–35, earthenware	
and 'Ironstone'	H.M. & J.
	printed with
	Royal Arms
then:	

Ridgway, Morley, Wear &   R.M.W. & CO.
Co., 1836–42, earthenware

              RIDGWAY, MORLEY
              WEAR & CO.

then: printed
Ridgway & Morley   R. & M.
1842–44
   various printed marks   RIDGWAY & MORLEY
   (backstamps) with
   names of pattern

Baddeley, Ralph & John   BADDELEY
1750–95, earthenware
   marks impressed   R. & J.
                BADDELEY

Bairstow & Co., P. E.   Fancies
1954–. earthenware   Fayre
and porcelain   England

Bentley, Wear & Bourne   BENTLEY, WEAR
1815–23, decorators   & BOURNE
   printed mark
(Bentley & Wear 1823–
   33)

Birch, Edmund John   BIRCH
1796–1814, Wedgwood-
type wares   E.I.B.
                impressed

Birch & Whitehead   B. & W.
1796, Wedgwood-type   impressed

Cockson & Harding
1856–62, earthenware
  marks printed or
  impressed
	C. & H.
	
	C. & H.
	LATE HACKWOOD

Cutts, James *c.* 1834–70, engraver and designer	J. CUTTS signature on prints
Dakin, Thomas early 18th century earthenware	THOMAS DAKIN sliptrailed
Hackwood & Son, Wm. 1846–9, earthenware	W.H. HACKWOOD printed
Harding, W. J. 1862–72, earthenware	W. & J.H. printed

Hicks & Meigh
1806–22, earthenware
  'Stone-China' & Royal
  Arms also used
	HICKS & MEIGH
	impressed or
	painted

Hicks, Meigh & Johnson
1822–35, earthenware
  'Stone-China' and
  Royal Arms also used
	H.M.J.
	
	H.M. & J.
	printed

Hollins, Samuel *c.* 1784–1813	S. HOLLINS

'Wedgwood-type' ware	HOLLINS impressed
Hollins, T. & J. *c.* 1795–1820, earthenware	T. & J. HOLLINS impressed
Howard Pottery Co. 1925–, earthenware printed mark of 1925–	
Keeling, Charles 1822–5, earthenware	C.K. printed
Meir John late 17th – early 18th- centuries, slipware	JOHN MEIR sliptrailed
Meir, Richard late 17th – early 18th- centuries, slipware	RICHARD MEIR sliptrailed
Phillips, Edward 1855–62, earthenware printed mark	EDWARD PHILLIPS SHELTON STAFFORDSHIRE
Read & Clementson 1833–5, earthenware	R. & C. printed
Read, Clementson & Anderson *c.* 1836, earthenware	R.C. & A. printed

Ridgway, John & William 1814–1830, general ceramics	J.W.R. J. & W.R. J. & W. RIDGWAY printed or impressed
Ridgway, William c. 1830–54, earthenware (also at Hanley from c. 1838–48)	W. RIDGWAY W.R. printed or impressed
'& Co.' added c. 1834 'QUARTZ CHINA' used from c. 1830–50	W.R. & CO.
Tittensor, Charles c. 1815–23, earthenware including figures	TITTENSOR impressed or printed
Twemlow, John 1795–7, earthenware and stoneware	J.T. rare initials
Washington Pottery Ltd. 1946–, earthenware (now Washington Pottery (Staffordshire) Ltd.)	
Worthington & Green 1844–64, earthenware and Parianware	WORTHINGTON & GREEN impressed

224

STOKE (Staffordshire)

Alton Towers Handcraft
Pottery (Staffs.) Ltd.
1953–, earthenware

printed or impressed

Arkinstall & Sons (Ltd.)
1904–24, bone-china

A. & S.
printed, 1904–12

  trade marks on
  souvenir wares 1904–
  24

ARCADIAN

ARCADIAN CHINA

(under various other
firms from 1908)

printed marks

Atlas China Co. Ltd.
1906–10, china
(name revived by
Grimwades Ltd. 1930–6)

'ATLAS CHINA' with
figure supporting
globe
printed

Bennett & Co., George
1894–1902, earthenware

G.B. & CO.
impressed or printed

Bilton (1912) Ltd.
1900–, earthenware
  current mark, printed
(now Biltons Tableware Ltd.)

Birks & Co., L. A.
1896–1900, general
ceramics

BIRKS
impressed

B. & CO.

Birks, Rawlins & Co. (Ltd.)
1900–33, bone-china
  other marks include
  trade-names of:
  SAVOY CHINA
  CARLTON CHINA

printed

Booth & Son, Ephraim   E.B. & S.
c. 1795, earthenware   impressed

Booth, Hugh   H. BOOTH
1784–9, earthenware   impressed
including creamware

Carlton Ware Ltd.
1958–, earthenware
(Arthur Wood & Son Group)

modern printed mark

Ceramic Art Co. (1905)   C.A. & CO. LTD.
Ltd., 1905–19, earthenware   printed or impressed

Close & Co.   CLOSE & CO. LATE
1855–64, earthenware   W. ADAMS & SONS
                                    STOKE-UPON-TRENT
                                    printed or impressed

Copeland & Garrett
Copeland, W. T., etc.
(*see under* Spode)

226

Coronation Pottery Co.
1903–54, earthenware

  'Ltd.' from 1947

printed or impressed

Crown China Crafts Ltd.
1946–58, general ceramics
  printed mark

Daniel, H. & R.   H. & R. Daniel
1820–41, pottery and
porcelain   H. Daniels & Sons
  fully named printed
  marks also used   written marks

Empire Porcelain Co.
1896–1967, earthenware
  printed mark, 1896–1912
(1958–67, Qualcast Group)

    Staffordshire
    England

  EMPIRE
  ENGLAND   *Shelton Ivory*

  late printed or impressed marks

Era Art Pottery Co.
1930–47, earthenware

  printed mark, 1936–

Featherstone Potteries 1949–50, earthenware marks impressed or printed	F.P. F.N.P.
Fielding & Co., S. 1879–, earthenwares (part of Crown Devon Group)	FIELDING impressed
'Crown Devon' trade-mark from *c.* 1930	S.F. & CO. (over crown and lion) printed
date-mark: 10th March 1954	FIELDING 10 M 54
Floyd & Sons, R. 1907–30, earthenware	 printed or impressed
Folch, Stephen 1820–30, earthenware	FOLCH'S GENUINE STONE CHINA impressed
Goss, W. H. 1858–1944, pottery and porcelain	W.H.G. W.H. GOSS
printed mark from *c.* 1862	

Greta Pottery   G
1938–41, earthenware   P
                                        printed or painted

Hamilton, Robert   HAMILTON
1811–26, earthenware   STOKE
                                        impressed or printed

Hancock & Co., F.
1899–1900, earthenware
  printed mark

Hancock, B. & S.   B. & S.H.
1876–81, earthenware   printed

Hancock & Sons, Sampson   S.H.
1858–1937, earthenware
(at Tunstall prior   S. HANCOCK
to 1870)   printed

  printed 1891–1935   S.H. & S.

                                          S.H. & SONS

  printed 1900–12
From 1935–37:–
S. Hancock & Sons
(Potters) Ltd.

Hancock & Whittingham   H. & W.
1873–9, earthenware   printed

229

Heath, Job
early 18th century
earthenware

JOB HEATH
sliptrailed

Jones, George
1861–1951, general ceramics

'& Sons', added on
crescent from 1873

in relief, impressed
or printed

Keys & Mountford
1850–7, 'Parian' ware

K. & M.

S. KEYS
& MOUNTFORD
impressed

Kirkham, William
1862–92, earthenware

W. KIRKHAM
impressed

Kirkhams Ltd.
1946–61, earthenware
(now Portmeiron
Potteries Ltd.)

Mayer, Thomas
1836–8, earthenware
(last three years at
Longport)

T. MAYER
T. MAYER, STOKE
printed

Meigh, W. & R.
1894–9, earthenware
    printed mark

Minton
1793–, general ceramics
(Royal Doulton Group from 1973)
Sèvres type mark used
on porcelain *c.* 1800–30,
sometimes with in blue enamel
pattern number

printed mark with
'M', 1822–1836

printed 1822–36

'M. & B.' for Minton &
Boyle partnership
1836–41, printed

'M. & Co.' Minton &
Co., 1841–73

'M. & H.', Minton &
Hollins partnership
1845–68

1862–71, 's' added
in 1873

MINTON
impressed

printed 1860–*c.* 69

impressed for 'BEST
BODY' mid-19th century

B.B.

'Globe-mark', 1863–72
'S' added to Minton
in 1871

impressed mark with
year 1875, used from
1868–80

18
MINTON
75

printed mark from 1873,
'England' added from
1891, and 'Made in
England' about 1910

impressed or moulded
c. 1890–1910

MINTONS
ENGLAND

'Globe-mark', *c.* 1912–50

standard factory-mark
adopted in 1951

'Ermine' mark used
from *c.* 1850 to identify
wares that had been
dipped in a soft-glaze
on which painting was
to be applied

relief mark of *c.* 1847–8
on 'Summerly's Art
Manufacturers' made
by Minton

Solon, Marc Louis, 1870–1904
decorator

signature on 'Henri Deux'　　　TOFT
reproductions
Mussill, W. (*d.* 1906)　　　W. Mussill
decorator in 1870s

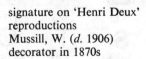

233

YEARLY MARKS OF MINTONS LTD., 1842–1942:

✳	△	▢	✕	⬭
1842	1843	1844	1845	1846
⌒	—	⋈	♣	∴
1847	1848	1849	1850	1851
V	♞	∿	✳	♀
1852	1853	1854	1855	1856
◇	♈	Ƭ	♌	⅄
1857	1858	1859	1860	1861
☦	♦	Ƶ	≋	✗
1862	1863	1864	1865	1866
⋈	Ⴚ	⊡	Ⓜ	ℕℂ
1867	1868	1869	1870	1871
⊗	✖	↓	Ɛ	◬
1872	1873	1874	1875	1876
◉	◭	◭	⚠	⊞
1877	1878	1879	1880	1881
⊗	◓	⊠	⋈	B
1882	1883	1884	1885	1886
♔	∞	S	T	⛨
1887	1888	1889	1890	1891

1892	1893	1894	1895	1896
1897	1898	1899	1900	1901
1902	1903	1904	1905	1906
1907	1908	1909	1910	1911
1912	1913	1914	1915	1916
1917	1918	1919	1920	1921
1922	1923	1924	1925	1926
1927	1928	1929	1930	1931
1932	1933	1934	1935	1936
1937	1938	1939	1940	1941
		1942		

At the commencement of 1943 the system of yearly date-marks that had operated from 1842 was discontinued, being replaced by figures denoting the year of production, preceded by a number allocated to the actual maker of the article, Number one was given to the factory's leading plate-maker, and plates he produces today have stamped in the clay 1–76, the last two digits representing the year.

Moore, Bernard
1905–15, art pottery and
porcelain, with
flambé glazes

painted

painted or printed

Mountford, G. T.
1888–98, earthenware

G.T.M.
STOKE
printed

Mountford, John
1857–9, 'Parian' ware

J. MOUNTFORD
STOKE
incised signature

Myott, Son & Co. Ltd.
1898–, earthenware
(now subsidiary of
Interpace Corporation)
(later Cobridge and
Hanley)

M S & Cᵒ
STOKE

1898–1902

late marks fully named

c. 1900–

S
& Vᶜᵒ
ENGLAND

236

Ollivant Potteries Ltd.
1948–54, earthenware

    printed marks, usually
    together with pattern

O.P.

O.P.L.

OLLIVANT

Plant & Co., J.
1893–1900, earthenware
    printed mark

STOKE POTTERY

Portmeirion Potteries Ltd.
1962–, earthenware

    printed mark

PORTMEIRION
POTTERY
STOKE-ON-TRENT
MADE IN ENGLAND

Ridgway Potteries Ltd.
1955, earthenware
(an Allied English
Potteries Ltd., company)

contemporary marks (1972)

Robinson & Leadbeater
1864–1924, 'Parian' ware
and bone-china
    'Ltd.' added to marks
    from *c.* 1905

impressed

Ruscoe, William
c. 1920– (to Exeter in
1944)
   full year-date added
   to initials from c. 1925

incised or painted

Shorter & Son, Ltd.
(member of Crown Devon
Group), 1905–
earthenware

late printed mark

Smith, James
1898–1924, general ceramics

JAMES SMITH

printed or impressed

printed

Spode, Josiah (*b.* 1733–
d. 1797) 1770–
earthenware
(Copeland & Garrett
from 1833)

Spode   SPODE
impressed or
in blue

   c. 1784–1805

SPODE   S
impressed

painted marks with pattern numbers, *c.* 1790–1820	SPODE 1989 2447 Spode
c. 1805–	SPODE printed
mark on stone-china, in black *c.* 1805–15, in blue *c.* 1815–30	 Stone China printed
painted	'Spode Stone China'
impressed 1810–15	SPODES NEW STONE
printed *c.* 1805–33	N.S. **Spode's** **Imperial**
printed in puce enamel on felspar porcelain *c.* 1815–27	
painted, impressed or printed *c.* 1797 to 1816	SPODE, SON & COPELAND

Copeland & Garrett
1833–47, general ceramics

C. & G.
painted or printed

printed in blue, with
name of pattern, *c.* 1833–47

COPELAND &
GARRETT

printed *c.* 1833–47

COPELAND & GARRETT
NEW
JAPAN STONE

Copeland & Sons, Ltd.,
W. T., 1847–
impressed or printed
c. 1847–67

COPELAND, LATE
SPODE

printed on Parian figures
c. 1847–55

COPELAND'S
PORCELAIN
STATUARY

printed, 1850–67

printed, *c.* 1847–51

printed, 1851–85

impressed on earthenware
1850–67

printed on porcelain
c. 1891–

SPODE
COPELANDS CHINA
ENGLAND

printed in various
colours on 'New Stone'
of this century

present-day mark

Alcock, S., decorator
c. 1890–

S. Alcock

Hürten, C. F., designer
1859–1897

C.F.H.

Steele & Wood
1875–1892, tiles

printed or impressed

Tittensor, Jacob
1780–95, earthenware

Jacob Tittensor
signature

Turner, Hassall & Peake   T.H.P.
1865–9, general ceramics

                                printed or impressed

Turner & Wood   TURNER & WOOD
1880–8, general ceramics   STOKE
                                 impressed

Wiltshaw & Robinson Ltd.
1890–1957, general
ceramics
    printed mark, 1894–
    various marks include
    trade-mark 'CARLTON
    WARE'

Winkle & Co., F.   F.W. & CO.
1890–1931, earthenware   ENGLAND

    printed or impressed   F. WINKLE & CO.
    marks, 1890–1910
    'Ltd.' added in 1911

    printed, 1890–1925

    misleading mark used
    by Winkle & Co., 1908–25
    (the wares of the
    18th century potter,
    Thomas Whieldon, were
    not marked)

242

Wolfe, Thomas 1784–1800, earthenware and later, *c.* 1811–18	WOLFE impressed
Wolfe & Hamilton *c.* 1800–11, earthenware	WOLFE & HAMILTON STOKE impressed or painted

TUNSTALL (Staffordshire)
  Adams & Sons (Potters)
  Ltd., William,

impressed, 1769–1800 (on creamware)	ADAMS & CO.
impressed, 1787–1864	ADAMS
on blue-printed wares 1804–40	
impressed on earthenware 1810–25	
impressed mark *c.* 1815	W. ADAMS & CO.
W. Adams & Sons 1819–64, printed	W.A. & S.

impressed on parian-ware, 1845–64	ADAMS
printed, mid-19th century	W. ADAMS
printed as 'back-stamp' with name of pattern, 1893–1917. 'ENGLAND' added in 1891	W.A. & CO.

printed from 1879–

printed from 1896– with varying names of ceramic bodies used, e.g. TITIAN WARE, IMPERIAL STONE WARE, etc.

impressed on Wedgwood-type jasperwares 1896 with confusing establishment date	ADAMS ESTBD 1657 TUNSTALL ENGLAND

printed mark, 1914–40

late impressed or printed mark	*Calyx Ware*
late printed mark *c.* 1950–	W. Adams & Sons England under crown
Adams, Benjamin *c.* 1800–20, earthenware and stoneware	B. ADAMS impressed
Adams, W. & T. 1866–92, earthenware printed mark	W. & T. ADAMS TUNSTALL under coat-of-arms
Beech & Hancock 1857–76, earthenware	B. & H. printed
Blackhurst, Jabez 1872–83, earthenware	JABEZ BLACKHURST printed
Booth & Son, Thomas 1872–6, earthenware	T.B. & S. printed
Booth, Thomas, G. 1876–83, earthenware name of pattern on strap	
Booth, T. G. & F. 1883–91, earthenware	T.G. & F.B. printed

245

Booth (Limited)
1891–1948, earthenware
   printed, 1891–1906

   painted or printed on
earthenware reproductions
of Worcester porcelain, 1905–

variety of marks used with 'Silicon China'
from about 1906. 'England' sometimes included

late mark of 1930–48

Boulton, Machin & Tennant
1889–99, earthenware

   mark printed or impressed

Bourne, Nixon & Co.
1828–30, earthenware
   mark impressed

   printed initials included
in backstamp

Bowers & Co., G. F.
1842–68, pottery &
   porcelain
   other printed or
impressed marks
include full name

BOURNE NIXON
& CO.

B.N. & CO.

G.F. B.B.T.
printed

246

Breeze & Son, John
1805–12, pottery & porcelain
(other potters of this
name were operating from
late 18th century to *c.* 1826)

BREEZE
incised or
painted

British Pottery Ltd.
1920–26, earthenware

mark printed

Brougham & Mayer
1853–5, earthenware

BROUGHAM &
MAYER
printed

Brownhills Pottery Co.
1872–96, earthenware

B.P. CO.
printed or impressed

printed marks of
c. 1880–96

Butterfield, W. & J.
1854–61, earthenware

W. & J.B.
printed

Challinor, Edward
1842–67, earthenware

E.C.

E. CHALLINOR
printed

247

Christie & Beardmore   C.B.   C.B.
1902–3, earthenware   F.

                      printed initials with
                      various backstamps

Clews & Co. Ltd., George
1906–61, earthenware
    printed 'globe' mark from
    1906, other marks all
    include full name

Clive, J. H.   CLIVE
1802–11, earthenware   impressed

Clive, Stephen   S.C.   S.C. & CO.
1875–80, earthenware   printed

Colley & Co. Ltd., A.
1909–14, earthenware
    mark printed or impressed

Cumberlidge & Humphreys   C. & M.
1886–9; 1893–5
earthenware   C. & M.
    marks printed or impressed   TUNSTALL

Dean & Sons, Ltd., T.
1879–1947, earthenware
    printed 1896–1947

1937–47

Eardley & Hammersley
1862–6, earthenware

E. & H.
printed

Edge & Grocott
c. 1830, earthenware
figures

EDGE & GROCOTT

Elsmore & Forster
1853–71, general ceramics

ELSMORE & FORSTER
printed with
variety of backstamps

Elsmore & Son, T.
1872–87, earthenware

ELSMORE & SON
ENGLAND

Emberton, William
1851–69, earthenware

W.E.
printed

Emberton, T. I. & J.
1869–82, earthenware

T.I. & J.E.
printed

Ford, Challinor & Co.   F.C.
1865–80, earthenware

F.C. & CO.
initials used with
various printed
marks

Gater & Co., Thomas
1885–94 (at Burslem)
earthenware

G.H. & CO.
later printed initials

Gater, Hall & Co.
1895–1943, earthenware
  printed mark of 1914–

printed mark from 1914–
(firm moved to Burslem
in 1907). Taken over
by:
Barratt's of Staffordshire
1943–. Some former
  marks continued:

  other marks include
  full name of Barratt's.
  'Delphatic' from 1957
(Barratt's now member of the manufacturing
division of G.U.S. Ltd.)

CORONA

CROWN
CORONA

G.H & CO
ENGLAND

Gem Pottery Ltd.
1961–, earthenware
  printed mark

printed

Goodfellow, Thomas
1828–59, earthenware

T. GOODFELLOW
printed

Grenville Pottery Ltd.
1946–, earthenware

Grindley & Co. Ltd., W. H.
1880–, earthenware
  printed mark to 1914
  ('England' included from 1891)

printed from 1914–25
'Ltd.' included from 1925
other marks include full
name of firm

modern printed mark

(W. H. Grindley & Co.
now a subsidiary of
Alfred Clough Ltd.)

Grindley Hotel Ware Co. Ltd.
1908–, earthenware
   mark printed from *c.* 1946–

Hall, Ralph	R. HALL
1822–49, earthenware	
printed in backstamp	
1822–41	
c. 1836	R. HALL & SON
1841–49	R. HALL & CO.
	R.H. & CO.
Heath & Co., Joseph	J. HEATH
1828–41, earthenware	printed
Heath, Joseph	J. HEATH & CO.
1845–53, earthenware	printed
Note: the letter 'J' is	J.H. & CO.
often printed as 'I'	printed

Holland, John 1852–4, earthenware	J. HOLLAND printed
Hollingshead & Kirkham 1870–1956, earthenware 1870–1900	H. & K. H. & K. TUNSTALL printed or impressed
mark of 1890 after take-over of Wedgwood & Co.	H. & K. LATE WEDGWOOD impressed

printed mark, 1900–24

later marks all include
name or initials of
firm

TRADE   MARK

HOLLINSHEAD & KIRKHAM
TUNSTALL
ENGLAND

Ingleby & Co., Thomas c. 1834–5, earthenware	T.I. & CO. printed

Keele Street Pottery Co.   K.S.P.
1915–, earthenware
   other later printed marks include full name

Keeling, Anthony & Enoch   A. & E. KEELING
c. 1795–1811, general ceramics

                              A.E. KEELING

Kirkland & Co. (Etruria) 1892–, earthenware	K. & CO.
printed on various backstamps	K. & CO. E

other various printed marks include full name
of Kirkland & Co. or K. & Co./E.

'Kirklands (Etruria Ltd.)'
from *c*. 1938, printed
'Kirklands (Staffordshire)
Ltd.' from *c*. 1947

Knapper & Blackhurst   KNAPPER AND
1867–71, earthenware   BLACKHURST
                impressed or printed

(1883–8 at Burslem)
   initials also probably used   K. & B.

Lingard Webster & Co. Ltd.
1900–, earthenware

   impressed or printed from
   c. 1946–

Maudesley & Co., J.   STONE WARE
1862–4, earthenware   J.M. & CO.
   (J.M. & CO. was also
   used by other firms)

Mayer & Maudesley   M. & M.
1837–8, earthenware   printed

Meakin Ltd., Alfred   ALFRED MEAKIN
1875–, earthenware   impressed or printed

253

'Ltd.' added in 1897
and omitted from *c.* 1930
early mark *c.* 1875–97

ALFRED MEAKIN
LTD.

Firm re-named 'Alfred
Meakin (Tunstall) Ltd.'
in *c.* 1913

printed mark from *c.* 1891
when the word 'ENGLAND'
was added

later marks include 'M. IRONSTONE'
'BLEU DE ROI', 'GLO-WHITE' and
'TRADITIONAL IRONSTONE, LEEDS'

Meir, John
c. 1812–36, earthenware

J.M.   I.M.
printed

Meir & Son, John
1837–97, earthenware
   initials used in various
   printed or impressed
   marks
   Date codes sometimes
   used e.g. 9 : Sept. 1875
$$\frac{9}{75}$$

J.M. & S.

             I.M. & S.

J.M. & SON

J. MEIR & SON

MEIR & SON

Pitcairns Ltd.
1895–1901, earthenware
   printed mark

Podmore, Walker & Co.   P.W. & CO.
1834–59, earthenware   printed in various
backstamps

Podmore, Walker &   P.W. & W.
Wedgwood, *c.* 1856–9
    various printed marks   WEDGWOOD
    included the confusing,
    name of 'Wedgwood'   WEDGWOOD & CO.
    Enoch Wedgwood being
    a partner. Name of firm changed to
Wedgwood & Co. in *c.* 1860

Rathbone, Smith & Co.   R.S. & CO.
1883–97, earthenware   printed
then:
Smith & Binnall
1897–1900, earthenware
    printed
then:
Soho Pottery, Ltd.
1901–6, earthenware
(1906–44 at Cobridge)
    other later marks include full name of
    firm and various trade-names, e.g.
    'SOLIAN WARE', 'AMBASSADOR WARE',
    'QUEENS GREEN', 'CHANTICLEER' and
    'HOMESTEAD', etc.
then:
Simpsons (Potters) Ltd.
1944–, earthenware
(at Cobridge)

Simpsons (Potters) Ltd. of Cobridge continue
to use many of the Soho Pottery Ltd.
trade-names plus 'MARLBOROUGH',
'Ironstone' and 'CHINASTYLE'
e.g.

Rathbone & Co., T.   T.R. & CO.
1898–1923, earthenware   TUNSTALL

   late printed mark :

Richardson, Albert G.   A.G.R. & Co. Ltd.
1915–34, earthenware   printed
(moved to Cobridge
in *c.* 1934)
   various printed marks including trade-
   name of 'Crown Ducal'

Salt Bros.   SALT BROS.
1897–1904, earthenware   TUNSTALL
(then 'taken-over' by   ENGLAND
T. Till & Sons of   printed or impressed
Burslem)

Selman, J. & W.   SELMAN
c. 1864–65, earthenware   impressed
figures

Shaw, Anthony   ANTHONY SHAW
1851–1900, earthenware

                              A. SHAW   A. SHAW
'& Son' added to   BURSLEM
mark in c. 1882–c. 98

                              SHAWS   SHAW
'& Son' replaced by   BURSLEM
'& Co.' from c. 1898
Shaws taken over by A. J. Wilkinson Ltd.
in c. 1900

Simpson, William   WILLIAM SIMPSON
late 17th- early 18th-   in slip-trailing
century, slip-trailed earthenware
(this name is also recorded at other
pottery towns in Staffs.)

Smith, Theophilus   T. SMITH
1790–c. 97, earthenware   impressed

Smith & Binnall   (*see* Rathbone,
1897–1900, earthenware   Smith & Co.,
                                  Tunstall)

Soho Pottery Ltd.   (*see* Rathbone,
1901–6, earthenware   Smith & Co.,
                                  Tunstall)

Summerbank Pottery Ltd. 1952–, earthenware (now Summerbank Pottery (1970) Ltd.)	SUMMERBANK printed
	COOPERCRAFT MADE IN ENGLAND

Tunnicliff, Michael
1828–41, earthenware toys
and figures

TUNNICLIFF
TUNSTALL

Turner, Goddard & Co. 1867–74, earthenware 'ROYAL PATENT IRONSTONE'	TURNER, GODDARD & CO. printed
Turner & Tomkinson 1860–72, earthenware	TURNER & TOMKINSON
printed in various marks	T. & T.
Turner & Sons, G. W. 1873–95, earthenware	TURNERS
	G.W.T. & SONS
various forms of initials used in a	G.W.T.S.
variety of backstamps sometimes in the form	G.W.T. & S.
of a Royal Arms 'England' added in 1891	G.T. & S.

Walker, Thomas   T. WALKER
1845–51, earthenware
  various printed   THOS. WALKER
  backstamps include
  name

Wedgwood & Co.   WEDGWOOD & CO.
(Enoch Wedgwood   impressed
(Tunstall) Ltd. from 1965)
  printed mark from *c.* 1862

'Ltd.' added from 1900

variety of printed marks used with the
following trade-names: 'IMPERIAL
PORCELAIN', 'WACOLWARE', 'WACOL
IMPERIAL', 'EVERWARE', 'ROYAL
TUNSTALL' and 'VITRILAIN'. From 1965
renamed Enoch Wedgwood (Tunstall) Ltd.
also producing former patterns of
Furnivals, 'Quail', 'Old Chelsea' and
'Denmark'

Wood & Challinor 1828–43, earthenware	W. & C. printed
Wood, Challinor & Co. *c.* 1860–64, earthenware	W.C. & CO. printed
Wood & Pigott 1869–71, earthenware	W. & P. printed
Wooliscroft, George 1851–3: 1860–4 earthenware	G. WOOLISCROFT or G. WOOLLISCROFT

ESHWATER (I.o.W.)
Island Pottery Studio
Lester, Joe
earthenware, 1956–
  'Freshwater' sometimes   printed or impressed
  added to mark

HIPPINGHAM (I.o.W.)
Isle of Wight Pottery
Saunders, S. E., *c*. 1930–40
earthenware
  (same monogram used at
  Carisbrooke Pottery Works, Newport, 1929–32)

CHANNEL ISLANDS

ERNSEY (Channel Islands)
The Guernsey Pottery Ltd.
red ware, studio pottery
1961–

SEY (Channel Islands)   JERSEY POTTERY
Jersey Pottery Ltd., 1946–   C.I.
earthenware   painted

1946–   1951
impressed or printed marks
261

ISLE OF MAN

Isle of Man Potteries, Ltd.
earthenware, 1963–

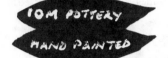

Isle of Man
Pottery
Handmade

NORTHERN IRELAND

PORTADOWN (Co. Armagh)
Wade (Ireland) Ltd., 1947–
porcelain, industrial
and artware
(subsidiary of Wade
Potteries, Ltd.)

printed

SCOTLAND

AIRTH (Central Region)
Dunmore Pottery Co.,
1903–11, earthenware,
c. 1860–1903
(Dunmore Pottery)

PETER GARDNER
DUNMORE POTTERY
DUNMORE
impressed

BO'NESS (Central Region)
McNay & Sons, Charles W.
earthenware, 1887–1958
'Dalmeny' trade-name

stick-on labels

Marshall & Co. Ltd., John   JOHN MARSHALL &
earthenware, 1854–99   CO.
  'Ltd.' added in 1897   printed

COATBRIDGE (Strathclyde)
  Crest Ceramics (Scotland)
  earthenware souvenirs,
  etc.

DUNOON (Strathclyde)
  West Highland Pottery Co. Ltd.
  earthenware, 1961–
    trade-names: 'Flow' ware,
    'Argyll', 'Cowal'
    printed

EDINBURGH (Lothian)   JOHN MILLAR
  Millar, John, 1840–82   printed
  retailer only

GLASGOW (Strathclyde)   B.M. & CO.
  Bayley, Murray & Co.   SARACEN POTTERY
  earthenware, 1875–   printed or impressed
  1900 (Saracen
  Pottery Co. from *c.* 1884)

  Britannia Pottery Co. Ltd.
  earthenware, 1920–35
    'HIAWATHA' trade-name
    from *c.* 1925   printed

Campbellfield Pottery Co. Ltd.   C.P. CO.
earthenware, 1850–1905
    'Ltd.' added *c.* 1884

    printed or impressed   CAMPBELLFIELD
    marks
                                 C.P. CO. LTD.

    printed mark of *c.* 1884–
    c. 1905
    or,
    'SPRINGBURN' with thistle

Cochran & Fleming   C. & F.   C. & F.
earthenware, 1896–   G
1920   ROYAL
                           IRONSTONE CHINA

    printed

PORCELAIN OPAQUE   COCHRAN & FLEMING
GLASGOW. BRITAIN   GLASGOW BRITAIN
FLEMING   printed

Cochran & Co., R.   R.C. & CO.
general ceramics   impressed
1846–1896

Geddes & Son, John
earthenware and porcelain
c. 1806–27
  '& Son' added in 1824

JOHN GEDDES
Verreville
Pottery
printed

Govancroft Potteries Ltd.
pottery, 1913–
  trade-names: 'Croft',
  'Hamilton', 'Lunar'
  1913–49

CROWN   GOVAN
printed or impressed

  printed 1949–

Grosvenor & Son, F.
pottery, c. 1869–1926

  printed mark from 1879

Kennedy & Sons Ltd., Henry
stoneware, 1866–1929

Lockhart & Arthur
earthenware, 1855–64
  marks impressed or
  printed

L. & A.

LOCKHART &
ARTHUR

265

Lockhart & Co., David   D.L. & CO.
earthenware, 1865–98   printed

Lockhart & Sons Ltd., David   D.L. & SONS
earthenware, 1898–1953
  printed in backstamps

Murray & Co. Ltd., W. F.
pottery, 1870–98
  mark impressed or
  printed

Nautilus Porcelain Co.
  porcelain, 1896–1913
  printed mark

North British Pottery   J.M. CO.
earthenware, 1869–75

  printed marks   J.M. & CO.   I.M. & CO.

Port Dundas Pottery Co. Ltd.   PORT DUNDAS
stoneware, *c.* 1850–1932   GLASGOW POTTERY

  impressed or printed

Possil Pottery Co.
general ceramics,
1898–1901

              printed

'Star Pottery'
stoneware and 'majolica'
1880–1907

impressed or printed

Thomson & Sons, John   J.T.
c. 1816– late 19th century   ANNFIELD
    '& Sons' added c. 1866

                                    J.T. & SONS
                                    GLASGOW

Williamson, John   WELLINGTON
pottery, 1844–94   POTTERY

    marks impressed or
    printed   WILLIAMSON
                                    WELLINGTON
                                    POTTERY

GREENOCK (Strathclyde)   CLYDE
    Clyde Pottery Co. Ltd.
    earthenware, c. 1815–
    1903   G.C.P. CO.
        'Ltd.' used c. 1857–63

                                    GREENOCK
                                    impressed or printed

Greenock Pottery   GREENOCK
earthenware, c. 1820–   POTTERY
60

    mark impressed or
    printed

267

Shirley & Co., Thomas   T.S. & COY.
earthenware, *c.* 1840–57

                                   T.S. & C.
                                  impressed

INVERDRUIE (Highland Region)
  Castlewynd Studios, Ltd.
  earthenware and stoneware
    trade-names, 'Castlewynd'
    'Aviemore'
  Started Edinburgh 1950
  moved to Gifford 1954
  (Castlewynd Studios
  (Highland China) 1974   printed
  at Fort William)

KIRKCALDY (Lothian)   R.H. & S.
  Heron & Son, Robert
  earthenware, *c.* 1850–
  1929
    Date of 1820 in mark
    is that of an earlier
    pottery taken over by Heron

                             printed

  Methven & Sons, David   D.M. & S.
  19th century–*c.* 1930
  earthenware

                          METHVEN

             D. METHVEN & SONS

NORTH BERWICK   Tantallon
(Lothian)   Ceramics
  Tantallon Ceramics   NORTH BERWICK
  earthenware, 1962–

PAISLEY (Strathclyde)
Brown & Co., Robert   BROWN PAISLEY
earthenware, 1876–1933

printed or impressed

PORTOBELLO (nr. Edinburgh, Lothian)
Buchan & Co. Ltd., A. W.
stoneware, 1867
    trade-name: 'Thistle'
    printed mark from 1949–

Gray & Sons, Ltd., W. A.   W.A. GRAY
pottery, *c.* 1857–1931   printed
    '& Sons' from 1870, 'Ltd.'
    from 1926

Milne Cornwall & Co.   MILNE CORNWALL
stoneware, *c.* 1830–40   & CO.
                   impressed

Rathbone & Co., Thomas   T.R. & CO.
earthenware, *c.* 1810–45

   marks printed or   T. RATHBONE
   impressed   P

Scott Brothers   SCOTT BROTHERS
earthenware, *c.* 1786–96

          SCOTT BROS.   SCOTT
   marks impressed   P.B.

PRESTONPANS (Lothian)   FOWLER THOMPSON
Fowler, Thompson & Co.   & CO.
earthenware, *c.* 1820–40   printed or impressed

269

Gordon's Pottery
earthenware, 18th century–
1832

GORDON
impressed

    initials in printed
    backstamps

G.G.

Watson's Pottery
earthenware, *c.* 1750–
1840

WATSON
impressed

    mark of *c.* 1800–40

WATSON & CO.
printed

WALES

CARDIFF AND SWANSEA
(Glamorgan)
    Primavesi & Son, F.
    retailers of earthenware
      c. 1850–1915 ('& Son'
      added *c.* 1860)

F. PRIMAVESI & SON
CARDIFF
Full name in a
variety of marks

CARDIGAN (Dyfed)
    Cardigan Potteries
    earthenware, *c.* 1875–90
      printed mark

CARDIGAN
POTTERIES
WOODWARD & CO.
CARDIGAN

CREIGIAU (nr. Cardiff)
    Creigiau Pottery, 1947–
    Southcliffe, R. G. & Co. Ltd.
    earthenware in copper
    lustre traditional style

'Creigiau'

LLANDUDNO (Gwynedd)
Cambrian Ceramic Co. Ltd.
(formerly Cambrian Pottery
Co. Ltd.), earthenware
1958–

CAMBRIAN
STUDIO
WARE
impressed or printed

LLANELLY (Dyfed)
Guest & Dewsbury
earthenware, 1877–1927
    printed initials in
    backstamps

G. & D.L.

G.D.
L

South Wales Pottery
earthenware, *c.* 1839–58
Chambers & Co.
c. 1839–54
Coombs & Holland
c. 1854–58

CHAMBERS
LLANELLY

S.W.P.

printed or impressed

NANTGARW (Glamorgan)
Nantgarw China Works
porcelain, 1813–14; 1817–22
Billingsley, William &
Walker, Samuel
    'C.W.' stands for 'China
    Works' (transferred to
    Swansea in 1814 until
    1817)

NANT-GARW
C·W·
impressed
(painted and stencilled
marks used, but
also found on later
copies)

SWANSEA (Glamorgan)
Swansea Pottery, Cambrian Pottery
c. 1783–1870, earthenwares

c. 1783–, mark impressed   SWANSEA

                                  CAMBRIAN POTTERY

impressed or printed   CAMBRIA
marks, c. 1783–1810

CAMBRIAN.

impressed or printed   DILLWYN & CO.
marks, c. 1811–17   SWANSEA

                                  D. & CO.

impressed from c. 1817–24   BEVINGTON & CO.

printed from c. 1847–50

impressed, c. 1847–50   CYMRO
                                  STONE CHINA

impressed, c. 1824–50   DILLWYN

Evans, David & Glasson   EVANS & GLASSON
pottery, c. 1850–62   SWANSEA
  impressed or printed   BEST GOODS
                                  CUBA

Evans, D. J. & Co.   D.J. EVANS & CO.
pottery, c. 1862–70

                              EVANS & CO.

printed, *c.* 1862–70

Swansea porcelain
impressed marks, 1814–22   SWANSEA

printed or written in red   *SWANSEA*
enamel
impressed, sometimes   *Swansea*
with 'SWANSEA'   DILLWYN & CO.

rare impressed mark   BEVINGTON & CO.
of *c.* 1820

Baker, Bevans & Irwin   BAKER BEVANS
Glamorgan Pottery   & IRWIN
earthenware, 1813–38   printed or impressed

example of printed mark

The name of Pellatt & Green, retailers
of St. Paul's Church Yard, London, is
sometimes seen on Welsh wares of *c.* 1805–30

Calland & Co., John F. Landore Pottery earthenware, 1852–56	C. & CO. CALLAND SWANSEA
YNYSMEDW (nr. Swansea) Ynysmedw Pottery earthenware, *c.* 1850–70	Y.M.P. Y.P. impressed

IRELAND

BELLEEK (Co. Fermanagh)
porcelain, 1863–
McBirney, David &
Armstrong, Robert

BELLEEK
CO. FERMANAGH

FERMANAGH
POTTERY
impressed

impressed or printed
mark of 1863–80

early version of usual
mark, 1863–91

post-1891 version
includes 'Ireland'
and 'Co. Fermanagh'
to comply with the
McKinley Tariff Act

printed

ORK
Carrigaline Pottery Ltd.
earthenware, 1928–

CARRIG WARE
CARRIGALINE

   printed marks   POTTERY

UBLIN
Chambers, John, *c.* 1730–
c. 1745
tin-glazed earthenware
  inscription painted on
  plate

Delamain, Captain Henry (*d.* 1757)
1752–*c.* 1771

Donovan & Son, John
decorator of English
pottery and porcelain
c. 1770–1829

DONOVAN

DONOVAN
DUBLIN
painted

  'DONOVAN' impressed on
  wares made to order

Vodrey's Pottery
earthenware, 1872–*c.* 85

VODREY DUBLIN
POTTERY

impressed

275

LIMERICK   Made by John Stritch
  Stritch, John, *c.* 1760   Limerick, 4th June 1761
  tin-glazed earthenware

                            inscription on plate

URNEMOUTH (Dorset)
Purbeck Pottery Ltd.
stoneware, Dec. 1965–

    printed marks

Purbeck
Pottery
England

OADSTAIRS (Kent)
Broadstairs Pottery Ltd.
stoneware, 1966–
    printed mark

UTON (Somerset)
Goddard Ltd., Elaine
earthenware, 1939–

    mark printed label

ESTERFIELD (Derbyshire)
Price, Powell & Co. Ltd.   No registered
earthenware, 1740–   trade mark
Ltd. from 1961)
Now subsidiary of Pearsons of Chesterfield

CHURCH GRESLEY
(Derbyshire)
  Mason, Cash & Co. Ltd.
  Pool Potteries, 1901
  domestic earthenware
  (Ltd. Co. since 1941)

products
unmarked

DARTMOUTH (Devon)
  Britannia Designs, Ltd.
  earthenware, 1959
    mark an applied label
    used from 1971

ELKESLEY (Nottinghamshire)
  Aston, Christopher S.
  stoneware, 1968
  (moved to Elkesley
  from Bawtry in 1971)

applied label

FARNHAM (Surrey)
  Harris & Sons, A.
  earthenware, 1872
  (established in 1864
  at Elstead, Surrey)

No special mark
used

HINDHEAD (Surrey)
  Surrey Ceramic Co. Ltd.
  Kingswood Pottery
  earthenware and
  stoneware, 1956–

LIVERPOOL (Merseyside)
Prince William Pottery Co.
earthenware, 1953–

'PRINCE WILLIAM'

LONDON
Macbride, Kitty
(Brown & Muntzer)
earthenware figures of
mice. Trade-name:
'The Happy Mice of
Berkeley Square'
1960–

Kitty MacBride
England

PAIGNTON (Devon)
Barn Pottery, Ltd.
earthenware, 1964

Trade-name 'Barn' ware

REDRUTH (Cornwall)
Foster's Pottery Co.
earthenware, 1949–

FOSTER'S
POTTERY
REDRUTH

stamped mark

STOKE D'ABERTON (Surrey)
Everson, Ronald
porcelain and bone-china
1953
mark in the form of
a dated signature

Ronald Everson

279

HANLEY (Staffordshire)
Mason's Ironstone China Ltd.
earthenware, March 1968
(from March 1974 name changed
to: Mason's Ironstone, a Division
of Josiah Wedgwood & Sons Ltd.)
printed marks

LONGTON (Staffordshire)
Anton Potteries, Ltd., Jon
ironstone, 1974–
(pottery established
c. 1874, 'Crown Clarence'
from *c.* 1953–1971
Jon Anton Potteries
1971–74)

mark on bone-china

Blyth Pottery (Longton) Ltd.
earthenware (taken over by John Tams Ltd.
in April, 1973 and no longer trading on own
account)

LONGTON (Staffordshire)
Hostess Tableware
Thomas Poole &
Gladstone China Ltd.
  'Royal Stafford' and
  'Hostess' bone china
  and 'Hostess' ironstone
  1971–

Hostess Tableware

FINE BONE CHINA
STAFFS, ENGLAND

& other full marks

Royal Albert Ltd.
(Royal Doulton Tableware
Ltd.) Ltd. added 1970
bone-china
  'Royal Albert' previously
  used by Thomas C.
  Wild & Sons Ltd.

printed

Royal Grafton Bone China
(A. B. Jones & Sons, Ltd.
part of Crown Lynn Potteries
Group, N.Z. from 1971–)
bone-china from 1959–

Royal Tuscan
bone-china, *c*. 1962–
(Division of Wedgwood
Group from 1966)

281

STOKE (Staffordshire)
  Baifield Productions Ltd.
  (S. Fielding & Co. Ltd., Crown
  Devon Group), 1963–

Blakeney Art Pottery
earthenware, 1968–
  'Flow Blue Victoria'
  printed ware, Kent
  Staffordshire figures
  and floral art containers.
M. J. Bailey & S. K. Bailey
Note the lion and harp
in coat-of-arms are in
reverse positions to the
authentic version

printed
backstamps in
blue

Similar Royal
Arms mark used,
with 'Romantic'
pattern

Blakeney Art Pottery (*cont.*)

IRONSTONE
STAFFORDSHIRE
ENGLAND

printed backstamp
in brown 'M.J.B.'
(Michael J. Bailey)

similar backstamp
used with:
FLO BLUE
T.M. STAFFORDSHIRE
ENGLAND

FLO BLUE
T.M. STAFFORDSHIRE
ENGLAND

Dorothy Ann Floral China
bone china floral
jewellery, 1946

STOKE ON TRENT
ENGLAND

TUNSTALL (Staffordshire)
Wedgwood (Tunstall) Ltd., Enoch
name changed from Wedgwood & Co. Ltd.
in 1965 (see p. 259)

283

APPENDIX A

Patent Office Registration Mark

From 1842 until 1883 many manufacturers' wares are marked with the following 'diamond-mark', which is an indication that the design was registered with the British Patent Office; ceramics and glass are Classes IV and III, as indicated in the topmost section of the mark, and gave copyright protection for a period of three years (see Appendix B and Preface, page 11).

The date of the 'diamond mark' only indicates the time of registration, but a popular form of decoration was often produced for far longer than the three years. Printed marks usually refer to the applied pattern, whereas impressed or moulded applied versions are more likely to relate to the form of the ware.

When checking date to determine the name of the manufacturer it will sometimes be the case that the design was registered by retailers, wholesalers or even foreign manufacturers.

'Diamond-marks' impressed into bone-china can often be more accurately read when held before a strong artificial light.

Example of ceramic
design registered on
23rd May 1842

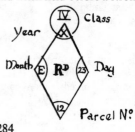

284

APPENDIX A

Index to letters for each year and month from 1842 *to* 1867:

Years

1842 X	1849 S	1856 L	1863 G
1843 H	1850 V	1857 K	1864 N
1844 C	1851 P	1858 B	1865 W
1845 A	1852 D	1859 M	1866 Q
1846 I	1853 Y	1860 Z	1867 T
1847 F	1854 J	1861 R	
1848 U	1855 E	1862 O	

Months

January	C	July	I
February	G	August	R ⎱ For September 1857
March	W	September	D ⎰ query letter R used
April	H	October	B from 1st–19th Sept.
May	E	November	K ⎱ For December 1860
June	M	December	A ⎰ query letter K used.

Index to letters for each year and month from 1868 *to* 1883:

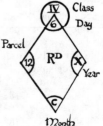

Example of ceramic design,
registered on 6th January 1868

Years			
1868 X	1872 I	1876 V	1880 J
1869 H	1873 F	1877 P	1881 E
1870 C	1874 U	1878 D	1882 L
1871 A	1875 S	1879 Y	1883 K

Months			
Jan. C	April H	July I	Oct. B
Feb. G	May E	Aug. R	Nov. K
Mar. W	June M	Sept. D	Dec. A

For Registration marks brought in with W for the year, see below:

From 1st to 6th March, 1878, the following Registra-tion Mark was issued:

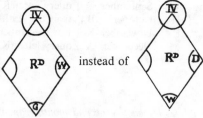

instead of

From 1884 this method of dating registrations ceased and the designs were numbered consecutively in the following manner: 'Rd. 12345' or 'Rd. No. 12345' The following table gives a guide up until 1910 to the range of numbers used within a year:

Registered in January		Registered in January	
1	1884	90483	1888
19734	1885	116648	1889
40480	1886	141273	1890
64520	1887	163767	1891

185713	1892	368154	1901
205240	1893	385500	1902
224720	1894	402500	1903
246975	1895	420000	1904
268392	1896	447000	1905
291241	1897	471000	1906
311658	1898	494000	1907
331707	1899	519500	1908
351202	1900	550000	1909

Information concerning the work of the full members of the Craftsmen Potters Association (modern studio-potters) is well provided by an excellent directory, *potters*, where the full particulars, including the mark and an illustration of the ware of 138 potters, are given. This directory may be obtained from the Craftsmen Potters Shop, William Blake House, Marshall Street, London, W.1., price 75p, plus postage.

The part of the Class IV Design Index in the Public Record Office that relates to pottery and porcelain is included in Appendix B, pages 288 to 392.

Index of Names and Dates of Manufacturer Retailers, Wholesalers and others who registered designs from 1842 to 1883

(See Appendix A, page 284, and Preface, page 12)

Date	Parcel No.	Patent No.	Factory, Retailer Wholesaler, etc	Plac
1842				
Sept 22	1	1694	James Dixon & Sons	Sheffie
Nov 2	1	2152	Joseph Wolstenholme	Sheffie
3	1	2163	idem	Sheffie
26	3	2503–4	Henry Hunt	Londc
Dec 2	3	2599–00	Joseph Clementson	Shelto
30	2	3346	James Edwards	Bursle
1843				
Jan 24	2	4296–7	John Ridgway & Co.	Shelto
Feb 3	4	4462	T. Woodfield	Londc
21	1	5266–70	Samuel Alcock & Co.	Bursle
Mar 21	5	5993–4	Josiah Wedgwood & Sons	Etruri
31	6	6266	Samuel Alcock & Co.	Bursle
May 2	4	6978	Josiah Wedgwood & Sons	Etruri
5	1	7037	W. S. Kennedy	Bursle
11	2	7074	idem	Bursle
13	4	7122	Jones & Walley	Cobri
June 14	5	7503–5	Samuel Alcock & Co.	Bursle
Aug 30	8	9678–80	James Edwards	Bursle
Oct 6	2	10370	idem	Bursle
Nov 10	3	11292	Minton & Co.	Stoke
28	5	11690	Thos. Dimmock & Co.	Shelto
Dec 14	10	12331	G. F. Bowers & Co.	Tunst

APPENDIX B

Date	Parcel No.	Patent No.	Factory, Retailer Wholesaler, etc	Place
4				
15	9	16264–5	Samuel Alcock & Co.	Burslem
20	4	16374–5	idem	Burslem
1	6	16687	Hamilton & Moore	Longton
5	3	16831	Mellor, Venables & Co.	Burslem
7	4	16871	J. & T. Lockett	Lane End
3	3	17566–72	Thos. Edwards	Burslem
11	4	17714	Hilditch & Hopwood	Lane End
y 7	4	18207	Thos. Dimmock & Co.	Shelton
e29	3	19182	idem	Shelton
20	5	19977–9	John Ridgway & Co.	Shelton
30	2	20332–4	Herbert Minton & Co.	Stoke
15	3	20779	King, Knight & Elkin	Stoke
21	7	21069–73	Herbert Minton & Co.	Stoke
9	7	21450	Cyples, Barlow & Cyples	Lane End
19	4	21700–1	Jn. Ridgeway & Co.	Shelton
21	2	21715	Henry Hunt	London
30	7	21960	Charles Meigh	Hanley
14	4	22158	Copeland & Garrett	Stoke
17	3	22192	Clementson, Young & Jameson	Shelton
30	4	22394–6	Herbert Minton & Co.	Stoke
6	4	22424	idem	Stoke
11	5	22490	James Edwards	Burslem
13	4	22499–500	John Ridgway & Co.	Shelton
22	4	22834	Thos. Dimmock & Co.	Shelton
26	3	22883	Ray & Wynne	Longton
2	3	22919–20	Copeland & Garrett	Stoke
7	4	23207–10	Thos. Edwards	Burslem
16	6	23593	Willm. Ridgway, Son & Co.	Hanley
24	2	23843	John Meir & Son	Tunstall
5				
11	6	24846	George Phillips	Longport

289

Date	Parcel No.	Patent No.	Factory, Retailer Wholesaler, etc	Plac
15	2	24996	Clementson, Young & Jameson	Shelto
21	6	25199	T. J. & J. Mayer	Longp
27	5	25273	John Rose & Co.	Coalp
Feb 26	5	26532–3	W. S. Kennedy	Bursle
27	3	26543	George Phillips	Longp
Mar 5	1	26608	Copeland & Garrett	Stoke
6	5	26617	Herbert Minton & Co.	Stoke
17	10	26939	idem	Stoke
20	1	26949	idem	Stoke
31	4	27034	Thos. Pearce	Londo
Apr 10	1	27202	idem	Londo
25	2	27350	Copeland & Garrett	Stoke
26	1	27352	George Pearce	Londo
26	3	27354	T. & R. Boote, Walley & Jones	Bursle Cobrid and Hanley
30	2	27383	Jacob Furnival & Co.	Cobrid
May 8	2	27451	Herbert Minton & Co.	Stoke
10	3	27482	Walley & T. & R. Boote	Cobrid and Bursle
31	1	27800	Francis Morley	Shelto
June 19	1	28150	George Phillips	Longp
26	3	28296	Minton & Co.	Stoke
July 5	1	28668–71	George Phillips	Longp
5	2	28672	Enoch Wood	Bursle
26	1	29173	William Adams & Sons	Stoke
Aug 28	3	29993	Joseph Clementson	Shelto
Sept 4	3	30161–3	Copeland & Garrett	Stoke
11	2	30286	Thos. Phillips & Son	Bursle
19	1	30383	Minton & Co.	Stoke
Oct 6	1	30543–4	H. Minton & Co.	Stoke
21	1	30699	Copeland & Garrett	Stoke

APPENDIX B

te	Parcel No.	Patent No.	Factory, Retailer Wholesaler, etc	Place
22	2	30701	Clementson & Young	Shelton
5	2	31128	Bayley & Ball	Longton
22	2	31329	Minton & Co.	Stoke
4	4	31670–3	John Ridgway	Shelton
27	2	32553	James Edwards	Burslem
29	2	32555	Joseph Clementson	Shelton
30	3	32601	Furnival & Clark	Hanley
7	2	32698	Joseph Clementson	Shelton
24	2	33319	Jacob Furnival & Co.	Cobridge
26	5	34031	T. J. & J. Mayer	Longport
2	4	34108	Minton & Co.	Stoke
11	2	34281–5	W. S. Kennedy	Burslem
7	1	34564–66	idem	Burslem
17	3	34684	Copeland & Garrett	Stoke
21	3	35030–1	H. Minton & Co.	Stoke
26	2	35116–7	idem	Stoke
6	1	35219	W. Chamberlain & Co.	Worcester
26	2	35777	H. Minton & Co.	Stoke
30	3	35795	John Goodwin	Longton
11	1	36047	J. K. Knight	Longton
16	1	36167	Ridgway, Son & Co.	Hanley
17	1	36263	John Ridgway & Co.	Shelton
21	1	36278	F. Morley & Co.	Shelton
1	2	36447–8	Josiah Wedgwood & Sons	Etruria
3	1	36450	idem	Etruria
3	2	36451–2	H. Minton & Co.	Stoke
3	2	37170	G. Phillips	Longport
3	3	37171–2	F. Morley & Co.	Shelton
4	4	37254	Copeland & Garrett	Stoke
26	2	37419–21	John Ridgway & Co.	Shelton
29	3	37586	T. J. & J. Mayer	Longport
26	1	37806	F. Morley & Co.	Shelton
26	5	37864	J. Edwards	Burslem

Date	Parcel No.	Patent No.	Factory, Retailer Wholesaler, etc	Pl.
Nov 3	1	37935	Ridgway & Abington	Hanl
5	2	37986	G. Phillips	Long
12	3	38068	C. Meigh	Hanl
16	2	38113	H. Minton & Co.	Stoke
21	2	38291–2	Thos. Furnival & Co.	Hanl
Dec 3	4	38606	Ridgway & Abington	Hanl
4	2	38610	H. Minton & Co.	Stoke
10	3	38786	Joseph Clementson	Shelt
14	3	39480	James Edwards	Burs
14	4	39481	Minton & Co.	Stoke
16	1	39519	John Goodwin	Long
17	2	39544–5	Copeland & Garrett	Stoke
26	5	39614	Henry Hunt	Lonc
29	2	39703	Edward Challinor	Tuns
31	3	39746	Josiah Wedgwood & Sons	Etrun
1847				
Jan 9	4	40104–5	John Ridgway & Co.	Shelt
9	7	40110	Copeland & Garrett	Stoke
Feb 2	7	41213	T. & R. Boote	Burs
8	5	41266–7	T. J. & J. Mayer	Long
15	4	41459–60	Copeland & Garrett	Stoke
Mar 17	3	42044	John Wedge Wood	Tuns
17	6	42047–8	John Ridgway & Co.	Shel
22	2	42233	Bailey & Ball	Long
23	7	42279	Herbert Minton & Co.	Stoke
30	1	42363	James Edwards	Burs
Apr 3	6	42435	Samuel Alcock & Co.	Burs
27	1	42804	idem	Burs
May 12	4	43154	Copeland & Garrett	Stok
14	1	43170–1	Herbert Minton & Co.	Stok
June 11	4	43536	James Edwards	Burs
11	6	43557	Joseph Alexander	Nor
21	5	43728	John Rose & Co.	Coal
25	2	43780	James Edwards	Burs

te Parcel No.		Patent No.	Factory, Retailer Wholesaler, etc	Place
5	5	43916–7	Mellor, Venables & Co.	Burslem
5	1	44014–5	idem	Burslem
6	5	44036–9	James Edwards	Burslem
27	3	44398	T. J. & J. Mayer	Longport
3	3	44872	John Rose & Co.	Coalport
6	2	45088	James Edwards	Burslem
17	2	45091–2	W. T. Copeland	Stoke
9	3	45175	H. Minton & Co.	Stoke
26	2	45367	James Edwards	Burslem
9	3	45730	William Taylor Copeland	Stoke
16	3	45822	idem	Stoke
25	5	45992	John Wedge Wood	Tunstall
1	4	46130	Thos. Peake	Tunstall
2	5	46192–4	John Ridgway & Co.	Shelton
4	3	46232	H. Minton & Co.	Stoke
8	4	46265	John Wedge Wood	Tunstall
13	1	46299	W. T. Copeland	Stoke
23	2	46516–8	H. Minton & Co.	Stoke
27	1	46529	John Ridgway & Co.	Shelton
11	4	46886	H. Minton & Co.	Stoke
23	4	47183	J. Wedgwood & Co.	Etruria
1	2	47417–20	John Rose & Co.	Coalport
10	3	47562–3	Minton & Co. & John Bell	Stoke
15	4	48130	Minton & Co.	Stoke
1	4	48540–2	Barker & Till	Burslem
6	4	48717	Geo. Grainger	Worcester
18	2	49040	W. T. Copeland	Stoke
11	3	49780–1	H. Minton & Co.	Stoke
29	12	50473	Minton & Co.	Stoke
4	4	50549	Minton & Co.	Stoke
7	1	50635–6	Ridgway & Abington	Hanley
14	2	50798	W. T. Copeland	Stoke
15	2	50803	idem	Stoke

Date	Parcel No.	Patent No.	Factory, Retailer Wholesaler, etc	Pl
20	7	50994	Wood & Brownfield	Cobr
27	8	51185–91	J. & S. Alcock Jnr.	Cobr
Apr 15	4	51542	John Ridgway & Co.	Shelt
17	6	51599	Frederick Harrison	Lond
22	3	51661	Josiah Wedgwood & Sons	Etrur
27	4	51763	idem	Etrur
28	5	51768	Giovanni Franchi	Lond
May 30	3	52162	Thos. Peake	Tuns
June 20	4	52402	G. F. Bowers & Co.	Tuns
30	2	52529	W. T. Copeland	Stoke
30	3	52530	Ridgway & Abington	Hanl
Aug 10	3	53782	Geo. Grainger	Worc
16	8	53876	Thos. Pinder	Bursl
23	2	54018	John Wedge Wood	Tuns
26	2	54067	John Meir & Son	Tuns
Sept 15	3	54438	W. T. Copeland	Stoke
18	4	54487	Charles Meigh	Hanl
25	4	54578–9	Giovanni Franchi	Lond
30	7	54662	John Ridgway & Co.	Shelte
Oct 17	3	54901	T. & R. Boote	Bursl
Nov 4	2	55174	W. T. Copeland	Stoke
13	4	55337	idem	Stoke
21	5	55456–7	Minton & Co.	Stoke
27	2	55766	John Ridgway & Co.	Shelte
Dec 16	3	56631–3	James Edwards	Bursl
28	2	56845	John Ridgway	Shelte
1849				
Jan 3	2	56978	William Adams & Sons	Stoke
20	2	57506–8	W. Davenport & Co.	Long
Feb 2	4	58069	Mellor, Venables & Co.	Bursl
16	5	58461	Minton & Co.	Stoke
16	11	58474	Ridgway & Abington	Hanl
26	2	58578	John Rose & Co.	Coalp
Mar 13	2	58874	Joseph Clementson	Shelte

APPENDIX B

e	Parcel No.	Patent No.	Factory, Retailer Wholesaler, etc	Place
6	5	59232	Minton & Co.	Stoke
7	2	59245	Cope & Edwards	Longton
1	2	59286	John Ridgway & Co.	Shelton
2	5	59308	Podmore, Walker & Co.	Tunstall
0	4	59400	W. T. Copeland	Stoke
6	6	59571	C. J. Mason	Longton
4	1	60081	Mr. Wedge Wood	Tunstall
7	3	60265	T. J. & J. Mayer	Longport
6	2	61347	Ridgway & Abington	Hanley
1	4	61865	W. T. Copeland	Stoke
5	2	61986	H. Minton & Co.	Stoke
7	2	62003	W. T. Copeland	Stoke
7	5	62316	Mellor, Venables & Co.	Burslem
4	6	62498	F. & R. Pratt & Co.	Fenton
8	6	62690–4	J. Ridgway	Shelton
0	2	62883	idem	Shelton
2	4	62914	Minton & Co.	Stoke
6	5	63267	J. Hollinshead	Shelton
8	6	63490	John Cliff Quince	London
9	4	63523	W. T. Copeland	Stoke
7	2	63718	Minton & Co.	Stoke
2	2	64319	W. T. Copeland	Stoke
0	5	64627	John Rose & Co.	Coalport
6	3	64739	W. T. Copeland	Stoke
5	4	64982	T. J. & J. Mayer	Longport
3	1	65884	W. Davenport & Co.	Longport
4	4	66266–7	J. Ridgway	Shelton
6	6	66862	G. Grainger	Worcester
3	1	67398	idem	Worcester
3	3	67413	J. & M. P. Bell & Co.	Glasgow
7	4	67783	G. Grainger	Worcester
9	3	67987	W. T. Copeland	Stoke
0	9	68489	John Rose & Co.	Coalport

APPENDIX B

Date	Parcel No.	Patent No.	Factory, Retailer Wholesaler, etc	Pla
Apr 4	4	68623	T. J. & J. Mayer	Longp
8	1	68720	J. Clementson	Shelto
13	7	68797	Minton & Co.	Stoke
18	11	68959	John Rose & Co.	Coalp
24	3	69142	William Pierce	Londo
25	3	69149	Minton & Co.	Stoke
June 4	1	69679	J. & M. P. Bell & Co.	Glasg
5	3	69685	Barker & Son	Bursle
21	4	69884	E. Walley	Cobri
July 2	2	70088	T. J. & J. Mayer	Longp
16	5	70364	C. & W. K. Harvey	Longt
Sept 9	5	71843	Thomas Till	Bursle
16	8	71952	J. & M. P. Bell & Co.	Glasg
16	9	71953–4	J. Ridgway	Shelto
19	2	71989	W. T. Copeland	Stoke
21	1	72057	Mellor, Venables & Co.	Bursle
Oct 9	2	72395–6	Minton & Co.	Stoke
17	6	72544	W. T. Copeland	Stoke
Nov 4	4	73327	J. Wedgwood & Sons	Etruri
20	7	73693	F. Morley & Co.	Shelto
22	3	73719	John Rose & Co.	Coalp
Dec 5	3	74138	F. Morley & Co.	Shelto
19	5	74785	John Rose & Co.	Coalp
19	6	74786	T. J. & J. Mayer	Longp
20	6	75148	W. T. Copeland	Stoke
1851				
Jan 20	4	75883–4	James Green	Lond
Feb 10	9	76664	William Brownfield	Cobri
Mar 17	13	77481–91	J. Ridgway & Co.	Shelto
31	4	77986	J. & M. P. Bell & Co.	Glasg
Apr 9	2	78268	Thos. Till & Son	Bursl
11	4	78309–10	J. & M. P. Bell & Co.	Glasg
11	6	78312	W. S. Kennedy	Bursl
14	7	78398–401	J. & M. P. Bell & Co.	Glasg

APPENDIX B

Date	Parcel No.	Patent No.	Factory, Retailer Wholesaler, etc	Place
26	3	78634	E. Walley	Cobridge
y 30	4	79085	W. T. Copeland	Stoke
ne 7	4	79164	J. Ridgway & Co.	Shelton
11	2	79183	W. T. Copeland	Stoke
11	3	79184	Ralph Scragg	Hanley
19	5	79300	W. T. Copeland	Stoke
y 10	3	79588	R. Britton & Co.	Leeds
14	3	79684	W. T. Copeland	Stoke
21	7	79750–3	T. & R. Boote	Burslem
24	2	79782	Thos. Till & Son	Burslem
26	3	79802	C. Collinson & Co.	Burslem
ug 16	2	80184	Ridgway & Abington	Hanley
ot 2	4	80365	T. J. & J. Mayer	Longport
19	3	80629–30	T. & R. Boote	Burslem
29	4	80815–16	James Edwards	Burslem
30	3	80826	idem	Burslem
t 1	1	80827	W. T. Copeland	Stoke
7	3	80887	Chamberlain & Co.	Worcester
10	4	80910–1	W. Brownfield	Cobridge
10	6	80913	T. & R. Boote	Burslem
14	4	80980	Thos. Till & Son	Burslem
16	4	80989	W. Brownfield	Cobridge
17	3	80997	George Bowden Sander	London
21	3	81057	Wm. Ridgway	Shelton
ov 1	5	81225–6	Geo. B. Sander	London
10	4	81492	Ralph Scragg	Hanley
12	6	81510–12	Minton & Co.	Stoke
13	2	81518	Charles Meigh & Son	Hanley
14	4	81558	Geo. B. Sander	London
ec 2	2	81815	T. J. & J. Mayer	Burslem
4	3	81843–4	Minton & Co.	Stoke
5	5	81864	John Ridgway & Co.	Shelton
8	8	81960	W. T. Copeland	Stoke
15	6	82052	Geo. B. Sander	London

APPENDIX B

Date	Parcel No.	Patent No.	Factory, Retailer Wholesaler, etc	Place
1852				
Jan 27	1	83342	W. & G. Harding	Burslem
Feb 17	1	83826	Venables & Baines	Burslem
Mar 4	2	84133–4	Wm. Brownfield	Cobridge
13	3	84239	Wm. Ridgway	Shelton
22	7	84385	Ralph Scragg	Hanley
24	3	84406	James Edwards	Burslem
24	4	84407	Minton & Co.	Stoke
25	1	84410	John Milner	Cobridge
26	3	84471	J. & M. P. Bell & Co.	Glasgow
Apr 1	1	84541	Thos. Till & Son	Burslem
8	4	84615	idem	Burslem
21	4	84837	George Ray	Longton
May 5	5	85001–2	J. M. Blashfield	London
6	5	85008	Geo. Bowden Sander	London
7	2	85010–3	J. M. Blashfield	London
14	5	85081	W. T. Copeland	Stoke
18	1	85102	Minton & Co.	Stoke
June 1	2	85224–5	J. M. Blashfield	London
5	5	85248	Minton & Co.	Stoke
14	4	85354	W. T. Copeland	Stoke
21	2	85404	J. & T. Lockett	Longton
July 5	3	85619	J. Pankhurst & Co.	Hanley
23	3	85803–4	Minton & Co.	Stoke
Aug 4	3	86070–1	W. T. Copeland	Stoke
13	5	86126	Thos. Till & Son	Burslem
25	4	86318	Chas. Meigh & Son	Hanley
25	5	86319	Geo. Bowden Sander	London
Sept 3	7	86473	Minton & Co.	Stoke
15	5	86649	Thos. Till & Son	Burslem
16	1	86657	Minton & Co.	Stoke
24	1	86815	idem	Stoke
27	3	86857	Warburton & Britton	Leeds
Oct 1	6	86931	W. T. Copeland	Stoke
7	5	87040	Ralph Scragg	Hanley

APPENDIX B

ate	Parcel No.	Patent No.	Factory, Retailer Wholesaler, etc	Place
23	4	87219	Davenports & Co.	Longport
25	2	87228	Wm. Brownfield	Cobridge
30	3	87464	Marple, Turner & Co.	Hanley
4	5	87541	John Holland	Tunstall
11	3	87633	Minton & Co.	Stoke
22	3	87883	J. Pankhurst & J. Dimmock	Hanley
25	4	88037	Keys & Mountford	Stoke
16	4	88350	John Rose & Co.	Coalport
27	1	88693	Warburton & Britton	Leeds
3	3	88808–9	W. T. Copeland	Stoke
12	6	88978	Thos. Goodfellow	Tunstall
14	3	88987	Davenports & Co.	Longport
18	2	89050	idem	Longport
4	9	89469	J. Pankhurst & J. Dimmock	Hanley
10	2	89626	Geo. Wooliscroft	Tunstall
11	6	89646	Thos. Worthington & J. Green	Shelton
12	3	89661–3	Minton & Co.	Stoke
17	4	89722–3	W. S. Kennedy & Co.	Burslem
26	5	89958	W. T. Copeland	Stoke
10	2	90253	J. & M. P. Bell & Co.	Glasgow
17	5	90360	J. W. Pankhurst & Co.	Hanley
19	2	90372	Minton & Co.	Stoke
4	6	90610	John Rose & Co.	Coalport
23	2	90876	Wm. Adams & Sons	Stoke
7	5	91121–4	John Alcock	Cobridge
7	3	91329	Geo. Wood & Co.	Shelton
14	2	91405–6	Livesley, Powell & Co.	Hanley
22	3	91469	Pankhurst & Dimmock	Hanley
24	3	91487	Geo. Wooliscroft	Tunstall
24	11	91512–3	Ridgway & Co.	Shelton

APPENDIX B

Date	Parcel No.	Patent No.	Factory, Retailer Wholesaler, etc	Pla
July 18	4	91737	John Edwards	Longt
20	2	91749–50	J. H. Baddeley	Shelto
Aug 8	1	92001	Anthony Shaw	Tunst.
10	2	92018	Holland & Green	Longt
Sept 3	2	92340	T. & R. Boote	Bursle
6	3	92364	F. Morley & Co.	Shelto
21	2	92631–2	James Edwards	Bursle
Oct 5	2	92768–70	Venables, Mann & Co.	Bursle
10	3	92859	Barrow & Co.	Fento
11	5	92864	Ralph Scragg	Hanle
12	3	92867	James Edwards	Bursle
12	4	92868–9	Livesley, Powell & Co.	Hanle
19	4	92952	Minton & Co.	Stoke
22	1	93008–9	T. J. & J. Mayer	Longp
Nov 24	2	93438–9	Thos. Till & Son	Bursle
26	2	93452	W. T. Copeland	Stoke
30	5	93483	Wm. Adams & Sons	Stoke
Dec 6	4	93536	J. Alcock	Cobri
24	3	93706–7	Samuel Moore & Co.	Sunde
24	4	93708	J. Alcock	Cobri
1854				
Jan 10	4	94326	W. & G. Harding	Bursle
13	1	94343–4	Deaville & Baddeley	Hanle
14	3	94632	Samuel Moore & Co.	Sunde
21	3	94727	J. & M. P. Bell & Co.	Glasg
30	4	94815	Samuel Alcock & Co.	Bursle
Feb 23	3	95163	W. T. Copeland	Stoke
Mar 11	4	95275	Samuel Alcock & Co.	Bursle
20	1	95388	Thos. Till & Son	Bursle
22	2	95397	James Edwards & Son	Longp
24	3	95420	Minton & Co.	Stoke
27	3	95448	Geo. Baguley	Hanle
27	6	95451	J. Deaville	Hanle
31	1	95469	Holland & Green	Longt

APPENDIX B

ate	Parcel No.	Patent No.	Factory, Retailer Wholesaler, etc	Place
1	4	95510	Wm. Brownfield	Cobridge
4	3	95523	Woollard & Hattersley	Cambdge
5	3	95542	Ralph Scragg	Hanley
6	3	95553	Samuel Alcock & Co.	Burslem
10	3	95575	J. Deaville	Hanley
10	4	95576	Samuel Alcock & Co.	Burslem
11	5	95587-8	Pearson, Farrall & Meakin	Shelton
15	1	95611	Geo. Baguley	Hanley
21	3	95646	Warburton & Britton	Leeds
y 4	3	95733	John Ridgway & Co.	Shelton
8	3	95751	Wm. Brownfield	Cobridge
e 3	2	96003	Thos. Till & Son	Burslem
9	2	96039	Chas. Meigh & Son	Hanley
21	5	96085-6	T. & R. Boote	Burslem
18	2	96296	idem	Burslem
18	4	96298	Alcock & Co.	Burslem
t 5	3	96773	Samuel Alcock & Co.	Burslem
12	2	96826	W. T. Copeland	Stoke
2	3	96980	Wm. Brownfield	Cobridge
6	4	97141	Davenports & Co.	Longport
9	4	97160	T. J. & J. Mayer	Longport
31	2	97508	Geo. Ray	Longton
10	5	97659	John Ridgway & Co.	Shelton
27	3	98640	Samuel Alcock & Co.	Burslem
27	4	98641	Pankhurst & Dimmock	Hanley
29	1	98648	F. & R. Pratt & Co.	Fenton
4	2	98696	Worthington & Green	Shelton
6	4	98786	Samuel Alcock & Co.	Burslem
15	2	99042	Pinder, Bourne & Hope	Burslem
15	4	99051	Brougham & Mayer	Tunstall
19	3	99086	Pankhurst & Dimmock	Hanley
30	1	99188	John Edwards	Longton

APPENDIX B

Date		Parcel No.	Patent No.	Factory, Retailer Wholesaler, etc	Place
Feb	3	4	99231	J. & M. P. Bell & Co.	Glasgo
	5	7	99282	Coomb(e)s & Holland	Llanell
	7	2	99310	John Alcock	Cobric
	17	3	99394	Pratt & Co.	Fenton
	26	3	99488	Lockett, Baguley & Cooper	Shelto
	28	4	99528	J. Ridgway & Co.	Shelto
Mar	1	5	99538–40	Minton & Co.	Stoke
	5	3	99579	Elsmore & Forster	Tunsta
	13	4	99653	Warburton & Britton	Leeds
	17	1	99679	Wm. Baker	Fenton
Apr	7	7	99814	W. T. Copeland	Stoke
	17	4	99876	Stephen Hughes & Son	Burslen
	26	1	99972–4	Wm. Brownfield	Cobric
	28	7	100008	Venables, Mann & Co.	Burslen
May	10	5	100094	Beech, Hancock & Co.	Burslen
	14	3	100116	Minton & Co.	Stoke
June	7	4	100246–7	John Alcock	Cobric
	11	3	100299	Saml. Alcock & Co.	Burslen
July	4	5	100624	J. Thompson	Staffs.
	24	1	100816	Chas. Meigh & Son	Hanley
Aug	6	1	101019	James Dudson	Shelto
	8	5	101026	J. Edwards & Son	Longp
	11	1	101082	Geo. Grainger & Co.	Worce
	20	3	101127	Thos. Ford	Shelto
	27	2	101229–31	Barrow & Co.	Fenton
Sept	27	4	101623–4	Saml. Bevington & Son	Shelto
Oct	3	2	101681	Geo. Mayor & Co.	Londo
	3	3	101682	Minton & Co.	Stoke
	17	8	101932	John Williamson	Glasgo
	25	3	102325	D. Chetwynd	Cobric
	29	6	102355	G. W. Reade	Bursle
Nov	1	3	102415	Josiah Wedgwood & Sons	Etruria
	22	4	102744	J. & M. P. Bell & Co.	Glasgo
	28	3	102785	Wm. Brownfield	Cobrid

APPENDIX B

ate	Parcel No.	Patent No.	Factory, Retailer Wholesaler, etc	Place
5	3	103103	J. Edwards	Longton
15	4	103404	James Pankhurst & Co.	Hanley
23	3	103506	J. Roberts	Kent (Upnor)
23	4	103507	Minton & Co.	Stoke
31	4	103616	Josiah Wedgwood & Sons	Etruria
11	1	104078	Davenports & Co.	Longport
12	3	104090	Pratt & Co.	Fenton
7	2	104313–16	A. Shaw	Tunstall
7	3	104317	J. & M. P. Bell & Co.	Glasgow
18	2	104392	Wm. Beech	Burslem
18	3	104393	Ralph Scragg	Hanley
18	6	104396	E. Walley	Cobridge
18	7	104397	Ridgway & Abington	Hanley
30	3	104602–3	Wm. Brownfield	Cobridge
8	2	104694	Minton & Co.	Stoke
22	1	104762	idem	Stoke
13	3	105059	Chas. Meigh & Son	Hanley
28	3	105223	Worthington & Green	Hanley
30	7	105258	J. Clementson	Shelton
28	3	105492	E. Challinor	Tunstall
30	5	105702	J. Edwards & Son	Longport
12	2	105871	F. & R. Pratt & Co.	Fenton
19	5	105926	idem	Fenton
22	4	105955–9	T. & R. Boote	Burslem
1	3	106161	W. T. Copeland	Stoke
2	3	106477	H. Baggaley	Hanley
16	2	106671–2	Minton & Co.	Stoke
22	3	106770	W. T. Copeland	Stoke
7	6	106950	F. & R. Pratt & Co.	Fenton
14	9	107038	Davenports & Co.	Longport
27	3	107708	idem	Longport
27	6	107714	Wm. Brownfield	Cobridge
29	1	107783–5	E. Walley	Cobridge

303

Date	Parcel No.	Patent No.	Factory, Retailer Wholesaler, etc	Plac
Dec 11	4	107955	W. T. Copeland	Stoke
18	2	108052	Mayer & Elliott	Longp
23	4	108105	idem	Longp
1857				
Jan 15	5	108605	F. & R. Pratt & Co.	Fenton
26	7	108785	J. Edwards	Longp
Feb 4	5	108854–5	John Meir & Son	Tunsta
9	4	108930	Minton & Co.	Stoke
17	3	109063	idem	Stoke
23	9	109180	Podmore, Walker & Co.	Hanley
Mar 20	4	109427	John Alcock	Cobrid
Apr 16	1	109738	John Alcock	Cobrid
29	1	109810	W. T. Copeland	Stoke
June 5	3	110096–7	Wm. Brownfield	Cobrid
19	1	110160	W. T. Copeland	Stoke
19	2	110161	Wilkinson & Rickhuss	Hanley
25	1	110247	J. & M. P. Bell & Co.	Glasgo
July 30	2	110780	Ridgway, Bates & Co.	Shelton
Aug 4	5	110806	Taylor, Pears & Co.	Fenton
11	3	110862	Kerr & Binns	Worce
Sept 7	2	111105	W. T. Copeland	Stoke
Oct 3	3	111495–6	Doulton & Watts	Londo
5	5	111515–6	idem	Londo
14	1	111585	Ridgway & Abington	Hanley
17	1	111642	Mayer Bros. & Elliott	Longp
17	2	111643–4	T. & R. Boote	Bursle
22	1	111677	Pratt & Co.	Fenton
Nov 3	3	111831–2	Maw & Co.	Brosele
28	2	112263	Kerr & Binns	Worce
Dec 4	4	112350	Minton & Co.	Stoke
9	2	112354	Wm. Brownfield	Cobrid

ate	Parcel No.	Patent No.	Factory, Retailer Wholesaler, etc	Place
29	3	112875	Cockson & Harding	Hanley
29	4	112876	E. & W. Walley	Cobridge
25	2	113290	Kerr & Binns	Worcester
9	2	113387	idem	Worcester
17	4	113456	Ridgway & Abington	Hanley
22	5	113565	T. & R. Boote	Burslem
30	5	113631	Minton & Co.	Stoke
6	4	113668	J. Edwards	Longton
25	4	113864	A. Shaw	Burslem
31	1	113900	Holland & Green	Longton
31	4	113903	Wm. Adams	Tunstall
2	1	113905–6	Wm. Brownfield	Cobridge
23	6	114048	Samuel Alcock & Co.	Burslem
13	2	114214	Mayer & Elliott	Longport
29	4	114532	Samuel Alcock & Co.	Burslem
24	2	114763	Wm. Brownfield	Cobridge
3	2	115120	Sharpe Bros. & Co.	Swadlncte
6	5	115197	James Edwards	Longport
10	3	115217	John Edwards	Longton
10	6	115343	Bridgwood & Clarke	Burslem
5	2	115901	Minton & Co.	Stoke
5	3	115902	Wm. Brownfield	Cobridge
7	1	115953	Ridgway & Abington	Hanley
18	3	116176	Minton & Co.	Stoke
29	2	116468	B. Green	Fenton
3	8	116585	James Stiff	London
5	5	116607	Wm. Savage	Winchstr
11	2	116737	E. & W. Walley	Cobridge
8	11	117336–8	T. & R. Boote	Burslem
8	12	117339	J. Clementson	Hanley
17	6	117443	W. T. Copeland	Stoke
23	2	117516	J. Clementson	Hanley
23	9	117530	W. T. Copeland	Stoke
27	4	117559	J. Clementson	Hanley

Date	Parcel No.	Patent No.	Factory, Retailer Wholesaler, etc	Plac
1859				
Jan 25	4	118119	W. T. Copeland	Stoke
Feb 2	3	118294	T. & R. Boote	Bursle
3	2	118303–4	Davenports & Co.	Longp
8	6	118415	Leveson Hill (Excrs. of)	Stoke
Mar 19	1	118827	Alsop, Downes, Spilsbury & Co.	Londo
21	7	118891	T. & R. Boote	Bursle
29	7	119137	idem	Bursle
May 7	1	119721–2	E. & W. Walley	Cobric
10	2	119760	Samuel Alcock & Co.	Bursle
20	1	119968	Wm. Brownfield	Cobric
26	1	120096	Lockett, Baguley & Cooper	Hanley
July 2	2	120560	W. T. Copeland	Stoke
Aug 6	7	121140	F. & R. Pratt & Co.	Fenton
27	6	121724	Samuel Alcock & Co.	Bursle
Sept 1	3	121833	James Edwards & Son	Longp
Oct 12	4	122959	Wm. Adams	Tunsta
14	4	123116	W. T. Copeland	Stoke
25	1	123389–91	Minton & Co.	Stoke
28	1	123604	Davenports & Co.	Longp
Nov 2	3	123738–40	Elsmore & Forster	Tunsta
5	4	123816	Wm. Brownfield	Cobric
17	4	124140–3	Minton & Co.	Stoke
23	4	124274	idem	Stoke
Dec 10	5	124653	Josiah Wedgwood & Sons	Etruri
14	2	124716	E. & W. Walley	Cobric
15	3	124725	Minton & Co.	Stoke
1860				
Jan 10	4	125365	W. T. Copeland	Stoke
23	7	125863	Mayer & Elliott	Longp
Feb 14	9	126446–7	W. T. Copeland	Stoke

te	Parcel No.	Patent No.	Factory, Retailer Wholesaler, etc	Place
1	2	126950	Bates, Brown–Westhead & Moore	Hanley
27	1	127513	idem	Hanley
5	1	127766	Geo. Grainger & Co.	Worcester
12	4	127965	Minton & Co.	Stoke
2	2	128476	John Meir & Son	Tunstall
19	9	129129	Lockett, Baguley & Cooper	Hanley
30	10	129578	Edward Corn	Burslem
6	4	129680–2	Wm. Brownfield	Cobridge
22	2	130106	Minton & Co.	Stoke
28	2	130135	Minton & Co.	Stoke
21	2	131943	John Wedge Wood	Tunstall
4	3	133411	Minton & Co.	Stoke
29	7	133788	idem	Stoke
3	5	134204	B. Green	Fenton
8	4	134519–20	Bates, Brown–Westhead & Moore	Hanley
9	4	134555–7	J. Clementson	Shelton
9	5	134558–9	Holland & Green	Longton
9	3	134936	Minton & Co.	Stoke
29	9	134968	Wm. Brownfield	Cobridge
3	9	136032	T. & R. Boote	Burslem
3	3	136285–6	Bates, Brown–Westhead & Moore	Hanley
2	3	136643	Bates & Co.	Hanley
8	6	137217	T. & R. Boote	Burslem
1	7	137529	Wedgwood & Co.	Tunstall
5	3	138356	J. Furnival & Co.	Cobridge
7	5	138535	James Edwards & Son	Longport
7	7	138861–2	Turner & Tomkinson	Tunstall
9	3	139053	W. T. Copeland	Stoke
9	4	139054–5	W. H. Kerr & Co.	Worcester

APPENDIX B

Date	Parcel No.	Patent No.	Factory, Retailer Wholesaler, etc	Pla
Apr 5	3	139360	Pinder, Bourne & Hope	Bursl
6	1	139369–72	Minton, Hollins & Co.	Stoke
12	3	139714–5	Davenports & Co.	Long
18	5	139881	T. & R. Boote	Bursl
20	6	139945	F. & R. Pratt	Fent
25	2	140200	James Dudson	Hanl
May 3	8	140367	W. T. Copeland	Stoke
6	3	140478	The Hill Pottery Co.	Bursl
6	5	140480–1	The Old Hall Earthenware Co.	Hanl
9	3	140578–9	Bates, Brown–Westhead & Moore	Hanl
13	7	140679	Minton & Co.	Stoke
14	2	140683	W. H. Kerr & Co.	Word
25	2	141055	idem	Word
31	3	141114	Cork, Edge & Malkin	Bursl
June 4	1	141214	Bates, Brown–Westhead & Moore	Hanl
7	5	141288	The Hill Pottery Co.	Bursl
11	2	141326–7	W. T. Copeland	Stoke
13	6	141369	Minton & Co.	Stoke
July 4	2	141715	Lockett & Cooper	Hanl
5	2	141727	Beech & Hancock	Tuns
6	2	141732	Wm. Brownfield	Cobr
18	4	141869–70	Josiah Wedgwood & Sons	Etru
Aug 19	7	142755	T. & R. Boote	Burs
22	7	142847	Wedgwood & Co.	Tuns
23	2	142850	G. W. Reade	Cobr
Sept 6	6	143313	Wm. Brownfield	Cobr
12	6	143400	J. & J. Peake	New
17	2	143702	W. T. Copeland	Stok
18	7	143769	Wm. Beech	Burs
26	7	144179	John Cliff & Co.	Lone
Oct 10	5	144757	W. H. Kerr & Co.	Wor
11	3	144767	Mountford & Scarratt	Fent

te	Parcel No.	Patent No.	Factory, Retailer Wholesaler, etc	Place
15	3	144896	Leveson Hill (Excrs of)	Stoke
18	3	145157	W. T. Copeland	Stoke
24	5	145499	Hulse, Nixon & Adderley	Longton
28	7	145686-7	Bates, Brown-Westhead & Moore	Hanley
15	3	146352-4	J. Clementson	Hanley
29	5	146924	Josiah Wedgwood & Sons	Etruria
4	7	147309-10	Wm. Brownfield	Cobridge
5	5	147322	Till, Bullock & Smith	Hanley
20	7	147820	Lockett & Cooper	Hanley
20	9	147823	Wedgwood & Co.	Tunstall
1	5	148517	Wm. Brownfield	Cobridge
25	3	148870	idem	Cobridge
1	4	149090	Elliot Bros.	Longport
10	6	149290	W. H. Kerr & Co.	Worcester
10	8	149292	Minton & Co.	Stoke
27	4	149673-4	James Dudson	Hanley
1	6	149716	T. & R. Boote	Burslem
13	6	149938	W. T. Copeland	Stoke
13	7	149939	Wm. Adams	Tunstall
14	8	149955	J. Knight	Fenton
14	9	149956	Wedgwood & Co.	Tunstall
14	10	149957-8	Wm. Brownfield	Cobridge
21	6	150100	Thompson Bros.	Burton-on-Trent
22	9	150152	T. & R. Boote	Burslem
27	1	150241	J. & M. P. Bell & Co.	Glasgow
28	5	150301-3	idem	Glasgow
29	3	150322	Minton & Co.	Stoke
1	5	150377	Josiah Wedgwood & Sons	Etruria
4	2	150455	Minton & Co.	Stoke
4	5	150458	J. & T. Furnival	Cobridge

Date	Parcel No.	Patent No.	Factory, Retailer Wholesaler, etc	Place
7	12	150515	Geo. Grainger & Co.	Worces
9	3	150538	The Old Hall Earthenware Co. (Ltd.)	Hanley
17	5	151029–30	Thompson Bros.	Burton
24	2	151141	Turner & Tomkinson	Tunsta
May 1	7	151351	Eardley & Hammersley	Tunsta
3	3	151378	G. L. Ashworth Bros.	Hanley
5	5	151456	John Cliff	Londc
9	9	151568–9	Brown–Westhead, Moore & Co.	Hanle
14	3	151672–3	Geo. Jones & Co.	Stoke
27	3	151995	E. Challinor	Tunsta
29	5	152013	J. Furnival & Co.	Cobri
June 24	5	152709	T. C. Brown–Westhead, Moore & Co.	Hanle
July 2	4	152859	Minton & Co.	Stoke
4	8	152963	J. Clementson	Hanle
12	4	153112	idem	Hanle
14	2	153127	Beech & Hancock	Tunst
19	6	153366	J. Clementson	Hanle
31	3	153476	Jones & Ellis	Long
31	4	153477	Minton & Co.	Stoke
Aug 16	5	153821	Richard Edwards	Long
16	7	153823	J. H. Baddeley	Hanle
18	4	153827	Hulse, Nixon & Adderley	Long
19	4	153844	G. L. Ashworth & Bros.	Hanle
25	3	154143–4	E. F. Bodley & Co.	Bursl
30	3	154220	Thos. Fell & Co.	Newc upon Tyne
30	4	154221	T. & R. Boote	Bursl
Sept 6	2	154401	Malkin, Walker & Hulse	Long
11	3	154678	Minton & Co.	Stok
12	2	154693	Thos. Cooper	Long

APPENDIX B

te	Parcel No.	Patent No.	Factory, Retailer Wholesaler, etc	Place
7	6	154812	Hope & Carter	Burslem
22	7	155103	Minton & Co.	Stoke
26	1	155220–2	Hope & Carter	Burslem
1	7	155263–4	Thos. Fell & Co.	Newcastle upon Tyne
9	3	155550	Hill Pottery	Burslem
5	2	156190	Turner & Tomkinson	Tunstall
23	8	156715–7	Wm. Baker & Co.	Fenton
1	3	157274	E. F. Bodley & Co.	Burslem
9	5	157547	Geo. Wooliscroft	Tunstall
28	4	157907	Minton & Co.	Stoke
3	5	158052–3	T. C. Brown-Westhead Moore & Co.	Hanley
5	2	158091	Wm. Brownfield	Cobridge
9	5	158221	Thomas Cooper	Hanley
7	5	158480	The Old Hall Earthenware Co. (Ltd.)	Hanley
8	3	158498	Geo. Jones	Stoke
2	6	159083	Davenport, Banks & Co.	Etruria
6	2	159123	Minton & Co.	Stoke
6	8	159153	Liddle, Elliot & Sons	Longport
29	1	159551	Josiah Wedgwood & Sons	Etruria
0	3	159573	T. & R. Boote	Burslem
2	3	159613	Minton & Co.	Stoke
7	4	159972	T. & R. Boote	Burslem
24	5	160110	James Stiff & Sons	London
6	2	160319	G. L. Ashworth & Bros.	Hanley
3	2	160456	Hope & Carter	Burslem
3	3	160457	Wilkinson & Sons	Hanley
0	8	160752	Worthington & Green	Hanley
20	9	160753–4	John Pratt & Co.	Fenton
21	2	160759	Beech & Hancock	Tunstall

Date	Parcel No.	Patent No.	Factory, Retailer Wholesaler, etc	Pla
21	4	160761	Hulse, Nixon & Adderley	Longt
21	5	160762	James Edwards & Son	Bursl
23	2	160791–2	Bodley & Harrold	Bursl
Apr 11	1	161404	J. Macintyre	Bursl
23	4	161852	T. C. Brown–Westhead Moore & Co.	Hanl
25	1	161861	Beech & Hancock	Tunst
30	3	162021	Wilkinson & Son	Hanl
May 4	6	162122	Harding & Cotterill	Burto on-T
11	3	162261–2	E. Pearson	Cobr
12	1	162267	Bodley & Harrold	Bursl
15	10	162304	Harding & Cotterill	Burto on-T
22	4	162618–9	W. T. Copeland	Stoke
26	9	162765	T. C. Brown–Westhead, Moore & Co.	Hanl
·June 4	5	162976	The Old Hall Earthenware Co. (Ltd.)	Hanl
8	15	163188	Minton & Co.	Stoke
8	16	163189	Wm. Brownfield	Cobr
July 14	2	164213	Turner & Tomkinson	Tuns
15	3	164221	H. Venables	Hanl
20	3	164353	Wm. Brownfield	Cobr
24	3	164468–9	W. T. Copeland	Stoke
28	6	164635	Minton & Co.	Stoke
Aug 11	3	165045–7	Turner & Tomkinson	Tuns
12	4	165171	Hancock, Whittingham & Co.	Burs
21	1	165317	J. Clementson	Han
28	5	165448	H. Venables	Han
Sept 7	6	165720	T. & R. Boote	Burs
28	4	166439	H. Venables	Han
28	6	166441–2	James Edwards & Son	Lon

312

APPENDIX B

Date	Parcel No.	Patent No.	Factory, Retailer Wholesaler, etc	Place
ct 2	5	166625	H. Venables	Hanley
6	5	166775	Thompson Bros.	Burton
14	7	167289	Wm. Brownfield	Cobridge
15	2	167299	F. Brewer & Son	Longton
17	1	167374	T. & R. Boote	Burslem
22	5	167536	Eardley & Hammersley	Tunstall
24	5	167560	Josiah Wedgwood & Sons	Etruria
26	7	167594–5	The Old Hall Earthenware Co. (Ltd.)	Hanley
28	8	167715	George Jones & Co.	Stoke
31	3	167761–3	Edmund T. Wood	Tunstall
ov 3	5	168132	John Meir & Son	Tunstall
4	7	168188	T. & R. Boote	Burslem
6	1	168234–5	Geo. Jones & Co.	Stoke
16	10	168765	Wm. Kirkham	Stoke
26	12	169553	Wm. Brownfield	Cobridge
27	3	169561	Bodley & Harrold	Burslem
ec 2	5	169774	J. W. Pankhurst	Hanley
2	6	169775	T. & R. Boote	Burslem
18	4	170294	F. & R. Pratt & Co.	Fenton
23	2	170418	Wm. Brownfield	Cobridge
30	1	170590	T. C. Brown–Westhead Moore & Co.	Hanley
54				
5	2	170759	Wm. Brownfield	Cobridge
11	5	170883	Malkin, Walker & Hulse	Longton
b 2	5	171421	Josiah Wedgwood & Sons	Etruria
5	5	171520	Hope & Carter	Burslem
6	3	171536	Thos. Goode & Co.	London
13	6	171673	W. T. Copeland	Stoke
22	7	171970	Cork, Edge & Malkin	Burslem
25	6	172060	Liddle, Elliot & Son	Longport
29	6	172183	J. & D. Hampson	Longton
ar 3	4	172212	Geo. L. Ashworth & Bros.	Hanley

Date	Parcel No.	Patent No.	Factory, Retailer Wholesaler, etc	Place
12	5	172559	Cork, Edge & Malkin	Burslem
18	1	172648	T. C. Brown–Westhead, Moore & Co.	Hanley
22	3	172815–6	Minton & Co.	Stoke
23	4	172876	Burgess & Leigh	Burslem
Apr 9	4	173200	Josiah Wedgwood & Sons	Etruria
15	4	173659	Geo. Jones	Stoke
18	5	173671	Minton & Co.	Stoke
21	4	173785	T. C. Brown–Westhead Moore & Co.	Hanley
21	8	173799	Liddle, Elliot & Son	Longpor
23	11	173996	Geo. L. Ashworth & Bros.	Hanley
26	3	174112	Bodley & Harrold	Burslem
27	4	174138	Hope & Carter	Burslem
29	2	174168	Wm. Brownfield	Cobridg
May 9	3	174424	R. T. Boughton & Co.	Burslem
10	5	174455–8	Geo. Jones & Co.	Stoke
11	3	174475	R. H. Grove	Barlasto
18	5	174795	Geo. Ray	Longtor
21	1	174817	J. & D. Hampson	Longtor
June 9	7	175330	Minton & Co.	Stoke
16	3	175500	Hope & Carter	Burslem
30	4	175927	Wm. Brownfield	Cobridg
30	10	175935	The Worcester Royal Porcelain Co. Ltd.	Worces
July 2	3	175959	Wood & Sale	Hanley
9	5	176164	Pinder, Bourne & Co.	Burslen
11	8	176235–6	idem	Burslen
18	6	176597	Bodley & Harrold	Burslen
18	7	176598	Evans & Booth	Burslen
19	4	176701	Hope & Carter	Burslen
19	8	176706	Wood & Sale	Hanley
28	4	176916	Holland & Green	Longto
Aug 10	2	177455	James Fellows	W/hmp
20	10	177912	Geo. Jones & Co.	Stoke

APPENDIX B

ate	Parcel No.	Patent No.	Factory, Retailer Wholesaler, etc	Place
26	5	178037	T. C. Brown–Westhead Moore & Co.	Hanley
6	5	178264	W. T. Copeland	Stoke
10	1	178410	Minton & Co.	Stoke
12	2	178433	idem	Stoke
14	4	178521	Bodley & Harrold	Burslem
16	6	178597–8	Geo. L. Ashworth & Bros.	Hanley
19	1	178680–1	Josiah Wedgwood & Sons	Etruria
21	1	178693–4	Minton & Co.	Stoke
22	6	178823–7	Josiah Wedgwood & Sons	Etruria
4	2	179445	Geo. Jones & Co.	Stoke
12	4	179656	Wm. Brownfield	Cobridge
27	4	180444	Evans & Booth	Burslem
28	2	180449	The Worcester Royal Porcelain Co. Ltd.	Worcester
28	4	180453	Bodley & Harrold	Burslem
28	9	180483	Minton & Co.	Stoke
29	2	180486	Chas. Collinson & Co.	Burslem
31	3	180569	Cork, Edge & Malkin	Burslem
1	7	180695	W. T. Copeland	Stoke
4	3	180713	Livesley, Powell & Co.	Hanley
10	2	181214–5	Elsmore & Forster	Tunstall
10	3	181296	Hope & Carter	Burslem
10	10	181286	Geo. Jones & Co.	Stoke
24	5	181722	T. C. Brown–Westhead Moore & Co.	Hanley
29	1	181843	Hope & Carter	Burslem
9	1	182203	Wm. Kirkham	Stoke
10	8	182249	Hope & Carter	Burslem
31	6	182699	Geo. Jones & Co.	Stoke
6	3	182806	Hope & Carter	Burslem
6	4	182807	Minton & Co.	Stoke
4	4	183331	Geo. Jones & Co.	Stoke

315

APPENDIX B

Date	Parcel No.	Patent No.	Factory, Retailer Wholesaler, etc	Pl.
Feb 1	1	183650–2	Minton & Co.	Stok
2	4	183706–7	Geo. L. Ashworth & Bros.	Han
13	7	183940	F. & R. Pratt & Co.	Fent
14	4	183945	Liddle, Elliot & Son	Long
27	4	184220	Livesley, Powell & Co.	Han
Mar 31	3	185473	Hope & Carter	Burs
Apr 1	4	185520	Wm. Brownfield	Cobr
3	4	185613	Minton & Co.	Stok
22	5	186266	Thos. Till & Sons	Burs
22	7	186273	James Edwards & Son	Burs
26	5	186325	idem	Burs
28	4	186349	Hope & Carter	Burs
28	7	186354	Henry Alcock & Co.	Cobr
29	3	186361	The Worcester Royal Porcelain Co. (Ltd.)	Wor
May 2	8	186477	Livesley, Powell & Co.	Han
15	2	186841	J. T. Hudden	Long
17	2	186901	Minton & Co.	Stok
June 6	6	187358–9	J. T. Hudden	Long
9	4	187403	The Worcester Royal Porcelain Co. (Ltd.)	Wor
13	5	187533	idem	Wor
14	6	187574	The Hill Pottery Co. Ltd.	Burs
15	2	187576	J. T. Hudden	Long
16	1	187583	Evans & Booth	Burs
17	5	187633	The Worcester Royal Porcelain Co. (Ltd.)	Wor
29	2	187847–8	Ed. F. Bodley & Co.	Burs
30	4	187861	The Hill Pottery Co. Ltd.	Burs
July 3	7	187972	T. C. Brown–Westhead, Moore & Co.	Han
12	3	188167	James Edwards & Son	Burs
Aug 21	6	189155	J. Furnival & Co.	Cob
23	5	189283	Josiah Wedgwood & Sons	Etru
Sept 11	4	189700	R. T. Boughton & Co.	Burs

316

APPENDIX B

ate	Parcel No.	Patent No.	Factory, Retailer Wholesaler, etc	Place
11	5	189701	Thos. Cooper (Excrs of)	Hanley
14	2	189718	T. C. Brown–Westhead, Moore & Co.	Hanley
18	6	189782	Liddle, Elliot & Son	Longport
28	4	190200	Minton & Co.	Stoke
30	4	190656	S. Barker & Son	Swinton
13	8	190903	T. C. Brown–Westhead, Moore & Co.	Hanley
24	4	191292	Edward Johns	Staffs.
30	4	191407–8	Wm. Brownfield	Cobridge
10	4	192236	Pinder Bourne & Co. & Anthony Shaw	Burslem
23	10	192793	The Old Hall Earthenware Co. Ltd.	Hanley
29	8	192963	James Edwards & Son	Burslem
2	3	193061	The Worcester Royal Porcelain Co. (Ltd.)	Worcester
23	3	193844	James Dudson	Hanley
2	4	194063	Pratt & Co.	Fenton
3	6	194194	J. T. Close & Co.	Stoke
13	2	194450	Ed. F. Bodley & Co.	Burslem
17	4	194537	Burgess & Leigh	Burslem
24	1	194696	Minton & Co.	Stoke
31	5	194840	James Edwards & Son	Burslem
2	7	194949	W. T. Copeland	Stoke
2	2	195644	Ford, Challinor & Co.	Tunstall
10	1	195841	The Old Hall Earthenware Co. (Ltd.)	Hanley
14	6	196551	Walker & Carter	Longton
14	7	196552–4	Geo. L. Ashworth & Bros.	Hanley
16	8	196619	The Old Hall Earthenware Co. (Ltd.)	Hanley
18	4	196651	James Edwards & Son	Burslem

317

Date	Parcel No.	Patent No.	Factory, Retailer Wholesaler, etc	Plac
20	7	196672–3	Wm. Brownfield	Cobrid
May 1	4	196987–8	J. Furnival & Co.	Cobrid
25	1	197705–6	Hope & Carter	Bursle
June 4	4	197857	James Broadhurst	Longto
12	1	198135–7	John Edwards	Fenton
21	4	198383–4	Pinder, Bourne & Co.	Bursle
30	4	198589	Thos. Minshall	Stoke
July 19	5	199186	J. T. Hudden	Longto
25	3	199295	Geo. Jones	Stoke
Aug 17	3	200006	Morgan, Wood & Co.	Bursle
29	4	200324	Ed. F. Bodley & Co.	Bursle
Sept 6	4	200599	F. & R. Pratt & Co.	Fenton
13	9	201040	T. & C. Ford	Hanle
15	8	201089	Geo. L. Ashworth & Bros.	Hanle
20	8	201495	Anthony Keeling	Tunsta
Oct 8	3	202103–5	Minton & Co.	Stoke
13	3	202493	Thos. Furnival	Cobrid
Nov 3	6	203173	Minton & Co.	Stoke
12	3	203538	W. T. Copeland	Stoke
14	8	203817	T. C. Brown–Westhead, Moore & Co.	Hanle
15	4	203912	Geo. Grainger & Co.	Worce
Dec 13	4	204764	Liddle, Elliot & Son	Longp
14	8	204794	Samuel Barker & Son	Swint
15	5	204863	T. C. Brown–Westhead, Moore & Co.	Hanle
19	5	205088	John Meir & Son	Tunst
24	2	205201	J. T. Hudden	Long
1867				
Jan 8	5	205372	James Edwards & Son	Bursl
17	3	205596	Ed. F. Bodley & Co.	Bursl
23	2	205759	The Worcester Royal Porcelain Co. (Ltd.)	Worc
Feb 9	1	206033	Ed. F. Bodley & Co.	Bursl

APPENDIX B

Date	Parcel No.	Patent No.	Factory, Retailer Wholesaler, etc	Place
23	5	206275	Worthington & Harrop	Hanley
2	7	206422	Josiah Wedgwood & Sons	Etruria
4	4	206497	T. C. Brown–Westhead, Moore & Co.	Hanley
5	6	206517	Powell & Bishop	Hanley
6	4	206522	The Old Hall Earthenware Co. (Ltd.)	Hanley
9	3	206564	John Edwards	Fenton
11	2	206662	Josiah Wedgwood & Sons	Etruria
14	1	206718	Davenport Banks & Co.	Etruria
15	7	206762–6	Wm. Brownfield	Cobridge
18	5	206867–8	Cockson & Chetwynd & Co.	Cobridge
19	5	206881	James Edwards & Son	Burslem
20	2	206887	Josiah Wedgwood & Sons	Etruria
21	10	206971	James Edwards & Son	Burslem
25	3	206994	Josiah Wedgwood & Sons	Etruria
26	4	207024–5	Minton & Co.	Stoke
3	5	207163	idem	Stoke
4	2	207165	Josiah Wedgwood & Sons	Etruria
4	9	207201	Elsmore & Forster	Tunstall
17	1	207564	Chas. Hobson	Burslem
23	3	207616	Adams, Scrivener & Co.	Longton
24	2	207636	W. T. Copeland	Stoke
6	3	207938	J. & M. P. Bell & Co.	Glasgow
7	4	207977	John Meir & Son	Tunstall
8	6	208002	T. C. Brown–Westhead Moore & Co.	Hanley
18	7	208394	Wm. McAdam	Glasgow
22	6	208434–5	Clementson Bros.	Hanley
6	3	208750	Josiah Wedgwood & Sons	Etruria
11	6	208819	Clementson Bros.	Hanley
11	7	208820	Cockson, Chetwynd & Co.	Cobridge
13	3	208891	W. & J. A. Bailey	Alloa
21	4	209057	Wm. Brownfield	Cobridge

319

APPENDIX B

Date	Parcel No.	Patent No.	Factory, Retailer Wholesaler, etc	Plac
21	8	209062	E. & D. Chetwynd	Hanley
24	4	209087	idem	Hanley
July 1	7	209290	Joseph Ball	Longt
4	5	209362	E. J. Ridgway	Hanley
8	3	209431	Geo. L. Ashworth & Bros.	Hanle
12	5	209530	Geo. Jones	Stoke
15	2	209556	Josiah Wedgwood & Sons	Etruri
17	2	209601	E. & D. Chetwynd	Hanle
25	3	209726	Hope & Carter	Bursle
Aug 28	10	210598	The Worcester Royal Porcelain Co. Ltd.	Worc
Sept 16	7	211275	Thos. Goode & Co.	Londo
17	3	211290	Wedgwood & Co.	Tunst
21	1	211536	Geo. L. Ashworth & Bros.	Hanle
25	9	211873–4	Powell & Bishop	Hanle
Oct 2	1	211995	Minton & Co.	Stoke
3	5	212054	Thompson Bros.	Burto on-Tr
3	6	212055	Minton & Co.	Stoke
7	4	212078	idem	Stoke
10	1	212194	Thos. Booth.	Hanl
24	5	212765	Ford, Challinor & Co.	Tunst
26	1	212881	W. T. Copeland & Sons	Stoke
28	4	212956	idem	Stoke
29	3	212964	Josiah Wedgwood & Sons	Etrur
30	3	212974	J. T. Hudden	Long
31	7	213065	Powell & Bishop	Hanl
Nov 6	7	213430	W. & J. A. Bailey	Alloa
7	4	213436	James Edwards & Son	Burs
18	9	214000	Ford, Challinor & Co.	Tuns
Dec 3	3	214618	W. T. Copeland & Sons	Stok
12	6	214981	F. & R. Pratt & Co.	Fent
20	3	215085	Josiah Wedgwood & Sons	Etru
27	1	215314	J. & J. B. Bebbington	Han

ite	Parcel No.	Patent No.	Factory, Retailer Wholesaler, etc	Place
3	1	215481	Minton & Co.	Stoke
7	8	215636	Thompson Bros.	Burton-on-Trent
7	11	215642	Cockson, Chetwynd & Co.	Cobridge
8	5	215674	T. & R. Boote	Burslem
9	7	215698	Taylor, Tunnicliffe & Co.	Hanley
10	2	215705	Cork, Edge & Malkin	Burslem
11	2	215725	Wm. Brownfield	Cobridge
13	2	215735	Geo. L. Ashworth & Bros.	Hanley
16	13	215879	The Old Hall Earthenware Co. (Ltd.)	Hanley
25	3	216186	Hope & Carter	Burslem
30	6	216333	J. Furnival & Co.	Cobridge
31	8	216347	Josiah Wedgwood & Sons	Etruria
31	14	216363	T. & R. Boote	Burslem
5	4	216451	Adams, Scrivener & Co.	Longton
5	8	216470	E. Hodgkinson	Hanley
10	8	216676–8	Minton & Co.	Stoke
12	1	216699	Josiah Wedgwood & Sons	Etruria
14	10	216821	John Mortlock	London
18	1	216895	Josiah Wedgwood & Sons	Etruria
18	2	216896–7	T. C. Brown–Westhead, Moore & Co.	Hanley
20	9	216988	Minton & Co.	Stoke
25	6	217070	John Rose & Co.	Coalport
27	5	217100	Alcock & Digory	Burslem
28	7	217112	W. & J. A. Bailey	Alloa
5	12	217208	Thos. Goode & Co.	London
5	15	217212	Minton & Co.	Stoke
25	7	217615	W. T. Copeland & Sons	Stoke
25	8	217616–7	The Worcester Royal Porcelain Co. (Ltd.)	Worcester
26	3	217630	Walker & Carter	Longton
1	6	217727	Minton & Co.	Stoke

Date	Parcel No.	Patent No.	Factory, Retailer Wholesaler, etc	Pla<
6	6	217938–9	Pinder, Bourne & Co.	Bursle<
16	7	218139	Geo. L. Ashworth & Bros.	Hanle<
21	6	218285	Beech & Hancock	Tunst<
23	8	218387	R. Hammersley	Tunst<
28	7	218466	T. G. Green	Burto< on-Tr<
May 13	1	218664	Adams, Scrivener & Co.	Longt<
14	2	218764	Hope & Carter	Bursle<
14	6	218773	Philip Brookes	Fento<
26	5	218951	T. C. Brown–Westhead Moore & Co.	Hanle<
26	6	218952	Pinder, Bourne & Co.	Bursle<
28	3	218967	Holdcroft & Wood	Tunst<
28	5	218969–71	Minton & Co.	Stoke
28	7	218973	J. & T. Bevington	Hanle<
30	4	219042	T. & R. Boote	Bursle<
June 8	4	219174	Burgess & Leigh	Bursle<
12	5	219316–7	Wm. Brownfield	Cobri<
16	4	219344	W. P. & G. Phillips	Londo<
22	5	219484	Minton & Co.	Stoke
July 10	3	219756	Josiah Wedgwood & Sons	Etruri<
16	3	219833	Hackney & Co.	Longt<
20	2	219942–3	Hope & Carter	Bursle<
24	4	219997	W. T. Copeland & Sons	Stoke
30	6	220183	Adams, Scrivener & Co.	Longt<
Aug 1	5	220236–7	T. & R. Boote	Bursle<
13	1	220772	Josiah Wedgwood & Sons	Etruri<
15	8	220821–4	James Edwards & Son	Bursle<
17	2	220828	Ed. F. Bodley & Co.	Bursle<
21	2	220906	Ralph Malkin	Fento<
31	7	221124	T. & R. Boote	Bursle<
Sept 1	1	221125–6	James Wardle	Hanle<
4	6	221203–4	Gelson Bros.	Hanle<
5	3	221214	T. C. Brown–Westhead, Moore & Co.	Hanle<

APPENDIX B

te	Parcel No.	Patent No.	Factory, Retailer Wholesaler, etc	Place
5	6	221217–9	McBirney & Armstrong	Belleek
9	4	221311	Hope & Carter	Burslem
9	5	221312	F. Jones & Co.	Longton
9	6	221313	Wedgwood & Co.	Tunstall
9	9	221316	J. & T. Bevington	Hanley
2	3	221521–2	Minton & Co.	Stoke
4	4	221548	Thos. Booth & Co.	Burslem
7	4	221688	T. C. Sambrook & Co.	Burslem
1	4	221814–7	George Ash	Hanley
25	4	221881–2	Minton & Co.	Stoke
5	13	222083–4	T. C. Brown–Westhead, Moore & Co.	Hanley
8	7	222460	Minton & Co.	Stoke
9	2	222476	J. Holdcroft	Stoke
9	3	222477	Hope & Carter	Burslem
9	5	222482–4	Davenports & Co.	Longport
4	8	222736	Geo. Jones	Stoke
7	4	223063	Minton & Co.	Stoke
1	8	223308	W. P. & G. Phillips	London
2	1	223309	McBirney & Armstrong	Belleek
2	5	223314–5	James Edwards & Son	Burslem
3	5	223817–8	Minton & Co.	Stoke
3	6	223819	T. C. Brown–Westhead, Moore & Co.	Hanley
6	13	224090	Powell & Bishop	Hanley
9	5	224172	Josiah Wedgwood & Sons	Etruria
6	3	224382	Knapper & Blackhurst	Tunstall
7	1	224389	Moore Bros.	Cobridge
1	5	224539	Minton & Co.	Stoke
4	5	224645	T. C. Brown–Westhead Moore & Co.	Hanley
5	4	224724	Cork, Edge & Malkin	Burslem
1	4	224953	T. C. Brown–Westhead, Moore & Co.	Hanley

Date	Parcel No.	Patent No.	Factory, Retailer Wholesaler, etc	Pla
3	5	225073–4	The Worcester Royal Porcelain Co. (Ltd.)	Worc
11	5	225410	Ed. T. Bodley & Co.	Bursl
12	4	225425	Wm. Brownfield	Cobri
14	7	225441	Cockson, Chetwynd & Co.	Cobri
23	5	225734	Minton & Co.	Stoke
23	6	225735	The Worcester Royal Porcelain Co. (Ltd.)	Worc
31	6	225993	Geo. L. Ashworth & Bros.	Hanl
31	7	225994	R. Hammersley	Tuns

1869

Date	Parcel No.	Patent No.	Factory, Retailer Wholesaler, etc	Pla
Jan 1	8	226051	Geo. Jones	Stoke
4	4	226098	Minton & Co.	Stoke
7	6	226131	Thos. Goode & Co.	Lond
21	6	226527–8	Minton & Co.	Stoke
22	5	226570	Gelson Bros.	Hanl
22	13	226581	T. C. Brown–Westhead, Moore & Co.	Hanl
25	3	226625	Worthington & Son	Hanl
28	5	226738	Minton & Co.	Stoke
28	10	226747–8	George Ash	Hanl
Feb 1	7	226910	T. C. Brown–Westhead, Moore & Co.	Hanl
2	4	226928	Geo. Yearsley	Long
9	5	227219	Minton & Co.	Stoke
11	10	227277	Geo. Jones	Stok
15	1	227307	Thos. Booth & Co.	Burs
19	2	227345	Josiah Wedgwood & Sons	Etru
22	6	227403	idem	Etru
22	11	227409	McBirney & Armstrong	Belle
22	13	227411	Pinder, Bourne & Co.	Burs
27	5	227518	Josiah Wedgwood & Sons	Etru
Mar 1	8	227556–8	Worthington & Son	Hanl
3	8	227619	Thos. Till & Sons	Burs

APPENDIX B

e	Parcel No.	Patent No.	Factory, Retailer Wholesaler, etc	Place
5	8	227668	F. Primavesi	Cardiff
8	6	227696	F. & R. Pratt & Co.	Fenton
	1	227743–4	Geo. Jones	Stoke
9	3	227746	idem	Stoke
0	10	227823	F. Primavesi	Cardiff
4	1	228141	J. F. Wileman	Fenton
4	1	228290	Wood & Pigott	Tunstall
2	6	228377	Wm. Brownfield	Cobridge
	7	228378	Minton & Co.	Stoke
5	3	228430	Baker & Chetwynd	Burslem
7	2	228455	Minton & Co.	Stoke
7	4	228457	The Worcester Royal Porcelain Co. (Ltd.)	Worcester
2	4	228572	Taylor, Tunnicliffe & Co.	Hanley
2	5	228573	Liddle, Elliot & Son	Longport
0	5	228764	idem	Longport
8	13	228937	J. & T. Bevington	Hanley
4	1	229319	Adams, Scrivener & Co.	Longton
4	16	229405	James Edwards & Son	Burslem
	1	229523	Worthington & Son	Hanley
5	4	229627	Thos. Booth	Hanley
	8	229642–4	Davenport & Co.	Longport
8	6	229837	McBirney & Armstrong	Belleek
8	7	229959	W. P. & G. Phillips & Pearce	London
0	5	230183–4	Wm. Brownfield	Cobridge
5	4	230429	James Edwards & Son	Burslem
5	9	230455	Minton & Co.	Stoke
8	9	230707–8	Josiah Wedgwood & Sons	Etruria
	3	230739	John Meir & Son	Tunstall
0	8	231101	James Wardle	Hanley
0	2	231124	Josiah Wedgwood & Sons	Etruria
	6	231153–4	George Ash	Hanley
8	6	231215	Minton & Co.	Stoke
4	4	231222	W. T. Copeland & Sons	Stoke

Date	Parcel No.	Patent No.	Factory, Retailer Wholesaler, etc	P
26	4	231241	Leveson Hill (Excrs of)	Stok
27	4	231256	J. T. Hudden	Lon
Aug 2	6	231504	W. T. Copeland	Stok
3	5	231602	John Edwards	Fen
4	4	231613	Tomkinson Bros. & Co.	Han
11	13	231812	W. P. & G. Phillips & Pearce	Lon
19	6	232307	W. T. Copeland & Sons	Stok
26	6	232474	idem	Stok
31	6	232586-7	John Pratt & Co.	Lan Delp
31	12	232598	W. T. Copeland & Sons	Stok
Sept 4	3	232822	Minton & Co.	Stok
8	5	232878	W. T. Copeland & Sons	Stok
8	6	232879	Pinder, Bourne & Co.	Burs
9	3	232890	John Pratt & Co.	Lan Delp
10	4	232903	Minton & Co.	Stok
21	7	233411	Gelson Bros.	Han
22	10	233527	W. & J. A. Bailey	Allo
30	8	233864-6	T. C. Brown-Westhead Moore & Co.	Han
Oct 1	3	233923-4	Minton & Co.	Stok
4	6	234016	idem	Stok
14	3	234465	McBirney & Armstrong	Bell
15	6	234486	Geo. Jones	Stok
23	4	235012	idem	Stok
26	2	235158	James Ellis & Son	Han
27	5	235168	McBirney & Armstrong	Bell
29	3	235399-400	Minton & Co.	Stok
29	4	235401-2	Powell & Bishop	Han
Nov 2	12	235589	Ed. Clarke	Tun
3	12	235691	T. C. Brown-Westhead, Moore & Co.	Han

Parcel No.	Patent No.	Factory, Retailer Wholesaler, etc	Place
1	235827–9	McBirney & Armstrong	Belleek
2	235830	T. C. Brown–Westhead, Moore & Co.	Hanley
11	235966	Tams & Lowe	Longton
3	235974	Wm. Brownfield	Cobridge
5	236184–5	McBirney & Armstrong	Belleek
8	236203–7	Liddle, Elliot & Son	Longport
5	236435	Alcock & Digory	Burslem
12	236478	The Worcester Royal Porcelain Co. (Ltd.)	Worcester
8	236533	Thos. Goode & Co.	London
9	236534	John Mortlock	London
1	236585	McBirney & Armstrong	Belleek
4	236628	Minton & Co.	Stoke
3	236653	idem	Stoke
3	236756	Geo. Jones	Stoke
9	236829	Wm. Brownfield	Cobridge
7	237224	Minton & Co.	Stoke
2	237229	Powell & Bishop	Hanley
3	237230	McBirney & Armstrong	Belleek
8	237358	George Ash	Hanley
7	237500	Geo. Jones	Stoke
1	237552	Gelson Bros.	Hanley
2	237565	John Pratt & Co.	Lane Delph
2	237644	Minton & Co.	Stoke
5	237691	T. C. Brown–Westhead, Moore & Co.	Hanley
4	237742	Geo. Jones	Stoke
9	237899	Pellatt & Co.	London
12	238147–8	Liddle, Elliot & Son	Longport
8	238388	Chas. Hobson	Burslem
3	238436	Minton & Co.	Stoke

APPENDIX B

Date		Parcel No.	Patent No.	Factory, Retailer Wholesaler, etc	Pl
Feb	1	6	238527–8	T. C. Brown–Westhead, Moore & Co.	Han
	3	13	238595–6	idem	Han
	4	7	238603	Powell & Bishop	Han
	7	5	238627	Wiltshaw, Wood & Co.	Burs
	7	6	238628	W. & J. A. Bailey	Allo
	9	2	238663	Josiah Wedgwood & Sons	Etru
	10	8	238688	Minton & Co.	Stok
	11	12	238761–2	W. P. & G. Phillips & Pearce	Lon
	15	6	238898–9	T. C. Brown–Westhead Moore & Co.	Han
	25	2	239139	Minton & Co.	Stok
	28	6	239239	idem	Stok
Mar	2	4	239304	idem	Stok
	7	6	239422	Chas. Hobson	Burs
	8	1	239424–6	Geo. Jones	Stok
	10	1	239474	idem	Stok
	10	9	239510	Powell & Bishop	Han
	11	8	239528	Leveson Hill (Excrs of)	Stok
	14	4	239548	T. C. Brown–Westhead, Moore & Co.	Han
	15	6	239585	Thos. Till & Sons	Burs
	16	2	239590–1	Minton & Co.	Stok
	17	4	239610–1	McBirney & Armstrong	Belle
	17	7	239622	The Worcester Royal Porcelain Co. (Ltd.)	Wor
	17	9	239628	J. Mortlock	Lon
	18	6	239642	Minton & Co.	Stok
	23	9	239793–4	J. Blackshaw & Co.	Stok
	25	4	239968	Hope & Carter	Burs
	25	5	239969–70	Minton & Co.	Stok
	26	1	240000–1	idem	Stok
	26	2	240002	Worthington & Son	Han

APPENDIX B

Date	Parcel No.	Patent No.	Factory, Retailer Wholesaler, etc	Place
28	9	240079	The Old Hall Earthenware Co. Ltd.	Hanley
r 7	9	240383	Cork, Edge & Malkin	Burslem
7	10	240384–5	Baker & Co.	Fenton
7	11	240386	Harvey Adams & Co.	Longton
9	1	240458	Minton & Co.	Stoke
11	3	240493	The Worcester Royal Porcelain Co. Ltd.	Worcester
13	4	240516	Thos. Goode & Co.	London
14	7	240570	Minton & Co.	Stoke
y 5	1	241231	James Oldham & Co.	Hanley
6	5	241264–5	McBirney & Armstrong	Belleek
10	4	241367–8	George Ash	Hanley
13	8	241474	T. C. Brown–Westhead, Moore & Co.	Hanley
17	7	241544	idem	Hanley
18	6	241567–8	Bates, Elliott & Co.	Longport
21	6	241649	The Old Hall Earthenware Co. Ltd.	Hanley
21	12	241666	James Edwards & Son	Burslem
25	7	241754	idem	Burslem
26	5	241960	Minton & Co.	Stoke
30	15	242077	Geo. Jones	Stoke
ne 3	8	242154	F. & R. Pratt & Co.	Fenton
7	15	242233	Hope & Carter	Burslem
7	16	242234	Thos. Booth	Hanley
9	3	242391	T. C. Brown–Westhead, Moore & Co.	Hanley
10	1	242392–4	Wm. Brownfield	Cobridge
11	3	242439	James Edwards & Son	Burslem
17	7	242503–8	Minton, Hollins & Co.	Stoke
22	1	242634–5	Harvey Adams & Co.	Longton
22	3	242637–8	Minton, Hollins & Co.	Stoke
22	4	242639	The Worcester Royal Porcelain Co. Ltd.	Worcester

329

APPENDIX B

Date	Parcel No.	Patent No.	Factory, Retailer Wholesaler, etc	Place
27	1	242715	Geo. Jones	Stoke
July 5	5	242859	Baker & Co.	Fenton
8	7	243049–50	James Wardle	Hanley
13	8	243176	James Edwards & Son	Burslem
14	9	243197–9	Minton, Hollins & Co.	Stoke
14	10	243200	The Worcester Royal Porcelain Co. Ltd.	Worceste
15	1	243207	W. T. Copeland & Sons	Stoke
16	2	243235	James Wardle	Hanley
19	6	243352	F. & R. Pratt & Co.	Fenton
20	5	243368	Thos. Booth	Hanley
21	1	243378	idem	Hanley
22	1	243385	Cork, Edge & Malkin	Burslem
27	1	243480	Beech, Unwin & Co.	Longton
Aug 1	2	243555	R. G. Scrivener & Co.	Hanley
4	4	243646	James Wardle	Hanley
4	5	243647–8	J. Broadhurst	Longton
9	2	243807	Wm. Brownfield	Cobridge
22	4	244137–8	T. & R. Boote	Burslem
23	6	244173	Geo. Jones	Stoke
25	5	244223	T. & R. Boote	Burslem
Sept 7	7	244703	Bailey & Cooke	Hanley
10	9	244741	Minton & Co.	Stoke
16	5	244961	idem	Stoke
19	2	244976	Wm. Brownfield	Cobridge
27	4	245227	Elsmore, Forster & Co.	Tunstall
27	6	245229	W. P. & G. Phillips & D. Pearce	London
28	11	245265	Gelson Bros.	Hanley
Oct 4	7	245463	Joseph Holdcroft	Longtor
4	8	245464	Minton & Co.	Stoke
6	4	245604	idem	Stoke
6	5	245605	James Broadhurst	Longtor
7	3	245620	Minton & Co.	Stoke
8	9	245668	Powell & Bishop	Hanley

APPENDIX B

Date	Parcel No.	Patent No.	Factory, Retailer Wholesaler, etc	Place
19	2	245985–6	Geo. Jones	Stoke
22	2	246149	Wm. Brownfield	Cobridge
25	6	246181	T. C. Brown–Westhead, Moore & Co.	Hanley
v 4	9	246927	idem	Hanley
9	8	247047	John Meir & Son	Tunstall
9	9	247048	Pellatt & Co.	London
10	5	247071–3	Minton & Co.	Stoke
10	10	247079–80	Wm. Brownfield	Cobridge
12	3	247248	McBirney & Armstrong	Belleek
12	8	247255	Minton, Hollins & Co.	Stoke
22	3	247944	Geo. Jones	Stoke
24	3	248041	Minton & Co.	Stoke
24	8	248049	Bates, Elliott & Co.	Longport
25	1	248051	Minton & Co.	Stoke
25	2	248052	Turner, Goddard & Co.	Tunstall
26	9	248114–6	T. & R. Boote	Burslem
: 1	7	248242	Wm. Brownfield	Cobridge
2	11	248294	T. C. Brown–Westhead, Moore & Co.	Hanley
5	4	248309–15	Minton, Hollins & Co.	Stoke
16	5	248869	Bates, Elliott & Co.	Longport
17	11	248899	idem	Longport
19	9	248953	Harvey, Adams & Co.	Longton
27	4	249104	James Edwards & Son	Burslem
2	2	249235	Gelson Bros.	Hanley
6	3	249331	Minton & Co.	Stoke
7	8	249356	Bates, Elliott & Co.	Longport
9	4	249388–93	McBirney & Armstrong	Belleek
10	7	249439	Geo. Jones	Stoke
11	4	249464	J. Mortlock	London
12	7	249479	McBirney & Armstrong	Belleek
12	12	249490	Soane & Smith	London

APPENDIX B

Date	Parcel No.	Patent No.	Factory, Retailer Wholesaler, etc	Place
24	4	249811	idem	London
26	8	249903–6	Minton, Hollins & Co.	Stoke
27	9	249927	The Worcester Royal Porcelain Co. Ltd.	Worces
30	2	249972	Gelson Bros.	Hanley
Feb 2	3	250020	James Edwards & Son	Burslem
6	5	250168–71	McBirney & Armstrong	Belleek
8	9	250231	James Macintyre & Co.	Burslem
11	9	250291	T. C. Brown–Westhead, Moore & Co.	Hanley
13	6	250366	Edge, Malkin & Co.	Burslem
13	7	250367	Worthington & Son	Hanley
13	9	250369	Powell & Bishop	Hanley
13	10	250370	Ed. F. Bodley & Co.	Burslem
15	7	250416–8	Powell & Bishop	Hanley
17	7	250440–1	Thos. Peake	Tunstall
20	2	250478–9	Elsmore & Forster	Tunstall
28	8	250657	The Watcombe Terra Cotta Clay Co. Ltd.	Devon
Mar 9	4	250865	J. & T. Bevington	Hanley
14	4	250954	John Pratt & Co.	Lane Delph
15	10	251013	Bates, Elliott & Co.	Longpc
27	1	251246	Wm. Brownfield & Son	Cobrid
29	1	251329	Thos. Furnival & Son	Cobrid
Apr 4	4	251453	McBirney & Armstrong	Belleek
22	4	251966	John Pratt & Co.	Stoke
24	4	251988	Josiah Wedgwood & Sons	Etruria
26	12	252068	Minton, Hollins & Co.	Stoke
27	7	252093–4	Wood & Clarke	Burslem
27	8	252095–7	W. P. & G. Phillips & Pearce	London
28	1	252128	Wood & Clarke	Burslem
29	6	252156	idem	Burslem
29	7	252157	James Edwards & Son	Burslem

332

APPENDIX B

Date	Parcel No.	Patent No.	Factory, Retailer Wholesaler, etc	Place
y 1	9	252171–3	T. C. Brown–Westhead, Moore & Co.	Hanley
2	3	252176	Ambrose Bevington	Hanley
2	4	252177–80	Wm. Brownfield & Son	Cobridge
3	4	252188	John Jackson & Co.	Rother'm
6	1	252258	W. P. & G. Phillips & Pearce	London
9	9	252387	Liddle, Elliott & Co.	Longport
11	13	252487	Powell & Bishop	Hanley
13	6	252503	Elsmore & Forster	Tunstall
22	9	252709	McBirney & Armstrong	Belleek
24	10	252756	John Meir & Son	Tunstall
e 2	4	253017	T. C. Brown–Westhead, Moore & Co.	Hanley
7	7	253069	Grove & Stark	Longton
16	9	253335	John Twigg	Rother'm
17	3	253339–40	Minton & Co.	Stoke
19	9	253378–9	Pinder, Bourne & Co.	Burslem
22	1	253472	Thos. Till & Sons	Burslem
23	9	253571	Bates, Elliott & Co.	Longport
4	8	253796–8	W. T. Copeland	Stoke
14	6	254013	Taylor, Tunnicliffe & Co.	Hanley
15	2	254030	Thos. Booth	Hanley
19	2	254074	Ambrose Bevington	Hanley
22	8	254130–3	Haviland & Co.	London and Limoges
25	12	254239	Bates, Elliott & Co.	Longport
29	6	254344	Hope & Carter	Burslem
2	3	254429	Robinson & Leadbeater	Stoke
9	7	254757	Bates, Elliott & Co.	Longport
18	10	254899	Pratt & Co.	Fenton
28	5	255267	James Wardle	Hanley
29	2	255274	Geo. Jones	Stoke
30	4	255320	Thos. Barlow	Longton

Date	Parcel No.	Patent No.	Factory, Retailer Wholesaler, etc	Place
31	9	255333	J. H. & J. Davis	Hanley
Sept 15	7	255821	J. Bevington & Co.	Hanley
15	10	255825	Thos. Barlow	Longton
19	2	255849	Minton & Co.	Stoke
25	8	256079	T. C. Brown–Westhead, Moore & Co.	Hanley
28	5	256215	Thos. Booth & Co.	Tunstall
Oct 4	7	256357–60	Minton & Co.	Stoke
4	9	256362	Pinder, Bourne & Co.	Burslem
6	6	256427–9	Moore & Son	Longton
9	8	256538	E. J. Ridgway & Son	Hanley
10	3	256582	J. T. Hudden	Longton
10	6	256586	T. C. Brown–Westhead, Moore & Co.	Hanley
11	4	256598	McBirney & Armstrong	Belleek
14	6	256687	Thos. Booth & Co.	Tunstall
14	7	256688	Josiah Wedgwood & Sons	Etruria
14	8	256689	McBirney & Armstrong	Belleek
18	4	256853	Moore & Son	Longton
19	6	256907	W. T. Copeland & Sons	Stoke
24	3	257126	Robert Cooke	Hanley
31	5	257258	Minton & Co.	Stoke
31	6	257259	Edge, Hill & Palmer	Longton
Nov 3	4	257364–5	R. G. Scrivener & Co.	Hanley
3	5	257366	J. F. Wileman	Fenton
15	4	257728	John Thomson & Sons	Glasgow
23	6	257944–6	Thos. Ford	Hanley
Dec 1	6	258095	Geo. Jones	Stoke
15	5	258773	Robinson & Leadbeater	Stoke
16	7	258816	McBirney & Armstrong	Belleek
22	6	258949	F. & R. Pratt	Fenton
23	3	258956–7	Geo. Jones	Stoke
29	10	259053	T. C. Brown–Westhead, Moore & Co.	Hanley

APPENDIX B

Date	Parcel No.	Patent No.	Factory, Retailer Wholesaler, etc	Place
1	5	259076	Moore & Son	Longton
1	6	259077	Edge Malkin & Co.	Burslem
5	3	259264	McBirney & Armstrong	Belleek
6	1	259271	Minton & Co.	Stoke
18	6	259801	The Worcester Royal Porcelain Co. Ltd.	Worcester
20	6	259854	Geo. Jones	Stoke
30	7	260081	W. T. Copeland & Sons	Stoke
2	2	260187	Moore & Son	Longton
2	11	260240–1	Turner & Tomkinson	Tunstall
3	4	260255–6	Geo. Jones	Stoke
7	3	260297	Ambrose Bevington	Hanley
15	3	260463	Powell & Bishop	Hanley
16	6	260503	McBirney & Armstrong	Belleek
16	7	260504–6	Geo. Jones	Stoke
19	6	260565	Wm. H. Goss	Stoke
20	4	260578	The Worcester Royal Porcelain Co. Ltd.	Worcester
22	3	260640	Minton & Co.	Stoke
4	3	260868	Geo. Jones	Stoke
4	4	260869–70	Minton & Co.	Stoke
4	6	260872	Minton, Hollins & Co.	Stoke
7	7	260992–3	Harvey, Adams & Co.	Longton
7	10	260998	Bates, Elliott & Co.	Burslem
8	5	261006–8	Minton, Hollins & Co.	Stoke
9	1	261016	McBirney & Armstrong	Belleek
13	8	261120	Minton, Hollins & Co.	Stoke
16	6	261190	Minton & Co.	Stoke
18	6	261207	idem	Stoke
20	10	261325	The Worcester Royal Porcelain Co. Ltd.	Worcester
21	14	261379	R. M. Taylor	Fenton
22	5	261391	J. Holdcroft	Longton

Date	Parcel No.	Patent No.	Factory, Retailer Wholesaler, etc	Place
22	8	261394	T. C. Brown–Westhead, Moore & Co.	Hanley
26	3	261453–4	Robinson & Leadbeater	Stoke
26	6	261458	Phillips & Pearce	London
Apr 5	4	261638	Wedgwood & Co.	Tunstall
5	5	261639	Minton & Co.	Stoke
6	1	261646–7	J. Holdcroft	Longton
9	6	261724	T. C. Brown–Westhead, Moore & Co.	Hanley
10	11	261749	Thos. Furnival & Son	Cobridge
17	13	261976	E. J. Ridgway & Son	Hanley
19	5	262013	Minton, Hollins & Co.	Stoke
24	5	262203	John Pratt & Co. Ltd.	Lane Delph
27	9	262354	Moore & Son	Longton
May 2	9	262425–6	Harvey Adams & Co.	Longton
2	11	262428–9	Thos. Furnival & Son	Cobridge
3	9	262471–2	Minton & Co.	Stoke
3	11	262474	Bates, Elliott & Co.	Burslem
6	3	262483–5	Moore & Son	Longton
6	8	262493	Bates, Elliott & Co.	Burslem
6	9	262494–5	Minton, Hollins & Co.	Stoke
10	1	262651	Moore & Son	Longton
11	4	262672	Thos. Booth & Sons	Hanley
27	1	262951	Geo. Jones	Stoke
27	3	262953	Minton, Hollins & Co.	Stoke
29	2	262990	Geo. Jones	Stoke
29	5	262993–4	Geo. Grainger & Co.	Worces
30	1	262999–3000	Minton & Co.	Stoke
June 3	6	263106	The Watcombe Terra Cotta Clay Co. Ltd.	Devon
5	3	263134	Hope & Carter	Burslem
6	6	263162	Wm. Brownfield & Son	Cobridge
7	4	263191	Minton, Hollins & Co.	Stoke

APPENDIX B

ate	Parcel No.	Patent No.	Factory, Retailer Wholesaler, etc	Place
11	5	263315	Josiah Wedgwood & Sons	Etruria
11	12	263348	W. T. Copeland & Sons	Stoke
18	3	263496–7	Geo. L. Ashworth & Bros.	Hanley
18	4	263498–9	Minton, Hollins & Co.	Stoke
21	7	263541–2	idem	Stoke
22	5	263561	Minton & Co.	Stoke
22	8	263565	Wm. Brownfield & Son	Cobridge
27	1	263771	T. C. Brown–Westhead, Moore & Co.	Hanley
2	2	263883–4	Robinson & Leadbeater	Stoke
2	3	263885	Josiah Wedgwood & Sons	Etruria
13	5	264081	Gelson Bros.	Hanley
15	4	264194	Robinson & Leadbeater	Stoke
16	5	264206–7	Minton, Hollins & Co.	Stoke
19	5	264299–303	R. M. Taylor	Fenton
20	3	264306–7	Geo. Jones	Stoke
24	2	264490	W. & T. Adams	Tunstall
29	7	264613	J. Dimmock & Co.	Hanley
31	3	264636–7	Minton & Co.	Stoke
2	1	264685–6	E. J. Ridgway & Son	Stoke
14	4	265105	T. Booth & Co.	Tunstall
16	1	265167–8	Wm. Brownfield & Sons	Cobridge
19	4	265254	W. E. Cartlidge	Hanley
19	5	265255	W. & J. A. Bailey	Alloa
2	3	265666	McBirney & Armstrong	Belleek
2	8	265687	Bates, Elliott & Co.	Burslem
12	6	265969	Minton, Hollins & Co.	Stoke
25	9	266628–31	Minton, Hollins & Co.	Stoke
26	2	266633	F. Jones	Longton
26	5	266636	W. E. Cartlidge	Hanley
7	7	266959	T. C. Brown–Westhead, Moore & Co.	Hanley
11	5	267060–4	Josiah Wedgwood & Sons	Etruria
12	10	267103–4	Bates, Elliott & Co.	Burslem

Date	Parcel No.	Patent No.	Factory, Retailer Wholesaler, etc	Plac
14	4	267112	Minton, Hollins & Co.	Stoke
17	8	267265	Josiah Wedgwood & Sons	Etruria
18	5	267317–9	Geo. Jones	Stoke
30	2	267523	J. F. Wileman	Fento
30	5	267527	The Brownhills Pottery	Tunsta
30	9	267534	Maw & Co.	Brosel
Nov 2	6	267588–91	The Worcester Royal Porcelain Co. Ltd.	Worce
4	3	267618	Geo. Grainger & Co.	Worce
11	2	267806	W. E. Cartlidge	Hanley
12	4	267839	Minton & Co.	Stoke
14	13	267893–5	Wm. Brownfield & Son	Cobri
14	14	267896	Moore Bros.	Longt
18	3	267972	Holland & Green	Longt
30	8	268309	Belfield & Co.	Presto pan
Dec 2	5	268322	T. C. Brown–Westhead, Moore & Co.	Hanle
4	3	268388	John Pratt & Co. Ltd.	Lane Delph
10	2	268724–5	Minton & Co.	Stoke
11	8	268748–9	The Old Hall Earthenware Co. Ltd.	Hanle
14	5	268806–7	Wm. Brownfield & Son	Cobri
24	1	269197	Cockson & Chetwynd	Cobri
27	4	269269	John Adams (Excrs of)	Longt
27	5	269270	R. G. Scrivener & Co.	Hanle
27	8	269275	John Meir & Son	Tunst
1873				
Jan 10	1	269585	Geo. Jones	Stoke
13	4	269621	W. T. Copeland & Sons	Stoke
14	8	269686	J. Defries	Lond
15	2	269690	Worthington & Son	Hanle

APPENDIX B

e	Parcel No.	Patent No.	Factory, Retailer Wholesaler, etc	Place
9	1	269993–70001	Minton, Hollins & Co.	Stoke
9	2	270002–4	Moore Bros.	Longton
1	1	270042–50	Minton, Hollins & Co.	Stoke
0	2	270298	W. & J. A. Bailey	Alloa
2	4	270354	Bates, Elliott & Co.	Burslem
5	1	270385	Minton & Co.	Stoke
9	14	270600–1	J. & T. Bevington	Hanley
5	6	270700	Geo. Jones	Stoke
7	4	270751	Thos. Till & Sons	Burslem
7	8	270755	Minton, Hollins & Co.	Stoke
6	1	271031–2	Minton & Co.	Stoke
6	9	271057	The Brownhills Pottery Co.	Tunstall
6	6	271561–2	Geo. Jones	Stoke
3	6	271851	Minton & Co.	Stoke
5	4	272091	Taylor, Tunnicliffe & Co.	Hanley
9	2	272206	Minton & Co.	Stoke
3	6	272293	Gelson Bros.	Hanley
8	5	272364–5	Powell & Bishop	Hanley
9	3	272384–5	Geo. Jones	Stoke
3	2	272637	Thos. Till & Sons	Burslem
3	7	272642–6	Wm. Brownfield & Son	Cobridge
3	8	272647–8	Minton & Co.	Stoke
6	2	272662	idem	Stoke
2	8	272835	T. C. Brown–Westhead, Moore & Co.	Hanley
4	7	272896–7	Moore Bros.	Longton
5	6	272983	Minton, Hollins & Co.	Stoke
7	4	272988–90	John L. Johnson & Co.	Longton
2	5	273089	Worthington & Son	Hanley
5	7	273158–9	Moore Bros.	Longton
5	8	273160	Soane & Smith	London
9	4	273246	Worthington & Son	Hanley
9	8	273251	Thos. Ford	Hanley

APPENDIX B

Date	Parcel No.	Patent No.	Factory, Retailer Wholesaler, etc	Pl...
30	15	273376	T. C. Brown–Westhead, Moore & Co.	Hanl
June 11	4	273662–3	Bates, Elliott & Co.	Burs
17	3	273736–7	Taylor, Tunnicliffe & Co.	Hanl
19	3	273804	Pinder & Bourne & Co.	Burs
28	4	274047	Thos. Goode & Co.	Lond
30	3	274054–5	Minton, Hollins & Co.	Stoke
July 3	9	274162	Minton, Hollins & Co.	Stoke
4	7	274183	T. C. Brown–Westhead, Moore & Co.	Hanl
28	2	274663	Chas. Hobson	Burs
28	8	274701	John Meir & Sons	Tuns
29	3	274704	McBirney & Armstrong	Belle
31	1	274725–6	Mintons	Stoke
Aug 5	2	274804	Baker & Chetwynd	Burs
14	10	275050	T. C. Brown–Westhead, Moore & Co.	Hanl
25	1	275514–5	Geo. Jones	Stoke
27	1	275600	The Worcester Royal Porcelain Co. Ltd.	Wor
30	2	275661	T. C. Brown–Westhead, Moore & Co.	Han
Sept 2	8	275755	Edge, Malkin & Co.	Burs
4	3	275816	Mintons	Stok
10	7	275994	Powell & Bishop	Han
15	3	276151	T. C. Brown–Westhead, Moore & Co.	Han
16	4	276159	idem	Han
17	8	276213	The Worcester Royal Porcelain Co. Ltd.	Wor
19	4	276338	T. C. Brown–Westhead, Moore & Co.	Han
25	8	276517	Harvey, Adams & Co.	Lon
25	10	276522	Jane Beech	Burs
29	2	276566	Wm. Brownfield & Son	Cob

APPENDIX B

Parcel No.	Patent No.	Factory, Retailer Wholesaler, etc	Place
3	276796–8	Moore Bros.	Longton
4	276799	Heath & Blackhurst	Burslem
6	276816–7	T. C. Brown-Westhead, Moore & Co.	Hanley
6	277136	Mintons	Stoke
3	277148–9	Geo. Jones	Stoke
6	277385	Mintons	Stoke
3	277844	Hope & Carter	Burslem
4	277845–7	Geo. Jones	Stoke
6	277969	Wedgwood & Co.	Tunstall
7	278169	T. C. Brown-Westhead, Moore & Co.	Hanley
3	278185	Worthington & Son	Hanley
6	278769–70	Taylor, Tunnicliffe & Co.	Hanley
6	278821	The Old Hall Earthenware Co. Ltd.	Hanley
1	278822	Harvey, Adams & Co.	Longton
8	278867	Wm. Brownfield & Son	Cobridge
12	279180	Geo. Jones & Sons	Stoke
7	279437	idem	Stoke
3	279476–7	Bates, Elliott & Co.	Burslem
15	279655–6	Davenports & Co.	London (and Longport)
3	279938	Powell & Bishop	Hanley
7	279964	W. T. Copeland & Sons	Stoke
5	280010	John Meir & Son	Tunstall
4	280153–6	Haviland & Co.	Limoges and London
4	280343	The Worcester Royal Porcelain Co. Ltd.	Worcester
5	280344	Bodley & Co.	Burslem

341

Date	Parcel No.	Patent No.	Factory, Retailer Wholesaler, etc	F
11	2	280350	Thos. Booth & Sons	Ha
14	9	280492	Worthington & Son	Har
19	1	280609	Geo. Jones & Sons	Sto
25	6	280785	Robinson & Leadbeater	Sto
25	7	280786	Geo. Jones & Sons	Sto
26	7	280802–4	Minton, Hollins & Co.	Sto
Mar 2	1	280853	McBirney & Armstrong	Bel
3	4	280907	Geo. Jones & Sons	Sto
4	3	280919	Mintons	Sto
4	8	280925	The Worcester Royal Porcelian Co. Ltd.	Wo
13	6	281106	J. Dimmock & Co.	Har
14	2	281129	Mintons	Sto
17	5	281190	Powell & Bishop	Ha
21	5	281301	idem	Ha
24	4	281319	Mintons	Sto
27	2	281404	Worthington & Son	Har
28	3	281429–30	Geo. Jones & Sons	Sto
30	1	281437	Worthington & Son	Ha
Apr 7	4	281639	The Worcester Royal Porcelain Co. Ltd.	Wo
14	4	281776	A. Bevington	Ha
15	7	281822	Mintons	Sto
20	7	281871–80	Minton, Hollins & Co.	Sto
21	8	281899	Geo. Jones & Sons	Sto
22	1	281902	Wm. Brownfield & Son	Co
23	8	281954	T. C. Brown–Westhead, Moore & Co.	Ha
25	2	281984	Geo. Jones & Sons	Sto
29	7	282088	Ridgway, Sparks & Ridgway	Ha
29	9	282091	T. Furnival & Son	Co
30	2	282098	Thos. Booth & Sons	Ha
May 5	3	282134	Bates, Elliott & Co.	Bu
9	3	282218–9	Geo. Jones & Sons	Sto

e Parcel No.	Patent No.	Factory, Retailer Wholesaler, etc	Place
1 2	282249–51	Moore Bros.	Longton
1 3	282252	J. Thomson & Sons	Glasgow
1 4	282253	Holland & Green	Longton
0 11	282497	Bates, Elliott & Co.	Burslem
1 5	282526	Mintons	Stoke
2 8	282555	idem	Stoke
3 4	282567–8	Geo. Jones & Sons	Stoke
1 7	282662	The Worcester Royal Porcelain Co. Ltd.	Worcester
6 2	282799–802	Wm. Brownfield & Son	Cobridge
6 5	282806	Chas. Ford	Hanley
6 6	282982	Cockson & Chetwynd	Cobridge
7 7	283041	Edge, Malkin & Co.	Burslem
8 1	283050	Mintons	Stoke
3 3	283201	Williamson & Son	Longton
3 7	283208	The Worcester Royal Porcelain Co. Ltd.	Worcester
5 5	283266–8	Thos. Ford	Hanley
6 4	283275	Pinder, Bourne & Co.	Burslem
0 2	283547	Mintons	Stoke
3 6	283570–1	T. C. Brown–Westhead, Moore & Co.	Hanley
7 1	283980	Hulse & Adderley	Longton
0 5	284053	Minton, Hollins & Co.	Stoke
1 8	284131–5	Mintons	Stoke
1 9	284136	Cockson & Chetwynd	Cobridge
6 7	284204	T. C. Brown–Westhead, Moore & Co.	Hanley
8 2	284254–5	Wm. Brownfield & Son	Cobridge
5 4	284417	Bates, Elliott & Co.	Burlsem
2 6	284562	J. T. Hudden	Longton
8 4	284699–700	Geo. Jones & Sons	Stoke
1 6	284779	T. J. & J. Emberton	Tunstall

APPENDIX B

Date		Parcel No.	Patent No.	Factory, Retailer Wholesaler, etc	P...
Sept	1	3	284791	Thos. Till & Sons	Burs...
	3	11	284883	Geo. Adler	Saxo... and Lon...
	3	12	284884–5	Cockson & Chetwynd	Cob...
	4	3	284897	Mintons	Stok...
	5	4	284916–7	The Worcester Royal Porcelain Co. Ltd.	Wor...
	5	7	284920	Furnival & Son	Cob...
	7	3	284936–7	Thos. Booth & Sons	Han...
	10	3	285013	Wm. Brownfield & Son	Cob...
	12	1	285181	Mintons	Stok...
	15	2	285281	Geo. Jones & Sons	Stok...
	16	7	285304	M. Bucholz	Lon...
	17	4	285322	R. Britton & Sons	Leed...
	30	4	285776	Wm. Brownfield & Son	Cob...
Oct	2	5	285826–8	Geo. Grainger & Co.	Wor...
	3	4	285841–4	Moore Bros.	Lon...
	6	3	286000	Mintons	Stok...
	6	4	286001	Grove & Stark	Lon...
	10	4	286134	Mintons	Stok...
	12	2	286171	Powell & Bishop	Han...
	17	8	286359–60	Bates, Elliott & Co.	Burs...
	21	8	286424	Geo. Jones & Sons	Stok...
	24	3	286504–5	Robinson & Leadbeater	Stok...
	27	1	286530	George Ash	Han...
	28	9	286563	Pinder, Bourne & Co.	Burs...
Nov	2	3	286715	James Edwards & Son	Burs...
	3	4	286720–2	W. & E. Corn	Burs...
	6	3	286759	Wm. Brownfield & Son	Cob...
	7	4	286774–80	Thos. Ford	Han...
	10	3	286794	Geo. Jones & Sons	Stok...
	12	3	286931	Mintons	Stok...
	12	12	286942	Bates, Elliott & Co.	Burs...
	20	12	287317	F. & R. Pratt & Co.	Fen...

344

APPENDIX B

Date	Parcel No.	Patent No.	Factory, Retailer Wholesaler, etc	Place
25	7	287438–9	Minton, Hollins & Co.	Stoke
ːc 1	5	287598	W. T. Copeland & Sons	Stoke
4	6	287638	Thos. Barlow	Longton
5	4	287676	Holmes & Plant	Burslem
7	8	287694–7	T. C. Brown–Westhead, Moore & Co.	Hanley
8	2	287699	Geo. Jones & Sons	Stoke
10	4	287731	Pinder, Bourne & Co.	Burslem
10	11	287752–6	The Worcester Royal Porcelain Co. Ltd.	Worcester
12	3	287776	Geo. Jones & Sons	Stoke
12	5	287785	Port Dundas Pottery Co.	Port Dundas
18	6	287982	Geo. Jones & Sons	Stoke
18	7	287983	Ambrose Bevington	Hanley
18	9	287985	Geo. Grainger & Co.	Worcester
18	11	287990–7	Minton, Hollins & Co.	Stoke
75				
ı 2	4	288241–2	T. C. Brown–Westhead, Moore & Co.	Hanley
6	3	288276–8	Minton, Hollins & Co.	Stoke
12	3	288366	The Worcester Royal Porcelain Co. Ltd.	Worcester
16	9	288502	The Brownhills Pottery Co.	Tunstall
18	8	288521	T. C. Brown–Westhead, Moore & Co.	Hanley
20	3	288552	Robinson & Leadbeater	Stoke
20	4	288553–6	Wm. Brownfield & Son	Cobridge
21	2	288682	Geo. Jones & Sons	Stoke
23	9	288755–8	T. C. Brown–Westhead, Moore & Co.	Hanley
28	5	288830	Mintons	Stoke
29	1	288861–2	Worthington & Son	Hanley
ɔ 3	7	288972	Chas. Ford	Hanley

Date	Parcel No.	Patent No.	Factory, Retailer Wholesaler, etc	Place
5	5	289076	T. & R. Boote	Burslem
6	2	289083	Moore Bros.	Longton
9	1	289172	Pinder, Bourne & Co.	Burslem
9	2	289173	Geo. Jones & Sons	Stoke
12	6	289280	J. Maddock & Sons	Burslem
15	2	289310	Moore Bros.	Longton
17	7	289334	Mintons	Stoke
23	5	289503	J. Maddock & Sons	Burslem
23	6	289504	Geo. Jones & Sons	Stoke
23	8	289507–8	George Ash	Hanley
24	3	289535	Stephen Clive	Tunstall
Mar 5	2	289769	Wm. Brownfield & Son	Cobridge
12	5	289874–6	Geo. Jones & Sons	Stoke
24	13	290153	Minton, Hollins & Co.	Stoke
24	14	290154–5	T. C. Brown–Westhead, Moore & Co.	Hanley
30	1	290186	Thos. Booth & Sons	Hanley
31	5	290209–10	Wm. Brownfield & Son	Cobridge
Apr 3	7	290259	J. Dimmock & Co.	Hanley
3	9	290261–2	E. F. Bodley & Son	Burslem
7	3	290352	Mintons	Stoke
9	6	290393–4	Wm. Brownfield & Son	Cobridge
10	7	290407–8	Powell & Bishop	Hanley
15	5	290500	R. Malkin	Fenton
17	1	290738	Pinder, Bourne & Co.	Burslem
20	1	290787	J. Dimmock & Co.	Hanley
20	2	290788	Mintons	Stoke
21	5	290812	Stephen Clive	Tunstall
22	3	290841–2	W. P. & G. Phillips	London
22	4	290843–6	Minton, Hollins & Co.	Stoke
May 3	8	290998	Soane & Smith	London
7	7	291109	Geo. Jones & Sons	Stoke
7	8	291110	Burgess & Leigh	Burslem
11	6	291229	Thos. Goode & Co.	London
20	1	291440	Bates, Elliott & Co.	Burslem

e Parcel No.	Patent No.	Factory, Retailer Wholesaler, etc	Place
0 3	291444	J. Dimmock & Co.	Hanley
2 1	291458	Holland & Green	Longton
6 6	291518–20	T. C. Brown–Westhead, Moore & Co.	Hanley
8 10	291556	Campbellfield Pottery Co.	Glasgow
8 12	291558	J. Mortlock	London
1 8	291568	Geo. Jones & Sons	Stoke
1 18	291611	Ridgway, Sparks & Ridgway	Hanley
2 9	291749–51	Minton, Hollins & Co.	Stoke
5 7	291870–1	W. P. & G. Phillips	London
7 3	291882	W. & T. Adams	Tunstall
8 4	291911	The Worcester Royal Porcelain Co. (Ltd.)	Worcester
10 6	292005	Wm. Brownfield & Son	Cobridge
12 5	292034	Chas. Stevenson	Greenock
12 6	292035	Maddock & Gater	Burslem
12 10	292042	Thos. Furnival & Son	Stoke
15 5	292080	Josiah Wedgwood & Sons	Etruria
19 6	292184	Thos. Till & Sons	Burslem
26 2	292367–70	Geo. Jones & Sons	Stoke
5 1	292542	Wm. Brownfield & Son	Cobridge
7 8	292579–80	Moore Bros.	Longton
8 5	292620	idem	Longton
20 4	292985	E. J. D. Bodley	Burslem
23 10	293035	T. C. Brown–Westhead, Moore & Co.	Hanley
27 5	293114	F. W. Grove & J. Stark	Longton
28 7	293129	Minton, Hollins & Co.	Stoke
19 7	293748	F. W. Grove & J. Stark	Longton
28 6	294038–9	W. P. & G. Phillips	London
2 3	294147	T. Elsmore & Son	Tunstall
13 2	294434–5	Geo. Jones & Sons	Stoke
14 9	294514	Minton, Hollins & Co.	Stoke
18 2	294571–2	Geo. Jones & Sons	Stoke

APPENDIX B

Date	Parcel No.	Patent No.	Factory, Retailer Wholesaler, etc	Plac
21	1	294595	R. Cochran & Co.	Glasgo
24	2	294657	H. Aynsley & Co.	Longto
25	3	294662	F. W. Grove & J. Stark	Longto
28	6	294768-9	T. C. Brown–Westhead, Moore & Co.	Hanley
30	4	294825-7	John Edwards	Fenton
Oct 2	6	294906	Josiah Wedgwood & Sons	Etruria
6	4	294936	R. Cooke	Hanley
11	4	295001	Powell & Bishop	Hanley
11	10	295014-5	The Brownhills Pottery Co.	Tunsta
16	8	295131	Burgess, Leigh & Co.	Bursler
28	3	295443	Minton, Hollins & Co.	Stoke
30	9	295473-4	W. P. & G. Phillips	Londo
Nov 5	3	295551-3	Geo. Jones & Sons	Stoke
8	4	295792-8	Minton, Hollins & Co.	Stoke
8	8	295803	W. T. Copeland & Sons	Stoke
12	1	295908	Geo. Jones & Sons	Stoke
12	2	295909	Burgess, Leigh & Co.	Bursler
13	8	295933	The Worcester Royal Porcelain Co. Ltd.	Worce
Dec 1	2	296475	Wm. Brownfield & Son	Cobrid
1	9	296508	Gelson Bros.	Hanley
3	4	296531	Geo. Jones & Sons	Stoke
6	8	296644	John Meir & Son	Tunsta
10	3	296770	Mintons	Stoke
11	5	296813	F. W. Grove & J. Stark	Longt
11	8	296818	Soane & Smith	Londo
13	8	296834-49	Minton, Hollins & Co.	Stoke
15	2	296939-40	Mintons China Works	Stoke
15	3	296941-5	Mintons	Stoke
24	4	297217-8	Chas. Ford	Hanle
24	6	297221	Bates, Walker & Co.	Bursle
29	5	297245	Edge, Malkin & Co.	Bursle
29	6	297246-7	T. C. Brown–Westhead, Moore & Co.	Hanle

ate	Parcel No.	Patent No.	Factory, Retailer Wholesaler, etc	Place
30	2	297250	Mintons	Stoke
30	8	297276	Mintons, Hollins & Co.	Stoke
4	4	297343	Mintons	Stoke
6	2	297471	Moore Bros.	Longton
11	7	297587	E. J. D. Bodley	Burslem
21	13	297791	Bale & Co.	Etruria
22	6	297809–11	Geo. Jones & Sons	Stoke
22	8	297813	Chas. Ford	Hanley
24	1	297817	Mintons	Stoke
24	4	297845	J. Friedrich	London
24	6	297863–4	Bates, Walker & Co.	Burslem
26	2	297977	Edge, Malkin & Co.	Burslem
26	3	297978	Powell & Bishop	Hanley
28	8	298018	James Edwards & Son	Burslem
29	3	298027–9	Wm. Brownfield & Son	Cobridge
1	2	298049	idem	Cobridge
2	7	298063	Josiah Wedgwood & Sons	Etruria
2	12	298069	Ridgway, Sparks & Ridgway	Hanley
3	5	298077	Powell & Bishop	Hanley
4	6	298103	Mintons	Stoke
4	12	298141–2	The Worcester Royal Porcelain Co. Ltd.	Worcester
8	9	298235	Bates, Walker & Co.	Burslem
19	5	298458	Geo. Jones & Sons	Stoke
21	4	298473	The Worcester Royal Porcelain Co. Ltd.	Worcester
22	3	298480–3	Minton, Hollins & Co.	Stoke
29	9	298693	J. Dimmock & Co.	Hanley
2	8	298821–4	T. Gelson & Co.	Hanley
2	11	298832	The Brownhills Pottery Co.	Tunstall
10	8	299076–8	Minton, Hollins & Co.	Stoke

APPENDIX B

Date	Parcel No.	Patent No.	Factory, Retailer Wholesaler, etc	Plac
14	5	299177	T. C. Brown–Westhead, Moore & Co.	Hanle
17	5	299236	Mintons	Stoke
18	3	299246	Robinson & Chapman	Longt
23	8	299366	E. J. D. Bodley	Bursle
24	7	299380	Bates, Walker & Co.	Bursle
28	8	299474	W. E. Withinshaw	Bursle
30	4	299497–9	Geo. Jones & Sons	Stoke
Apr 8	6	299773	Bates, Walker & Co.	Bursle
11	4	299819	Thos. Gelson & Co.	Hanle
12	4	299830	Powell & Bishop	Hanle
12	11	299852	J. Dimmock & Co.	Hanle
21	7	300020	Minton, Hollins & Co.	Stoke
21	10	300037–8	Furnival & Son	Cobri
22	5	300105	The Worcester Royal Porcelain Co. Ltd.	Worce
27	3	300260	Mintons	Stoke
May 8	7	300421–3	T. C. Brown–Westhead, Moore & Co.	Hanle
10	3	300463	Geo. Jones & Sons	Stoke
11	9	300491	F. & R. Pratt & Co.	Fento
16	7	300603–4	Mintons	Stoke
22	3	300682	Moore Bros.	Longt
22	4	300683–5	Josiah Wedgwood & Sons	Etruri
23	7	300734–7	Haviland & Co.	Limo, and Lond
24	3	300746	Mintons	Stoke
25	6	300779	Moore Bros.	Longt
29	8	300809–10	Geo. Jones & Sons	Stoke
June 3	2	301030	Mintons	Stoke
3	5	301035–7	E. J. D. Bodley	Bursl
7	1	301087	Thos. Gelson & Co.	Hanl
8	4	301099	Mintons	Stoke
9	6	301164	W. T. Copeland & Sons	Stoke

ate	Parcel No.	Patent No.	Factory, Retailer Wholesaler, etc	Place
15	1	301254	Henry Meir & Son	Tunstall
15	9	301267–9	Minton, Hollins & Co.	Stoke
19	2	301302	Josiah Wedgwood & Sons	Etruria
19	9	301310	J. Holdcroft	Longton
21	4	301330	Mintons	Stoke
22	4	301342	Thos. Gelson & Co.	Hanley
23	5	301402	Mintons	Stoke
26	6	301443–4	Minton, Hollins & Co.	Stoke
28	8	301543	J. Aynsley	Longton
1	3	301589–90	Mintons	Stoke
1	4	301591	John Tams	Longton
3	2	301596	Ford & Challinor	Tunstall
5	1	301619	Thos. Till & Sons	Burslem
5	7	301641	W. T. Copeland & Sons	Stoke
10	3	301877	Thos. Gelson & Co.	Hanley
12	2	301926	E. J. D. Bodley	Burslem
18	3	301984	Soane & Smith	London
26	3	302125	Geo. Jones & Sons	Stoke
28	10	302178	Thos. Gelson & Co.	Hanley
28	11	302179	Powell & Bishop	Hanley
31	8	302220	G. Grainger & Co.	Worcester
8	1	302384	Robinson & Chapman	Longton
25	8	302901	F. & R. Pratt & Co.	Fenton
5	5	303289–90	Bates & Walker & Co.	Burslem
6	9	303308	Pinder & Bourne & Co.	Burslem
6	10	303309	Wm. Brownfield & Sons	Cobridge
9	8	303455	Worthington & Son	Hanley
9	9	303456–7	T. C. Brown–Westhead, Moore & Co.	Hanley
11	1	303459	E. J. D. Bodley	Burslem
12	6	303522–3	Geo. Jones & Sons	Stoke
18	10	303677	G. L. Ashworth & Bros.	Hanley
20	3	303731–2	Hollinshead & Kirkham	Burslem
22	3	303757	Powell & Bishop	Hanley
26	5	303853	Hope & Carter	Burslem

APPENDIX B

Date		Parcel No.	Patent No.	Factory, Retailer Wholesaler, etc	Pla
	26	10	303918	T. C. Brown–Westhead, Moore & Co.	Hanle
	28	2	303926–7	Moore Bros.	Longt
	28	10	303942	Hope & Carter	Bursle
Oct	7	2	304128	Wm. Harrop	Hanle
	7	3	304129–31	Wm. Brownfield & Sons	Cobri
	7	4	304132–3	Josiah Wedgwood & Sons	Etruri
	7	6	304144–5	Wm. Adams	Tunst
	9	1	304149–50	Geo. Jones & Sons	Stoke
	12	8	304321	Ambrose Bevington	Hanle
	17	4	304376	T. C. Brown–Westhead, Moore & Co.	Hanle
	17	9	304383	Wardle & Co.	Hanle
	19	3	304428	Burgess, Leigh & Co.	Bursle
	20	2	304454–66	Mintons	Stoke
	21	3	304473	Edge, Malkin & Co.	Bursl
	23	2	304489	Mintons	Stoke
	31	2	304910–4	Wm. Brownfield & Sons	Cobri
Nov	1	2	304926	Moore Bros.	Longt
	7	3	305065	Robert Jones	Hanle
	8	3	305080	Geo. Jones & Sons	Stoke
	8	9	305090	Wm. Brownfield & Sons	Cobri
	9	10	305150	Belfield & Co.	Preste par
	11	9	305173	Moore Bros.	Long
	13	3	305181	Mintons	Stoke
	14	2	305189	Josiah Wedgwood & Sons	Etrur
	14	8	305195	Clementson Bros.	Hanle
	17	3	305222	Banks & Thorley	Hanle
	18	3	305233	Minton, Hollins & Co.	Stoke
	18	7	305264	Minton, Hollins & Co.	Stoke
	18	9	305266	The Worcester Royal Porcelain Co. Ltd.	Word
	23	5	305312	Wm. Adams	Tuns
	24	15	305461–2	Thos. Furnival & Sons	Cobr

352

APPENDIX B

te	Parcel No.	Patent No.	Factory, Retailer Wholesaler, etc	Place
28	2	305510	W. Hudson & Son	Longton
29	11	305568	Thos. Furnival & Sons	Cobridge
5	2	305684	Wedgwood & Co.	Tunstall
1	2	305829	John Tams	Longton
2	11	305885	The Campbell Brick & Tile Co.	Stoke
4	1	305934	Harvey Adams & Co.	Longton
4	11	305973	J. Dimmock & Co.	Hanley
8	9	306100	James Beech	Longton
20	7	306184	J. & T. Bevington	Hanley
21	2	306202	F. W. Grove & J. Stark	Longton
23	5	306282	Chas. Ford	Hanley
27	15	306341	The Campbell Brick & Tile Co.	Stoke
28	6	306367	Harvey Adams & Co.	Longton
4	10	306564	The Campbellfield Pottery Co.	Glasgow
7	5	306953	The Worcester Royal Porcelain Co. Ltd.	Worcester
20	2	307028	F. W. Grove & J. Stark	Longton
24	10	307213	Wm. Brownfield & Sons	Cobridge
25	6	307236	Wood & Co.	Burslem
25	7	307237-9	Geo. Jones & Sons	Stoke
26	3	307258	Mintons	Stoke
26	4	307259	Powell & Bishop	Hanley
1	6	307432	James Edwards & Son	Burslem
2	7	307495-7	The Worcester Royal Porcelain Co. Ltd.	Worcester
3	4	307506-7	Minton, Hollins & Co.	Stoke
5	2	307525-7	McBirney & Armstrong	Belleek
7	3	307551	Holland & Green	Longton
7	7	307570-2	Wm. Brownfield & Sons	Cobridge
9	7	307603	Robinson & Co.	Longton

APPENDIX B

Date	Parcel No.	Patent No.	Factory, Retailer Wholesaler, etc	Pl
9	11	307613	T. C. Brown–Westhead, Moore & Co.	Han
12	3	307646	James Beech	Lon;
14	16	307782	The Worcester Royal Porcelain Co. Ltd.	Wor
15	10	307794	Minton, Hollins & Co.	Stok
16	9	307866	John Rose & Co.	Coal
19	2	307877	Wm. Brownfield & Sons	Cob
20	8	307892	G. Grainger & Co.	Wor
21	6	307906	Mintons	Stok
21	9	307909	W. T. Copeland & Sons	Stok
24	3	307983	Thos. Hughes	Burs
27	2	308010	Mintons	Stok
Mar 1	4	308116–21	Hallam, Johnson & Co.	Lon
8	14	308329	W. T. Copeland & Sons	Stok
10	7	308357	Geo. Jones & Sons	Stok
14	9	308493	The Campbell Brick & Tile Co.	Stok
20	3	308650–2	Clementson Bros.	Han
20	8	308662	J. Dimmock & Co.	Han
22	14	308718	E. J. D. Bodley	Burs
24	1	308781–2	Powell & Bishop	Han
31	7	308916	E. F. Bodley & Co.	Burs
Apr 3	1	308918	Powell & Bishop	Han
4	5	308932	J. Mortlock	Lon
5	2	308934	Ford, Challinor & Co.	Tun
12	11	309233	J. Dimmock & Co.	Han
23	4	309617	John Tams	Lon
26	2	309680	J. & T. Bevington	Har
26	7	309696	The Worcester Royal Porcelain Co. Ltd.	Wo
27	10	309746	John Rose & Co.	Coa
May 2	2	309818–21	Geo. Jones & Sons	Stoi
4	13	309917	The Old Hall Earthenware Co. Ltd.	Har

354

APPENDIX B

Date	Parcel No.	Patent No.	Factory, Retailer Wholesaler, etc	Place
5	4	309922	Josiah Wedgwood & Sons	Etruria
12	7	310034	Thos. Furnival & Sons	Cobridge
16	5	310175	Wm. Brownfield & Sons	Cobridge
18	6	310267	Josiah Wedgwood & Sons	Etruria
22	5	310359–61	Wm. Brownfield & Sons	Cobridge
24	8	310448	T. C. Brown–Westhead, Moore & Co.	Hanley
30	13	310556	T. Furnival & Sons	Cobridge
e 1	2	310599	J. & R. Hammersley	Hanley
5	6	310670	E. J. D. Bodley	Burslem
7	1	310709	idem	Burslem
7	2	310710	Joseph Holdcroft	Longton
8	7	310761–4	Minton, Hollins & Co.	Stoke
9	3	310775–6	Baker & Co.	Fenton
13	2	310909	idem	Fenton
15	7	310972	Ridgway, Sparks & Ridgway	Hanley
19	4	311031	Ford & Challinor	Tunstall
19	6	311033	Murray & Co.	Glasgow
22	3	311141	Walker & Carter	Stoke
22	13	311181–6	Steele & Wood	Stoke
22	14	311187	E. F. Bodley & Co.	Burslem
26	11	311366	T. Furnival & Sons	Cobridge
28	9	311423	idem	Cobridge
29	10	311448–9	Sherwin & Cotton	Hanley
2	3	311523	W. T. Copeland & Sons	Stoke
6	2	311626	Mintons	Stoke
7	4	311684	Ridge, Meigh & Co.	Longton
9	2	311711	Minton, Hollins & Co.	Stoke
14	2	311883–4	John Tams	Longton
17	9	312019–21	James Edwards & Son	Burslem
20	7	312062–4	Haviland & Co.	London and Limoges
20	15	312113	Taylor, Tunnicliffe & Co.	Hanley

APPENDIX B

Date	Parcel No.	Patent No.	Factory, Retailer Wholesaler, etc	Plac
23	2	312125	John Edwards	Fento
25	5	312187	Ford, Challinor & Co.	Tunsta
26	6	312311–4	Minton, Hollins & Co.	Stoke
31	1	312421	McBirney & Armstrong	Bellee
31	2	312422	Minton & Hollins & Co.	Stoke
Aug 1	4	312434	Holmes, Stonier & Hollinshead	Hanle
3	14	312521	The Campbell Brick & Tile Co.	Stoke
13	5	312909	Haviland & Co.	Londc and Limog
15	7	313009	The Campbell Brick & Tile Co.	Stoke
17	11	313080	Ridgway, Sparks & Ridgway	Stoke
18	6	313099–101	Minton, Hollins & Co.	Stoke
18	7	313102	Furnival & Son	Cobri
23	6	313280	W. Hudson & Son	Longt
25	2	313324	Wm. Wood & Co.	Bursle
25	3	313325–9	Minton, Hollins & Co.	Stoke
28	9	313381	T. C. Brown–Westhead, Moore & Co.	Hanle
Sept 11	3	314046	G. W. Turner & Sons	Tunst
19	5	314292	Minton, Hollins & Co.	Stoke
20	3	314385	Josiah Wedgwood & Sons	Etruri
22	7	314470–1	Mintons	Stoke
22	13	314480	Minton, Hollins & Co.	Stoke
25	5	314548	Mintons	Stoke
28	9	314675	J. Holdcroft	Long
Oct 2	7	314890	Bates, Walker & Co.	Bursl
3	2	314896	Robinson & Leadbeater	Stoke
4	4	314906–7	J. & T. Bevington	Hanle
10	3	315102	John Edwards	Fento

356

APPENDIX B

Date	Parcel No.	Patent No.	Factory, Retailer Wholesaler, etc	Place
10	5	315104–5	Wm. Brownfield & Sons	Cobridge
15	2	315271–2	Geo. Jones & Sons	Stoke
16	6	315400–1	Powell & Bishop	Hanley
19	8	315473	Minton, Hollins & Co.	Stoke
19	13	315479	T. C. Brown–Westhead, Moore & Co.	Hanley
24	10	315565	F. W. Grove & J. Stark	Longton
24	14	315574	F. & R. Pratt & Co.	Fenton
30	7	315684	Wedgwood & Co.	Tunstall
31	6	315765	Geo. Jones & Sons	Stoke
5	4	315918	Powell & Bishop	Hanley
6	11	315954–6	Wm. Brownfield & Sons	Cobridge
7	1	316087–9	E. J. D. Bodley	Burslem
7	2	316090	Mintons	Stoke
7	10	316101	Pinder, Bourne & Co.	Burslem
9	8	316122	Taylor, Tunnicliffe & Co.	Hanley
15	12	316309	T. C. Brown–Westhead, Moore & Co.	Hanley
20	9	316502	James Edwards & Sons	Burslem
21	8	316526	Davenports & Co.	Longport
22	1	316542–3	The Old Hall Earthenware Co. Ltd.	Hanley
22	13	316560	B. & S. Hancock	Stoke
24	7	316605	J. Dimmock & Co.	Hanley
29	3	316723	J. Holdcroft	Longton
1	5	316763	J. Holdcroft	Longton
1	6	316764	Oakes, Clare & Chadwick	Burslem
5	2	316842	E. J. D. Bodley	Burslem
6	4	316863	Mintons	Stoke
7	14	316912	J. Unwin	Longton
14	1	317112	J. Dimmock & Co.	Hanley
15	10	317203	The Worcester Royal Porcelain Co. Ltd.	Worcester
21	6	317404	Mintons	Stoke

APPENDIX B

Date	Parcel No.	Patent No.	Factory, Retailer Wholesaler, etc	Pla
21	10	317410	T. Furnival & Sons	Cobri
22	5	317427–8	Wm. Brownfield & Sons	Cobri
29	6	317494	T. C. Brown–Westhead, Moore & Co.	Hanl

1878

Date	Parcel No.	Patent No.	Factory, Retailer Wholesaler, etc	Pla
Jan 3	4	317537–9	Minton, Hollins & Co.	Stoke
9	4	317692–4	The Brownhills Pottery Co.	Tuns
10	12	317733	J. Mortlock & Co.	Lond
14	1	317756	J. Maddock & Sons	Bursl
14	2	317757	Cotton & Rigby	Bursl
14	3	317758	Wm. Adams	Tuns
14	6	317763	Minton, Hollins & Co.	Stoke
15	5	317780	Josiah Wedgwood & Sons	Etrur
18	5	317826	Taylor, Tunnicliffe & Co.	Hanl
22	6	317940	J. Dimmock & Co.	Hanl
24	6	318041	W. T. Copeland & Sons	Stoke
25	9	318107–8	Wm. Brownfield & Sons	Cobr
28	11	318141	T. C. Brown–Westhead, Moore & Co.	Hanl
30	3	318158–9	Geo. Jones	Stoke
30	15	318189–90	The Brownhills Pottery Co.	Tuns
31	1	318210	B. & S. Hancock	Stoke
Feb 1	4	318239	Geo. Jones & Sons	Stoke
1	11	318265–6	Minton, Hollins & Co.	Stoke
1	16	318275–9	The Derby Crown Porcelain Co. Ltd.	Derb
5	5	318397	The Campbell Brick & Tile Co.	Stoke
9	6	318469	J. Dimmock & Co.	Hanl
11	5	318543–4	T. C. Brown–Westhead, Moore & Co.	Hanl
12	5	318556–63	Derby Crown Porcelain Co. Ltd.	Derb
20	6	318800	Minton, Hollins & Co.	Stoke

e	Parcel No.	Patent No.	Factory, Retailer Wholesaler, etc	Place
0	7	318801	The Worcester Royal Porcelain Co. Ltd.	Worcester
1	10	318821	W. E. Cartlidge	Burslem
2	8	318843	The Campbell Brick & Tile Co.	Stoke
8	3	319041	Dunn, Bennett & Co.	Hanley
5	2	319190	F. W. Grove & J. Stark	Longton
6	5	319201	Minton, Hollins & Co.	Stoke
7	4	319219	John Edwards	Fenton
9	1	319278-9	The Brownhills Pottery Co.	Tunstall
9	8	319293	Moore Bros.	Longton
9	11	319296	Powell & Bishop	Hanley
1	1	319310-1	Taylor, Tunnicliffe & Co.	Hanley
3	1	319370	Mintons	Stoke
3	7	319387	J. & T. Bevington	Hanley
3	10	319394	W. T. Copeland & Sons	Stoke
5	10	319507	John Rose & Co.	Coalport
3	8	319634-6	Derby Crown Porcelain Co. Ltd.	Derby
5	9	319679	F. J. Emery	Burslem
7	6	319725-6	G. W. Turner & Sons	Tunstall
7	15	319867-72	Minton, Hollins & Co.	Stoke
2	6	320030	Belfield & Co.	Preston-pans
0	4	320281	Mintons	Stoke
3	9	320373	McBirney & Armstrong	Belleek
7	4	320482	Mintons	Stoke
7	14	320568-9	Ridgway, Sparks & Ridgway	Stoke
0	2	320606	Thos. Furnival & Sons	Cobridge
0	6	320616	The Worcester Royal Porcelain Co. Ltd.	Worcester
4	2	320669	Wm. Brownfield & Sons	Cobridge
7	12	320793	McBirney & Armstrong	Belleek
0	7	320874-5	Josiah Wedgwood & Sons	Etruria

APPENDIX B

Date	Parcel No.	Patent No.	Factory, Retailer Wholesaler, etc	Plac
May 3	2	321028	Josiah Wedgwood & Sons	Etruri
3	9	321163	Robinson & Leadbeater	Stoke
8	9	321231–2	Bates & Bennett	Cobri
14	6	321361	Elsmore & Son	Tunsta
17	12	321575	J. Dimmock & Co.	Hanle
20	9	321632–4	Derby Crown Porcelain Co. Ltd.	Derby
21	11	321693	Banks & Thorley	Hanle
23	3	321704	Josiah Wedgwood & Sons	Etruri
23	4	321705	Moore Bros.	Longt
24	2	321726	Josiah Wedgwood & Sons	Etruri
27	20	322007	E. J. D. Bodley	Bursle
29	9	322039	Minton, Hollins & Co.	Stoke
June 1	5	322130	J. Mortlock & Co.	Londo
4	9	322168	F. Furnival & Sons	Cobri
5	14	322223–4	W. T. Copeland & Sons	Stoke
7	1	322309	Geo. Jones & Sons	Stoke
8	8	322390	Wm. Wood & Co.	Bursle
12	10	322471	Harvey Adams & Co.	Long
13	2	322476	John Tams	Longt
13	3	322477	McBirney & Armstrong	Bellee
19	7	322597–8	E. F. Bodley & Co.	Bursl
21	8	322662	Allen & Green	Fento
27	7	322931–2	Josiah Wedgwood & Sons	Etrur
29	1	322948	Wood, Son & Co.	Cobri
July 1	1	322971	Burgess & Leigh	Bursl
3	2	323132	Mintons	Stoke
6	7	323315–20	Joseph Cliff & Sons	Leed
8	6	323396	Josiah Wedgwood & Sons	Etrur
9	8	323434	Mintons	Stoke
9	9	323435	Josiah Wedgwood & Sons	Etrur
9	10	323436	J. Dimmock & Co.	Hanl
10	14	323508	Bates & Bennett	Cobr
11	1	323521	Soane & Smith	Lond
11	11	323596	W. & J. A. Bailey	Alloa

APPENDIX B

Date	Parcel No.	Patent No.	Factory, Retailer Wholesaler, etc	Place
12	4	323604	Josiah Wedgwood & Sons	Etruria
12	13	323626	Samuel Lear	Hanley
12	15	323628	T. C. Brown–Westhead, Moore & Co.	Hanley
15	1	323650–1	Pratt & Simpson	Fenton
17	9	323774–5	Wm. Adams	Tunstall
18	2	323778	Ambrose Bevington	Hanley
20	1	323847	J. Bevington	Hanley
20	6	323893	John Meir & Son	Tunstall
20	11	323910–1	E. J. D. Bodley	Burslem
26	3	324177	Josiah Wedgwood & Sons	Etruria
30	2	324324	idem	Etruria
30	6	324336	Powell, Bishop & Stonier	Hanley
30	12	324347	E. Clarke	Longport
31	8	324383	Mintons	Stoke
31	13	324388	James Edwards & Son	Burslem
6	3	324576	Moore Bros.	Longton
7	3	324730	Thos. Hughes	Burslem
9	10	324848	Derby Crown Porcelain Co. Ltd.	Derby
9	12	324870–2	Craven, Dunnill & Co. Ltd.	Jackfield
14	4	325029–34	S. H. Sharp	Leeds
16	9	325094	The Campbell Brick & Tile Co.	Stoke
23	1	325278	Moore Bros.	Longton
23	7	325319	J. Dimmock & Co.	Hanley
3	12	325612	G. & L. Wohlauer	Dresden
5	3	325716	Moore Bros.	Longton
9	5	325992–4	Wm. Brownfield & Sons	Cobridge
10	2	326006	Josiah Wedgwood & Sons	Etruria
12	6	326146	J. Bevington	Hanley
13	5	326155	G. L. Ashworth & Bros.	Hanley

APPENDIX B

Date	Parcel No.	Patent No.	Factory, Retailer Wholesaler, etc	P
13	16	326198	The Worcester Royal Porcelain Co. Ltd.	Wor
20	19	326482	R. Wotherspoon & Co.	Glas
24	3	326785	T. Bevington	Han
28	5	326970–1	Minton, Hollins & Co.	Stok
30	1	327000	Mintons	Stok
Oct 2	2	327035	Mintons	Stok
3	8	327110	J. T. Hudden	Lon,
4	8	327227	F. & R. Pratt & Co.	Fen
5	4	327235	Jones Bros. & Co.	W/h
5	13	327271	The Worcester Royal Porcelain Co. Ltd.	Wor
8	6	327359	Moore Bros.	Lon
8	7	327360	Bates, Gildea & Walker	Burs
9	9	327392	Josiah Wedgwood	Etru
11	8	327556	Minton, Hollins & Co.	Stok
14	8	327625–6	W. T. Copeland & Sons	Stok
23	1	328018	The Brownhills Pottery Co.	Tun:
23	11	328144–5	Pinder & Bourne & Co.	Burs
24	1	328146	T. Furnival & Sons	Cob
24	2	328147	J. Dimmock & Co.	Han
24	13	328274	The Worcester Royal Porcelain Co. Ltd.	Wor
26	4	328320	Wm. Brownfield & Sons	Cob
30	3	328436–7	Minton, Hollins & Co.	Stok
30	5	328439–40	Mintons	Stok
Nov 1	3	328620	J. Bevington	Han
4	1	328699	Edge, Malkin & Co.	Burs
5	11	328774	H. Burgess	Burs
5	17	328790–2	E. J. D. Bodley	Burs
6	3	328795	Samuel Lear	Han
13	13	329075	John Rose & Co.	Coa
15	1	329108	Craven, Dunnill & Co. Ltd.	Jack
15	11	329147	F. & R. Pratt & Co.	Fen
16	5	329157	J. Dimmock & Co.	Han

APPENDIX B

Parcel No.	Patent No.	Factory, Retailer Wholesaler, etc	Place
13	329378	Cliff & Tomlin	Leeds
2	329456	E. & C. Challinor	Fenton
14	329673	T. & R. Boote	Burslem
9	329709	J. McIntyre & Co.	Burslem
14	329782–3	W. & E. Corn	Burslem
7	329901	T. C. Brown–Westhead, Moore & Co.	Hanley
8	329902	J. F. Meakin	London
9	329922	J. McIntyre & Co.	Burslem
2	329939	Wm. Brownfield & Sons	Cobridge
3	330061	Mintons	Stoke
2	330097	A. Shaw	Burslem
8	330485	Thos. Hughes	Burslem
13	330677	T. & R. Boote	Burslem
4	330687	J. Gaskell, Son & Co.	Burslem
7	330920	W. T. Copeland & Sons	Stoke
11	330965–6	Minton, Hollins & Co.	Stoke
8	330997–8	Wm. Brownfield & Sons	Cobridge
5	331152	The New Wharf Pottery Co.	Burslem
6	331153	The Campbell Brick & Tile Co.	Stoke
3	331228	B. & S. Hancock	Stoke
13	331342	F. & R. Pratt & Co.	Fenton
15	331418–9	Derby Crown Porcelain Co. Ltd.	Derby
4	331458	Dunn, Bennett & Co.	Hanley
11	331597	W. T. Copeland & Sons	Stoke
2	331600	T. Furnival & Sons	Cobridge
3	331601	T. Bevington	Hanley
15	331677	E. J. D. Bodley	Burslem
13	331775	Clementson Bros.	Hanley
1	331777	Josiah Wedgwood & Sons	Etruria

363

APPENDIX B

Date	Parcel No.	Patent No.	Factory, Retailer Wholesaler, etc	Pl
5	7	331892–3	Mintons	Stok
8	1	332030	Mintons	Stok
14	4	332251	T. Furnival & Sons	Cob
15	2	332266	The Campbell Brick & Tile Co.	Stok
17	6	332296	McBirney & Armstrong	Belle
24	2	332606	W. P. Jervis	Stok
24	3	332607–9	W. & T. Adams	Tun:
25	4	332642	Mintons	Stok
28	1	332823	E. Chetwynd	Stok
28	7	332831	Clementson Bros.	Han
Mar 1	1	332837	T. Furnival & Sons	Cob
4	4	332938	F. W. Grove & J. Stark	Lon,
6	10	333047	Powell, Bishop & Stonier	Han
12	4	333210	Edge, Malkin & Co.	Burs
12	12	333235–6	W. T. Copeland & Sons	Stok
13	1	333241–4	Wm. Davenport & Co.	Lon,
13	14	333301	Clementson Bros.	Han
14	9	333319	E. Clarke	Lon
17	2	333368	Powell, Bishop & Stonier	Han
18	1	333431	Josiah Wedgwood & Sons	Etru
19	2	333485	J. Hawthorn	Cob
26	17	333751–2	The Worcester Royal Porcelain Co. Ltd.	Wo
28	6	333801	Clementson Bros.	Har
29	4	333813	Beck, Blair & Co.	Lon
Apr 3	9	334030	T. C. Brown–Westhead, Moore & Co.	Han
4	12	334052–3	Pinder, Bourne & Co.	Bur
9	5	334137	H. Alcock & Co.	Cob
10	12	334200	T. C. Brown–Westhead, Moore & Co.	Har
12	1	334206	The Worcester Royal Porcelain Co. Ltd.	Wo

e Parcel No.	Patent No.	Factory, Retailer Wholesaler, etc	Place
5	6	334241–2	T. C. Brown–Westhead, Moore & Co.	Hanley
3	8	334508	T. C. Brown–Westhead, Moore & Co.	Hanley
4	3	334531	Josiah Wedgwood & Sons	Etruria
2	5	334803	A. Bevington	Hanley
5	1	334860–1	T. Furnival & Sons	Cobridge
5	6	334897	Bates, Gildea & Walker	Burslem
6	7	334923–5	Sampson Bridgwood & Son	Longton
7	11	334978	The Worcester Royal Porcelain Co. Ltd.	Worcester
9	15	335057	idem	Worcester
3	4	335148–51	Pinder & Bourne & Co.	Burslem
3	8	335167–8	Clementson Bros.	Hanley
4	9	335182	T. C. Brown–Westhead, Moore & Co.	Hanley
4	13	335187–8	E. J. D. Bodley	Burslem
9	1	335308–9	Wm. Brownfield & Sons	Cobridge
1	5	335496	Harvey Adams & Co.	Longton
3	2	335551–2	Sampson Bridgwood & Son	Longton
3	14	335608	Harvey Adams & Co.	Longton
9	2	335715	John Tams	Longton
9	12	335739–40	Pinder, Bourne & Co.	Burslem
0	3	335744	McBirney & Armstrong	Belleek
0	10	335791	J. Dimmock & Co.	Hanley
0	12	335793	F. W. Grove & J. Stark	Longton
1	4	335805	Minton, Hollins & Co.	Stoke
0	4	336030	T. Furnival & Sons	Cobridge
1	8	336075	Thos. Till & Sons	Burslem
3	13	336132	T. C. Brown–Westhead, Moore & Co.	Hanley
8	4	336185	F. W. Grove & J. Stark	Longton
4	11	336415	Josiah Wedgwood & Sons	Etruria
5	1	336417	Clementson Bros.	Hanley

APPENDIX B

Date	Parcel No.	Patent No.	Factory, Retailer Wholesaler, etc	P
26	13	336471–4	Haviland & Co.	Lim and Lon
27	11	336496	Shorter & Boulton	Stok
30	12	336586–7	Birks Bros. & Seddon	Cob
July 2	2	336676	Josiah Wedgwood & Sons	Etru
7	2	336917	J. F. Wileman	Fen
8	1	336930	Mintons	Stok
8	16	336967–8	T. C. Brown-Westhead, Moore & Co.	Han
9	12	337058	idem	Han
10	2	337060	T. Bevington	Han
10	3	337061	Moore Bros.	Lon
16	4	337157–8	A. Bevington & Co.	Han
16	14	337177	T. C. Brown-Westhead, Moore & Co.	Han
25	4	337497	Mintons	Stok
26	6	337536	Minton, Hollins & Co.	Stok
31	2	337660	Mintons	Stok
Aug 2	2	337814	H. M. Williamson & Sons	Lon
5	12	337945–7	J. Mortlock & Co.	Lon
6	6	337958	Wardle & Co.	Han
13	2	338135	F. W. Grove & J. Stark	Lon
22	4	338559	McBirney & Armstrong	Bell
27	13	338872	Bates, Gildea & Walker	Burs
Sept 4	6	339193	T. C. Brown-Westhead, Moore & Co.	Han
10	13	339373	idem	Han
17	4	339685–6	Wm. Brownfield & Sons	Cob
18	10	339979	T. C. Brown-Westhead, Moore & Co.	Har
26	4	340431	J. T. Hudden	Lon
29	3	340569	Edge, Malkin & Co.	Bur
Oct 9	6	341137	Bates, Gildea & Walker	Burs

APPENDIX B

te Parcel No.	Patent No.	Factory, Retailer Wholesaler, etc	Place
10 2	341151	T. C. Brown-Westhead, Moore & Co.	Hanley
11 5	341229–30	E. J. D. Bodley	Burslem
15 1	341347	Mintons	Stoke
16 5	341466	J. Roth	London
16 16	341500	Minton, Hollins & Co.	Stoke
17 2	341502	G. L. Ashworth & Bros.	Hanley
18 3	341629	Josiah Wedgwood & Sons	Etruria
23 12	341864	C. Pillivuyt & Co.	London
24 4	341882–3	The Campbell Brick & Tile Co.	Stoke
27 9	341997	E. F. Bodley & Co.	Burslem
29 5	342098	Mintons	Stoke
29 7	342100	Clementson Bros.	Hanley
29 15	342152	F. D. Bradley	Longton
30 4	342158	Mintons	Stoke
3 12	342396	Minton, Hollins & Co.	Stoke
3 14	342398	Tundley, Rhodes & Procter	Burslem
6 2	342461	Josiah Wedgwood & Sons	Etruria
6 3	342462–3	Moore Bros.	Longton
6 4	342464–72	Burmantofts (Wilcock & Co.)	Leeds
12 11	342769	The Worcester Royal Porcelain Co. Ltd.	Worcester
15 12	342921	C. Ford	Hanley
15 16	342925–7	W. T. Copeland & Sons	Stoke
17 2	342929	Powell, Bishop & Stonier	Hanley
19 5	343017	idem	Hanley
20 4	343070–1	Elsmore & Son	Tunstall
21 6	343148	Mintons	Stoke
21 14	343166	Soane & Smith	London
22 7	343219	The Worcester Royal Porcelain Co. Ltd.	Worcester
28 5	343530	Wm. Brownfield & Sons	Cobridge

APPENDIX B

Date	Parcel No.	Patent No.	Factory, Retailer Wholesaler, etc	Pla
28	6	343531	A. Bevington & Co.	Hanl
29	3	343585	Mintons	Stoke
29	4	343586	T. C. Brown–Westhead, Moore & Co.	Hanl
Dec 1	2	343618	J. Holdcroft	Long
2	4	343652–3	T. C. Brown–Westhead, Moore & Co.	Hanl
2	5	343654	Elsmore & Son	Tuns
2	17	343716	J. Aynsley & Sons	Long
6	2	343815–6	T. & R. Boote	Bursl
10	14	344077	Clementson Bros.	Hanl
11	4	344082–4	Moore Bros.	Long
17	11	344387	Ridgways	Stoke
19	1	344452	Clementson Bros.	Hanl
19	3	344454	Burmantofts (Wilcock & Co.)	Leed
20	5	344478	Josiah Wedgwood & Sons	Etrur
22	2	344503	Mintons	Stoke
24	2	344568	Sherwin & Cotton	Hanl
1880				
Jan 3	1	344838	Sherwin & Cotton	Hanl
7	3	344961–2	T. Bevington	Hanl
7	4	344963	T. & R. Boote	Bursl
7	5	344964–9	Soane & Smith	Lond
7	8	344972	Minton, Hollins & Co.	Stoke
8	9	344997	The Old Hall Earthenware Co. Ltd.	Hanl
9	3	345003	Sherwin & Cotton	Hanl
9	12	345045	T. G. Allen	Lond
13	1	345131	T. C. Brown–Westhead, Moore & Co.	Hanl
14	11	345184–5	The Worcester Royal Porcelain Co. Ltd.	Worc
16	8	345288	S. Fielding & Co.	Stoke

368

APPENDIX B

Date	Parcel No.	Patent No.	Factory, Retailer Wholesaler, etc	Place
16	14	345299	Brockwell & Son	London
21	7	345469–71	Pinder, Bourne & Co.	Burslem
22	2	345481	Mintons	Stoke
22	8	345493–4	Minton, Hollins & Co.	Stoke
23	5	345511	Mintons	Stoke
26	11	345719	Wm. Brownfield & Sons	Cobridge
27	13	345798	Wardle & Co.	Hanley
28	3	345801	T. C. Brown-Westhead, Moore & Co.	Hanley
28	4	345802	J. Aynsley & Sons	Longton
28	12	345833	Powell, Bishop & Stonier	Hanley
29	9	345860–1	E. J. D. Bodley	Burslem
30	2	345864	Taylor, Tunnicliffe & Co.	Hanley
3	11	345952	Powell, Bishop & Stonier	Hanley
9	18	346202	Whittingham, Ford & Riley	Burslem
10	4	346208–10	Mintons	Stoke
11	10	346344	T. Bevington	Hanley
12	4	346360	W. A. Adderley	Longton
12	7	346363	Wm. Brownfield & Sons	Cobridge
14	14	346467	Bates, Gildea & Walker	Burslem
18	12	346594	The Derby Crown Porcelain Co. Ltd.	Derby
24	2	346832	Mintons	Stoke
24	11	346870	Wm. Harrop & Co.	Hanley
25	18	346920	Clementson Bros.	Hanley
25	23	346945	Sherwin & Cotton	Hanley
26	6	346952–3	Minton, Hollins & Co.	Stoke
26	7	346954	Moore Bros.	Longton
3	6	347138	J. Holdcroft	Longton
4	8	347203	Soane & Smith	London
8	4	347344	T. Furnival & Sons	Cobridge
8	10	347360	W. Harrop & Co.	Hanley
12	4	347476	W. A. Adderley	Longton
16	3	347599	J. F. Wileman & Co.	Fenton
16	11	347645	Sherwin & Cotton	Hanley

Date	Parcel No.	Patent No.	Factory, Retailer Wholesaler, etc	Pl
16	12	347646–7	J. Macintyre & Co.	Burs
17	6	347660	Josiah Wedgwood & Sons	Etru
18	3	347690–6	Moore Bros.	Lon;
22	4	347838	Powell, Bishop & Stonier	Han
23	4	347872	Taylor, Tunnicliffe & Co.	Han
25	6	348018	Mintons	Stok
30	4	348110	Sherwin & Cotton	Han
31	3	348114	Thos. Peake	Tuns
Apr 12	6	348606–8	Bates, Gildea & Walker	Burs
15	11	348761	Ridgways	Stok
19	11	348911–3	The Worcester Royal Porcelain Co. Ltd.	Wor
22	11	349025–6	Sherwin & Cotton	Han
22	5	349027	W. H. Grindley & Co.	Tuns
26	1	349221	T. Furnival & Sons	Cob
27	11	349239–41	Moore Bros.	Lon;
27	13	349318–23	The Worcester Royal Porcelain Co. Ltd.	Wor
29	4	349340–1	Mintons	Stok
30	6	349380	T. Furnival & Sons	Cob
May 3	3	349438–43	Wm. Brownfield & Sons	Cob
5	13	349528	S. Fielding & Co.	Stok
10	6	349693	Powell, Bishop & Stonier	Han
11	15	349791	Soane & Smith	Lon
13	8	349852–3	Mintons	Stok
13	15	349869	Minton, Hollins & Co.	Stok
14	26	349939	Bates, Gildea & Walker	Burs
25	4	350098	Wm. Brownfield & Sons	Cob
26	6	350142	Mintons	Stok
June 1	4	350251	Mintons	Stok
2	3	350353	Sherwin & Cotton	Han
7	6	350476	J. Dimmock & Co.	Han
8	1	350477	Geo. Jones & Sons	Stok
10	3	350554	Sherwin & Cotton	Han
10	4	350555	E. J. D. Bodley	Burs

Date	Parcel No.	Patent No.	Factory, Retailer Wholesaler, etc	Place
10	12	350613	J. Dimmock & Co.	Hanley
11	3	350616	Josiah Wedgwood & Sons	Etruria
14	12	350842	J. Roth	London
15	4	350848	Buckley, Wood & Co.	Burslem
16	3	350972	Wedgwood & Co.	Tunstall
17	4	351025	Samuel Lear	Hanley
17	15	351058	Ridgways	Stoke
17	16	351059	J. Macintyre & Co.	Burslem
17	20	351063	The Crystal Porcelain Co.	Hanley
17	21	351064	J. Dimmock & Co.	Hanley
19	11	351186	Josiah Wedgwood & Sons	Etruria
19	15	351190	J. Roth	London
22	1	351259	W. H. Grindley & Co.	Tunstall
26	13	351496–7	The Worcester Royal Porcelain Co. Ltd.	Worcester
y 5	11	351866	Westwood & Moore	Brierley Hill
7	4	351909	Sherwin & Cotton	Hanley
7	5	351910	Mintons	Stoke
7	15	351928	F. J. Emery	Burslem
12	4	352094	Mintons	Stoke
13	12	352138	Thos. Barlow	Longton
15	3	352192	Dunn, Bennett & Co.	Hanley
15	4	352193	F. W. Grove & J. Stark	Longton
16	9	352224	Sherwin & Cotton	Hanley
16	10	352225	Moore Bros.	Longton
16	19	352278	S. Fielding & Co.	Stoke
28	2	352872	The Brownhills Pottery Co.	Tunstall
31	8	353079	The Old Hall Earthenware Co. Ltd.	Hanley
4	3	353108	Pinder, Bourne & Co.	Burslem
11	14	353543	Clementson Bros.	Hanley
14	12	353713–4	Wm. Davenport & Co.	Longport
17	6	353746	Sherwin & Cotton	Hanley
18	3	353818	Josiah Wedgwood & Sons	Etruria

APPENDIX B

Date	Parcel No.	Patent No.	Factory, Retailer Wholesaler, etc	Plac
21	2	354026	Sherwin & Cotton	Hanley
21	10	354081	W. A. Adderley	Longte
23	5	354092	Jackson & Gosling	Longte
23	6	354093-4	T. C. Brown–Westhead, Moore & Co.	Hanley
24	10	354154	E. J. D. Bodley	Bursle
Sept 3	3	354639	T. C. Brown–Westhead, Moore & Co.	Hanley
4	7	354766-7	J. Beech & Son	Longte
11	3	355091–100	Wm. Brownfield & Sons	Cobri
14	6	355169	Mintons	Stoke
15	6	355231	G. L. Ashworth & Bros.	Hanley
15	12	355255-7	Minton, Hollins & Co.	Stoke
23	3	355575	Ambrose Wood	Hanle
25	6	355651-4	Minton, Hollins & Co.	Stoke
27	5	355745-6	John Marshall & Co.	Bo'ne Scotla
29	3	355947-8	The Brownhills Pottery Co.	Tunst
30	4	355987	The Worcester Royal Porcelain Co. Ltd.	Worc
Oct 1	3	356014	Wade & Colclough	Bursle
6	4	356163	Josiah Wedgwood & Sons	Etruri
12	4	356514	Mintons	Stoke
13	5	356532	Josiah Wedgwood & Sons	Etruri
20	10	356970	Burgess & Leigh	Bursle
21	13	357033-5	The Worcester Royal Porcelain Co. Ltd.	Worc
22	4	357039	E. F. Bodley & Son	Bursle
22	12	357088	J. Aynsley & Sons	Long
26	13	357298-9	Minton, Hollins & Co.	Stoke
27	5	357305	Taylor, Tunnicliffe & Co.	Hanle
27	20	357429	J. Tams	Long
27	21	357430	G. Woolliscroft & Son	Etrur
28	2	357466	Sherwin & Cotton	Hanle

APPENDIX B

Date	Parcel No.	Patent No.	Factory, Retailer Wholesaler, etc	Place
30	6	357560	Jones & Hopkinson	Hanley
2	2	357609	W. H. Grindley & Co.	Tunstall
4	4	357656–7	W. & T. Adams	Tunstall
4	15	357724–5	Minton, Hollins & Co.	Stoke
9	4	357954	Josiah Wedgwood & Sons	Etruria
10	2	358062–3	Wilcock & Co. (Burmantofts)	Leeds
10	13	358141	Bednall & Heath	Hanley
18	3	358466	S. Radford	Longton
18	14	358500	Mintons	Stoke
19	15	358552	The Crown Derby Porcelain Co. Ltd.	Derby
24	4	358747	F. W. Grove & J. Stark	Longton
24	5	358748	Bates, Gildea & Walker	Burslem
6	2	359292	Powell, Bishop & Stonier	Hanley
7	10	359321–6	Pinder, Bourne & Co.	Burslem
8	5	359342–3	Wittmann & Roth	London
15	15	359668–71	Wm. Brownfield & Sons	Cobridge
18	2	359784	Bates, Gildea & Walker	Burslem
24	8	359997	T. C. Brown–Westhead, Moore & Co.	Hanley
29	7	360042–4	Doulton & Co.	Lambeth
31	1	360100	The Old Hall Earthenware Co. Ltd.	Hanley
31	4	360103–5	Sherwin & Cotton	Hanley
5	7	360326	J. Roth	London
6	2	360331	B. & S. Hancock	Stoke
6	8	360355	F. D. Bradley	Longton
7	13	360484	Sherwin & Cotton	Hanley
12	5	360633	idem	Hanley
14	10	360747	The Worcester Royal Porcelain Co. Ltd.	Worcester
14	18	360799	E. J. D. Bodley	Burslem

373

Date	Parcel No.	Patent No.	Factory, Retailer Wholesaler, etc	Plac
15	4	360806–7	Holmes, Stonier & Hollinshead	Hanley
20	3	360900	Mintons	Stoke
21	11	360954	W. & T. Adams	Tunsta
26	4	361116–7	Minton, Hollins & Co.	Stoke
27	15	361151	The Worcester Royal Porcelain Co. Ltd.	Worce
28	3	361170	G. Woolliscroft & Son	Hanley
Feb 8	5	361537	F. W. Grove & J. Stark	Longt
8	6	361538–41	Wm. Brownfield & Sons	Cobric
11	10	361668	F. J. Emery	Bursle
15	6	361748	W. A. Adderley	Longt
16	3	361784	F. D. Bradley	Longt
17	2	361813	Murray & Co.	Glasg
18	3	361868	S. Radford	Longt
19	15	361927	S. S. Bold	Hanle
21	4	361937	Taylor, Waine & Bates	Longt
24	8	362086	Wm. Harrop & Co.	Hanle
25	14	362166	J. Macintyre & Co.	Bursle
28	9	362242	E. J. D. Bodley	Bursle
Mar 3	5	362423	J. Dimmock & Co.	Hanle
7	11	362545	J. Aynsley & Sons	Longt
8	3	362548	F. W. Grove & J. Stark	Longt
14	1	362815	E. J. D. Bodley	Bursle
17	9	362992	Shorter & Boulton	Stoke
19	4	363026–7	Mintons	Stoke
23	4	363157	Mintons	Stoke
24	2	363206–7	T. S. Pinder	Bursle
24	3	363208	W. A. Adderley	Long
29	6	363421	T. A. Simpson	Hanle
31	2	363461	J. T. Hudden	Longt
Apr 7	2	363720	Sherwin & Cotton	Hanle
7	9	363732	The Old Hall Earthenware Co. Ltd.	Hanle
8	2	363738	W. Harrop & Co.	Hanle

APPENDIX B

te	Parcel No.	Patent No.	Factory, Retailer Wholesaler, etc	Place
8	3	363739	Wedgwood & Co.	Tunstall
8	14	363785	The Worcester Royal Porcelain Co. Ltd.	Worcester
9	5	363793	R. H. Plant & Co.	Longton
11	1	363800	A. Bevington & Co.	Hanley
12	4	363849–50	Mintons	Stoke
14	10	363975	Mintons	Stoke
16	17	364110	J. Marshall & Co.	Bo'ness, Scotland
19	3	364116	Sherwin & Cotton	Hanley
19	5	364118	T. & R. Boote	Burslem
21	4	364172	Sherwin & Cotton	Hanley
21	5	364173–4	E. J. D. Bodley	Burslem
23	7	364238	J. F. Wileman	Fenton
28	12	364488	W. T. Copeland & Sons	Stoke
30	3	364528	Trubshaw, Hand & Co.	Longton
30	4	364529	Josiah Wedgwood & Sons	Etruria
3	4	364604	Wm. Wood & Co.	Burslem
3	5	364605	Sherwin & Cotton	Hanley
4	2	364624	idem	Hanley
4	3	364625–7	Wm. Brownfield & Sons	Cobridge
5	2	364648	W. & T. Adams	Tunstall
6	4	364736	R. H. Plant & Co.	Longton
11	3	364941	J. Tams	Longton
13	2	365005	Mintons	Stoke
16	2	365066	Josiah Wedgwood & Sons	Etruria
17	9	365134–5	J. Mortlock & Co.	London
20	11	365206	W. A. Adderley	Longton
21	3	365211	Powell, Bishop & Stonier	Hanley
24	5	365391	G. L. Ashworth & Bros.	Hanley
24	6	365392–3	Mintons	Stoke
24	7	365394	F. J. Emery	Burslem
25	3	365424	Powell, Bishop & Stonier	Hanley
25	9	365442–4	The Worcester Royal Porcelain Co. Ltd.	Worcester

APPENDIX B

Date	Parcel No.	Patent No.	Factory, Retailer Wholesaler, etc	Pla
25	10	365445–6	Josiah Wedgwood & Sons	Etrur
26	7	365461	G. Woolliscroft & Son	Hanl
30	1	365539	T. Furnival & Sons	Cobr
30	2	365540	The Decorative Art Tile Co.	Hanl
June 1	3	365730	Mintons	Stok
1	13	365793	J. Mortlock & Co.	Lond
3	4	365827	S. P. Ledward	Cobr
4	3	365852	T. Furnival & Sons	Cobr
4	4	365853	The Decorative Art Tile Co.	Hanl
7	3	365875	E. F. Bodley & Son	Burs
7	4	365876–7	The Decorative Art Tile Co.	Hanl
7	17	365914–6	The Worcester Royal Porcelain Co. Ltd.	Wor
8	6	365955	The Crystal Porcelain Co.	Hanl
13	1	366015	S. Lear	Hanl
16	8	366078–9	S. Fielding & Co.	Stok
18	1	366093	Jackson & Gosling	Long
21	13	366220–2	Birks Bros. & Seddon	Cobr
21	20	366246	Gildea & Walker	Burs
July 2	1	366634	McBirney & Armstrong	Belle
2	5	366643	T. Furnival & Sons	Cobr
6	7	366809	Josiah Wedgwood & Sons	Etru
9	10	366922–3	Wardle & Co.	Hanl
14	6	367133–4	T. C. Brown–Westhead, Moore & Co.	Hanl
15	5	367150	Wm. Corbitt & Co.	Rthr
16	3	367213	Trubshaw, Hand & Co.	Long
18	4	367249	G. Hall	Wor
19	2	367259	The Dalehall Brick & Tile Co.	Burs
25	2	367418	J. H. Davis	Han
28	3	367516	McBirney & Armstrong	Belle

APPENDIX B

ate	Parcel No.	Patent No.	Factory, Retailer Wholesaler, etc	Place
28	4	367517	A. Wood	Hanley
28	14	367538	Ridgways	Stoke
29	2	367542–3	Sherwin & Cotton	Hanley
29	3	367544	Whittmann & Roth	London
30	3	367549	Sampson Bridgwood & Son	Longton
30	4	367550	Sherwin & Cotton	Hanley
30	5	367551	Mintons	Stoke
30	15	367590	W. T. Copeland & Sons	Stoke
2	1	367608	E. J. D. Bodley	Burslem
5	12	367892–3	Pinder, Bourne & Co.	Burslem
10	13	368044	The Old Hall Earthenware Co. Ltd.	Hanley
20	11	368686	The Worcester Royal Porcelain Co. Ltd.	Worcester
23	3	368802	F. W. Grove & J. Stark	Longton
24	11	368942	T. & R. Boote	Burslem
27	3	369202	S. Lear	Hanley
27	9	369215–8	Gildea & Walker	Burslem
29	7	369248	W. & T. Adams	Tunstall
2	4	369389	Dale, Page & Goodwin	Longton
3	11	369526	T. A. Simpson	Hanley
6	1	369538	The Derby Crown Porcelain Co. Ltd.	Derby
7	10	369654	Adams & Sleigh	Burslem
9	11	369731	The Worcester Royal Porcelain Co. Ltd.	Worcester
10	12	369778–81	J. Roth	London
16	10	370093	Geo. Jones & Sons	Stoke
22	9	370400	Bold & Michelson	Hanley
23	21	370470–2	Minton, Hollins & Co.	Stoke
27	9	370611	Pinder, Bourne & Co.	Burslem
28	4	370620	E. J. D. Bodley	Burslem
28	13	370633	Gildea & Walker	Burslem
29	3	370636	Geo. Jones & Sons	Stoke
30	3	370702–3	Davenports Ltd.	Longport

APPENDIX B

Date	Parcel No.	Patent No.	Factory, Retailer Wholesaler, etc	Pl
30	15	370725–8	Mintons	Stok
Oct 4	6	370885	Wm. Brownfield & Sons	Cob
6	5	370998	J. & R. Boote	Burs
6	7	371000	The Campbell Brick & Tile Co.	Stok
7	27	371098	Mintons	Stok
8	3	371102	Adams & Sleigh	Burs
11	16	371247	The Worcester Royal Porcelain Co. Ltd.	Wor
12	14	371330–1	Mintons	Stok
13	3	371337	Adderley & Lawson	Long
13	5	371339	T. & R. Boote	Burs
20	1	371866	Thos. Begley	Burs
20	2	371867	Robinson & Chapman	Long
22	1	371959	Mintons	Stok
26	8	372138	Mintons	Stok
26	16	372171	T. C. Brown–Westhead, Moore & Co.	Han
27	1	372185	Robinson & Chapman	Long
29	3	372347	T. & R. Boote	Burs
29	4	372348	Wm. Brownfield & Sons	Cob
29	11	372376	Wardle & Co.	Han
29	14	372379	Minton, Hollins & Co.	Stok
31	11	372464	T. A. Simpson	Han
Nov 2	1	372489–90	T. C. Brown–Westhead, Moore & Co.	Han
3	12	372613	The Worcester Royal Porcelain Co. Ltd.	Wor
4	24	372727	idem	Wor
8	1	372918	T. & R. Boote	Burs
9	6	372979	F. W. Grove & J. Stark	Long
9	7	372980–2	E. J. D. Bodley	Burs
10	2	372995	Brough & Blackhurst	Long
19	3	373541	Sampson Bridgwood & Son	Long

378

e	Parcel No.	Patent No.	Factory, Retailer Wholesaler, etc	Place
9	12	373573	The Worcester Royal Porcelain Co. Ltd.	Worcester
1	1	373575	J. Bevington	Hanley
2	9	373615	J. Tams	Longton
2	17	373647	Ambrose Wood	Hanley
3	13	373707	Shorter & Boulton	Stoke
5	1	373821	Adams & Sleigh	Burslem
5	15	373860	J. Roth	London
9	10	374058	The Worcester Royal Porcelain Co. Ltd.	Worcester
2	16	374229	J. Roth	London
5	11	374376	John Rose & Co.	Coalport
8	9	374498	Adderley & Lawson	Longton
9	2	374516	E. J. D. Bodley	Burslem
0	7	374579	T. C. Brown–Westhead, Moore & Co.	Hanley
2	12	374628	John Fell	Longton
6	3	374782	Mintons	Stoke
0	9	374948	Bednall & Heath	Hanley
1	3	374955	F. Grosvenor	Glasgow
1	9	374987	The Worcester Royal Porcelain Co. Ltd.	Worcester
4	5	375054	J. Broadhurst	Fenton
3	6	375415	Holmes, Plant & Maydew	Burslem
4	2	375426–7	W. T. Copeland & Sons	Stoke
4	7	375439	J. Roth	London
4	9	375444	F. & R. Pratt & Co.	Fenton
7	2	375494	W. H. Grindley & Co.	Tunstall
7	11	375580	Ridgways	Hanley
0	5	375599	S. Lear	Hanley
1	1	375709–12	Minton, Hollins & Co.	Stoke
3	4	375815–6	The Decorative Art Tile Co.	Hanley

APPENDIX B

Date	Parcel No.	Patent No.	Factory, Retailer Wholesaler, etc	
18	10	376032	Robinson & Son	Lo
26	5	376425	J. T. Hudden	Lo
26	16	376443	S. Fielding & Co.	Sto
27	8	376461	Craven, Dunnill & Co. Ltd.	Jac
30	2	376528	Hollinshead & Kirkham	Tu
30	3	376529	F. W. Grove & J. Stark	Lo
Feb 1	1	376580	Edge, Malkin & Co.	Bu
3	4	376672–3	T. C. Brown–Westhead, Moore & Co.	Ha
4	10	376754	Minton, Hollins & Co.	Sto
6	4	376764–6	The Campbell Tile Co.	Sto
7	2	376798	Wm. Mills	Ha
8	7	376839	Wardle & Co.	Ha
15	4	377048	F. W. Grove & J. Stark	Lo
16	6	377135–7	Mintons	Sto
18	5	377273	J. F. Wileman & Co.	Fe
23	17	377488–9	Minton, Hollins & Co.	Sto
24	3	377492	Taylor, Tunnicliffe & Co.	Ha
Mar 1	11	377779	The Worcester Royal Porcelain Co. Ltd.	Wo
1	12	377780	Minton, Hollins & Co.	Sto
7	7	378051	idem	Sto
13	3	378252	J. T. Hudden	Lo
15	3	378337	Powell, Bishop & Stonier	Ha
15	4	378338	Murray & Co.	Gl
20	5	378643	W. A. Adderley	Lo
23	2	378739	W. & T. Adams	Tu
23	15	378823	T. A. Simpson	Ha
27	3	378937	D. Chapman	Lo
27	10	378959	Shorter & Boulton	Sto
28	12	378988	Ambrose Wood	Ha
28	16	378993–4	A. Bevington & Co.	Ha
30	13	379076	John Rose & Co.	Co
30	17	379080	S. Fielding & Co.	Sto
31	3	379088	A. Bevington & Co.	Ha

APPENDIX B

Parcel No.	Patent No.	Factory, Retailer Wholesaler, etc	Place
2	379212–3	Wm. Brownfield & Sons	Cobridge
6	379434	Geo. Jones & Sons	Stoke
7	379435–6	Minton, Hollins & Co.	Stoke
7	379767	Sampson Bridgwood & Son	Longton
14	380072	The New Wharf Pottery Co.	Burslem
5	380194	G. L. Ashworth & Bros.	Hanley
1	380199	S. Radford	Longton
2	380401	Wood, Hines & Winkle	Hanley
5	380418	Powell, Bishop & Stonier	Hanley
6	380419–20	Whittaker, Edge & Co.	Hanley
18	380549–50	Davenports Ltd.	Longport
3	380553–4	H. Alcock & Co.	Cobridge
4	380555	Whittaker, Edge & Co.	Hanley
7	380558	Wm. Brownfield & Sons	Cobridge
11	380564	Minton, Hollins & Co.	Stoke
4	380571–2	John Edwards	Fenton
14	380676	S. Fielding & Co.	Stoke
6	380789	Geo. Jones & Sons	Stoke
2	380869–70	E. J. Bodley	Burslem
4	381376	Minton, Hollins & Co.	Stoke
21	381434	Doulton & Co.	Burslem
11	381480	W. A. Adderley	Longton
3	381568	Samuel Lear	Hanley
5	381611	W. H. Grindley & Co.	Tunstall
6	381805	Mintons	Stoke
7	381806	Wood, Hines & Winkle	Hanley
3	381964	Hall & Read	Burslem
4	381965–6	W. A. Adderley	Longton
11	382126	A. Shaw & Son	Burslem
14	382130–1	Wardle & Co.	Hanley
4	382406	Wm. Lowe	Longton
5	382407–8	Sampson Bridgwood & Son	Longton
11	382472	The Old Hall Earthenware & Co. Ltd	Hanley

Date	Parcel No.	Patent No.	Factory, Retailer Wholesaler, etc	P
23	1	382593–4	Josiah Wedgwood & Sons	Etr
23	5	382598	Burgess & Leigh	Bu
28	2	382721	The Derby Crown Porcelain Co.	De
July 1	8	382829	Taylor, Tunnicliffe & Co.	Ha
3	2	382842	Mintons	Sto
3	3	382843	E. J. D. Bodley	Bu
4	3	382859	Wright & Rigby	Ha
6	4	383020–1	Wm. Brownfield & Sons	Co
14	3	383436–7	Geo. Jones & Sons	Sto
14	10	383468	Wardle & Co.	Ha
14	14	383482	Beech & Tellwright	Co
17	8	383549	Wood & Son	Bu
19	7	383641	Wardle & Co.	Ha
20	1	383694–6	John Edwards	Fe
22	8	383802	Geo. Jones & Sons	Sto
25	3	383855	F. Grosvenor	Gla
25	9	383869–71	The Brownhills Pottery Co. Ltd.	Tu
26	4	383893	Adderley & Lawson	Lo
28	3	384078	Hawley & Co.	Lo
31	2	384160–1	Sampson Bridgwood & Son	Lo
31	9	384171–2	Mintons	Sto
Aug 5	4	384353–4	Wm. Brownfield & Sons	Co
10	5	384464	Wright & Rigby	Ha
21	2	385106	John Tams	Lo
21	8	385129	Adams & Bromley	Ha
25	2	385411	Mintons	Sto
26	4	385490	Wm. Wood & Co.	Bu
28	2	385527	Belfield & Co.	Pr
28	9	385544	Mintons	Sto
29	12	385623	Wm. Brownfield & Sons	Co
30	14	385693	The Worcester Royal Porcelain Co. Ltd.	W

te	Parcel No.	Patent No.	Factory, Retailer Wholesaler, etc	Place
1	3	385701	A. Bevington & Co.	Hanley
6	2	385954	Hawley & Co.	Longton
8	5	386085–6	Mintons	Stoke
9	3	386126	Taylor, Tunnicliffe & Co.	Hanley
1	4	386178	Adams & Bromley	Hanley
6	2	386388–9	Hulme & Massey	Longton
9	2	386542	W. H. Grindley & Co.	Tunstall
8	4	387147–8	T. C. Brown–Westhead, Moore & Co.	Hanley
8	22	387229	Bridgett & Bates	Longton
9	2	387231–2	The Brownhills Pottery Co.	Tunstall
6	2	387598–603	Mintons	Stoke
9	3	387771	W. T. Copeland & Sons	Stoke
9	4	387772	Dean, Capper & Dean	Hanley
1	3	387958–60	Sampson Bridgwood & Son	Longton
1	4	387961	Wood & Son	Burslem
2	17	388200	T. Furnival & Sons	Cobridge
6	4	388296	Wood & Son	Burslem
9	4	388395	Lowe, Ratcliffe & Co.	Longton
1	2	389136	Wm. Lowe	Longton
1	14	389201	Stonier, Hollinshead & Oliver	Hanley
4	19	389390	The Worcester Royal Porcelain Co. Ltd.	Worcester
8	2	389554	Mintons	Stoke
0	10	389793	Ridgways	Stoke
0	12	389795–7	Pratt & Simpson	Fenton
1	2	389801	Powell, Bishop & Stonier	Hanley
3	1	389893	Edge, Malkin & Co.	Burslem
3	2	389894	Sampson Bridgwood & Son	Longton
4	3	389911–2	Ed. Steel	Hanley
5	7	390004–5	S. Fielding & Co.	Stoke
6	3	390023	Taylor, Tunnicliffe & Co.	Hanley
1	4	390255	J. Holdcroft	Longton

Date	Parcel No.	Patent No.	Factory, Retailer Wholesaler, etc	P
21	8	390264	Gildea & Walker	Bur
22	11	390285	S. Fielding & Co.	Sto
24	19	390588	Minton, Hollins & Co.	Sto
27	3	390617	H. Alcock & Co.	Cob
27	4	390618	The Derby Crown Porcelain Co. Ltd.	Der
27	5	390619	J. F. Wileman & Co.	Fen
Dec 2	8	390976	Minton, Hollins & Co.	Sto
4	7	390985	A. Bevington & Co.	Har
6	2	391068-9	T. C. Brown–Westhead, Moore & Co.	Har
13	4	391361-2	Mintons	Sto
13	5	391363-4	Josiah Wedgwood	Etru
14	6	391409	S. Lear	Har
15	3	391460	The Old Hall Earthenware Co. Ltd.	Har
18	9	391596	J. Lockett & Co.	Lon
19	3	391620	H. Kennedy	Gla
21	4	391768	E. J. D. Bodley	Bur
21	5	391769	Wood, Hines & Winkle	Ha
22	2	391818	F. W. Grove & J. Stark	Lor
22	14	391846	Lorenz Hutschenreuther	Bav
23	4	391855	J. F. Wileman	Fen
23	12	391917	The New Wharf Pottery Co.	Bur
23	14	391922-7	The Worcester Royal Porcelain Co.	Wo
27	1	391929	The New Wharf Pottery Co.	Bur
1883				
Jan 2	2	392166	The Derby Crown Porcelain Co. Ltd.	De
3	1	392176	Wm. Hines	Lo
3	14	392362	T. Furnival & Sons	Co

APPENDIX B

Date	Parcel No.	Patent No.	Factory, Retailer Wholesaler, etc	Place
3	18	392388–9	John Rose & Co.	Coalport
4	5	392403	T. C. Brown–Westhead, Moore & Co.	Hanley
8	5	392590	W. T. Copeland & Sons	Stoke
8	12	392621	The Worcester Royal Porcelain Co. Ltd.	Worcester
9	3	392626	Powell, Bishop & Stonier	Hanley
9	4	392627	E. F. Bodley & Son	Longport
9	5	392628–30	Hall & Read	Hanley
9	11	392652	Davenports Ltd.	Longport
10	17	392693	Gildea & Walker	Burslem
12	3	392725	Holmes, Plant & Maydew	Burslem
13	6	392760	Moore & Co.	Longton
13	17	392809	T. & R. Boote	Burslem
16	1	392855	Blair & Co.	Longton
17	3	392888	W. H. Grindley & Co.	Tunstall
23	8	393099	E. F. Bodley & Son	Longport
23	10	393102–3	W. T. Copeland & Sons	Stoke
24	1	393107	Sampson Bridgwood & Son	Longton
24	2	393108–9	Wm. Brownfield & Sons	Cobridge
25	3	393177	The Brownhills Pottery Co.	Tunstall
26	8	393258	Wm. Lowe	Longton
27	8	393298	G. W. Turner & Sons	Tunstall
29	6	393310	Wm. Brownfield & Sons	Cobridge
29	7	393311–2	W. H. Grindley & Co.	Tunstall
30	1	393323	E. F. Bodley & Son	Longport
30	12	393362	Wedgwood & Co.	Tunstall
31	14	393413	Minton, Hollins & Co.	Stoke
1	3	393418	Sampson Bridgwood & Son	Longton
1	17	393474	E. J. D. Bodley	Burslem
2	4	393495	S. Hancock	Stoke
2	17	393539	Wedgwood & Co.	Tuhstall
3	3	393548	Mintons	Stoke
5	2	393647	J. Holdcroft	Longton
6	1	393668	Wood, Hines & Winkle	Hanley

Date	Parcel No.	Patent No.	Factory, Retailer Wholesaler, etc	Pla
7	4	393714	Hawley & Co.	Long
7	5	393715	Mountford & Thomas	Hanl
9	9	393979	E. J. D. Bodley	Burs
12	3	394086	Dunn, Bennett & Co.	Hanl
14	3	394185	W. H. Grindley & Co.	Tuns
15	5	394215	J. H. Davis	Hanl
17	13	394371	G. W. Turner & Sons	Tuns
19	1	394374	W. A. Adderley	Long
20	13	394443	Davenports Ltd.	Long
20	17	394448	Gildea & Walker	Burs
21	3	394452	Geo. Jones & Sons	Stok
22	6	394556–61	Hall & Read	Hanl
22	20	394599	The Worcester Royal Porcelain Co. Ltd.	Wor
22	21	394600	The Old Hall Earthenware Co.	Han
24	12	394676	Josiah Wedgwood & Sons	Etru
24	13	394677	The Worcester Royal Porcelain Co. Ltd.	Wor
26	6	394687	Williamson & Sons	Lon
28	3	394765	Thos. Till & Sons	Burs
Mar 8	5	395284	M. Massey	Han
8	20	395316–7	E. F. Bodley & Son	Lon
14	3	395560	The Derby Porcelain Co. Ltd.	Der
15	3	395622	T. Furnival & Sons	Cob
16	6	395688	J. Broadhurst	Fen
17	8	395703	Mintons	Stok
20	3	395818	E. A. Wood	Han
20	4	395819	Josiah Wedgwood & Sons	Etru
24	3	396056	Sampson Bridgwood & Son	Lon
30	1	396200–1	Mintons	Sto
30	9	396245	Minton, Hollins & Co.	Sto
Apr 2	3	396313	T. & E. L. Poulson	Cas
3	3	396316	E. Warburton	Lor

APPENDIX B

Date	Parcel No.	Patent No.	Factory, Retailer Wholesaler, etc	Place
6	14	396576	G. & J. Hobson	Burslem
10	1	396648	Banks & Thorley	Hanley
19	3	397090	R. H. Plant & Co.	Longton
21	1	397227	J. F. Wileman & Co.	Fenton
24	7	397311	G. L. Ashworth & Bros.	Hanley
25	14	397376	Pratt & Simpson	Fenton
27	17	397512	C. Littler & Co.	Hanley
27	18	397513	J. H. Davis	Hanley
27	19	397514	Powell, Bishop & Stonier	Hanley
2	4	397609–11	T. C. Brown–Westhead, Moore & Co.	Hanley
5	4	397751	Whittaker, Edge & Co.	Hanley
7	8	397819	S. Fielding & Co.	Stoke
8	6	397829–30	T. G. & F. Booth	Tunstall
11	5	398059	R. H. Plant & Co.	Longton
16	12	398280	T. A. Simpson	Stoke
22	11	398425	Powell, Bishop & Stonier	Hanley
22	12	398426	Burns, Oates	London
23	7	398436	T. G. & F. Booth	Tunstall
23	8	398437–8	E. A. Wood	Hanley
24	3	398479	The Brownhills Pottery Co.	Tunstall
25	4	398519	W. A. Adderley	Longton
28	2	398577–80	O. G. Blunden	Poling
31	17	398784	Wardle & Co.	Hanley
2	9	398849–55	Minton, Hollins & Co.	Stoke
4	8	398877–8	Clementson Bros.	Hanley
8	2	399068	H. Alcock & Co.	Cobridge
9	2	399135–6	Sampson Bridgwood & Son	Longton
9	6	399143	Mintons	Stoke
11	2	399147	F. W. Grove & J. Stark	Longton
11	8	399161	J. Matthews	Westons-s'-Mare
11	9	399162	idem	Westons-s'-Mare

Date	Parcel No.	Patent No.	Factory, Retailer Wholesaler, etc	Plac
13	3	399319	Belfield & Co.	Presto pan
13	7	399336	Pratt & Simpson	Stoke
14	2	399367–70	F. W. Grove & J. Stark	Longt
18	11	399554	John Tams	Longt
18	12	399555–9	Wm. Brownfield & Sons	Cobri
20	3	399640	T. & R. Boote	Bursle
20	4	399641	Mintons	Stoke
20	16	399675	W. & E. Corn	Bursle
21	22	399822	Wardle & Co.	Hanle
23	4	399875	Josiah Wedgwood & Sons	Etruri
25	5	399891	Ford & Riley	Bursle
25	10	399897–8	Wm. Brownfield & Sons	Cobri
July 2	4	400146	Edge, Malkin & Co.	Bursle
3	3	400176	J. Aynsley & Sons	Longt
3	4	400177	Moore Bros.	Longt
4	7	400348	Wm. Brownfield & Sons	Cobri
5	6	400367	F. W. Grove & J. Stark	Longt
5	19	400462	T. Furnival & Sons	Cobri
5	21	400464	Owen, Raby & Co.	Long
6	2	400467	Blackhurst & Bourne	Bursl
10	9	400582	Ambrose Wood	Hanl
10	11	400583–4	J. Macintyre & Co.	Bursl
11	1	400596	Josiah Wedgwood & Sons	Etrur
19	4	400941	Davenports Ltd.	Long
19	21	400994	Geo. Jones & Sons	Stok
20	11	401035	Hollinshead & Kirkham	Tuns
21	3	401040	Bridgett & Bates	Long
23	3	401087	Josiah Wedgwood & Sons	Etru
26	1	401296	W. A. Adderley	Long
27	4	401410	T. C. Brown–Westhead, Moore & Co.	Han
27	13	401426–7	Wm. Bennett	Han
30	10	401553	Wm. Brownfield & Sons	Cob
31	3	401593	T. & R. Boote	Burs

APPENDIX B

te	Parcel No.	Patent No.	Factory, Retailer Wholesaler, etc	Place
1	3	401623	Wagstaff & Brunt	Longton
1	4	401624	Geo. Jones & Sons	Stoke
1	9	401653	T. C. Brown–Westhead, Moore & Co.	Hanley
2	3	401663–4	Davenports Ltd.	Longport
3	17	401769	E. J. Bodley	Burslem
8	9	401842	J. & E. Ridgway	Stoke
9	15	401897–9	Haviland & Co.	France and London
17	5	402346	E. J. D. Bodley	Burslem
20	8	402514	The Worcester Royal Porcelain Co. Ltd.	Worcester
22	1	402560–1	The Brownhills Pottery Co.	Tunstall
23	2	402625–6	Grove & Cope	Hanley
24	12	402736	Mountford & Thomas	Hanley
25	11	402839	Wm. Brownfield & Sons	Cobridge
29	3	402950	J. Aynsley & Sons	Longton
31	6	403110	W. & E. Corn	Burslem
31	7	403111	J. F. Wileman & Co.	Fenton
1	10	403204	S. Fielding & Co.	Stoke
5	3	403298–9	Wm. Brownfield & Sons	Cobridge
7	4	403486	The Derby Crown Porcelain Co. Ltd.	Derby
7	19	403513–4	Powell, Bishop & Stonier	Hanley
11	4	403665	Josiah Wedgwood & Sons	Etruria
13	17	403802–3	H. Aynsley & Co.	Longton
14	1	403805–6	W. & T. Adams	Tunstall
14	2	403807–9	Mintons	Stoke
17	14	403978	The Derby Crown Porcelain Co. Ltd.	Derby
20	12	404171–5	Hall & Read	Hanley
20	13	404176	The Derby Crown Porcelain Co. Ltd.	Derby

Date	Parcel No.	Patent No.	Factory, Retailer Wholesaler, etc	Pla
21	4	404196	T. C. Brown–Westhead, Moore & Co.	Hanle
24	9	404317	Jones & Hopkinson	Hanle
25	4	404328	F. W. Grove & J. Stark	Long
25	5	404329–30	Sampson Bridgwood & Son	Long
27	21	404466	Meigh & Forester	Long
28	4	404473	Blair & Co.	Long
28	5	404474	E. J. D. Bodley	Bursl
29	4	404571	Sampson Bridgwood & Son	Long
Oct 2	15	404643	Mellor, Taylor & Co.	Bursl
2	22	404652–3	Meigh & Forester	Long
4	4	404745	Sampson Bridgwood & Son	Long
4	5	404746	Whittaker, Edge & Co.	Hanl
4	24	404809	The Worcester Royal Porcelain Co. Ltd.	Worc
6	2	404870	W. H. Grindley & Co.	Tuns
8	1	404900	Hollinson & Goodall	Long
8	2	404901–2	T. G. & F. Booth	Tuns
8	3	404903–5	Hall & Read	Hanl
9	9	405016–8	A. Bevington & Co.	Hanl
11	2	405215	Wittmann & Roth	Lond
12	13	405336	Bridgetts & Bates	Long
13	3	405341	Wood & Son	Burs
13	11	405363–4	Wm. Brownfield & Sons	Cobr
17	5	405466	The New Wharf Pottery Co.	Burs
17	6	405467–8	Hall & Read	Han
20	3	405724	W. A. Adderley	Long
20	4	405725–9	Wm. Brownfield & Sons	Cob
23	6	405855	J. Dimmock & Co.	Han
24	11	405946–8	Minton, Hollins & Co.	Stok
25	17	406032–3	Taylor, Tunnicliffe & Co.	Han
26	7	406043	Jones & Hopkinson	Han
27	1	406046	The Brownhills Pottery Co.	Tuns

e Parcel No.	Patent No.	Factory, Retailer Wholesaler, etc	Place
0	2	406140	J. Marshall & Co.	Bo'ness, Scotland
0	3	406141	The New Wharf Pottery Co.	Burslem
0	17	406187	J. Robinson	Burslem
1	1	406223	A. Bevington & Co.	Hanley
1	25	406370	Wood, Hines & Winkle	Hanley
1	26	406371	S. Fielding & Co.	Stoke
1	27	406372	Davenports Ltd.	Longport
2	19	406464–9	The Worcester Royal Porcelain Co. Ltd.	Worcester
5	13	406511	H. Alcock & Co.	Cobridge
6	3	406516	E. & C. Challinor	Fenton
7	2	406561	W. & E. Corn	Burslem
10	9	406781	Taylor, Tunnicliffe & Co.	Hanley
10	10	406782	Wm. Brownfield & Sons	Cobridge
13	10	406875	T. G. & F. Booth	Tunstall
14	3	406893	Stonier, Hollinshead & Oliver	Hanley
15	17	407063	T. Furnival & Sons	Cobridge
17	2	407155	The Derby Crown Porcelain Co. Ltd.	Derby
21	3	407333	F. J. Emery	Burslem
22	3	407385	S. Fielding & Co.	Stoke
23	7	407587–8	Minton, Hollins & Co.	Stoke
24	3	407601	Powell, Bishop & Stonier	Hanley
26	2	407623	W. A. Adderley	Longton
26	3	407624	Sampson Bridgwood & Son	Longton
28	12	407805–10	The Worcester Royal Porcelain Co. Ltd.	Worcester
1	3	407913	idem	Worcester
3	10	407943	James Wilson	Longton
5	2	408035	Malkin, Edge & Co.	Burslem
5	3	408036	The Derby Crown Porcelain Co. Ltd.	Derby

Date	Parcel No.	Patent No.	Factory, Retailer Wholesaler, etc	Pl
8	8	408136	J. F. Wileman & Co.	Fent
14	4	408288	The Brownhills Pottery Co.	Tuns
15	13	408356	T. G. & F. Booth	Tuns
15	14	408357	Hollinson & Goodall	Long
29	4	408849	Powell, Bishop & Stonier	Han

Index

394

399

402

407

414

415

419

Index

420

Index

422

428